THE
SILENT
KOOKABURRA

LIZA PERRAT

TRISKELE BOOKS

To my wonderful family, near and far.

Chapter 1

Knuckles blanch, distend as my hand curves around the yellowed newspaper pages and my gaze hooks onto the headlines.

HAPPY AUSTRALIA DAY. January 26th, 1973. 165-year anniversary of convict ships arriving in Sydney.

Happy? What a cruel joke for that summer. The bleakest, most grievous, of my life.

I can't believe my grandmother kept such a reminder of the tragedy which flayed the core of our lives; of that harrowing time my cursed memory refuses to entirely banish.

Shaky hands disturb dust motes, billowing as I place the heat-brittled newspaper back into Nanna Purvis's box.

I try not to look at the headline but my gaze keeps flickering back, bold letters more callous as I remember all I'd yearned for back then, at eleven years old, was the simplest of things: a happy family. How elusive that happiness had proved.

I won't think about it anymore. I mustn't, can't! But as much as I wrench away my mind, it strains back to my childhood.

Of course fragments of those years have always been clear, though much of my past is an uncharted desert — vast, arid, untamed.

Psychology studies taught me this is how the memory magician works: vivid recall of unimportant details while the consequential parts — those protective breaches of conscious recollection — are mined with filmy chasms.

I swipe the sweat from my brow, push the window further open.

Outside, the sun rising over the Pacific Ocean is still a pale glow but already it has baked the ground a crusty brown. Shelley's gum tree is alive with cackling kookaburras, rainbow lorikeets shrieking and swinging like crazy acrobats, eucalyptus leaves twisted edge-on to avoid the withering rays.

But back in my childhood bedroom, behind Gumtree Cottage's convict-built walls, the air is even hotter, and foetid with weeks of closure following my parents' deaths.

Disheartened by the stack of cardboard boxes still to sift through, uneasy about what other memories their contents might unearth, I rest back on a jumble of moth-frayed cushions.

I close my eyes to try and escape the torment, but there is no reprieve. And, along with my grandmother's newspaper clipping, I swear I hear, in the rise and dump of its swell, the sea pulling me back to that blistering summer of over forty years ago.

Chapter 2

'Oh god, not again!' my mother cried out from the bathroom. 'Why, why, *why*?'

A lizard flip-flopped in my belly, slithered up my throat, closing it tight. Was that same thing happening to Mum; the thing I couldn't understand but knew was shocking and terrible for her, and for my father? I flung aside my *Real Life Crime* magazine, bolted from the bedroom.

I cracked open the bathroom door. One hand pressed against her belly, the fingers of my mother's other hand clenched the sink. Bloody underpants dangled around her knees, green tiles stained red with wobbling jellyfish-clots.

I rushed in, clutched her arm. 'What's wrong with you, Mum?'

'What are you doing in here, Tanya?' She looked up, face ghost-white, shaking off my hold. 'Go away, get out now.'

'But all the blood, are you sick?' I stared in horror at the fresh blood trickling down the insides of her thighs.

'Nothing's wrong. Just go outside and play.' She made flapping motions at me. 'Shut the door behind you. And don't worry, I'll be fine.'

'You're not fine, Mum. And I know this's happened before. I've seen it, lots of times. Why won't you tell me what's wrong?'

'Go, Tanya, please. Really, I'm not sick. I'll be fine ... soon.'

But as I reeled back from that swishing arm I knew my mother would not be fine.

Dad was hurrying down the hallway, pushing past me into the bathroom. I peered through the slit where he'd not properly closed the door.

He circled his arms around Mum. Her head resting on his shoulder, she sobbed.

'Another one flushed away, Dobson. Like some scrap of toilet paper. How much longer can we keep trying? How many more do I have to lose?'

My grandmother came in from her hairdresser's, her curls a darker blue than this morning.

'Oy quit that racket, youse two,' she said to the yapping dogs. But as ever, Billie-Jean and Bitta took not the slightest notice of Nanna Purvis.

She glanced up at me, still standing outside the bathroom door, my mother's cries bleating down the hallway. 'What's going on, Tanya?'

'It's Mum. Dad's in the bathroom with her ... there's blood everywhere. What's wrong with her?'

Nanna Purvis threw her veiny arms in the air. 'Aw strewth, not *another* one gone. You come away from there. No ten-year-old should see such a thing.'

My grandmother went into the kitchen to make a pot of tea, the dogs on her heels, and the awful truth hit me like an axe blow to the head. Suddenly I understood what was going on; what had been happening all those other times when they'd refused to explain it to me.

'Too young. '

'You won't understand, Tanya.'

They'd stopped discussing names, cots and prams; my mother stopped talking altogether. I knew this was the latest in the long and sad string of my mother's failed babies.

I wanted to rush into the bathroom and hug her but it was obvious Mum wanted only my father.

'It's all right, Eleanor, you'll be okay, love.' Dad was patting her back, stroking her hair, sadness puckering his sun-wrinkled face. 'We'll get through this … like we got through the others.'

'I can't bear it any longer. There's something wrong with me. Has to be.'

'There's nothing wrong with you, love,' Dad said. 'Maybe we're just … just meant to have only one.'

'No, Dobson, not just one. You know I need a boy to … to make up for …'

'I know, love. But that's over, in the past — '

'Didn't get a chance to hold him,' she sobbed. 'Those bitches snatched him away before I could even *see* him.'

Didn't get a chance to hold who? What does she need a boy to make up for?

My cat wrapped himself about my ankles and meowed. I picked Steely up, stroked him, shivered as an ice block slid from my shoulders, down my back, my legs. Frozen; knowing, dreading the misery that was creeping up on my mother.

Waiting for that enormous beach dumpster to crash over her, swallow her down to the seabed, almost drown her. Until she could fight her way up to the surface and breathe again.

* * *

My mother was slumped over a cup of tea at the kitchen table. No "Hi Tanya, how was school?" No smile or kiss. No "Tell me about your day. Are you thirsty?" Just The Invisible Girl and a mother staring at air. Like every afternoon since that gruesome bathroom episode a few weeks ago.

'Come on, Eleanor, drink the cuppa,' Nanna Purvis said. 'Make ya feel better.'

'I'll make you a fresh one, Mum.' I kicked off my shoes, peeled away sweaty socks and sat beside her, my palm hovering over her bent back, not daring to touch. 'This one's gone cold.'

'It's Friday, so no homework,' I added, my palm making circles between her shoulder blades, like she did to me when I woke from a nightmare. 'I can help you with the housework or cook tea, or something?'

My mother sipped her cold tea, sat there. A mute person. She was gone again to that mysterious lost-babies seabed.

Dad strode in from another day of bricklaying, kissed Mum's brow and ruffled my hair.

'Hey, I've had a beaut idea.' He threw his Akubra hat, boomerang-style, onto the table. 'Let's go camping? Would you fancy that, Eleanor?'

Mum sighed, didn't look up at Dad.

'Come on, love, weather forecast's great and it'll take your mind off … off things.'

'Camping?' Nanna Purvis said, as if Dad had suggested rocketing off to Mars. 'What with me wonky hip and me very cow's veins? Stark-raving mad you are, Dobson.'

'*Varicose* veins,' I said to my grandmother. 'Nothing to do with cows.'

'Who said you're invited, Pearl?' Dad sniffed and lit a fag.

Nanna Purvis muttered, '*Humpf*', hobbled into the living-room with her dog and switched on the television.

Dad clamped a dusty hand on Mum's shoulder. 'What about it, Eleanor?'

She shook her head. 'No, I couldn't … maybe some other time.'

'Come on, Mum. We'll cook sausages and toast marshmal-lows over the campfire like last time. It was great fun, remember? And we'll go to the beach *all day* Saturday and Sunday.' I looked up at my father. 'Won't we, Dad?'

'You bet, Princess.'

Mum pushed away the teacup and stood up. 'All right then, if you insist.'

'That's my girl. I'll get the tent packed.' Dad pecked her cheek and hurried out through the kitchen flyscreen door, down to the storage shed.

'I'll get the food ready, Tanya,' Mum said, trying to sound enthusiastic as she took a pack of sausages and a loaf of bread from the freezer. 'You grab the swimmers and towels, okay?'

'Sure thing! Don't forget the tomato sauce.' I skipped down the hallway to my bedroom, wanting to shriek a whoop of excitement at the smile that had crept back onto my mother's face, and into her eyes.

* * *

We left Wollongong around five o'clock, Dad driving the Holden to the Royal National Park, which was halfway up to Sydney.

While my father wrangled with the tent pegs, amidst foraging currawongs and crimson rosellas, Mum and I kindled up a campfire and roasted the snags.

'Look at him.' I pointed to a large flat rock. Behind it, a shy wallaby peeked out at us, rubbing its forepaws together as if clapping at our show.

'Aw, what a sweetie,' Mum said, handing me a sausage sandwich smothered in tomato sauce.

A magpie swooped over us, clacking her bill. '*Quardle, oodle, ardle, wardle, doodle.*'

'Defending her nest,' Mum said as we toasted the marshmallows.

Dad smiled, gave her leg a pat. 'Like all good mothers.'

And in the falling darkness of the coastal breeze we followed the scents of the night creatures: long-nosed bandicoots, brush-tailed possums, sugar gliders and many others whose names I didn't know.

The shriek of a sulphur-crested cockatoo woke me on the Saturday morning. I struggled from my sleeping bag, stepped outside the tent, walked towards the smouldering campfire and almost trod on a snake. Its slimy scales gleamed in the pearly dawn light.

I almost peed myself, but held it in, not daring to cross my legs; afraid to budge an inch. A blob of sweat dribbled into my eye.

'Dad, quick, snake!'

My father lurched from the tent as the black snake reared up, its thick underbelly a streak of fire. Head pointed, forked tongue out, it fixed one dark eye on me and hissed.

My throat seized up, crazy moths flapped about in my heart. I wanted to run, to scarper from the snake as fast as I could, but Dad was holding up a warning hand.

'No quick movements, Tanya. Just wait, it'll slither away if you don't scare it.'

Tears pricked at my eyes. 'No, no, it's going to bite me … to kill me. Get rid of it, Dad!'

Mum clutched Dad's arm, a hand flying to her cowlick. 'Do something, Dobson … just stay very still, Tanya.'

My schoolteacher's voice clanged through my mind. *Blackies can be dangerous … can hurt you badly but they likely won't kill you.*

The red-bellied black snake sure looked deadly to me. My bladder was about to burst; my legs wobbled — jelly left out of the fridge in a heatwave.

Go snake. Just please go away, please.

As if it had read my mind, the snake lowered its head and slithered away into the bushes.

'Relax, Princess,' Dad said. 'It won't be back. You know they don't actually search for humans to bite … only if they're scared.'

'Okay,' Mum said, 'can we just try and forget about the snake and eat something so we can get down to the beach?'

It was only early November, but the day was hot as mid-summer and after our damper bread and billy tea breakfast — the snake incident almost forgotten — we traipsed down through the rainforest to a sea the bright green shade of a dragonfly.

Gulls *hark, harked* overhead and on an outcrop of shiny rocks that looked like mudflats, herons strutted about on thin legs and cormorants kept an eye out for fish.

'Look, Tanya.' Dad pointed to the coal tankers on the horizon, sailing to and from Port Kembla harbour. 'Those pirate ships are sailin' the high seas again, m'lady.'

Mum laughed.

'Oh Dad, I'm not a kid anymore.' Though I couldn't help laughing too, remembering how terrified I'd been as a kid of those "pirate ships" but feeling safe with him. My father would always protect me, keep me safe from everything. Even red-bellied blackies.

We drove back to Wollongong on the Sunday evening, the first violet jacaranda and red flame tree flowers, blooming. Mum and Dad chatted and laughed together in the front seat, my smiley mother returned from her sad seabed place.

Yes, she was back with us, almost the same as before. But not quite, because each flushed-away baby always took a smidgeon of her happiness with it to its toilet grave.

Chapter 3

'I'm going to have a baby, again.' Mum smiled, laid a hand over her flat belly. I'd never seen it swell in the slightest. None of them — besides me, if I was *not* adopted that is — had ever made it that far. 'The doctor confirmed it today.'

It was a few months after the camping weekend, around February of 1972, and I'd almost forgotten that last bathroom episode in the excitement of beach trips, Christmas presents, turkey lunch and long, warm evenings playing Monopoly with Mum and Dad. Another lost baby would put a stop to all that.

Dad, Nanna Purvis and I fell silent; stopped chewing the chops, mash and beans my mother had just served out.

'Aren't you going to say something?' Mum looked around at us. 'Aren't you all pleased?'

'That's beaut news.' Dad gave my mother his fake smile and kissed her cheek.

'Yep, great news, Mum.'

Only it wasn't. I was almost sorry it was happening, sure this one would end the same as all the others and my mother would, once again, slip away from us. My appetite fled and I gathered Steely into my arms and stroked him.

'Well, let's hope *this* horse makes it the whole way round the race-track,' Nanna Purvis said. 'But me hairdresser, Rita, reckons after losing so many there's Buckley's Chance of one making it to the finish line.'

'Jesus bloody Christ thanks for your optimism, Pearl.' Dad shoved away his plate of half-eaten tea. 'Really helpful.'

'Gotta stare the goanna in the guts, Dobson,' Nanna Purvis said.

My mother's face pinked up. She stared down at the kitchen lino. No one said anything else.

Dad lit a fag and flicked ash into one of his push-button ashtrays. *Click-click, click-click.*

I cleared away the plates, shovelled the uneaten food into the rubbish bin, and outside, cicadas whirred into the dusk light, louder, more screechy.

* * *

During those first three months of my mother's new pregnancy — the dangerous period, I'd learned — the whole of Gumtree Cottage quivered. It could have been the westerly wind though, that blasted for over a month, gales whistling through the fig, gum and jacarandas, sneaking beneath the low-slung verandah eaves and rattling the stone foundations.

'*Not another one, not again,*' the house whisper-shrieked.

Or perhaps the house seemed to shake from all of us tip-toeing around it, barely speaking, holding our breath. Just waiting for those cries from the bathroom.

My mother pottered about pretending everything was normal, but not getting any jobs done. Half-jobs, flitting from one thing to another.

'Let me do the vacuuming,' I'd say, taking the Hoover from her, while Nanna Purvis cooked tea.

'I'll do the washing up, Eleanor,' Dad said each night after we'd eaten. 'You go and put your feet up.'

'But I haven't done a thing all day,' Mum would say. 'None of you will let me do anything. I'm not sick you know.'

'I know, love,' he said. 'But still ...'

Dad didn't clean the cot or dust down the night-feeds rocking chair. We didn't discuss names, or mention the pregnancy to friends, family or neighbours.

But those dangerous three months went by. Then four and five. Six! Nanna Purvis's horse hadn't made a false start or stumbled; it had made its way around two-thirds of the racetrack.

Mum's stomach ballooned, her grin a fair clown's, her face a pretty pink rose. 'A miracle… it's a miracle,' she kept saying.

A month before the baby was due, I patted her huge belly. 'Will I have a sister or a brother?'

'Ah, that's the big surprise, Tanya.'

'But you want a boy, don't you?'

'What makes you think that?'

'Because I heard you say that to Dad … the last time. "You know I need a boy to make up for …" is what you said. Make up for what?'

A crimson flush crept up Mum's neck. 'You must've heard wrong, Tanya. Now come on, let's have a nice cool lemonade together and you can tell me your favourite boy and girl names. We'll have to choose soon.'

Three weeks later the birth pains came. Dad flapped around like a crazy galah, jamming the last things into Mum's suitcase; a frantic search for his car keys which were lying on the kitchen table in plain sight; phoning the work boss to say he wouldn't be in today.

I heated towels in hot water, pressed them against Mum's lower back where the pain was worse as she paced, breathing deeply. Nanna Purvis made a dozen cups of tea.

'Can I watch it being born?' I bounced about on the spot. 'Please, Mum?'

'Don't be ridiculous,' Nanna Purvis said. 'They don't even let husbands in and it sure ain't a place for a ten-year-old.'

I rolled my eyes at Nanna Purvis. 'I'm *eleven* now, did you forget?'

'You stay here with your grandmother,' Dad said. 'I'll call you the minute the baby's born and you can come and visit.'

The dogs barked and charged through Gumtree Cottage as if sensing this was an exciting moment. Exciting, but at the same time terrifying, because anything could go wrong. Or the baby could be born dead.

But I wouldn't think about that. Everything *had* to be all right.

Chapter 4

'Drive like the blazes, mate,' Nanna Purvis hollered at the driver as we jumped into the taxi. 'Me daughter's just given birth, but they've had to rush her to the operating theatre.'

Without a word, the driver put his foot down and zoomed his taxi all the way to the Wollongong Hospital. I held my breath, the entire trip it seemed, clenching my hands to stop them shaking. Dad had sounded panicked — hysterical — when he'd phoned from the maternity ward and told us there'd been a problem after the birth. My mother was bleeding too much.

'Is the baby alive?' I'd said, tugging on Nanna Purvis's elbow. But my grandmother had hung up and was dialling the taxi number.

'We'll find out everything when we get there, Tanya,' she'd said, grabbing her crocheted handbag.

As the taxi raced towards Crown Street, Wollongong's main street where the hospital was, I thought of that story in *Real Life Crime* about a mum who bled to death after giving birth, so the husband went and murdered the doctor. 'Mum can't die,' I said. 'And what about the baby, is it all right?'

'I told you I know nothing,' Nanna Purvis said. 'But don't you worry, ya father said the doctors are doing all they can to save Eleanor.'

In the maternity ward, Dad was pacing, stiff-legged, arms straight down by his sides. Robot-like.

'What went wrong, Dobson?' Nanna Purvis barked.

Dad glanced up. His face was grey, his brow creased in dried mud-track ruts. He mumbled something about retained placenta, oxygen mask, blood transfusion, but couldn't explain anything properly.

'Is the baby okay?' I said.

Dad nodded. 'Yes, thank Christ for that at least. It's a girl.'

A nurse gave us cups of tea while we waited, Nanna Purvis and me sitting on the plastic chairs. Dad went back to pacing the corridor, head bent, one hand swiping at his tangle of dark curls.

'Please tell me Mum will be okay,' I kept saying to him. 'Please.'

But he still couldn't tell me exactly what had gone wrong, or if my mother would survive. I rubbed at my cowlick, kicked my heels against the chair.

'Quit ya fidgeting, Tanya,' Nanna Purvis said. 'Making me all nervy.'

'Why're they taking so long?' I said. 'Why can't we know *now*?'

Finally, a doctor wearing operating theatre gear appeared. From the way he looked at us I couldn't suss out if it was good news or bad.

'We've managed to stop Mrs Randall's bleeding,' he said.

'Thank bloody Christ for that.' Dad let out a long breath. 'Thank you. Thanks so much.'

'And stabilised her, for now,' the doctor went on. 'But the next hours will be critical. We'll keep you informed of her progress.'

'Can we see Mum?' I asked. 'And where's our baby, can we see her?'

'The baby's fine, but I suggest you all go home and have a good rest. Leave Mrs Randall to rest too, and visit them both tomorrow.'

'But I want to see my baby sister.'

'The baby's in an incubator for the moment,' the doctor said, already walking away from us, obviously in a hurry. 'As I said, rest and come back tomorrow.'

'How are we supposed to *rest*?' I clamped my arms across my chest as Nanna Purvis steered me and Dad outside to the carpark. 'Until we're sure Mum and the baby are okay. Anyway, why's the baby in an incubator? There must be something wrong with her.'

* * *

'Well, she's got all her bits at least,' Nanna Purvis said the following day, looking the baby over from her head to her toes. Of course my grandmother wouldn't hold her; didn't touch a single downy curl.

'She's beautiful and Shelley's a pretty name ... a beach name,' I said, looking down at that little rose-cheeked girl lying in my mother's arms; her almost see-through skin, raspberry lips and the thickest dark hair I'd ever seen on a baby.

'Look at my three girls,' Dad said, standing beside the hospital bed, the silliest smile showing off his yellow-stained teeth. He stretched an arm along the bedrail above my pale, weakly smiling mother and my sleeping sister, and gathered me into the curve of his other arm.

A flurry of pink cards, balloons, flowers and stuffed animals encircled the four of us — a happy-family photograph. The baby had all her bits; nothing wrong with her at all. My mother was weak but the doctor said she *would* recover. I couldn't think of a single reason why the happiness wouldn't last, this time.

On account of the bleeding, my mother had to stay longer in hospital, but at last, in October of 1972, she and Shelley came home to Gumtree Cottage. Dad carried Mum's bag in one hand. With the other, he opened the door and ushered her and the baby inside like important guests.

My mother couldn't stop smiling, as if making up for all the unsmiling times. Bitta and Billie-Jean yelped and dashed around Mum and Shelley.

'Enough noise, youse two,' Nanna Purvis said, but the dogs kept barking, sensing a lot of excitement was worth a lot of noise.

'Can I hold Shelley, Mum?' I held out my arms.

'Be careful you don't drop her,' Nanna Purvis said. 'You know how precious this one is.'

I scowled at my grandmother. 'As if I'd drop my own sister. Anyway, every baby is precious, even if it doesn't …'

'Why don't you all go into the living-room,' Dad said, obviously not wanting us to dwell on the sorrow of those never-born babies. 'I'll get us some drinks. And food, maybe.' He patted my mother's arm. 'Fancy a bite to eat, love? Doc said you need to eat properly, build up your strength.'

'Just a cuppa and a biscuit would be nice, thanks,' Mum said, sitting beside me on the sofa.

Nanna Purvis groaned, the plastic slats of her fold-up chair squeaking as she eased herself onto her banana lounge and started flipping through her *Only for Sheilas* magazine.

I wanted to ask my grandmother how she could act as if this was any normal day, and not the amazing thing that it was, but there was never any point questioning Nanna Purvis's stony routines.

The baby started mewling and my mother took her from me, settled back into the sofa and lifted her top. Shelley suckled, Mum grinning down at her, one elbow supporting the baby's head, the other hand brushing dark swirls of hair from her forehead.

I grabbed a little foot that had come loose from her cotton wrap. 'Look, her toes all work perfectly, just like mine.' And my mother's smile washed over me — a cool swim on a blistering day.

On the coffee table, Dad placed the tray loaded with a bottle of KB Lager for him, two cups of tea, green cordial for me and a plate of Anzac biscuits. There was also a packet of Nanna Purvis's Iced VoVos, but they were only for her. My grandmother never shared her biscuits with anyone.

'Here you go,' Dad said, holding the teacup to my mother's lips. 'Your hands are full.'

'Such a chivalrous gentleman, Dobson,' Mum said in a mock-posh voice.

Nanna Purvis rolled her eyes, kept flipping the magazine pages with one hand and feeding biscuit morsels to Billie-Jean with the other.

Mum swapped Shelley to the other breast and as the baby suckled we all fell silent; still couldn't believe our good luck at having this beautiful — alive! — baby. And my mother too, back from the almost-dead.

My father's grin spread across his cheeks to his dark side-burns and I could see the relief in his unhunched shoulders as he lifted the beer bottle to his lips, and the easy way he spread his long legs out in front of him.

Shelley gave a loud burp. 'Come on, Tanya, I'll show you how to change her nappy,' Mum said.

In my parents' bedroom, Mum lay Shelley on the bed, removed her plastic pants and slid the wet nappy into a bucket that smelled like a swimming pool. 'This is how it's done.' She folded a clean nappy into a triangle and showed me how to poke in the pins without jabbing the baby's skin.

'She's so warm and cuddly, isn't she?' I kissed Shelley's soft head, pushed my nose into her liquorice-twist curls. 'Smells yummy too — like lamington cakes hot from the oven.'

'A cake baked to perfection,' Mum said with a laugh as she put Shelley to sleep on the lambskin rug in her cot which sat next to my mother's side of the bed.

She sat on the stool in front of her dressing table. 'Brush my hair for me, Tanya?'

I stood behind her and brushed her hair until it shone so silky it slipped off the bristles.

As she applied eyeshadow, mascara and lipstick, lots of blush over her pale cheeks — things she'd never done through those gloomy seabed days — I raked the brush through my own hair.

I clamped it down over my ears with bobby pins, but that just looked ridiculous. Besides, the pins slid straight out and back went my hair behind the bat-wing ears.

Mum sprayed her Cologne 4711 perfume onto her slender neck and wrists, and misted my chubby arms.

'Remember when I was a kid and drew an elephant with your Tropical Coral lipstick right there?' I nodded at the wall behind Shelley's cot. 'And you said, "Oh what a nice rhinoceros," and I said you were silly … that it was an elephant.'

Mum let out a giggle, the same as when I'd made the elephant sketch then clomped about in her cork-heeled platforms still clutching the Tropical Coral lipstick.

'I think we deserve something nice for tea to celebrate the new baby,' Mum said, as Steely jumped onto the dressing table. His bum in our faces, the cat stalked between the bottles, tubes and jars: all my mother's things that made her look beautiful once again. 'What do you want, meat pies or sausage rolls?'

'Both!' I said, trying on her coloured bracelets, jangling them right up to my elbow.

'Okay, we'll have both. Your dad will go to the shop.' And we both smiled at the side-by-side happy faces in the mirror.

* * *

Over the next few weeks, in the afternoons and evenings after school, I played with my little sister, shaking her rattle at her, showing her how to stroke the cat and dogs. 'Gently, Shelley, like this, so you don't scare them.'

I held her close to the sweet-smelling pink and white flowers that climbed the back-yard fence. 'This is jasmine, my favourite. It might be yours too, Shelley, when you're old enough to smell flowers.'

I imitated the squawky sound of a sulphur-crested cockatoo, the shrieky '*Eep, eep*' of a galah. 'Then you'll know what each bird is,' I told her.

I pointed up into the red-flowering gum. 'Look, there's our kookaburra. Mr Kooka, he's called.

'*Garooagarooagarooga*,' I said, imitating the kookaburra's laugh.

'*Garooagarooagarooga*,' he cackled back, which made me laugh more than the bird.

Sometimes I went with my mother when she took Shelley to the Baby Health Clinic for weighs and check-ups, and each time the clinic nurse assured Mum that our baby girl was perfectly healthy.

'There's no need to bring her every day, Mrs Randall,' the nurse said. 'Once a week will do fine.'

After her feeds, Mum took Shelley into the backyard and laid her in her pram, permanently parked in shade of the eucalyptus which — as well as being Mr Kooka's gum tree — I'd named "Shelley's gum tree".

Still tired and weak from the bleeding, my mother would rest beside the pram, staring at Shelley, so cute in her pink matinee jacket, her arms thrown above her head, scarlet lips puckered like she was kissing the air, chubby legs splayed outwards as if she didn't have a care in the world. Which she didn't!

Mum never took her eyes off Shelley's chest, rising and falling as she slept beneath the pram netting. As if she was afraid our baby wasn't real, but a doll from some kid's fairy-tale; a happily-ever-after story that was too good to be true.

'How's my little gumnut girl today?' Dad would say when he came in from work each afternoon. He loped down to the gum tree, pulled funny faces at her, and I swore Shelley laughed at his grimaces along with Mum and me.

'You sure it's a good idea to park Shelley's pram under the gum tree, Eleanor?' Nanna Purvis said one afternoon. 'What of them widow-maker stories? Just the other day it was on the news again: wind ripped off a branch ... fell on some campers and killed one of them.'

'Don't be silly,' Mum said. 'The chances of a branch falling on

Shelley are so slim it's not worth worrying about. Besides, there's not a breath of wind and the gum tree shade is the coolest spot for her to sleep.'

Dad raised his eyebrows, making them join in the middle, and winked at me. 'Your grandmother and her ridiculous superstitions.' He turned to Nanna Purvis. 'If you had your way, we'd all spend our days watching television in the safety of our own living-room. What kind of a life is that, Pearl?'

'Go ahead, make fun of me, Dobson … take no notice of what I say,' Nanna Purvis said. 'You never do, but if something happens to this baby don't say I didn't warn you.'

Mavis and Mad Myrtle Sloan, the sisters from next door at number fifteen, came to admire Shelley.

'What a sweetie, am I allowed a cuddle?' Mavis said.

'Of course.' Mum sat Mavis down and placed the baby in the old woman's arms. 'She's such a good little girl. Never cries or even wakes up even when we pass her around to people.'

It was true, even visitors' chatter, or the Longbottoms' television bleating out from next door at number eleven, or the breeze moving her feathery hair across her face, never woke Shelley.

'I'm so lucky,' Mum said, a fingertip caressing Shelley's cheek, 'to have such an easy baby.'

'Maybe you're just a good mother?' I said, and Mum smiled and kissed *my* cheek.

'Yeah, thank our lucky dilly bag she's not like you were, Tanya,' Nanna Purvis said.

'Not like me? Why, what was I like?'

'You? You really gave us the run-around, barely sleeping and whingeing nonstop.' Nanna Purvis poked a Pooch Snax into her dog's mouth and scratched his head. 'Eh, Billie-Jean? Thought she'd drive us all crackers, didn't we?'

'Your dog wasn't even here when I was born.' I turned to my mother. '*Was* I a terrible baby?'

'Oh Tanya, I don't remember,' Mum said as Mavis handed Shelley back to her. 'It was so long ago and so much has happened …'

Yes, so much had happened. So many failed babies. So much sadness. But that was over now. Beautiful and well-behaved Shelley had magicked the happiness back to us.

Perhaps Shelley had even broken the bad spell — the curse that drooped over Gumtree Cottage as heavy as the boughs of the dead fig tree Dad had got cut down.

And on it went like that: Shelley being the best baby in the whole of Australia and Mum, Dad, Nanna Purvis and I drifting about Gumtree Cottage as if we were floating on those powdery puffs of spring cloud.

Until the day at the beach.

Chapter 5

The thermometer rose to thirty degrees that Sunday in November and North Beach was thick with noise and people, colourful beach umbrellas and laid-out towels. It was Shelley's first outing from Gumtree Cottage, besides the daily Baby Health Clinic trips.

As usual Nanna Purvis hadn't wanted to come. 'I'll mind the ranch,' she'd said. 'Got me telly and Billie-Jean to keep me company.'

I spread out the towels amongst mothers chasing toddlers, slapping on the hats they'd thrown off, and older children, brows furrowed in concentration, modelling towers for sandcastles. Beyond the crowded sand, beneath the sun, the sea glistened like gold-shot turquoise silk.

Barely noticeable amidst the flock of ordinary seagulls, kelp gulls — with black upperparts and wings and yellow bills — called their strident 'ki-och'. I wished I could be a kelp gull and blend in so easily. Though people immediately saw I wasn't the same as other girls, especially at the beach. Until I could rush into the surf and hide under the water, that is. Then I was just another normal-sized girl splashing about in the waves.

Once Dad got the umbrella up, Mum handed Shelley to him and rummaged through the beach bag. She passed me the tube of zinc. 'Don't want that pretty face to burn.'

'Pretty?' I mumbled, slapping a T-shape of thick, greasy zinc across my cheeks, down my nose. 'Pretty plain more like it.'

It was nice of Mum to say that, but I was fully aware not only of my bat-wing ears, but also of why the kids at school called me Ten-ton Tanya.

Nearby, a group of girls in crocheted bikinis, limbs shiny with coconut oil, laughed and whispered to each other, sinking nail-polished toes deep into the sand, seeking the cool beneath the burning surface. If I were slim, I too could wear a crocheted bikini instead of this ungroovy one-piece. I wished they were my mates. At least I had Angela — my one friend. I'd invite Angela to the beach with us this summer, that's what I'd do. Then I'd have someone to talk to on the sand, and swim with.

The girls were giggling at a knot of surfie boys wearing board shorts and plastic shark's tooth charms on silver necklaces. Ignoring the girls' shrieks, the boys picked them up and carried them down to the water.

As their thin bodies scraped against the boys' muscles, the heat rose about me, pressing against my fat rolls. And when the boys dumped them onto ridden-out waves, the girls' squeals rose louder than the seagulls' crowing.

Idiots. As if getting chucked in the surf on a hot afternoon is so terrible.

'Race you, Tanya,' Dad said. 'Last one in's a rotten egg.'

Mum waved us off, holding up one of Shelley's little hands in a wave.

'Ow, ouch,' I squealed racing across the scalding sand, sighing with relief once we reached the cool, wet shoreline.

'Under this one,' I shouted, as the set of waves rolled in. I dived beneath the breaker, clutched the sandy bottom so the dumpster wouldn't pick me up and hurl me about like some ragdoll. Down I dived, again and again, and when the break came, Dad and I surfaced, laughing, breathing fast and flipping the hair from our faces.

'Let's get ice-creams,' Dad said when the skin on my hands was wrinkly soft, the bum of my swimmers sagging with sand.

We hitched a ride into shore on the back of a wave, dried off and dashed across the sand up to the kiosk.

Clutching our chocolate Paddlepops, we hurried back to Mum and Shelley, and slurped our ice-creams in the shade of the umbrella. But as fast as I licked, the quicker it melted, chocolate running down my chin, my arm, blobbing onto the sand. And Mum and Dad were laughing at me getting chocolate everywhere.

The afternoon breeze wafted away the dense heat, the air turning cooler, lighter and I just knew it. This was only the beginning of loads of happy summers of sea water cooling hot skin, of ice-creams and fish and chips wrapped in newspaper. Mum, Dad, Shelley and me all together.

'Why don't you go for a swim with Dad?' I said to Mum. 'I'll mind the baby.'

'Okay, why not? Shelley's just had a feed so she should be all right for a while.' And my parents scampered off across the hot sand, hand in hand like the young lovers in *Dolly* magazine.

I held my sister upright, close to my face, and stared into our father's chocolate-coloured eyes. Unlike mine, which were small, too close together and a boring greeny-brown shade. 'Isn't the beach great, little one? And soon you'll be old enough to swim in the surf with me. Then the real fun will start.'

Of course Shelley was too young to even smile, let alone answer, but I was convinced she did smirk as I touched a finger to her smooth cheek. She sensed I loved her; was old enough — responsible enough — to take care of her in our mother's absence. I was no longer a kid building silly sandcastles, or turning cartwheels and falling over in a heap, my mother having to brush off my faceful of sand.

'I'll always stick up for you, Shelley,' I said, swaying her gently. 'Even if you turn into an ugly and uncool kid like me.'

* * *

Through the blistering sunlight, I squinted at my parents lurching from the surf, walking away from the boisterous crowd of people swimming between the flags.

Dad's arm slung across my mother's shoulders, their hips touched as they strolled along the shoreline, curving sideways together to avoid obstacles: cracked seashells, daggery shards of cuttlefish, sharp driftwood.

I was so busy staring at my lovey-dovey parents that at first I didn't notice Shelley's whimpers. Her little fists began thrashing and she struggled in my arms. I hoisted her over my shoulder as I'd seen my mother do, jiggled around, patting her back to get up her wind.

The whimpers grew louder, weakened once she burped, then rose again. I bounced on the spot. 'Shush, shush, Shelley, you'll be all right.'

But Shelley was not all right. The cries turned to screams. People began staring as if they suspected I might be hurting her.

I laid her on the towel, checked her nappy. Clean and dry.

'Maybe you're too hot?' I stripped off her cotton top, her singlet.

'What *is* wrong with you?' I gathered my shrieking, scarlet-faced sister into my arms. 'You can't be hungry, and you've burped. What is it?'

Her body stiffened, her legs outstretched, stubby feet pummelling my chest.

'You're hurting somewhere. But where, and from what?'

Despite the umbrella shade, the sun beat down harder, hotter on my back. 'What *is* wrong, little one?'

The heat heightened her screams, trapping them in that scalding air, her little body sweat-slick against mine. More beach-goers were gawking at us, wives muttering to husbands — advice probably, about how *they'd* be able to stop a baby screaming.

'Why won't you tell me then?' I wanted to snap at them. 'I don't know what to do.'

Finally Mum and Dad were making their way back, hurrying when they realised it was Shelley making more noise than the crashing waves.

'She won't stop crying ... I don't know what's wrong.' I shovelled Shelley into my mother's arms. 'I didn't do anything ... just held her, like you showed me.' My fingers darted to my cowlick, pressing, rubbing.

'It's all right,' Mum said. 'Probably just a bit of stuck wind.'

'I promise I didn't do anything to make her cry.'

'No one's blaming you, Princess.' Dad dragged my fingers from the cowlick. 'She'll be right soon, you'll see.'

But the stare in Shelley's wide dark eyes seemed to plead: '*Do something ... stop my pain. Please!*'

Hiccups. Sobs. Louder hiccups, more crying and Mum pacing around, patting her back.

'Guess we should head off home,' Dad said, jamming down the umbrella. I bundled our things into the beach bag and we sprinted back to the Holden, Shelley shrieking the whole way.

* * *

Gumtree Cottage was a fifteen-minute drive from the main Wollongong beaches, but as we passed South Beach, at the end of Crown Street, then drove along Corrimal Street, alongside the Sewage Treatment Works and finally up the Gallipoli Street hill, Shelley's wailing made the trip seem like hours.

Later, when the sun vanished over Mount Kembla and dusk fell, Shelley was still yelling. She muffled the dogs' yelping as they ran circles around each of us — whoever was holding her, trying to calm her down.

'Sounds like the colic to me,' Nanna Purvis said as Mum sat on the sofa and tried to feed her again.

Shelley jerked her face away and beat her fists against the swollen breast as if saying: '*No, that's not what I want!*'

'Tanya had the colic, don't you remember, Eleanor?' my grandmother said, scurrying out to the kitchen, the dogs on her heels. 'Screamed the place down for weeks. We'll try that hot-towel trick we used on her.'

'A hot towel in this heat?' Dad scowled at Nanna Purvis who handed a sodden, steaming towel to Mum.

'Well, if you're the colic expert, Dobson,' Nanna Purvis said, 'what do *you* suggest?'

Dad shrugged, flicked fag ash into one of his push-button ashtrays. *Click-click, click-click.*

'Oh yes, I'd forgotten this trick,' Mum said laying Shelley tummy-down on the hot towel. 'It's been so long.'

'Yeah, should move that nasty gas, eh, Shelley?' Nanna Purvis threw my father a triumphant smirk as her shrieks waned to exhausted little whimpers.

'Thank goodness for that … poor poppet.' My mother stroked Shelley's head. The baby's eyelids fluttered closed and Mum left her on her lap. I don't think she dared move her to the cot for fear of starting up the crying again.

'Righto, I'll be off down the pub,' Dad said, slapping on his Akubra hat and jingling his car keys in his pocket.

'Typical,' Nanna Purvis said, 'leaving us here on our own to cope with a sick baby.'

'Shelley's not sick,' Dad said. 'Just a touch of colic. She's fine now.'

'Oh just let him go to the pub for a few beers,' Mum said. 'He's right, she *is* fine now.'

Dad kissed Mum's brow and touched a yellow-stained fore-finger to the baby's cheek. 'Won't be long, love, quick schooner and I'll be back.'

But my father had been at The Dead Dingo — aka The Dead Dingo's Donger — for only half an hour when Shelley woke and started crying again.

We tried the hot towel-trick again which only made her scream louder. Mum filled the bathtub and lowered Shelley into the warm, deep water.

Her face red as a waratah bloom, sweat pearls dotting her forehead, Shelley thrashed about in the tub, fists bunched as if she wanted to punch something.

Of course Nanna Purvis wouldn't attempt to pacify her, so after that bath I took Shelley, sat in the night-feeds chair and rocked back and forth as I sang: '*Baa baa black sheep, have you any wool, yes, sir …*'.

But she must have sensed the tension in me, the strain seeping right through Gumtree Cottage and, hating my tight and desperate embrace, her wailing stifled my words.

'Sorry, I give up,' I said, handing Shelley back to my mother.

I went into my own room and pulled the latest issue of *Real Life Crime* from its hiding place, rolled up inside *Dolly* — a magazine I was allowed to read. I flung my horrible rose-patterned bedspread onto the floor, and flopped onto the sheet.

Right from when I was a kid and Mum had bought it on special at Kmart, that ugly bedspread had given me nightmares — frightening dreams about a burglar breaking into Gumtree Cottage and stabbing me. I was bleeding to death but Mum and Dad didn't realise because they couldn't see my blood among those huge red roses.

Shelley eventually settled. Mum fell asleep. Nanna Purvis's snores rattled down the hallway but I couldn't sleep for the heat. A thick carpet of it unravelling into my room from the hot darkness outside.

A sound just beyond my window, a muted kind of cough, made me leap from the bed. Sparrows beat their wings in my chest as a shadow slipped past the window. A shadow too long, the wrong shape, to be my cat. It was the shadow of a person. Too frightened to peek through the Venetian blind slats, I stood there trembling, sweat droplets trickling down my cheeks. I didn't want to go running to my mother like a little kid. Besides, she was still exhausted from the birth, and the bleeding, to deal with any extra dramas.

Then the shadow was gone and there was only silence and darkness, and my short and quick breaths.

Later, footsteps coming down the hallway startled me. I bolted up in my bed, listening for that cough, watching for the shadow. It was only Dad though, back from The Dead Dingo. But his noise had woken Shelley too, who started wailing.

My poor little sister cried right through the night and as the sun peeped over the Pacific horizon we all straggled from our beds, battle-weary soldiers after an entire night of Shelley's bombardment.

Chapter 6

Home from school, I opened the front door. No crying Shelley like almost every afternoon since she'd started two weeks ago at the beach. Just an echoey quiet.

'Mum?'

'In the bedroom, Tanya.'

My mother was lying on her bed reading *Women's Weekly*, Shelley sleeping on her lambskin in the cot, a thumb stuck in her mouth.

'Just grabbing a quick rest,' Mum said, patting a place beside her. 'The clinic nurse gave me a new colic remedy. This peppermint mixture. And it's working. Your sister's been quiet all day.'

'That's great.' I kicked off my shoes and sat on her bed.

She closed her magazine, put it aside. 'Good day at school?'

'Okay, same as always.' I didn't mention the usual fat, batwing ear taunts; didn't want her to fuss. She had enough to worry about with Shelley's colic and "building up her strength".

'It's *so* hot, isn't it?' I said, then as if the idea has just leapt into my head: 'Shelley's sleeping, so maybe Nanna Purvis would mind her and you could take me to the beach?'

'Oh Tanya, I'd love a swim with you, but after weeks of your sister's crying I'm just flagged out, up all night and day with her. Don't even know where I'll find the energy to get off this bed to cook tea.'

'We could just go for an hour? We'll have the quickest swim ever. Then I'll help you cook tea.'

'Maybe tomorrow, or the next day. If this peppermint mixture does the trick I'll be much better in a few days. Then we'll
go to the beach, I promise.'

For two weeks she'd been saying she'd take me to the beach
soon. But soon never came. My mother's promises meant nothing. I shoved her hand from my thigh.

'Tanya, please ...'

'Oh, just forget about it,' I said in my sulkiest voice, stomping
out of the room. 'I'm taking Steely for a walk.'

I stuffed *Real Life Crime* into the Indian shoulder bag Dad
had bought me at a beachside fair, snagged Steely's leash from
the hook and clipped it onto his collar.

I knew all the neighbours thought I was a weirdo, taking
Steely for walks, and this afternoon was no different. Mad
Myrtle and Mavis Sloan at number fifteen peered through their
Venetian blind slats. Old Lenny Longbottom at number eleven
winked and smiled — the smile you'd give a lunatic. I ignored
their stares, marching out with my cat into Figtree Avenue.

The Anderson boys were playing cricket on the footpath
outside their house at number ten, opposite ours, which they
did each day after school. Come six o'clock their mother, Mrs
Coralie Anderson, would open her front door and call out:
'that's enough cricket for today, boys. Time for tea.'

'Hey, Tanya, wanna play?' the oldest, Terry, asked. Terry and
Wayne never really wanted me to play, since my cricket skills
— like every other sport — were terrible, but you needed three
for a proper game: batter, bowler, wicket-keeper. I was usually
keen, the Anderson boys being the only kids besides my friend,
Angela Moretti, who didn't call me nasty names.

'Maybe tomorrow,' I said, too miffed at my mother to feel like
cricket.

'Is your baby sister sick or something?' Wayne asked. 'What
with all her hollering?'

'Just a bit of colic,' I said. 'She'll get over it soon.'

'Our mother reckons there's something not right with

Shelley,' Terry said. 'And that your mum should figure out how to shut her up.'

'Nobody in this whole street can sleep anymore,' Wayne said.

'The nurse gave my mother a new colic mixture,' I said. 'And it's working. Shelley will be better now.'

The sun roasted my face, arms and legs as I hurried up Figtree Avenue to the bush track that led to the old abattoir.

I let out a groan as I saw Stacey Mornon playing elastics with two of her friends at the end of the cul-de-sac.

Oh no, not bloody Stacey Mornon-the-moron.

'*England, Ireland, Scotland, Wales. Inside, outside, monkey's tails,*' the friends chanted as Stacey jumped over the taut elastic, blonde curls shiny and bouncing in the sun.

I picked up Steely, tried to hide his leash.

'Ha ha,' Stacey said, with a sneer. 'We know you're walking that cat of yours, Ten-ton Tanya. Who*ever* takes a cat for a walk? How uncool, even for Miss Adopted Batgirl.'

'People walk their dogs,' I said, 'so why not their cat?'

Their laughter seared, hot arrows through my back, as I scurried away from them and onto the bush track.

I reached my special place in a clearing, sat on my flat rock in the flimsy bush shade and pulled *Real Life Crime* from the Indian bag. Steely started sniffing around.

I was so engrossed reading the story about the Faraday School kidnappings in Victoria, when two kidnappers took a teacher and her six pupils for a one-million-dollar ransom, that I didn't notice the man approaching me.

A shadow blackened the page. My heart somersaulted in my chest and I leapt to my feet. *Real Life Crime* slid to the ground.

I gripped Steely's leash and stared up at the tall, thin man with dark curly hair and eyebrows to match.

'Who are you?' My voice was a trembly mouse-squeak, and I was sure he could hear my heart still doing gymnastics.

* * *

'Hello, Tanya. Don't be scared.' The man's voice was soft and feathery, and, hands nestled in the pockets of an ankle-length Driza-Bone coat, his shoulders looked wide and hulky.

'I'm not scared,' I said. And I wasn't. The longer I stared at the man the less afraid I became. I didn't know why but he seemed familiar, so I felt no *Real Life Crime* stranger fears.

'Who are you?' I repeated. 'Did you follow me up here?'

'I know you come here some afternoons with your cat, Tanya, I've seen you before.'

His words bobbed up and down. A ripple on a calm sea. He stepped closer, his breath hot and heavy on my cheeks.

'You're really like your mother up close,' he said. 'Her lovely hair too — same tawny shade as a dingo.'

Lovely hair? The most boring, thin and straight hair the colour of a mouse.

My fingertips flew to my cowlick, pushed at my brow.

'You even rub that cowlick like your mother did when she was nervous, or anxious. I told you, Tanya, don't be scared, I won't hurt you.'

I dragged hair clumps over my ears, which made him grin.

'And the same ears that stick out just that bit,' he said. 'But you'll work out — as your mum did — that you can camouflage those small flaws just by wearing your hair a certain way.'

'Who *are* you? And how do you know my name ... and my mother?'

'Call me Uncle Blackie, and I knew your mum a long time ago.' He smiled but not at me. A faraway smile, secretive, mysterious.

He pulled a paper bag from his coat pocket and pushed it into my hand. 'I got you some Redskins and Milk Bottles, your favourite lollies.'

'How do you know they're my favourites? Anyway I'm not supposed to take lollies from strangers ... I'm not even supposed to talk to them.'

'I told you, Tanya, I'm no stranger. I'm your dad's brother.'

'My father hasn't got a brother,' I said, even as I saw Dad's same thick black eyebrows that joined into one long and furry caterpillar, same dark hair and eyes, boxy face and sideburns.

This Uncle Blackie might look like Dad, though a bit more handsome, but I remained vigilant (word learnt from *Real Life Crime*), wary he could be lying. Adults could be liars. My father lying about how many beers he was drinking lately, for example.

'Dad's only got an awful sister who Nanna Purvis calls "That Bitch Beryl". Anyway, if you're his brother we'd know you. We'd *see* you.'

'Ah, your Nanna Purvis put a stop to that long ago.'

'Why would she do that?'

'Put it this way, I'm sort of a secret that bossy Nanna Purvis doesn't want people to know about.'

'So you know my bossy grandmother too?'

'She was just Mrs Pearl Purvis back then.' He broke into the same chuckle as Dad's. 'But if you call her "my bossy grandmother" it sounds like she hasn't changed.'

'Yeah real bossy. Tells us what to do, all the time.'

Steely meowed, struggled against his leash as a paw swiped at a blowfly. 'It's all right, Steely,' I said stroking him.

'Why don't you sit back down, Tanya?' Uncle Blackie sat on my rock and patted the sun-baked spot next to him. 'Yes, Steely, you too.'

So we sat, the three of us, in that hot and airless bushland cleft, Uncle Blackie's long legs bent up before him in an awkward pyramid.

'Steely's a funny name for a cat,' he said, staring at my tongue rolling around a Milk Bottle as if it was the most interesting thing he'd ever seen.

This brother of Dad's is a bit weird.

'Because he's grey and brown like the Port Kembla Steelworks and fluffy. You know, same as the chimney smoke. I won him at the school fete when I was a kid. I really wanted to win him so I got Dad to buy all the tickets in the kitten lottery.'

'He's a good friend?'

I shrugged. 'He's just a cat. Not a *real* friend.'

'I'd love to be your real friend.' Uncle Blackie smiled, the eyebrows meeting above his nose.

I stroked Steely hard, as if I'd stroke the fur right off him, scratched at my cowlick. I finished the Milk Bottles and started sucking on a Redskin.

'So if you're my father's brother, you'd know if I was adopted?'

'I wasn't around when you were born,' Uncle Blackie said. 'But whatever makes you think you're adopted?'

'Stacey Mornon-the-moron reckons I am. That girl's my number one enemy … lives up at number twenty-five.' I waved in the direction of Figtree Avenue. 'The house at the end of the cul-de-sac with all the garden gnomes. That's because her father's a gnome-maker. They've even got a dog and cat gnome … completely daggy.'

Uncle Blackie nodded. 'Oh yes, the height of dagdom. But it sounds as if this Stacey might just be being spiteful, don't you think?'

'Another reason is this gene thing our teacher was talking about. You know, when kids inherit the dark genes because they're dominant, over pale ones? Like my baby sister got Dad's dark genes. Wouldn't I've got them too?'

'I don't think it's as simple as that,' Uncle Blackie said. 'Besides, I just told you how much you resemble your mother.'

'I'm really like her?'

'Exactly, Tanya. You even smell like her. What was that perfume she wore?' He closed his eyes, took a deep breath. 'That's it, Cologne 4711.' His elbow nudged my ribs. 'Been nicking your mum's perfume, eh?'

I jerked away and we fell silent as the sun slid down its westering arc, the orange light sliding through the tangle of bush and finding the bare parts of my body. The only sound in the still, afternoon heat was the rustle of a creature slithering into the scrub.

'That could be a snake,' I said. 'Our teacher reckons that of the world's ten most venomous snakes, over half are Australian.'

'Goodness, you'd better hold my hand then.'

'Your skin's rough. Are you a brickie too, same as Dad?'

'Nah, got these from too much gardening.'

'What do you grow in your garden?'

Uncle Blackie dropped my hand as if a bee had stung him. He looked away, in the direction of the distant abattoir.

'Not much ... nothing really. *Therapeutic* gardening they called it.'

'Oh right,' I said; didn't ask him what *therapeutic* gardening actually was, and risk appearing an idiot.

'What's that about?' He nodded at *Real Life Crime*, still lying on the ground.

'My favourite magazine, about true crimes. Nanna Purvis reckons I'm obsessed with crime and that no kid of eleven should be reading such rubbish.' I giggled, short and shrill. 'So you can never tell them I read it.'

'Don't you worry, I'm the best secret-keeper.' Uncle Blackie winked. 'And speaking of secrets, I think you're old enough to understand we have to keep this meeting a secret.'

'Why, do Mum and Dad want to keep you a secret too?'

'Probably best not to say anything. Besides, it's pretty cool having secrets from your parents, not to mention bossy grand-mothers, isn't it? And it wouldn't be fair to stop a girl seeing her own uncle, would it?'

'My lips are sealed,' I said and ran my pinched thumb and forefinger across my clamped mouth.

'That's my girl.'

We both fell quiet again. I didn't really know what else to say to this new and mysterious uncle.

The last heat burned my arms and legs, the top of my head, the sky darkening to the colour of a new bruise. I slapped at a mosquito settling on my arm and glanced at my watch.

'Gotta go. Nanna Purvis will be hopping mad if I'm late for tea because that'll make her late for her telly shows.' I leapt to my feet, smoothed down my school dress.

'So soon, Tanya? Didn't you enjoy it here, friends chatting together?'

'Course I did.'

Uncle Blackie stood too, long and ropy as the gum tree shadows, and replaced his Akubra hat. The same fur-felt one as Dad's — the wide-brimmed hat worn by most men who worked outdoors.

'What if I tell you where I live and give you my phone number?' he said. 'For if you ever want to come over to visit, as a friend, you know. That's what friends do, visit each other. If it gets too tough at home like I know it has been ... your baby sister crying all the time. Your mum down in the doldrums. You could come over for a break whenever you wanted?'

'Dunno, maybe ...' I hesitated. 'Well, since you're Dad's brother it should be okay.'

'Can you remember this?' Uncle Blackie said in the floaty voice, and recited his address and phone number. 'Mightn't be a good idea to write it down in case bossy boots Nanna Purvis finds it.'

'Nanna Purvis *would* find it,' I said with a nervous giggle. 'She finds out everything.'

'I bet she does,' Uncle Blackie said. 'And you wouldn't want her to stop you doing what you wanted, would you?

'No way.'

'And remember, Tanya, our secret, eh?'

I nodded, hurried off down the dirt track, clutching Steely against my heart pattering faster than my feet.

The last light seeped from the summer sky as I scurried down Figtree Avenue. The sun slunk behind Mount Kembla, which loomed like a dark and scruffy monster. Street and house lights flickered on.

I was breathless not only from hurrying, but with the shuddering inside me — as if a can of Coca-Cola was being shaken up in my belly, and like pins being stuck into me, though I felt no pain. Uncle Blackie's sea-ripple voice — saying nice things that made me feel good — had driven from my mind Shelley's colic and my mother's refusal to take me to the beach. But as I reached Gumtree Cottage it all chilled me once more — the first gust of a southerly buster after days of scalding heat. I put Steely down, rubbed my goose-pimpled arms.

If Uncle Blackie truly is my uncle, why hasn't Dad ever said? He would've told me if he had a brother … he doesn't keep secrets from me. And why doesn't Nanna Purvis want us to see him?

Maybe this Uncle Blackie wasn't Dad's brother, but some crazed kidnapper lying about knowing us just to get me to go off with him. My magazine was full of those kinds of stories.

Then I relaxed because if he *did* kidnap me I knew what to do — same as that girl in *Real Life Crime*. I'd just make friends with my kidnapper so he wouldn't murder me. Easy as that. No worries.

'Where you been, Tanya?' Nanna Purvis hollered from the living-room as I slipped inside. 'Beyond the black stump? You know tea-time's half past six, before me telly shows start.'

'Bossy old boots,' I hissed to Steely as I spooned out his food and filled his water bowl. As if I'd tell Nanna Purvis where I'd been. Or about my new and exciting secret friend.

Chapter 7

It was a scorching day in early December, almost the end of fifth grade — and summer holidays! — when I arrived home to the same racket since the peppermint colic mixture had stopped working: Shelley's cries and my mother's vacuum cleaner. And Billie-Jean and Bitta's barks, louder, yappier, competing with the other noise.

Something had sucked all the air from the stifling house. From every ceiling hung long, spinning coils of sticky flypaper, black with bodies, but still my mother freaked out at the smallest speck of fly dirt on her scrubbed furniture.

The dogs on my heels, I went into Mum and Dad's room. In her cot, my red-faced sister was writhing like a worm. After a month of crying I wondered if Shelley now did it out of habit; as if that was the only thing she'd learned to do. She turned her screwed-up stare to me that seemed to beg: *'Do something.'*

'Poor little gumnut girl.' I picked her up, cuddled her tight as if that could squeeze out the terrible pain from her belly.

'Maybe she's hungry, Mum?' I called out.

'She's just had her bottle,' she shouted back over the Hoover hum.

The bottle, yes, because my mother had abandoned the breastfeeding. She thought she didn't have enough milk; that that's what Shelley's trouble was. Or there was something wrong with it. But whatever the problem, the Baby Health Clinic nurse had advised her to stop breastfeeding altogether.

'Formula might help settle the colic,' the nurse had said.

I cooled a flannel under the kitchen tap and wiped Shelley's hot brow, face and neck.

'There you go, that's better, isn't it?'

My sister cooed, her dark gaze following mine as I stole a packet of Nanna Purvis's Iced VoVos from the pantry. Supporting the baby upright over my shoulder, I licked the strip of pink coconut-sprinkled fondant off four biscuits, then the raspberry jam, watching my mother run the Hoover across the same patch of living-room carpet. She was wearing her orange-flowered cleaning shift which was about the only thing she wore now.

Shelley gurgled, tried to grab the Iced VoVo. 'No, no,' I said. 'Not yet, but soon you'll be allowed bikkies. And I bet they won't give you that nasty colic.'

I kept cramming the biscuits into my mouth, feeling better with each one. Until I felt sick.

Stop eating, piggy-girl. Why can't you just stop? I hate you.

I wanted to vomit them all into the kitchen sink but down they stayed, sitting heavy in my belly.

Still holding the half-eaten biscuit packet in one hand, Shelley in the other, I marched into the living-room and stood before my mother.

'You vacuumed yesterday, how can it be dirty again?' Iced VoVo crumbs tumbled from my mouth.

'The clinic nurse says the vacuum cleaner noise, or washing machine, can distract a baby from colic pain.' Her gaze travelled from my face down to my feet, and to the biscuit crumbs sprinkled over her freshly-vacuumed carpet. She pushed the Hoover over the crumbs, back and forth, three times.

'Anyway, no amount of walking or back-patting will help, Tanya,' she said, shovelling the Hoover back into the linen cupboard. 'Don't you think I've tried that? Tried *everything*? Now can't you go and do something — surely you've got homework — and let me get this house clean?' She darted an arm at the dogs. 'And take them with you; they're just getting under my feet. All day, barking and in my way.'

'Bitta, Billie-Jean, come boys.' I clicked my fingers. The dogs trotted over, circled my ankles and wagged their tails as if this were all a game.

Mum almost knocked me over, lifting the plastic strips with which she'd covered the hallway carpet. Still holding Shelley, I followed her as she lugged the strips out the back, shook each one and draped it over the peeling paint on the verandah rail.

'Let's go to the beach,' I said. 'It's so hot, and the clinic nurse said a moving car could help calm colic, remember?'

'Not this beach thing *again*. I told you, Tanya, I've still got a hundred jobs to get through.' Her voice had become raspy and light as if she was having trouble breathing.

'But there's no dirt left to clean, Mum! And anyway, why won't you hold Shelley anymore?' I tried to push my sister into my mother's folded arms but she swivelled away and made shooing motions like I was some irritating blowfly. 'Have you stopped loving your baby?'

Mum swung back, snatched Shelley from me. She marched over to the gum tree and laid Shelley beneath the pram netting. 'Fresh air might settle her,' she mumbled.

But the air was not fresh. It was hot, still and thick — walking into an oven.

My mother removed the pillow she used to prop up Shelley when she was sitting in the pram, and stored it on the lower shelf. She'd heard that pillows and sleeping babies are a dangerous combination; that a baby could pull it over its head and suffocate.

I wished she'd stop all this housework and sit down with me for a cool lemonade, but she loped back inside. Along with the dust and crumbs, she'd hoovered away all her happiness. Sunk to that seabed again and we were back to the misery. The same gloom that came with each lost baby.

I dawdled back to the kitchen and poured myself a glass of green cordial. From the cupboard under the kitchen sink, I plucked her cans of disinfectant and threw them into the bin, deep beneath the other rubbish.

I gave Bitta some of Billie-Jean's Pooch Snax. Billie-Jean skittered over and nipped my ankle. 'Nasty little beast.' I kicked a foot at Nanna Purvis's dog.

'You giving that mongrel Billie-Jean's expensive Pooch Snax again?' Nanna Purvis called from her banana lounge on the back verandah.

'Why should Billie-Jean get them and not Bitta?' I said, pulling Bitta onto my lap, named because he was a bit 'a this and a bit 'o that.

Nanna Purvis's dog was an Australian Terrier she'd named after her favourite tennis star, Billie-Jean King, because my grandmother loved tennis before she got the crippled knees and varicose veins. Now she could barely walk, let alone wield a tennis racquet.

I'd pointed out that Billie-Jean was a boy dog, but my grandmother said Billie-Jean King was so fabulous she'd name her dog after her, boy *or* girl.

I went back outside and rocked the pram but Shelley still wouldn't settle. The neighbour, Old Lenny, turned up the sound on his television set.

Lenny Longbottom over at number eleven next door kept a tatty sofa and a television on his back verandah and most days he sat out watching telly all afternoon. We'd hear him blathering on to his son and daughter-in-law, who he lived with, the *chack-chack* of beer bottles opening and, of course, whatever show they were watching.

Nanna Purvis kept her gaze on her magazine. Shelley cried harder. The Longbottoms' television grew louder.

My grandmother snapped shut *Only for Sheilas* and staggered from her banana lounge. 'Gonna give that Lenny Longbum a gobful.'

'Turn that thing down, you telly-head,' she hollered. 'Ain't you heard about respect for neighbours?'

Old Lenny's craggy face appeared over the fence. Bald on top, a ratty grey plait trailed halfway down his back.

'You shut that kid up, Pearl, and I won't have to turn up me telly so loud. Weeks now, we've been putting up with her racket. What with this heat it's sending us mad as cut snakes. Youse need to shut her up.'

'You shut up,' I shouted at Lenny Longbottom.

'Mind your manners, Tanya,' Nanna Purvis said.

'You ever think it might be that house of yours?' Lenny said, with a flick of the plait and a swig of beer. 'The Gumtree Cottage curse? Been bringing bad luck to youse Randalls for years, ain't it? I've said it before, Pearl, move away, that's your best bet. I know a good builder … might be able to get youse a cheap deal on a new place.'

'Bad luck for years, you say?' Nanna Purvis said. 'What would you know of *years*, Lenny Longbum? You've been away for the last twenty-odd.'

Every Figtree Avenue resident knew the story of Lenny Longbottom and how he'd been away for years, though I'd quickly worked out "away" had meant gaol.

Everyone also knew about the curse lurking over Gumtree Cottage, the bungalow my father told me his convict ancestors — freed after seven years hard labour — built with hand-carved sandstone bricks, honest sweat and a great deal of pride. He said there were whispers of gold rush too, of stolen nuggets, a bush-rangers' lair. A bungalow built on blood money, whatever that was. Dad didn't know the details but said there'd been tragedies too.

'Calamities that made Gumtree Cottage an ill-starred place,' Nanna Purvis had said. 'Not to mention all their ghosts still hanging around.'

Old Lenny lumbered away. The television blared across both yards.

'Why don't *you* try and stop Shelley crying?' I said to Nanna Purvis. 'You must know about babies, you've had one. Why don't you pick her up for once?'

'Me?' Nanna Purvis said as if I'd asked her to fly to the moon.

'No point asking her,' my mother said as she came outside, panting and lugging her Venetian blinds down the verandah steps. *Clunk, clunk, clunk.* 'Your grandmother never picked me up or cuddled me, not once that I can remember.'

'Aw, I wasn't one for all that mollycoddling,' Nanna Purvis said. 'Didn't seem to do you any harm though.'

Oh yes, I certainly knew Nanna Purvis wasn't one for mollycoddling, that she hated anyone touching her too. Except her hairdresser fiddling with her hair.

'Can we do anything to help?' The faces of Mad Myrtle and Mavis Sloan appeared over the number fifteen side fence.

'Poor little mite's been crying for weeks,' Mad Myrtle said.

'Doesn't the clinic nurse know what's wrong with her, Pearl?' Mavis said.

'It's just colic,' I said. 'It'll pass, we just have to be patient.'

'I heard warmed-up vegetable oil works,' Mad Myrtle said. 'A teaspoon in her bottle three times a day.'

'*Humpf,*' Nanna Purvis muttered, as if she thought the sisters had no idea about anything,

'Just call out if you need something,' Mavis said.

'Nosy old biddies should mind their own bananas,' Nanna Purvis said as the women hobbled off, back inside their house.

'They're only trying to help,' I said.

My mother lugged the blinds towards the washing line. Without a glance at Shelley crying in her pram, she grunted and struggled to fling them over the Hills Hoist. Arcs of sweat stained her underarms, dribbled down her forehead.

'Let me help,' I said.

My mother gave me a crazed kind of smile, as if my help would be just a piss in the ocean of household jobs swelling about her, but together we managed to heave the blinds over the washing line.

Mum turned on the tap, grabbed the hose and directed a fierce jet onto each slat. Slashing away the dust and dirt. Grime easily hosed away because there was barely any on those well-washed blinds.

* * *

My mother tramped back inside. I rocked the pram again. Like every summer, our gum tree had burst into flower — an explosion of red fireworks. Back when I was a kid, Mum had told me about the eucalyptus legend.

'If you walk under a gum tree and one of its blossoms falls onto your head your luck will change,' she'd said. And her kiss on my cheek was soft as a gumnut flower.

I laid a palm against my cheek: no blossom, no kiss, just one tear that I swiped at in frustration.

A bold lizard darted out to sun itself on a rock beneath the jasmine, fat tongue lolling in the heat. The sun hopscotched between the blue-tinged eucalyptus leaves, the light chasing the shade across Shelley's face, lulling her to sleep. The hot westerly had flattened the Pacific Ocean glassy green, the gusts tugging off the gum tree blossoms and dumping them in a ragged red circle around the trunk.

'*Garooagarooagarooga*,' Mr Kooka laughed from his branch above the baby's pram, where he sat like some guard watching over her. *'I'll get Shelley to sleep. I'll fix her up,'* he cackled, winking at me with a white, sharp eye.

'That's a good girl, now you have a nice long sleep,' I whispered as her eyelids drooped and closed. 'When you wake up I bet that nasty colic will be gone. And soon you'll grow up and my mother will take us *both* to the beach. If there's two of us nagging her, no way she'll be able to refuse.'

A single scarlet blossom had somehow sneaked beneath the pram netting. It mustn't have bothered Shelley because she slept on, so I left the flower where it had fallen onto her little chest, rising and falling with her gentle breaths.

'Phew, bit of peace at last,' Nanna Purvis said, as I hurried across the parched grass to the verandah shade, out of that brutal heat my grandmother claimed sent people mad; pushed them to do strange and terrible things they normally wouldn't dream of.

I grabbed the half-eaten packet of Iced VoVos and plonked down on the wooden verandah boards as far as possible from the annoying grandmother and her smelly dog.

I swung my legs over the edge, faster and faster, stuffing biscuits into my mouth, watching the baby sleeping.

'Oy, who said you could eat me Iced VoVos?' Nanna Purvis said.

'You don't pay for the biscuits. Dad does, so that gives me more right to eat them than you.'

'Ah, Tanya, I've told ya before, if you want them nasty school-kids to stop their teasing, you'll have to cut out the bikkies.'

'Who cares?' I shovelled the last biscuit into my mouth, but that full, warm feeling of a bellyful of biscuit didn't last. The sickness was surging from my gut. I swallowed hard, blinked away my tears. I did care. Hated myself for gobbling so much food; disgusted at the blobs that quivered around my middle every time I moved.

'Don't know what's got into ya,' Nanna Purvis went on, 'eating like there's no tomorrow.' She shook her blue curls, turned back to *Only for Sheilas*.

I snatched up my yoyo, Steely's gaze moving around, up and down, a paw swiping at the string as I dangled the yoyo over the verandah edge for "walk the dog" and "around the world".

'And another thing,' Nanna Purvis said. 'Noticed you've had a bit of a growth spurt in the boobies department these last months. Ya mum needs to get you a training bra or they'll end up hanging around ya knees like mine. Only natural, now ya got the monthly curse.'

Oh my god, how totally embarrassing. I stared at Nanna Purvis as she hobbled off into the kitchen. How dare she talk about that thing which had happened only once, and which you did not talk about with your *grandmother*.

I chucked the yoyo over the verandah edge faster, harder, thinking about that pamphlet — *The Birds 'n the Bees* — my mother had given me to read which told you nothing apart from the fact that you could now make babies.

Sullen puffs of smoke from the copper smelter stack of the Port Kembla Steelworks pumped into the sky, and the patch of Pacific Ocean in the distance taunted me with its woodsy-green coolness.

'Wouldn't I love to be in that sea right now, Steely?' I threw the yoyo aside, started picking at rust-coloured flakes of paint from a verandah post. 'I know Mum's having a hard time of it with Shelley's colic, Steely-boy, but I reckon she could still take me to the beach. It's not fair, is it?'

No, fairness was only for happy people, which poor little Shelley and her colic had stolen from the Randall family.

Chapter 8

It was almost dusk when the Holden lurched into the driveway — Dad, back from downing schooners with his mates at the pub. At the same time, another car roared off down Figtree Avenue, but my Venetians were closed so I couldn't see who was scarpering off in such a hurry.

I closed *Real Life Crime*, slid from my bed, kicked at the hateful rose-pattered bedspread from where I'd chucked it on the floor, and watched my father stagger into the hallway.

His eyes were stained red, breath filling the house with the reek of beer. Same as every afternoon now. He bent down to pat Bitta and Billie-Jean, tripped over the quivering bundles of fur and stumbled. I thought he was going to lose his balance and fall over, but he righted himself with a hand on the plastic carpet strip, and scratched the dogs' heads.

'Wearing the wobbly boot *again*, Dobson,' Nanna Purvis said, as I pushed past him into the kitchen to feed Steely. My mother didn't look up from where she was bent over scrubbing the oven. 'If you didn't spend so much time down that pub … if you were home a bit more,' my grandmother went on, 'things might be easier for us with Shelley's colic and crying.'

'Easier for *us*?' Dad said. 'Doesn't strike me you're helping much with the baby, Pearl.' He slapped his Akubra onto the table, flung his hands in the air. 'Eleanor, can't you do *something*? It's not normal for a kid to scream nonstop. Can you at least look at me when I'm talking to you?'

'The clinic nurse says if a baby is healthy and gaining weight,' Mum said, her gaze fixed on the oven, 'it's only colic, which will pass. I just have to be patient and not worry too much. Leave her be and get on with things.' She scrubbed so hard every word shook. 'So that's what I'm doing, getting on with things.'

Dad disappeared into the bedroom, returning with the crying Shelley slung over one shoulder, like a sack containing something tight and hard.

'Well you still need to stop all this bloody cleaning, Eleanor,' he went on, jigging around, patting the baby's back. 'Every time I come home it's clean, wash, scrub. Clean, wash, scrub. Just look at the state you're in.'

She gazed up at him from eyes sunk into their sockets, hollow as a green-brown sea swell, hair hanging about her shoulders like dirty rope. She'd always been thin but her bones now stuck out as if her skeleton was on the outside.

Still holding Shelley, he laid his free hand on Mum's shoulder, gave it a gentle squeeze. 'I'm just worried about you, love,' he said, the snap fading from his voice. 'This is getting too much for you ... too much for *all* of us.'

'That's what I've been trying to tell her,' Nanna Purvis said. 'Put ya feet up with a cuppa, I keep saying. But she's always flat out like a lizard drinking.'

My mother stood up, hands black with oven grease, a slick of it slashed across her brow.

'Put my feet up? You must be joking ... so much to do around this place.' She couldn't stop shaking her head and waving the greasy hands. 'And the baby... the baby ...'

'Lenny Longbum might have a point,' Nanna Purvis said. 'And it's this cursed house what's making Shelley sick. I've always known something wasn't right about Gumtree Cottage. Never has been. Well, what can you expect from number thirteen in any street?' She gathered Billie-Jean into her arms and took him out to the backyard.

Dad raised his eyebrows in that dark, furry line; threw me

a small smile. 'Your grandmother and her silly superstitious legends.'

He handed me the baby, lit a fag, took a bottle of KB Lager from the fridge and popped the top. *Click-click, click-click* went his push-button ashtray. Dad had one in every room of the house because he'd got a batch of them on special for fifty-nine cents each.

I wanted to agree with him; to say yes, Nanna Purvis was spouting her rubbish, but instead I said, 'Haven't you had enough beer for today?'

'Last one, Princess.' He winked, and as he drank it down in one long swallow, Old Lenny appeared at the flyscreen door in his usual faded blue singlet and baggy shorts.

'Youse still can't do a thing about that kid's noise?' he said.

Red-hot anger rose from my belly, caught in my throat. 'How dare you say that when we're trying everything — *everything* — to stop her?' I stamped towards the door.

'Don't, Tanya,' Dad said, grabbing my arm.

'A mate of mine reckons Coca-Cola did the trick for his grandkid's colic,' Old Lenny said, holding up a can of Coca-Cola. 'Mix it with water … shake the fizz out before youse put it in her bottle. I bet me money on it, that'll stop her noise.'

'Stop her noise … stop it, stop it.' Mum's voice came from her dark seabed — muffled, liquidy.

Stop it. Stop it.

The words clanged back at me as if Gumtree Cottage were shuddering, its walls — solid that they were — straining and buckling beneath the din. I wedged two slices of bread into my mouth, chewed as if I'd been starved for days. My jangly nerves settled.

'Quit eating, Tanya, you'll spoil ya tea,' Nanna Purvis said, and the bread churned in my guts, knotting it like tangled ropes.

I prepared Shelley's bottle, Old Lenny hovering about, checking I added the right amount of Coca-Cola. I sat back at the kitchen table and everyone except my mother watched in silence as I fed Shelley.

She finished her bottle, burped loudly, let out a sigh and lay peacefully in my arms, her dark gaze shifting over us as if she was wondering why we were all staring at her.

'Told youse it'd work,' Old Lenny said with a victorious smirk. 'I got a whole carton of the stuff if youse need it. Got it cheap off a mate. Give you a good price for a dozen, Dobson?'

Dad nodded and Old Lenny limped back next door to his pokey flat, converted from his son and daughter-in-law's garage.

'Maybe the answer's as simple as that?' Dad said. 'Coca-Cola?'

My mother shrugged and shook her head as if nothing he said was even worth a reply. Or as if the answer to Shelley's colic couldn't possibly be that simple.

* * *

I straightened out the cot sheet and Shelley's lambskin, lined up her fluffy teddy bear, dolphin and cat against the bars.

'Gently, don't wake her,' I said, as Dad eased her down onto the lambskin. He patted a fingertip to his lips as we crept out of the bedroom.

Shelley slept right through tea. Nobody spoke, not even Nanna Purvis. All of us so slain with fatigue we didn't have the energy to eat and speak at the same time. Either that or we had nothing to say to each other.

'Tanya and I'll clear up the tea things,' Dad said to Mum as he lurched over to the sink with the dirty plates. A knife clattered onto the floor. My mother jumped at the noise. Nanna Purvis scowled. We held our breath, waiting for Shelley to start crying. But she didn't, and our relieved exhalations filled the hot kitchen air.

'Off you go to bed, love,' Dad said to Mum. 'Have an early night. Can I get you anything? Nice hot cuppa?'

'I'll just heat up some milk,' Mum said, as Nanna Purvis went into the living-room and settled herself on the sofa to watch her evening television shows with Billie-Jean and a nip of sherry.

Mum took a Valium with her milk, the pills the doc had prescribed for anxiety and sleeplessness in those sad times after the unborn babies. She crushed part of another tablet into the bottle she made up for Shelley's night feed, along with a dose of Old Lenny's Coca-Cola.

I took Steely into my bedroom, shut the door, slumped on my bed and opened *Real Life Crime* to the story I'd been reading earlier. A pair of moths swirled around the ceiling light in that hot, thick air. Inside, though, I was frozen — iced up with Shelley's pain and crying, my mother's rising misery and her crazy cleaning. And my father's guzzling more and more beer.

I'd lived all my life in Gumtree Cottage, always slept in the same bedroom, so it had come as a shock a few years ago when Mum said: 'You'll have to give your bedroom to Nanna Purvis, Tanya. She's old and will be cooler in your east-facing room.'

Nanna Purvis used to live with Pop Purvis — my mother's father — in a standard red-brick house in Gallipoli Street, but when Pop Purvis died of a dicky ticker while sitting on the toilet, she and Billie-Jean moved into Figtree Avenue with us.

My mother had made me shift all my stuff into one of the hot, west-facing bedrooms that gave onto the front verandah, and the street.

The eaves dropping low across the front verandah, and the ugly cream wallpaper patterned with posies of violets, made the bedroom dark, stuffy and dingy-looking. I'd never forgiven Mum or Nanna Purvis for stealing my light and airy bedroom on Gumtree Cottage's sea-facing side.

From my bedside table drawer, I took the bag of Jelly Babies I'd bought on the way home from school. I started on the red ones, dragged down the box of Barbies from the top shelf of the wardrobe and sat cross-legged on the floor.

I hadn't done the Barbies' hair and makeup since I was a kid, so I don't know what made me tip them out onto the carpet and line them up in a row: Twiggy, Ken, Skipper, black Christie, Miss America and Sunset Malibu Barbie.

No more red Jelly Babies. I started munching through the green ones. 'That's how skinny you have to be, Steely,' I said, holding Twiggy Barbie before my cat's face. 'If you want to become a famous fashion model on telly and the cover of magazines all over the world, *Vogue, The Tatler* and stuff. Can you imagine that?'

I finished off the Jelly Babies — the black ones last — and kicked the packet under the bed where I couldn't see it. I pinched my belly blubber until it hurt.

You're stupid and hopeless and fat and I hate you.

Steely sat up straight, ears pointed, as a light *tap-tap-tap* came on my window. Someone knocking? I stayed very still, on the floor, too afraid to open the Venetians; terrified it might be that nightmares' burglar with his stabbing knife. There it was again: *tap-tap-tap.*

I was just about to yell out to Dad when he appeared in my doorway. He'd had more beer. I could smell it on his breath, see it from the way he leaned against the frame as if it was holding him up.

The knocking stopped and I figured I must have imagined it. I didn't say anything to my father, wouldn't want him to think I was a stupid kid scared over nothing.

'Before tea, you said that was the last beer, Dad?'

As usual he changed the subject. 'School tomorrow, Princess, time for lights out.'

'What're we going to do about Shelley's colic, Dad? She must be hurting so bad, to scream all the time. And the Coca-Cola won't work forever, you know it won't! And what about Mum cleaning all the time? I'm helping her as much as I can, with the baby and everything, but it's never enough.'

Dad ruffled my hair. 'I know you're helping your mum, I know. Let's just hope this colic thing passes soon.'

Shelley's colic did not pass. On and on it lingered, right through those blazing December days and nights, the hottest — and maddest — month of 1972.

Oh, there were times when it wasn't too bad. She'd often sleep after her morning feed through till lunchtime. As if making up for the wakeful afternoons, evenings and most nights — the nights my mother forgot to crush Valium into her bottle, or the next remedy on the list failed.

But this particular night Shelley slept right through. There was no more mysterious knocking on my window, and the night was silent. Someone had turned off a machine that had been running for so long we'd become used to the noise. And it was not the noise, but the silence, that was strange.

Chapter 9

'A meet up is a beaut idea,' Uncle Blackie said. My hand gripping the phone shook, my gaze skittering about watching for Mum or Nanna Purvis to catch me. 'Give me half an hour, Tanya.'

'See you then,' I whispered.

I hadn't seen Uncle Blackie again, but his address and phone number were still firmly secreted in my mind. I'd gone back to our secret bush spot several times in the hope he'd be there, though he never was.

But walking home from school each day, I'd sensed my uncle close by. Amidst the dense gum and fig tree leaves, and all the flowers, I was certain I'd glimpsed the oily brown swirl of his Driza-Bone. Ghost-like, he was watching me, out of sight, just waiting for the right time when there was nobody around to leap from behind a bottlebrush bush and surprise me.

Over those two weeks I'd kept asking myself if I should go to his place. After all, he *had* given me his address, so it wouldn't be like I was turning up uninvited.

As I'd trudged up the Figtree Avenue hill after school, the purple jacaranda and red flame blossoms were nodding in the warm breeze as if saying: '*Phone him. Go on, don't be scared. He looks so like your Dad; not a bit like a kidnapper or any other kind of thug. Of course you can phone your own uncle, you silly goon.*'

I'd called Uncle Blackie as soon as I got home.

'Who was that on the phone, Tanya?' Nanna Purvis called

from the kitchen as I jammed down the receiver. 'Didn't even know ya'd got in from school.'

'None of your business. But if you really want to know, it was Angela,' I lied. 'I was calling her to check our homework.'

'What've I told you about hanging around with that foreign girl?' Nanna Purvis hobbled into the hallway. 'Can't ya find any Aussie mates?'

'Why do my mates have to be Aussie?' I said, stuffing *Real Life Crime* into the Indian bag. 'Angela's my best friend and I don't need you to pick my mates for me.'

I scurried into my parents' bedroom, leaned into the cot over the whining Shelley and planted a gentle kiss on her soft pink cheek. 'See you later, little gumnut girl … we'll play with your teddy bear together.'

'So where you off to now?' Nanna Purvis said as I hurried back down the hallway and clipped Steely's leash onto his collar.

'Taking my cat for a walk, isn't that obvious?'

'Gawd, whatever,' she said as I shut the front door behind me.

I had plenty of time but I wanted to get away from Gumtree Cottage — to see my new and exciting friend — as quickly as possible. So I hurried up the street, keeping to the wide shade of the Moreton Bay figs.

Once I reached the bush spot I slumped down onto my rock in the sparse shade and pulled out *Real Life Crime*.

Steely nosing around the sun-baked ground, I started reading a story about an eight-year-old boy who was murdered after his parents won the lottery and suddenly there was Uncle Blackie — gangly and handsome and smiling down at me.

* * *

'Hey, Tanya, great to see you,' he said in the dreamy ocean voice. He sat beside me on my rock, scratched Steely's head and handed me another bag of Redskins and Milk Bottles.

'Yum. Thanks, Uncle Blackie.'

We sat in silence while I munched through the Milk Bottles.

'Did you know he's the best camouflaged lizard?' I said, pointing to a frilled-neck lizard the same colour as the rock on which it was sunning itself.

'Oh yes, a master chameleon,' Uncle Blackie said. 'So, managing to keep your chin up at home, Tanya? I gather things've got pretty bad?'

I shrugged, my fingers flying to the cowlick. 'Yeah, pretty bad what with … with everything.'

'I'm sorry you're having a hard time. I'm guessing you're a strong girl who can cope with a lot, but just know I'm here if you need to talk about things.'

Uncle Blackie swiped at a fly buzzing around my leg. A hand slid down onto my knee, rough fingers rubbing at the scar. 'What happened here?'

'Banged into Mum's Hill's Hoist.'

'That must've hurt.'

I shrugged again, my leg jerking away from his touch. 'A bit.'

He cupped a hand under my chin and lifted my face to meet his dark gaze. 'Your mum could've been a model,' he said. 'Just like you could be, Tanya.'

'Me, a model? Oh yeah, sure.'

'Yeah, sure,' he said. 'And you know what? After I met you up the bush track that first time, I had this idea.'

'What idea?'

'Have you thought about entering Miss Beach Girl 1973, Tanya?'

'What's Miss Beach Girl 1973?'

'A beauty quest,' Uncle Blackie said. 'Early next year, the organisers will walk around Wollongong beaches picking out beautiful girls. The winner gets a trip to New York and a guaranteed six-month photographic modelling contract. So, the chance to become a famous model.'

'Be cool to be a model but I've got Buckley's Chance of *that* ever happening.'

'Don't be silly, you've got every chance in the world,' Uncle

Blackie said, and as he told me about the photographers who would photograph me in the latest-fashion clothes with jewellery and make-up that would make my eyes glitter like amber and emeralds, my cheeks grew hotter.

'I could take some photos of you, Tanya, show you what it's all about. If you want, that is, then you'd know exactly what it is to be a model. What do you say?'

'Nah, everybody reckons I've got bat wings for ears. "Batgirl" they call me — and I *am* fat. I know I am.'

'You'll slim down, don't worry,' he said. 'Besides, those models aren't as beautiful as they're made out, you know, Tanya. It's all camera angles and make believe. They're quite plain in real life in fact. And I already told you, just wear your hair a different way and nobody will notice your ears. The same as your mum did when she was young.'

'You're really a photographer, Uncle Blackie?'

'Yeah, I'm pretty good with a camera. So what do you say? No pressure, only if you want.'

'Okay, if you really think I've got a chance at this beauty quest, why not?'

Chapter 10

It was morning recess and Angela and I sat in the shade of a fig tree forcing sips of our warm milk.

'This is disgusting,' I said, a hand shading my eyes from the sun's glare as I threw the half-finished milk carton into the bin.

'If it didn't sit outside in those crates all morning before we got to drink it,' Angela said, 'it wouldn't taste so awful.'

'Or they could keep it in a fridge?'

'You'd never find a fridge big enough for all the school milk,' Angela said. 'Oh well, only one more year of primary school, then we won't have to drink disgusting warm milk anymore.'

'I hope they won't make us drink it in high school?'

'No, my brother told me they don't,' Angela said. 'I can't wait for high school, primary's *so* boring.' She held up her hands enlaced with the cat's cradle string. 'Your turn.' I hooked my thumbs and forefingers around the string.

Angela Moretti had started at my primary school in the middle of last year. She came from Cringila, a southern Wollongong migrant suburb right next to the Port Kembla Steelworks.

Dad told me that Cringila had started out as just a few shacks and tents for the steelworkers, and was originally called Steeltown.

The school often kept the foreign kids back a year, as if they were dumb and needed to catch up to the Aussie kids. But they weren't dumb, especially not Angela, who always put her hand up first in class and answered every question correctly. So even though she was in my class, Angela was eight months older than me — almost twelve years old — and could've easily managed sixth grade this year.

I never understood why she'd wanted to be friends with me. Maybe because I was one of the few schoolkids who spoke to her, except to call her a dirty *Eyetie*, even though she spoke exactly like an Aussie. Or perhaps because Angela was a bit tubby too.

'Anyway, soon we'll get a whole six weeks of *no* school and not having to listen to them,' I said, nodding at Stacey Mornon and her moron friends, sunning their legs and blowing gum.

I stiffened, sensed the taunts hovering on their lips as Stacey and her friends got up and sauntered over to us.

'That's so sweet,' Stacey said with a sneer. 'Miss Adopted Batgirl Ten-ton and Miss *Eyetie* are best friends.'

'How's your dad's drug business going, Angela?' one of Stacey's friends said, which made them all explode into giggles.

Angela leapt to her feet. 'Drug business?'

I stood too, one hand on Angela's arm, trying to urge her away. 'Let's go, we don't need to listen to them.'

But the girls marched off into the sweltering air, laughing and holding onto each other as if it was so funny they might fall over.

'What drug business?' Angela said with a frown. 'What are they talking about?'

'It's nothing, just rubbish for sure,' I said. Of course I wasn't going to tell Angela that my grandmother reckoned her father, the carpet-layer, peddled drugs in his rolls of carpet. Nor that Nanna Purvis had forbidden me to be friends with "that foreign *Eyetie* girl".

'And anyway, why does Stacey keep saying you're adopted?' Angela said. 'How does she know?'

'Because her birthday's the same day as mine, and Stacey's mum told her my mother was not in Wollongong Hospital having me when she was having Stacey. But as if I'd believe anything that moron says.'

'You could've been born in another hospital?' Angela said.

'What other hospital? There's only Wollongong Hospital to have babies, isn't there?'

'Why don't you just ask your mamma and papa?'

'I have. All they say is: "why do you keep asking that, Tanya?" I thought Uncle Blackie would know the truth but he wasn't around back then.'

'Who's Uncle Blackie?'

'He's Dad's brother, but you can't say anything about him because Uncle Blackie's a kind of secret.'

'Where was he then?' Angela said. 'And why's he a secret?'

'Dunno, probably just my grandmother's usual bossiness, telling us who we can and can't see. And I don't know where he was ... somewhere he had to do lots of gardening, apparently. Anyway I think he's some far-out photographer because he wants me to go over to his place to do a photo shoot. You know, like practise for the Miss Beach Girl 1973 quest.'

'Wow, groovy,' Angela said.

'Yeah, he thinks I might have a chance of winning, but I completely doubt that. Anyway, Uncle Blackie reckons Stacey's only being spiteful, which is probably due to her parents getting divorced.'

'Why're they getting divorced?'

'Nanna Purvis says it's because of Mrs Mornon's totally uncool orange lipstick and her stiff hair, and that daggy net she wears to be sure the hair won't move. Can you imagine a *net*?' My lip curled. 'Anyway, her face is so misery guts and she's always grumpy ... Mr Mornon couldn't stand it so he ran off with his secretary.'

'How do you know all this?'

'My grandmother's hairdresser told her the whole story.'

'Oh right,' Angela said as the end of recess bell started ringing. 'Hey, you'll have to come over to my place in the holidays for a swim.'

'You've got a swimming pool? Wow your dad must be rich.'

'You should've seen the crummy little Cringila shack we lived in before Papa worked really hard,' Angela said over the din of the clanging bell, 'and could afford the house in Bottlebrush Crescent.'

We'd driven through Cringila once or twice, and I did recall the small and shabby-looking houses, many of them painted blue.

'Steelworks' paint,' my father had said. 'They get it cheap.'

'Papa was a good swimmer when he was a boy,' Angela said as we hurried to class beneath the sun's blaze, and I thought longingly of the days my mother used to take me to the beach.

'They were really poor when they left Naples and came to Australia, but he told Mamma he'd work a lot so one day he'd have a swimming pool in his own backyard, like successful Australians do. So would your mamma let you come to my place?'

'My mother doesn't care what I do anymore. She's too busy cleaning the house. That's all she ever does. I even threw out all her cleaning stuff but the very next day there were new cans of the same disinfectants in the cupboard. Oh I know she's just trying to block out the noise — and the *problem* — of Shelley's colic crying but ...'

'Your sister's *still* got the colic?' Angela said. 'Poor little baby.'

'Yeah, poor Shelley. But when she's not crying she's the cutest baby. You'll have to come over and see her sometime.'

'One of my little cousins had colic,' Angela said, as we walked into class. 'And her mamma would mix olive oil with salt and rub it on the baby's belly, back and legs. Maybe your mamma could try that?'

I nodded and realised, with a twang of guilt, that up to now, I hadn't thought once about Shelley's colic, or my mother's frantic cleaning. I was too busy glowing with the warmth of my first best friend — a friend who smelled nutty and exotic, and nothing like garlic or pizza as Nanna Purvis claimed.

Someone to laugh with, to swap stories and secrets. Like a mysterious uncle.

* * *

But after school, Shelley's cries battered my eardrums as I thumped across the rickety verandah boards, and that king-tide swamping me once more.

The front of Gumtree Cottage reminded me of an old person's face: a bit worn out and ragged. The corrugated iron roof was a hat sitting over a sandstone-brick face, sloping low across the verandah as if to hide half the face. The windows of my bedroom and my parents' were boxy eyes staring out onto Figtree Avenue, watching everyone who went up and down the street, all those who'd ever come to the bungalow. The front door was a thin straight nose, the full-length verandah a wide mouth. Of the jasmine creeping along the side fences, and the bottlebrush lining it, I imagined bushy tufts of hair jutting from the old person's ears. And each time my mother's misery set in, the face took on a scowl, the house sinking lower into the sun-parched earth.

The day had not cooled off — the temperature only soaring — without the slightest whiff of sea breeze to shift the stifling air. And even if my mother had the time, without her real and imagined cleaning tasks, she'd never take me to the beach because she'd stopped driving altogether; had pretty much stopped leaving the house. As if Gumtree Cottage had taken her prisoner — trapped her like all of its old ghosts.

'Okay, that's enough crying, Shelley,' I said, taking my scarlet-cheeked sister from her cot. There was no sign of our mother, though I could hear her washing machine sloshing away down in the back-yard laundry shed.

I carried her into the bathroom and bathed her face, arms and neck with a cool washer. I held her, tummy down, over my forearm and swayed. 'Shush, shush, you'll be better soon.'

I made up a mixture of olive oil and salt, undressed her and rubbed it over her squirming little body. She quietened down and gurgled at me. I kept cradling Shelley as I sat at the kitchen table, glugged down some green cordial and chomped through four slices of bread and cheese. I was becoming a master of the one-handed task.

I laid Shelley on the small patch of living-room carpet my mother hadn't covered with plastic, and took her favourite plastic ball from the toy box. I gave it a little push and the transparent ball rocked to and fro. Shelley's eyes widened as the little creatures inside the ball — a penguin, a duck, a pony — moved. She grabbed at it, clumsy fingers not yet able to grasp the big ball. I moved it again, she cooed and dribbled and gave me a gummy smile.

Steely slunk up to us, a paw toying with the ball. The penguin, duck and pony wobbled faster and I giggled at Shelley shrieking in wonder.

'Thank god Dad said he'd take me for a swim, eh Shelley? That's if he ever gets home before dark.' But Shelley wasn't listening to me. She'd managed to grab Billie-Jean's plastic bone, and was trying to ram it into her mouth.

'Yuck, give me that.' I took the slobbery bone, chucked it aside, and when Shelley smiled I saw the faintest white sliver of her first tooth.

I took her hand, stroked Steely with it. 'And when you're grown up, we'll swim at the beach together. I'll push you on the swings too and give you see-saw rides. It'll be great when you're old enough to really play.'

But Shelley had fallen asleep, there on the living-room floor. Mum would freak out if she saw the baby sleeping on her supposedly dirty carpet, though no way did I dare move her to the cot.

Steely and Shelley sleeping side by side, I opened the packet of Riviera Fags I'd bought at the corner shop. I took one of the musk-flavoured lollies, sucked on the end, frowning at the other red-tipped end. Same as Dad did with his real fags.

My father had promised to come straight home from work to take me to the beach. But he didn't. When he finally arrived I could tell he'd stopped off at The Dead Dingo's Donger because his breath stank of beer and his eyes were red, glassy and slightly crossed. I was still sitting on the carpet beside Shelley and Steely sleeping, the empty packet of Riviera Fags ripped to shreds beside me.

'Ready to ride the waves, Princess?' he slurred. He kissed Shelley's brow, ran a hand through her liquorice twirls of hair. 'Where's your mother?'

'Down in the laundry I think ... haven't seen her since I got home.'

As if she'd heard Dad talking about her, my mother came trudging inside, clutching her washing basket overflowing with clothes fresh off the washing line.

'Why's the baby sleeping on this grubby carpet, Tanya?' she said.

'I was playing with her and — '

'Get her off the floor.' The hair hanging in greasy clumps about Mum's shoulders shook in time with her voice.

'Leave Tanya be,' Dad said. 'The baby's sleeping at least. And if you stopped all this bloody cleaning and paid Shelley a bit more attention, Tanya wouldn't have to take care of her all the time.'

'I do all I can for that baby,' Mum said, staring down at her bony bare feet. 'I can't do any more ... can't ...'

Dad shook his head. 'Jesus bloody Christ, what's happened to you?'

'N-nothing,' Mum stammered. She looked up at us, gloom clinging to her like the ugly sweat-stained cleaning shift. Her eyes filled with tears. 'I don't know. Nothing ... everything's fine.'

Dad sighed. His voice grew louder, snappier. 'Oh yeah, Eleanor. I can see everything's fine. Just fine and bloody dandy!'

Chapter 11

It was still sweltering at North Beach but I was glad I'd got my father away from yelling at my mother — from the tautest elastic stretched between them.

Over the westward mountains, white cloud puffs hovered, their dolphin-grey underbellies hugging the escarpment but over the sea the sky was blue and cloudless.

Wet-suit-clad surfers, boards tucked under one arm, hands shading eyes, stood on the shoreline searching for the best surfing spot.

'What're you waiting for?' Dad said, stripping down to his Speedos. 'Thought you were so hot you'd be in the water the second we arrived?'

'Coming.' I slapped zinc cream onto my face, silently willing Dad to go on ahead of me. It was becoming totally embarrassing to be seen with my father wearing Speedos. They were only for little kids and old men, and I wished he'd wear board shorts over them, like the surfies did.

The sun searing holes through my back, Dad weaved alongside me, puffing out his beery breath as we skittered towards waves thick with foam. As if someone had squeezed whipped cream across the rim.

'Watch out for the plovers' eggs,' I said, as we scattered a crowd of the tiny red-capped birds. 'That's what my teacher said, be careful of their scraped-out nests, and their eggs.'

'Don't worry, plovers lay their eggs in January,' Dad said. 'I think.'

But as we ran into the cool shallows, I thought how easy it would be to accidentally crush those unborn plovers. I wondered how any of them survived to hatch out. And even if they did make it beyond the egg, who's to say they'd not be immediately squashed; murdered by some careless human?

As Dad dived beneath a wave and swam out, I sat in the shallows thinking about the poor murdered plovers, the salt on the offshore breeze whipping my cheeks, stinging my eyes, two coal tankers — pirate ships! — slipping across the horizon.

A couple swimming beyond the breakers had drifted outside the flags and a surf-lifesaver was blowing his whistle at them. He waved his arms, motioning at them to get back in between the flags.

'Stay between the flags,' everyone always says. 'It's only safe between the flags.' As if an inch either side of the red and yellow flags the surf becomes suddenly dangerous.

The surf-lifesaver jogged along the shore, still waving his arms and blowing his whistle, harder, louder. But it was obvious the couple was in trouble, the rip tugging them further out to sea. The people around me had stopped squealing and jumping around in the surf, all heads turned to the swimmers getting smaller and smaller.

Three more lifesavers appeared and the four of them dragged the longboat down to the water. As they started rowing out over the breakers, I was reminded of the story of Australia's Lost Prime Minister. Harold Holt had gone for a swim one day in 1967 and was never seen again. Vanished. Forever probably.

Some reckoned a Chinese submarine kidnapped Harold Holt. Others, Nanna Purvis, for example, said a shark got him. But the surf-lifesavers were certain a rip had carried him off — those dangerous currents running at angles to the shore which we are powerless to control or fight.

The longboat bow bounced over the waves, tilting to an almost vertical angle.

Dad came and stood beside me, squinting at the distressed swimmers, eddies of white wash clinging to him like Pavlova meringue.

The longboat reached the swimmers, and someone cried out: 'Got 'em.'

'You bewdie,' shouted another and the onlookers resumed their frolicking, no longer thinking about lives that could be lost in a minute of being caught in the wrong place.

'Come on, Princess,' Dad said. 'Surf's great.' His voice was clear and sharp; the cool water had washed clean the beer slur.

I followed him out, struggled to get beyond the breakers, feeling the thrill as each wave pulled me up to the urgent curve of its peak.

And when I judged — because it was all in the exact timing — that the wave would crash on top of me, I dived deep, hunched into a ball against the drag of the sea. Scaring off schools of tiny gleaming fish, I gripped the rippled sandy bottom, listening to the murmur of its own special language as the silky arc broke above my head.

A break in the sets and Dad and I surfaced, and caught our breath.

I looked out at the deeper, dark water. If I stared for long enough I always imagined I could see the black bob of a whale or the menacing fin of a shark. But if I steadied my gaze, I realised there was nothing there at all. That it was only my brain tricking me.

'Hope there's no sharks,' I said.

Dad smiled. 'I won't let any silly shark eat you.'

I so wanted to believe him, like when I was a kid and believed everything my parents said because I'd thought adults always told the truth, believed they understood everything.

But now I knew otherwise, and I imagined the sharks speeding in from the deep, their fins boat propellers cutting through the water. They reached me, started circling. No escape. Trapped prey. They closed in on me, bit my body in half. My head, arms and trunk sank to the dark and murky seabed.

'I'm getting out of the water,' I yelled. 'Gotta get out!'

I thrashed about, breathless, riding on waves that tossed and tumbled me into the shallows.

I stumbled from the surf, giddy, sweeping hair from my eyes and hacking salty water from my throat.

Panting hard, I stood on the shoreline amidst clots of seaweed the leaving tide had thrown up. Some were like rags of lettuce, others were dark and wavy — the stolen curls of mermaids who now glided, bald, across the seabed. Another was a delicate green fern, fragile as Shelley.

A dead crab lay upside down amidst a cigarette butt, a discarded zinc tube and a child's sandal.

'Why're the crabs always upside down?' I asked my father. 'Do they flip over before or after they die?'

'Oh for god's sake, Tanya, who knows? And who cares?'

'Can we buy meat pies for tea?' I said. 'Mum probably won't have cooked anything at home.'

'I know your mother's a bit ... distracted, but you gotta understand the strain she's under. The strain we're *all* under.'

'I do, Dad. But that doesn't mean she can ignore everyone and everything except the housework.'

'I know. But I'm betting our little gumnut girl will be right soon and things ... Mum, will get back to normal.'

Oh sure. Another lie.

* * *

We sat on the grassy area over at Belmore Basin to eat our pies, chucking bits of tomato-sauce-sodden pastry to squawking seagulls. The ocean breeze ruffled their feathers as if airing them out.

Dad had brought two bottles of DA in the beach bag — the longnecks he called Dirty Annie's — which he swilled down with his pie.

A mother was pushing her little girl on the swing, and a stab, like the point of a fishing spear, jabbed at my heart. I remembered when my mother pushed me on swings, those times when she'd recover from the sadness of the last lost baby. In the state she was in now, I could never imagine her pushing Shelley on a swing. But I would. As soon as she was old enough, I'd make sure my baby sister was happy all the time.

The little girl squealed in glee, which sent the gulls off into a majestic grey and white flight and the whole beach seemed to rise into the sky with their shadows. *Thud, thud* went the see-saw, children's laughter a song against that sun darkened with seagull shadows.

It was twilight by the time we got back to the Holden, the hum inside a seashell still in my ears, the tang of salt still in my throat and nostrils.

House and street lights flickered on as Dad drove along the South Beach road, Wollongong's other main beach, mainly for surfers. From the Port Kembla Steelworks, furnace flames and smoke chugged into the dusk air.

A few moments later, on Corrimal Street, as we passed the Wollongong Golf Club, the Holden veered into the middle of the road. An oncoming car honked.

'Dad!'

My father jumped in his seat, rubbed his eyes with one hand, the other tightening on the wheel.

'You almost dozed off, didn't you?'

'Sorry, Princess.'

'Are you okay?'

'I'm fine, Tanya. Just a bit tired from your sister crying all night, and hard days at work.'

Of course Dad was tired from our wakeful nights. Shelley's crying had exhausted us all. But it wasn't only that and his hard bricklaying days making him sleepy. It was also too many schooners of beer.

A minute later I spotted the rabbit on the road in front of us, so enormous it might've been a hare. My father — bleary gaze fixed on something in the distance — didn't seem to notice it.

'Dad!' I grabbed the steering wheel; the Holden swerved madly.

He slammed on the brakes. The tyres squealed as the car skidded across the road.

The rabbit didn't budge, just stared straight into the Holden's oncoming headlights, and the last thing my father probably saw was the rabbit rising from the bumper bar through the twilight in a beige and red explosion of fur, blood and guts.

The car careened off the road. I screamed with the thud, my ears, my mind filling with the roar of crumpling metal, exploding glass. Then silence as the Holden came to rest, bonnet buried in the roadside ditch.

I looked across at my father. His arms hung limp, straight down beside him, his head resting against the steering wheel. A trickle of blood leaked down between his closed eyes.

Chapter 12

'Ya can't bring Shelley with us,' Nanna Purvis said a few days later, when the hospital said we were allowed to visit Dad. 'What if she yells the place down? Think of all them sick people.'

'I can hardly leave the baby on her own, can I?' Mum said. 'I'll stay here with her, you two go. Besides, the carpets need a good vacuum.'

'Why don't you want to see Dad?' I said. 'Anyway, the car trip will calm down Shelley.'

After the accident three days ago, when the ambulance had rushed Dad to Wollongong hospital, I couldn't stop shaking; could barely utter a single word, so they'd taken me too, for a check-over.

'You've had a shock,' the nurse said, 'but apart from a few bruises, no nasty injuries. You'll be right as rain in a day or so, love.'

Nanna Purvis and Old Lenny had come in Lenny's van to take me back to Gumtree Cottage; Mum stayed home with Shelley. I was still all trembly, couldn't think straight or make a proper sentence.

'Off to bed with you right now, Tanya,' my mother had said, popping half a Valium into a steaming cup of tea.

'Yeah, Eleanor, come and visit Dobson with us,' Nanna Purvis said. 'Do you good to get away from these four walls. Even if I am going to give Dobson a gobful, tell him how irresponsible he is, driving a kid around with all that grog under his belt. Downright dangerous it is.'

For once my grandmother wasn't talking rot. My father's beer-drinking could've killed me, and I was still half-angry at him for that. But half-glad he was still alive.

'And thank me lucky dilly bag you had that beach bag on ya lap, Tanya,' Nanna Purvis went on, 'or you'd have hit the windscreen like ya father thunked into the steering wheel.'

Mum looked around as if uncertain she could leave the safety of the house. 'All right, I'll come to the hospital, since you both insist,' she said, and dragged her cleaning shift over her head.

During the taxi ride, Shelley lay quietly on Mum's lap in her pink frilly dress. I grabbed a finger and she gave me a gummy smile, and gurgled as if she was trying to talk to me. Then she fell asleep.

'We ought to drive her around *every* night,' Nanna Purvis said with a grim smirk.

'Cute baby,' the taxi driver said, as we reached the Wollongong Hospital. 'Real well-behaved too.'

I had an urge to roll my eyes at him.

'Which ward is Dobson Randall on, please?' Nanna Purvis said to the hospital receptionist.

'Robson,' my mother cut in. '*Robson* Randall.'

Everybody forgot that Dad's mother, Nanna Randall, had actually named my father "Robson". But the person who'd written out his birth certificate had made the "R" stroke too short and everybody'd thought it was a "D". And since Nanna Randall had bled to death a year later and Pop Randall couldn't read or write, my father had ended up being called "Dobson" all his life.

Dad was in the end bed of a row of five down either side of the ward. All the patients were lying on their beds, wearing pyjamas or white hospital gowns, coughing, yawning or talking to visitors.

A wide bandage, spotted with dark blood, encircled my father's forehead. Purple bruises ringed both his eyes.

Nanna Purvis and Mum — holding Shelley — sat on the green plastic chairs beside the bed. I was still annoyed at Dad but I leaned over, kissed his cheek. His skin was clammy and cool against my lips.

There were only two chairs so I slumped, cross-legged, onto the floor in the corner.

Dad opened his eyes a crack and frowned. One shaky hand reached out, trying to touch my mother's, but Mum kept her hands around the bundle of Shelley, just beyond his grasp. Dad seemed too weak to reach any further and Mum didn't move closer. Her blank gaze began skimming the white hospital walls, probably checking for dirty marks, or to avoid looking at her husband.

He sighed and closed his eyes. Nobody spoke, the three of us sitting there in silence, staring at Dad. Shelley slept in Mum's arms. I picked at strips of loose paint on the wall behind me.

After a few minutes Dad opened his eyes, frowned again. 'Blackie … think … saw him outside house …'

Nanna Purvis straightened in her chair, gnarly hands gripping her crocheted handbag. 'Blackie … what do you mean you saw him?' She glanced sharply at my mother, who turned her attention from the walls to Dad.

My fingers stilled on the peeling paint, my ears burning.

'Saw … Blackburn …' Dad managed to say before his voice trailed off and the eyelids drooped shut.

'Why's he gabbling on about seeing Blackie, Eleanor?' Nanna Purvis glared at my mother. 'Impossible. That bad egg's still locked up. At least I hope he is, and the key flushed down the dunny for what he did to that Carter girl.'

The man in the next bed stared across at us.

'Mind your own bananas, you,' Nanna Purvis said to the man, and reefed closed the curtain separating the beds.

Mum said nothing but a strange look came over her face. A kind of odd, half-smile which vanished as quickly as it had appeared.

'Who's that Carter girl?' I said.

'Nobody.' Nanna clamped her lips into a firm line.

My grandmother wouldn't tell me about that Carter girl. Well, too bad, Uncle Blackie would. I bet my groovy secret uncle would tell me anything I wanted to know.

* * *

I dawdled over to Dad's bedside table, flicked through his "get well" cards, mostly from his brickie and pub mates. There was also one from Mavis and Mad Myrtle Sloan next door. Another, from the Andersons across the road, was decorated in fuzzed-out roses like a sympathy card. I hoped we wouldn't be needing any of those "death" cards. There were two from the Mornons — one from Mrs and the other from Mr — because they'd divorced by now. The Longbottoms had sent nothing, which wasn't surprising. If Old Lenny's constant over-the-fence complaints about Shelley's noise were anything to go by, they probably hated us.

The biggest and brightest card, along with the largest and prettiest bouquet of flowers, came from Angela's parents. But you couldn't see the card properly because Nanna Purvis had slid it to the back behind the others.

'This is the nicest one,' I said, moving the Morettis' card to the front so it half-hid all the others.

'Bought with drug money no doubt,' Nanna Purvis said, 'along with those fancy flowers. Laundering they call it. Now put it back out of sight, Tanya.'

'What's *laundering*?' I said. 'And how can you say that about my best friend's family? Anyway, Angela's invited me over to her place in the holidays to swim in her pool and you can't stop me going.'

Nanna Purvis shook her blue curls. 'I can't allow that, Tanya. What if you fall into drugs or something? With your mother barely in the game these days,' she went on, nodding at Mum who'd gone back to staring at the hospital walls, 'and your father always down The Dead Dingo's Donger — when he's not in the hospital that is — it's my job to protect you from people such as that Moretti mob.'

'You can't stop me seeing my friends,' I said. '*You're* not my parent.'

Nanna Purvis glared at me as a nurse came over to Dad's bed. She looked like a tidy white parcel in her thick stockings that the heat must've stuck to her legs, her white uniform, and her cap that made me think of two seagulls glued together on top of her head.

She took Dad's pulse, blood pressure and temperature, and shone a torch into his eyes.

'Just checking your dad's okay after the accident,' she said, and wrote on a chart at the end of his bed.

'Is my father going to die?'

'Your dad's going to be fine,' the nurse said with the kind of friendly smile you'd give a small kid. The kind of lie you'd tell someone so as not to upset them. 'He's had a nasty knock on the head but you see, he'll be better soon.'

'He's confused, nurse,' Nanna Purvis said. 'Seeing things — people — who can't be there. That normal?'

'Oh yes, confusion and hallucinations *can* be concussion symptoms.'

'Me hairdresser, Rita, said her neighbour's brother had hallucinations,' Nanna Purvis said. 'Another one what wore the wobbly boot.'

'Will he wake up properly?' I said.

'I don't know … er, yes of course,' the nurse said. 'And if … when he does wake up, you should tell your dad to get seat belts fitted in his car.'

'Right, it seems Dobson's in good hands,' Nanna Purvis said after ten more minutes of us watching Dad sleep. She bounced the crocheted bag on her lap again. 'We'd best be getting home.

Billie-Jean'll be wanting his tucker and I haven't even defrosted his meat yet.'

Shelley cried all the way back to Figtree Avenue. The taxi driver — a different one — kept glancing at us in his rear-vision mirror.

'She's got colic,' I said.

'My missus reckons a few drops of eucalyptus oil in a hot bath does the trick,' he said, pulling up outside Gumtree Cottage. 'Well, good luck.'

Mum hurried inside with Shelley, Nanna Purvis hobbling along behind her. As they disappeared down the hallway, I caught a rustling noise. It came from behind the wide trunk of the fig tree closest to our house. I held my breath, swivelled around, squinted into the twilight. I stood still, listened. But there was nothing. No people. No birds or dusk creatures. I was sure I felt it though. There was someone, or some*thing*, out there.

I wasn't hanging around to find out what it was though, and I scurried inside, closed the door and locked it, Nanna Purvis's ghost tales rattling through my head.

* * *

'I dunno how long Dobson's planning on staying in that hospital,' Nanna Purvis said, spooning out Billie-Jean's kangaroo meat. 'But if it's too much longer, the housekeeping money'll never cover these taxi trips. We'll have to save more grocery money, I'll have a look at the Specials in the newspaper. Eleanor?'

My mother didn't answer though I was sure she could hear Nanna Purvis because Shelley had quietened. They were so strange, those small bouts of silence sitting heavy on the hot air, that I couldn't get used to them.

'Need to give these old knees and very cow's veins a rest,' Nanna Purvis said, tugging off her shoes.

'*Varicose* veins,' I said.

'You might stop ya cheek, young girl.' She frowned as she slipped on her furry blue slippers. 'And help me fix our tea since ya mum's vanished again.'

She eased herself onto a chair at the kitchen table. One wrinkly hand flipped the pages of the *Illawarra Mercury* to the Specials page, the slipper on her crossed leg jerking up and down like a kid's battery-powered toy — bob-bob, bob-bob.

'Coles've got Rolled Leg Ham for ninety-nine cents a pound,' she said as I fed Bitta and Steely. 'Now that's a real bargain.'

Billie-Jean burped up his last meat morsel onto the floor and farted. The stink of mouldy cheese filled the kitchen.

'Smelly beast.' I kicked a foot at him. I hadn't touched the dog but Billie-Jean yelped and skittered over to Nanna Purvis.

'I've told ya, Tanya, leave me dog alone. Come here, yes. Come to Mummy, baby.'

She lifted the trembling Billie-Jean onto her lap, stroking him, and I was sure that dog smirked at me. 'How're we off for dunny paper, Eleanor?' she hollered. 'It's on special for twenty-eight cents ... assorted colours.'

I padded into the bathroom. Mum was not checking the toilet paper stock, she was giving Shelley a warm and deep eucalyptus-scented bath.

'She loves it,' I said, watching my baby sister rock about over Mum's arm, all pink and limp and relaxed.

'Yes, let's hope this is the answer,' Mum said with the faintest flicker of a smile. She lifted the baby from the bath and wrapped her in our softest towel.

Shelley found just enough strength to drink her bottle, then I took her from Mum, burped her and laid her on the cot lambskin.

'That's a good girl.' I smoothed out the sheet around her as she fell asleep. 'You'll be all better soon, and when you're a big girl, you won't even remember how awful the colic was. You'll see, we'll have so much fun together when you're grown up.'

Shelley slept on and I thought Mum would've gone and sat

down with a cup of tea. But no, after her absence at the hospital, she prowled through the house from one room to the next, checking for untidiness, dust and grime. I could see her making a mental list of what needed to be done to get Gumtree Cottage shipshape again.

'Aw crikey, it's too late in the day to think about cleaning,' Nanna Purvis said. 'Come and sit down with us. Tanya's made spaghetti on toast.'

That's all it was, since Mum had stopped cooking: opening a can of spaghetti or baked beans and slapping it on toast. Spaghetti or baked beans. Baked beans or spaghetti. Or Spam if you wanted. Whatever came from a can.

My mother shook her head. 'Not hungry.'

She looked starved. Reedy as a blade of grass, face pale as sour milk, the skin slouched in pockets beneath her dull eyes, the corners of her bloodless lips turned down. She'd begun to stoop too, like a bag of stones was sitting on her small shoulders.

'I've said it before,' Nanna Purvis said, Mum shuffling about the kitchen, her feet barely lifting from the lino as if she was afraid they'd rise and she'd fly off for good. 'You're no longer fit to look after anyone. And with me wonky knees and veins, neither am I. So if Dobson dies, I don't know what's to become of your daughters.'

'Dad's not going to die!' The fear jangled like murdering hands around my neck. My fork clanged onto the plate which made my mother blink and jump.

'Ya gotta be prepared for all eventualities in life, Tanya,' Nanna Purvis said.

'But that nurse said Dad's going to be fine ... "soon he'll be just fine" she said.' I wanted so much to believe that but my chest pressed tighter, and I feared the seagull nurse had been lying.

My eyes burned with unshed tears, my appetite vanished for once, and for the rest of teatime I sat at the table, staring at the awful kitchen wallpaper. Once a bright yellow sunflower pattern, it had paled to a mustardy yellow — the colour of a sick person's skin. The only sound was Nanna Purvis cutting, chewing and swallowing, bellowing through my eardrums louder than a Steelworks' explosion.

Once Nanna Purvis and I had cleared away the tea things, she settled herself for her television shows, Billie-Jean curled up beside her on the white sheet covering the sofa.

Hungry again, I took one of my grandmother's Violet Crumble bars that she hid at the back of the pantry for "special occasions", grabbed *Real Life Crime* and sat outside on the back verandah.

Cicadas beating away in the wattles, the stink of rotted jacaranda blossoms — pretty purple gone dirty brown — thick in my nostrils, I dangled my legs over the edge and flipped through the magazine, searching for the goriest story.

I stroked Steely, poking bits of chocolate-covered honeycomb between my lips, almost groaning with pleasure when it melted all through my mouth.

Soon, though, the honeycomb began to feel like paste on my palate. I no longer tasted anything. I tried to stop myself finishing the Violet Crumble but the whole lot ended up disappearing.

The flyscreen door creaked behind me — slow and quiet. I didn't look around but from the silence, and the smell of madness that clung to her like poison to the oleander, I knew it was my mother. I didn't bother hiding *Real Life Crime* from her view.

She stood to my side, behind me, not too close. 'The doctors are doing everything for your father, Tanya. Trying to make him better. I'll feel better soon too … as soon as your sister gets over her colic.'

Mum didn't touch me, and her voice barely caught the words that slid from her tongue. As if she could be saying any old thing. I swivelled around to look at her properly. Her eyes reflected in the light coming from the kitchen were a brighter hazel, her breath sharp and hot as acid and she gave off the musty smell of old and damp clothes.

I wanted to ask her how she could spend so much time

cleaning the house and hardly ever washing her own body, but my mother was beyond understanding the simplest question, let alone answering it.

Chapter 13

I got off the bus and trudged up Figtree Avenue. It was another hot December afternoon, mushrooms of brown smoke swelling from the Port Kembla chimney stack. But as I thought back over my school day, at how Angela and I had laughed and swapped secrets, it didn't seem so stifling, the hill not nearly as steep.

The heat still scorched and bubbled the road asphalt. The pale brown grass still screamed for water. The sun still burned the part in my hair and made me squint. The sweat still plastered my uniform to my body. But it didn't bother me so much; the bullying taunts didn't drag me down like they had before I met Angela Moretti.

I couldn't face Gumtree Cottage — a yelling baby and the mother who ignored her, and me, so I plonked down on the kerb in the shade of a fig tree, and kicked stones along the gutter.

I thought of Dad, who I'd been to see twice more at the hospital. His smile was still weak, his footsteps wobbly, but he wasn't the least bit confused and he'd not mentioned seeing Uncle Blackie again.

When Nanna Purvis had started spouting her usual rubbish, Dad had winked at me. So I figured if my ally was well enough to joke about my grandmother with me, he'd be home soon. And things at Gumtree Cottage would get better.

'You wanna bowl today, Tanya?' Terry said, as the Anderson

boys came charging out of number ten to play cricket.

'Okay,' I said as Wayne pounded the stumps into the grass with the bat.

I grabbed the ball and bowled it to Terry at his wicket-keeper spot, Wayne hitting it before it reached the stumps. *Clack, clack* went the ball, against the screeching chorus of the rainbow lorikeets on the gum tree boughs, the shrieking mob of sulphur-crested cockatoos.

'Our mother reckons your mum might've gone crackers,' Terry said. 'On account of your baby sister still crying day and night.'

'Has she gone loony?' Wayne asked. 'Like she was before ... even before Shelley's colic started. Our mother reckons she went loony every time a baby died in her guts.'

My fist tightened around the cricket ball. 'My mother's not loony ... never has been. You're the loonies!' Snarling, I swung back and hurled the cricket ball right over the roof of their house, and into the bushland behind.

'Whatcha do that for?' Wayne said. 'We'll never find it now.'

'Bloody *Catholics*,' I hissed, stamping away from the cricket pitch.

I was so mad I almost walked straight into Stacey Mornon, riding her shiny blue bike down Figtree Avenue, rainbow-coloured streamers flying from the handlebars. Just the kind of bike I'd love to own.

'Watch where you're going, Ten-ton Tanya.' Stacey stopped pedalling, planted her feet on the ground and perched on the edge of the flowered seat. 'You almost barged right into me. With that weight you could've knocked me, *and* my bike, over.'

Bright green eyes stared at me from a suntanned face ringed in sea-foam white curls.

'You'd better get out of my way then,' I said, 'or I *will* knock and your sissy bike over.' I strode on, my elbow nudging the basket, which made the entire bike wobble.

'Nasty, nasty,' Stacey said, regaining her balance. 'Not my

fault your mother's gone crazy and will soon be carted off to a mental asylum. No use blaming others.'

'What would *you* know?' I tried to stop my voice quaking, to shake off the fear uncoiling before me like that red-bellied black snake. 'And if you believe everything you hear, you're even more of a moron than you look.'

Stacey sighed and shrugged as if she was sorry for me. 'And you'd better get your mum — if she's not too crazy, that is — to get you a training bra. You bounce around more than that silly cricket ball.' With a nasty little wave, curls bouncing around her shoulders, she rode off down Figtree Avenue, streamers waving from the handlebars like mad dancers.

A dented and rusty blue Kingswood rumbled up the hill, drove past Stacey and stopped beside me.

'Uncle Blackie! What are you doing here?'

* * *

He wound down the window. 'Haven't seen you in a few weeks, Tanya … been worried about you after your dad's accident. You're okay, aren't you?' He reached over and opened the passenger door, beckoning hand and breezy voice urging me into the Kingswood. 'Come and sit with me for a minute?'

I jumped into the passenger seat. 'I'm fine … I just hope my father will be fine too.'

'Aw, I'm sure he'll recover, but in the meantime I'm here if you need anything.' He smiled, pushed another bag of lollies into my hand.

'Choo Choo bars for a change,' he said. 'I know you love those too.'

As I bit into the liquorice-flavoured lolly, he nodded down the road, where Stacey had disappeared. 'Was that your number one enemy cycling off, this Stacey girl?'

'That's her. But blue bikes are *so* ordinary. If I could have a bike I'd want a red one … I love red.'

Uncle Blackie reached into a bag on the floor beside me and pulled out the latest issue of *Real Life Crime*. His hand grazed my shin, sending shivers right up my leg. 'It's not a red bicycle but I thought you deserved a treat what with your dad in the hospital.'

'How do you know about Dad? How do you know nearly *everything* about us?'

'Not everything, Tanya.' The eyebrows joined above his nose as he grinned.

'Well, thanks for the magazine,' I said, flipping through the pages, chewing on the Choo Choo bar and trying to ignore Nanna Purvis's words jabbering at my brain.

… that bad egg's still locked up. At least I hope he is, and the key flushed down the dunny for what he did to that Carter girl.

'Who's that Carter girl, Uncle Blackie?'

'Carter girl?' The smile slid from Uncle Blackie's face and he looked away, out the window, up and down Figtree Avenue. 'Whatever made you ask me that?'

'Oh nothing … probably just my grandmother's stupid gossip. She's always prattling on with some kind of rubbish.'

'Never mind, grandmothers *can* be a bit funny, kind of old-fashioned, sometimes,' he said. 'Hey, I wondered, with the accident and all, if you'd forgotten about our photo shoot?'

He glanced up and down the street again but there was nobody out in this heat except the Anderson boys, who must have found another cricket ball. Uncle Blackie swatted at a fly, and, in the same movement, stretched his arm across my shoulders.

'You'd make the best model,' he said.

He must have felt my shoulders fluttering like a sparrow trapped in a hot verandah because his arm slid back to the steering wheel, gripping it far too tightly for someone who wasn't actually driving. 'Are you sure you're still keen on these photos?'

I didn't answer straightaway; didn't truly know if I was that keen.

'Course I am,' I said. 'I'll come soon …'

'Soon?'

'Tomorrow,' I said. 'Tomorrow afternoon.'

'You will? That's great,' Uncle Blackie said. 'I'll look forward to it. Now you'd better run off home before that bossy grandmother catches you in my car, eh?'

'Yeah sure.' With a nervous giggle I leapt from the Kingswood, a rush of heat swelling from my belly up to my chest as the car did a U-turn and my secret friend zoomed off down the street like he was in a tearing hurry.

I lumbered up the front verandah steps, the kookaburra cackling his happy, *'Garooagarooagarooga,'* into the afternoon heat as if he was grinning along with me.

'Almost human they are, those kookas,' Nanna Purvis would say. 'Ain't got an ounce of fear in them either, peering from the trees with their clever eyes, imitating any kind of sound.'

She also reckoned that when our Mr Kooka laughed he was sending a message that it would rain soon, or a storm or something else, was brewing.

I shook my head at my grandmother's ridiculous stories. For someone who talked almost nonstop, she didn't know much about anything.

Chapter 14

The next morning — the big photo shoot day — I leapt from my bed. Outside my window, a magpie's '*Quardle, oodle, ardle, wardle, doodle,*' and the '*Waarrk, waarrk,*' reply of a koel filled the morning air.

'I'll walk with you to the bus stop,' my mother said as I buttered my Vegemite sandwich. 'We'll take Shelley. Do her, both of us, good.'

She smiled a quick, silly grin, but it was not a real smile, rather one cut from a magazine and pasted onto her face.

'Oh, okay,' I said, surprised but pleased she was making an effort to be the jolly mum.

While my mother brought the pram around to the front, I packed my sandwich and an apple into my schoolbag. Not that I'd need my lunch. Uncle Blackie would give me something far more interesting to eat at his place before the photo shoot.

I fed Steely and Bitta, stole back into my parents' bedroom, and squirted Mum's Cologne 4711 onto my neck and wrists. My body wasn't crash hot but at least I should smell nice for the photos.

Mum was waiting for me out the front, Shelley's pillow propping her upright, a position we'd found was less painful than lying flat. The dawn chill was long gone but there was no sting to the sun as yet, and the damp-dew smell hung in my nostrils.

Shelley looked up at me, her chocolate-brown eyes reminding

me, as always, of our father's. And Uncle Blackie's. I swore she smiled at me again, her stretched lips the same blood-red as the bottlebrush and flame tree flowers in springtime.

'Let's go then,' I said, starting down the hill.

My mother didn't move — her feet cemented to the footpath.

'So steep,' she said, gazing down the Figtree Avenue slope as if she'd never seen it before, as if it was a sheer cliff-face. 'Might fall.' Her voice had slowed to slug's pace, the words almost breaking up before they got out.

'Don't be silly, you won't fall.'

Her bony knuckles paled, gripping the pram handle. 'Can't go down there … too steep.'

'Now you *are* being silly, Mum. Come on, I'll miss the bus.'

'No, have to get back inside …' She turned around, the pram swivelling with her, head bent, shoulders hunched as she pushed it back into the yard without another glance at me.

I'd never admit it to them, but they were right — Terry and Wayne Anderson, and Stacey Mornon. And all the rest of them.

My mother had definitely gone crazy.

* * *

The morning dragged by. As soon as the lunch bell rang I hurried out of the schoolyard, glancing over my shoulder to make sure no teachers saw me leave. I kept going over Uncle Blackie's address.

Number eight, or was it eighteen? The name of his block of flats in Wattle Road … Albany, that's it.

I knew Wattle Road. My mother bought the good ham at the Wattle Road delicatessen if Dad got a work bonus. Or rather *used* to buy, before she stopped leaving Gumtree Cottage. There was a TAB — a betting shop — next to the deli, and The Monitor Arms pub on the other side.

Instead of turning right into Figtree Avenue as if I was going home, I kept walking along Gallipoli Street. I trudged up and over the big hill, then the long stretch down the other side.

The sun broiled my head, my arms, my legs and I squinted against the bright rays, trying to keep to the stingy gum tree shade. By the time I reached Wattle Road my soles were burning through my school shoes and my throat was dry as a summer riverbed.

Albany was number eight, a block of four flats. I slowed my pace as I walked up the pathway of the dirt-coloured brick building. I gagged on the stench of rotting food overflowing from rubbish bins. Supermarket pamphlets spilled from letterboxes and a swollen-bellied spider bobbed in a web cartwheeling from the eaves.

'Beretti, Armstrong, Papa-dop-ou-lous,' I read from the doorbells. I pressed the one marked "Randall"; heard the ring from inside. No answer.

I rang again. A silky black cat slunk up to me, meowed, rubbed its head against my legs. 'Hello pretty cat.' It looked up at me, its eyes the greeny-yellow of a sunrise. I stroked its back. 'I'd love to take you home with me but Steely'd have a fit.'

Still no answer. I rang a third time, waiting and wondering what I was missing at school. A creature rustled in the bushes beside the front door. Lizard, snake? The teacher's voice clanged through my mind.

The funnel web is the deadliest spider in the world. It can kill in less than two hours and the fangs can even bite through gloves and fingernails.

'Uncle Blackie, are you home? It's me … Tanya.'

I wondered what I was doing here, at this filthy, scary kind of place. But beyond the grime and stink — and my fear — the thrill of something new prickled my skin. Something exciting.

The door to one of the two downstairs flats cracked open and my uncle's head popped out.

'Tanya? Wasn't expecting you till later.' His voice was still mellow but the words staggered from him in a cloud of whisky fumes. I knew the smell because Uncle Bernie, husband of Dad's sister, That Bitch Beryl, drank whisky and smelled the same.

'I decided to miss school this afternoon. It's Christmas holidays in two days so nothing much is happening.'

'You'd better come in then.' He opened the door wider and the nice black cat slipped inside. Red-rimmed eyes narrowed against the sun, Uncle Blackie glanced up and down Wattle Road, and glared at a purple-haired woman frowning from behind her front gate across the street.

'Is this your cat?' I said, following it inside.

'Don't know who it belongs to but it's always coming inside, meowing for food and a saucer of milk.'

Uncle Blackie's flat stank of rotted fruit and unwashed socks, and in the dimness of the closed Venetian blinds everything looked grey, old and grubby. Except two posters stuck to a wall: one of a tropical beach, the other with fuzzed-out red roses on a pink background, which looked somehow strange on Uncle Blackie's walls.

I bent down and stroked the cat. It meowed, wove between my feet, pushing its silky face against my leg.

Uncle ran a hand through his curls that stuck out at all angles, and rubbed at his watery eyes. 'You must be thirsty after such a long walk … let's find you something to drink.'

I followed Uncle Blackie and the black cat into a tiny kitchen, where he poured milk into a saucer for the kitty, then made up a jug of orange cordial from a jar of Tang.

'Here you go.' He filled a cloudy glass with cordial and nodded at one of three tatty chairs.

While I drank, and the cat lapped, Uncle Blackie opened a cupboard, rustled around. A cockroach the size of a mouse scuttled out, which would have given my mother a fit. I shuddered, lifted my feet. Kitty swiped a paw but it got away, scurrying into a dark corner.

'Gotta be *something* to eat in here,' Uncle Blackie said, almost losing his balance crouched down like that. 'Must get to the shops …'

'It's okay, I've got my lunch.' I unwrapped my sandwich, scraped off a wodge of Vegemite and let the cat lick it from my finger.

'Look, Kitty loves Vegemite,' I said. 'Just like Steely.'

As if he hadn't heard me, Uncle Blackie pulled out a half-eaten packet of dried-up-looking biscuits. 'Not the most appetising, but when I take you home later we'll stop at the corner shop for something nice. How about that?'

'Okay, whatever. Don't you go out to work during the day, same as my father?'

'Yep. I just work different hours than most people, shift work.' He told me about his job at the TAB down the road, where people gambled away all their wages betting on horses and greyhounds. He was silent for a minute, then said, 'What's wrong, Tanya? You're not your usual self.'

'Well, apart from my baby sister's constant crying, which is sending us all a bit crackers, and my dad still in hospital, my mother's gone crazy.'

I put down my sandwich and bit into a biscuit. The packet was torn, the writing so faded I couldn't read the brand name, but it tasted like one of those plain buttery things — the type old ladies dip into tea.

'Don't you worry too much, Tanya. Your mum can't help the way she is right now.' One of Uncle Blackie's hands slid onto my shoulder, the other cupped under my chin which he lifted, forcing me to look straight into the brown, red-tinged eyes. 'Your mum doesn't want to be unhappy but she just can't help it, so the doctor needs to give her some pills to calm her down and make her happy again.'

The biscuits were so pasty I understood why you needed to dip them in tea, but still I chomped through one after the other, Uncle Blackie's fingertip caressing my chin, my moving jaw.

'She'll be better once your baby sister stops the constant screaming,' he said. 'That'd be enough to send anyone crackers, wouldn't it?'

His sea-ripple voice was unlike any I'd heard. The complete opposite of Nanna Purvis's screechy holler. So unlike Dad's raspy bark or Mum's airy, sluggish nonsense. It was different too, but just as musical, as Angela Moretti's teensy-bit-Italian voice.

'But what if Shelley's colic doesn't stop? What if Mum stays like this and my father dies from the car accident?'

'Do you trust me, Tanya?' Uncle Blackie touched a forefinger to the spot below my bottom lip. Dust-blown sunlight caught the creases on his face as he smiled.

I kept chewing the biscuit, nodding.

'Good girl. So just believe me when I say your mum will get better. And your dad too. But while they're … out of action, shall we say, I'm here.'

Of course I trusted my own uncle. If he said everything would be all right with my mother, then it *would* be.

'So how did you know Mum, when she was young?'

'We met at the beach. Summer of '57-'58 it was, before she married your dad.' He glanced away, at the cockroach cupboard, and the black cat grooming itself. 'Your mother preferred my brother in the end.'

His gardening hand dropped from my hair, trailed across my shoulder. Sandpaper fingers. He inhaled deeply. '*Mmn*, Cologne 4711 again. It smells as nice on you as it did on her.'

I didn't know what to say; couldn't help shivering with embarrassment, with the strange mixture of excitement and fright filling me up. The kind of fear that is tangled up with worry. The fingers scraped down my arm, settled in the crook of my elbow. Tracing circles. Feather-soft dandelion seeds blowing in a breeze. I shivered but didn't pull away, too afraid he'd think I was a stupid kid. Besides, it was nice having someone take care of me.

'Why're there no photos of you in Mum and Dad's wedding album?'

'Because I'd left Wollongong by the time your parents got married.'

'Left Wollongong?' I said. 'Nanna Purvis reckons you were locked up in a place for doing something to a girl named Carter. Is that true?' I realised he hadn't answered me yesterday when I'd asked him about that Carter girl.

Uncle Blackie took a step back, said nothing, both hands sweeping back dark curls and I wondered whatever could have happened to the Carter girl.

What is *it that men do?*

He finally let out a chuckle. 'And here's me thinking you're too smart to believe silly gossip, Tanya. You know your grandmother talks a lot of rot ... said so yourself only yesterday.'

'Yeah, she sure does talk rubbish ... but I don't believe a word of it.'

'Course you don't, clever girl like you.' He jabbed a finger at the newspaper on the table. 'Now what about this Miss Beach Girl 1973 Quest we talked about? You'll miss out if you don't enter soon,' he said as I kept reading:

A WIN-TV team will soon be scouting beaches to select three beautiful girls as entrants for final judging.

'And what do you reckon about this photo shoot, eh?' He gestured at the fancy wall posters. 'Against these nice backdrops.'

'We're doing the photo shoot today?' I said. I'd agreed to it only yesterday, but hadn't thought we'd do it just yet.

My gaze swept across the peeling wall paint, the rusty taps, the bubbled and grimy floor lino. And up to the posters — turquoise water lapping smooth white sand, palm leaves waving at me. Pretty red roses on a fuzzy pink background.

... those models aren't as beautiful as they're made out you know, Tanya. It's all camera angles and make believe. They're quite plain in real life, in fact.

Uncle Blackie cleared his throat, spoke in the day-dreamy voice: 'Only if you want to, Tanya ... if you're game.'

I poured myself another glass of cordial, thought how much more thrilling it was to be here with Uncle Blackie than at boring school with Stacey Mornon having a go at me.

I gulped down the drink and stood up. 'Course I'm game.'
The silky black cat leapt from his chair.

Chapter 15

I stood before Uncle Blackie as he instructed me: legs slightly apart, palms clamped on my hips, one hip bent sideways. It was a lot to remember at once, as well as trying to look like a *Dolly* magazine model.

Click-clack went the camera. *Click-clack*.

'That's beaut, Tanya. You look smashing … just like a model.'

I was in a ship sailing off to unknown tropical islands. Amazing, palm-tree places where I'd make incredible discoveries.

After he'd taken a dozen or so shots, Uncle Blackie placed his camera on the table. 'Super job, Tanya. Ready for a break now? Let's have a drink … and a bit of a chat.'

From the cupboard above the sink, he took a bottle labelled: "Johnnie Walker Red Label". He poured himself a glassful, his hands a little shaky so that some of the whisky sloshed across the bench top.

He held the bottle up to me. 'Want to try some?'

'No thanks, I already tried whisky,' I said, remembering the furtive sip I'd taken from Uncle Bernie's glass. 'It's yuck.'

'Have some more cordial then.' Uncle Blackie poured me another glassful, sat beside me at the table and clinked his glass against mine.

'Cheers to us, Tanya. Cheers to the future top model.'

That made me smile and, together, we drank our drinks. I stroked the black cat, curled up again on the chair beside me.

'Come with me,' he said taking my hand. 'I've got some things I want to show you.'

'What things?' I trotted after him into the bedroom, which smelled as if he never opened the window to air out the room, like Mum did every morning.

He nodded at the bed. 'Have a seat, don't be shy.'

I perched on the edge, trying not to look at the tangle of wrinkled sheets with some kind of stains. I imagined my mother ripping those sheets from the bed, scrubbing at the stains, then shovelling the sheets through her wringer washer. Twice.

Uncle Blackie creaked open the wardrobe door and pulled out a cardboard box.

He sat beside me on the bed and took from the box a little sculpture of a girl wearing white socks, black shoes and a checked dress like my school uniform. She had long hair, blue eyes and a small nose and mouth. 'What do you think, Tanya?'

He took out more sculptures — another girl and two boys. There were many more in the box. All of girls and boys in school uniform.

'I made lots of them,' he said. 'Back when I had so much time to spare …'

'What are they made from?' I turned each one over in my hand, amazed at the fine detail: buttons on the clothes, shoe-laces, eyebrows and long lashes.

'Salt dough. It's easy. I could teach you to make some too … if you wanted?'

I nodded, handing him back the figures. 'That'd be groovy.'

'You said you're on holidays soon, right? Why don't you come back to Albany then … we could take a few more photos, and I'll show you how to make salt-dough sculptures?'

'Okay,' I said, pleased to have somewhere exciting to go, something to do during what would be long, hot and boring holidays with my mother making up excuses not to take me for a swim. Or anywhere else.

'That's beaut,' Uncle Blackie said with a pat on my thigh. 'And

I have a feeling there'll be a nice surprise waiting when you do come back, my sweet Tanya.'

'What surprise?'

He winked, the hand rubbing my thigh. 'Ah ha, you'll find that out when you come back to Albany.'

* * *

Back in Gumtree Cottage, after our tea of Spam on toast, I filled the bathtub, stripped off my school uniform and stood before the mirror in my singlet and undies. My body looked the same only it didn't feel the same. It felt like the body of a grown-up woman, more powerful than my child's body.

… you look smashing.

Uncle Blackie was right, I thought, stepping into the tub. If I was ever going to win Miss Beach Girl 1973 and become a model I'd have to stop feeling bad about my body.

I lathered the flannel with Pears' soap. "Matchless for the complexion", the *Illawarra Mercury* ad said, and scrubbed until my skin was raw and tingling.

As I dried myself, the ringing phone made me jump. I slipped on my nightie, dashed into the hallway and answered it. 'Dad!'

'Good news, Tanya. They're letting me out of the hospital. I'll be home tomorrow.'

'Really? That's so cool, Dad.' My heart soared right out of my chest and buzzed over my head like a toy helicopter and I completely forgot I was still a bit mad at him for causing the car accident.

But as I sat on my bedspread, the red-rose pattern — against the ghastly violets wallpaper pattern — tinted the room a shade of dirty pink and it became stuffy and airless once more. Something worn and olden — a convict-ancestor's room that we no longer used.

I tipped out the box of Barbie dolls, picked up Twiggy

Barbie. Pretty and skinny Twiggy. I pinched a glob of my belly fat, inhaled deeply. The glob was still there and I did not feel so smashing.

I'll never be that *thin.*

I kicked stupid Twiggy Barbie and the other stupid Barbies under my bed and pulled *Real Life Crime* from inside *Dolly* magazine.

The night was hot and still. A mosquito buzzed deep in my ear as if it was stuck inside my skull. My ear hummed, itched like mad. I wanted to tear it off. I thrashed about, eyes wide open, staring at the horrible violet-patterned walls.

The clock chimed another hour and the whole neighbourhood — even Shelley — was quiet. But still I couldn't sleep, thinking about Uncle Blackie's photo shoot, trying to hold onto the excitement, and to fend off the swirling doubt.

I sweated and shifted, slid off the nightmare bedspread and padded into my parents' bedroom. Shelley was asleep in her cot, my mother lying on her bed, facing away from the door.

'Can I have a new bedspread?'

'What?' Mum's voice was caked in a pastry crust, same as the Longbottoms' and Dad's, after too many schooners. Though by now I knew it was the Valium that slurred her voice.

'I hate my bedspread,' I said. 'Can I have a new one?'

'That bedspread cost me over half the housekeeping money, thought you liked it.'

'I don't. Never have. I always wanted a Holly Hobbie one but I don't now, they're for little kids.'

No answer. She stayed curled up, facing the wall.

'Dad's coming home from hospital tomorrow. Isn't that good?'

'Oh,' she said, as if she didn't care one way or the other.

Chapter 16

'Stop it, Shelley! Stop your crying … Jesus bloody Christ, stop.'

I ran into my parents' room, Nanna Purvis hobbling along behind me. Dad was holding my scarlet-faced, shrieking sister high up. And shaking her.

'That's *enough*, Shelley,' he yelled again.

I was shocked; my father rarely shouted, except at Nanna Purvis.

'Stop shaking her, Dad!'

My father had arrived home from hospital only a few hours ago, to a forty-degree furnace. The hottest day of 1972, just before Christmas, and already things were not better with him back at Gumtree Cottage. No, they were worse.

'Put Shelley down, Dobson,' Nanna Purvis said. 'Everyone knows shaking a kid like that can kill it.'

'How could you shake her, Dad?' I snatched Shelley from my father and hurried down the hallway with her, the screams echoing back at me from the walls. 'It's okay, little gumnut girl,' I soothed. 'Your big sister will make it all better.'

I made up another olive oil and salt mixture, took her into my bedroom and undressed her. I made wide, massaging motions, rubbing the mix over her little body. 'That's it, nice and calm. Poor baby.'

Once she quietened down, I took the bottle from the fridge

that Mum had prepared, sat down and fed Shelley. After her burp, I put her in her pram beneath the gum tree — the only shade in that god-awful heat. There was still no sign of my mother but from the noise coming from the laundry shed, I figured she was busy washing again.

'Fancy a trip down to Eastbridge, Tanya? Think I'll get those seat belts fitted in the Holden,' Dad said, loping out onto the back verandah, calm as ever, as if he hadn't been shaking his baby so angrily just half an hour ago. There wasn't a trace of the desperate rage in his smile, in the one eyebrow raised like Uncle Blackie's. As if my father was two completely different people.

When the Holden got repaired after the accident, Dad had wanted to get seat belts fitted but Nanna Purvis kept insisting he wait until they were on special.

'Kmart are selling those seat belts for just under six dollars at the moment, including installation,' he said. 'And maybe we'll find something nice for you too?'

I nodded, walked over to the pram to check on Shelley before we left. Her eyes were still closed but instead of its usual rosy shade, her face was pale. Ghost-white. She wasn't moving, not even a fingertip.

She was too calm, too *asleep*. I stared at her chest, waiting for it to rise and fall. It stayed still.

I turned to my father. 'I can't see her breathing, Dad!'

Mum scuttled out from the laundry, wide-eyed. 'Not breathing?'

'What?' my father cried, reaching the pram before my mother. He reefed Shelley from it.

The baby opened her eyes wide, as if in great surprise. She howled. We all let out our breath, long and slow.

And for once Shelley's cries were a welcome noise.

* * *

While we waited for the seat belts to get fitted, we bought groceries in Coles which, being almost Christmas, was heaving with shoppers. Dad went to hold my hand but I pulled it away. 'Only kids hold their father's hand, Dad.'

I hadn't seen Uncle Blackie since the photo shoot; hadn't had a chance to sneak back to Albany for more pics, and that mix of thrill, shame and fear still churned me up. As if I'd swallowed a Redskin lolly whole, and it had got stuck in my throat.

If I was honest with myself, I wasn't even certain I did want to go back to Albany. It ended up being fun shopping with Dad, who bought me three of the week's USA Top 40 singles: Helen Reddy's *I Am Woman*, The Temptations' *Papa Was A Rollin' Stone* and Carly Simon's *You're So Vain*.

'Fancy one of these nice crocheted jackets, Princess?' he said, as we wandered through the Ladies Clothes section. 'Or how about a halter-neck frock?' The frocks were nice, with a smocked bodice and a pattern of tiny red apples, but I started to ask myself why my father wanted to buy me all these things. Something wasn't right. Was he trying to make up for the car accident, or for shaking Shelley like that?

On the drive back home, strapped snugly into the new seat belts, I found out what was bugging him.

'I'm going away for a while, Tanya.'

'Away?' Goosebumps broke out along my arms as he turned into Gallipoli Street. 'But why ... and where?'

'There's not many brickie jobs around in the summer holidays so I'm heading up to Mount Isa to work in the mines ... I'll earn a lot of money. You'll be able to buy anything you want.'

'But Mount Isa's so far away. Isn't it all the way up to Queensland?'

'It is,' he said. 'But the money's good and ... and it won't be for long.'

Ants crawled up my arms: hundreds of them, itchy tingling. 'When are you leaving?'

'Don't worry, I'll stay around for Christmas and the holidays

… wouldn't want to miss our beach trips, would I?' He gave me a thin smile but his hand patting my leg trembled.

As we drove up Figtree Avenue, I didn't believe his going to Mount Isa had anything to do with earning a lot of money. No, my father was planning on leaving us.

Well, never mind, I thought, breathing away the weight squeezing the air from my lungs. I no longer needed Dad to buy me things, or to do stuff with me. I had Uncle Blackie now.

Chapter 17

'Oh boy, it's for *me*, Uncle Blackie?' I sat on the flowered seat of the sparkly red bicycle and pushed the bell. *Tring, tring, tring*. I ran my fingers through the brightly-coloured streamers dangling from the handlebars. 'It's really mine?'

'It sure isn't for me,' Uncle Blackie said with a laugh. 'Course it's for you, Tanya.'

With Dad still at home recovering from the car accident, it was after Christmas before I'd got a chance to sneak back to Albany. But I'd finally made it, and I couldn't believe Uncle Blackie's far-out surprise. Better than any of the ordinary Christmas presents at home.

'I can't take the bike back to Gumtree Cottage,' I said. 'They'll ask where it came from and you're … you're a secret.'

'Why not leave the bike here, Tanya? You can ride it up and down Wattle Road every time you come and visit me.'

'Okay,' I said, disappointed I couldn't show it off to Stacey Mornon. But I understood I still had to keep my new friend a secret.

'What about if I take a photo of you on the bike?' Uncle Blackie said, turning away from me to pour himself a whisky and a Tang cordial for me. 'So you can look at it when you're at home. That's if you're still up for more photos?'

He downed the whisky in a single gulp. 'Or still too embarrassed about your lovely body?'

'Nope, not embarrassed,' I lied, wincing at the taste of the Tang cordial — kind of strong and bitter. But I was thirsty and finished it off. 'And don't worry, I'll keep the bike photo hidden, I've got some beaut hiding places at home.'

'That's my girl,' he said as I hitched up my frock to sit astride the bike again.

'How's this, Uncle Blackie?'

'Perfect.' He pointed the camera at me. 'Just like those models on bicycles and motorbikes.' *Click-clack. Click-clack.* 'Smile a bit more. Yeah, fabulous!'

Click-clack. Click-clack.

'You looked fabulous in your school uniform for the last lot of photos,' he said, laying the camera on the table, 'but as you're not wearing it this time, I've got a better idea.'

'Course I'm not wearing my uniform, we're still on holidays,' I said. 'What idea?'

'Did you know,' Uncle Blackie said, in the dreamy voice, 'that famous models sometimes have to be photographed in their underwear?'

'Only their underwear? No, no, no … I didn't know that. Oh boy!'

'It's fine, Tanya. It's just art. That's what art's all about.'

'You want to take photos of me in my *underwear*?' I said. 'I can't … I'm so fat.' I was starting to feel strange, like my brain was swirling around inside my too-heavy head. A doll being swept out to sea on a current. I hoped I wasn't coming down with a flu or something.

'That's just how *you* see yourself. You're a beautiful girl, almost a woman.'

The heat rose up my throat, spread across my face. 'You really don't think I'm fat?'

'Course you're not. You need to ignore those nasty kids,' Uncle Blackie said. 'And listen to me, someone who knows what he's talking about.'

I didn't move; too shy to take off my sun frock.

No way can I do this!

Uncle Blackie cocked his head to one side and gave me the meltiest smile. 'You said you trusted me, Tanya?'

'I do … I do.' Why had my voice had gone sluggish, slurry like Dad's beer-voice?

'So?' He got up and took two long paces, so close to me the whisky breaths fanned my hot brow. 'You can do this … I just *know* you can.'

'I can?' I sidled towards my beautiful red bicycle. 'Should I sit on the bike like before?'

'Oh no, not on the bike this time, Tanya. You see, these sorts of photos must be taken lying down on a bed. Because, in that position, I know how to make you look real slim and curvy … just like those magazine girls.'

My head spun as he took my hand and led me into the bedroom. The palm-beach and red-roses posters were stuck to the wall, which was weird. I was certain they'd been on the living-room wall before, but maybe I was mistaken.

Slowly, gently, he turned me around, unbuttoned my dress. I hoped he couldn't feel me shaking as he swivelled me back around to face him and dragged the sun frock over my head.

The caterpillar eyebrow twitched as his fingers brushed against the wisps of hair lining my armpits. Uncle Blackie threw my dress aside, his gaze travelling from my face down to my singlet, my belly. Stopping at the shadow beneath my undies.

I clamped my arms across my chest. Sure my nipples had gone all pointy, I wished I had a training bra beneath my singlet to hide the flabby little boobies. But my mother was too busy —too crazy! — to get me one, or even think I might need one.

'Okay, Tanya?'

I nodded.

'Lie back then. That's right, good.' He took his camera, loomed over me and started shooting. *Click-clack. Click-clack.*

'Arms down by your sides. Great … you're the spitting image of a world-famous model,' Uncle Blackie said. 'Smile, don't forget to show the photographer those white teeth. Excellent, that's the way, my girl.'

'A world-famous model, really?' Despite my lead-brain, I couldn't help giggling, lips pouty, body slim.

After a few moments Uncle Blackie laid the camera on the bed and pulled me up to a sitting position. I thought we were about to have another drink break but that Tang had tasted so awful I didn't want any more of it.

'And now,' he said, 'are you up for the best part, Tanya ... the biggest challenge to a model?'

'Challenge?'

'Yes. You know by now that models are photographed in clothes *and* underwear, don't you?'

I nodded.

'But did you know that sometimes they have pictures taken with no clothes at all?'

'What, totally *naked*?' My cheeks flushed hot just imagining that. But I must have heard Uncle Blackie wrong; he couldn't have meant that at all.

* * *

'Oh don't worry, Tanya, the photographers are used to it. They don't even see the body in front of the camera ... too busy trying to get the best shot. And the models *want* to show off their bodies. They love it.'

'No way, Uncle Blackie, I could *never* do that.' Not only my cheeks burned; my whole body was a furnace. A drop of sweat leaked from my forehead into my eye. I hunched into a sitting ball, arms wrapped around my knees.

'That's okay, Tanya.' Uncle Blackie let out a sigh, poured himself another glass of whisky. He took a sip, licked his lips. 'No worries, but I did think ... thought you trusted me?'

He fell silent, finished the whisky, poured another. He wasn't looking at me anymore but staring out through the window, at some point beyond the overflowing garbage bins. He looked so unhappy.

'I *do* trust you, Uncle Blackie.'

Of course I trusted Dad's brother who spoke like a mermaid would if mermaids could speak. My uncle who bought me groovy presents, who cared about me, unlike my own parents.

'Well then?' Uncle Blackie didn't move from his chair.

I breathed deeply; still couldn't imagine taking off all my clothes. It was bad enough sitting there in my singlet and undies. I shook my head.

'Ah, never mind,' Uncle Blackie said with a shrug. 'I must have misunderstood you … just imagined you were ready to be a grown-up model. But I got it wrong, you're still only a child. I'm sorry, Tanya, really I am.' He zipped up the camera in its case.

I followed his gaze out to the living-room, to my sparkly new bicycle. I felt so ungrateful, so selfish.

'Is the bike still mine?' For some reason I was afraid he was going to take it away from me.

'Of course it is, you silly thing,' Uncle Blackie said with a sad little smile. 'Why don't you go and ride it right now? We'll think more about grown-up modelling and photo shoots in a year or two, when you're old enough.'

'I *am* old enough.' I stamped my foot. 'Right now, I'm old enough.'

Uncle Blackie smiled again and shook his head. 'It seems you're not, Tanya. Not old enough for a model's biggest challenge. Look, just don't worry about it, forget I ever mentioned it.'

'Okay,' I said with a sharp nod. I hoped he hadn't heard the tremble in that one short word; couldn't hear my heart thumping against my chest, my brain ricocheting against my skull. 'I'll do it.'

He stared at me. 'You're absolutely certain you're not too young for this?'

'Certain.'

And before I knew it, Uncle Blackie was sitting on the bed beside me, removing my underwear. I couldn't help myself, and clamped my arms over my breast buds, crossed my legs.

'Come on, Tanya, stand up in front of those nice palm trees, show the camera how lovely you are. And don't you worry, nobody else'll see the photos,' Uncle Blackie went on in the ripply voice. 'Because they're just for you, to show you what a beautiful girl you really are. Besides, I develop them myself, right here in my own bathroom.'

I pulled my arms away, hung them by my sides, limp and awkward, breathing deeply to fend off the giddiness.

Click-clack. Click-clack. 'That's it. Side on now, Tanya. Throw that pretty head back over your shoulder. Smile … fabulous!'

His voice, rising with excitement, spurred me on. *Click-clack. Click-clack.*

'Now shift a bit to the left, in front of the rose poster. That's right … beaut. Don't look so anxious, a model must look relaxed, confident. Perfect, you look just like Twiggy.'

Me, the famous and skinny super model Twiggy?

The warmth bubbled inside me and I threw my arms up in a dramatic pose, a hip cocked sideways. Thin and beautiful Twiggy.

It must have been the way I angled my head so that, through the doorway into the bathroom, I caught a glimpse of myself in the mirror above the sink.

Suddenly the sickness gorged up from my guts and it all felt wrong. I was swamped — a great frothy wave crashing over my head, dumping me onto the sand. It mashed up my face, my body, into fat and ugly Tanya once again.

'No more photos.' I groped about for my underwear, my dress, hands fumbling, trying to cover my nakedness. 'I'm no Twiggy … '

Uncle Blackie placed his camera on the table, came over and wrapped his arms around me. Same as any caring uncle. 'I told you before, don't listen to those teasing kids, you're beautiful to me.'

I looked up to his smile, inhaled the whisky fumes.

'I have to get home.' I pulled away from him; from something hard in his trousers pressing against me. I almost fell over in my hurry to put on my clothes; to cover myself as quickly as possible.

'You're okay, aren't you, Tanya?'

'Sure ... just have to get home, that's all.'

'I'll drive you back to Figtree Avenue. We'll stop at the corner shop, get you some lollies ... or anything else you want?'

I shook my head. 'Prefer to walk.'

'Okay, but remember this is our secret. Because modelling photo shoots are only for adults and you're almost a grown woman now, not a silly kid anymore. It's nobody's business but ours.'

'I'm no silly kid.'

Clutching my sandals in one hand, my Indian bag slung over the other shoulder, I hurried away from Albany without looking back.

Chapter 18

The afternoon sun scalded the cricks of my knees as I trudged back up the Gallipoli Street hill, the sizzling rays burning their mark into my skin, branding me like one in a herd of cows. Clouds of grey-brown smoke surged from the Port Kembla chimney stacks.

Things were different. Something had changed but I didn't know what. I didn't feel like a child any longer but this new adult world didn't make sense. Something told me it was wrong of Uncle Blackie to take those naked photos, but he — an adult *and* Dad's brother — knew better than me how things went; what was right and what was wrong. He was probably this minute thinking what an idiotic kid I was, when I'd so wanted him to think I was grown up. He *had* made me feel grown up, the way he'd spoken to me — looked at me — as if I was a real model. Until I'd lost my stupid nerve.

Dried grass spikes pierced my feet, the bindiis needles through my soles.

'Ah, ouch, ouch.' I limped from the bindii patch to the kerb, sat down and slipped on my Roman sandals.

By the time I reached Figtree Avenue, the sky over Mount Kembla had darkened to ash-grey, a giant effortlessly pushing storm clouds towards the Pacific.

The wind turned squally, my nostrils flaring with the fruity smell of approaching storm, the gusts twisting the gum trees as if they were flimsy frocks.

I was a sailor lost at sea, unable to get my bearings. My ship was rocking about in a night-storm, jerking and tilting against gigantic, chevron-spiked waves, keel all askew.

The wind scattered dust from the western plains across the escarpment. As it surged through that dent between mountain and sea, the air around me became tainted with it — the stink a dead beast at the roadside. It strewed leaves across the road and the yards of houses, slid beneath my dress and grazed my skin. It chased me up the hill, blowing hair into my mouth, grit down my throat.

'*Run, Tanya, run,*' it hissed.

I panted, every breath dustier than the last. The inside of my nose was caked with it, my throat rough as the road.

The gales buffeted the yellow crests of cockatoos sitting high in the gum trees. Head cocked, eyes twinkling, the huge white birds peered down at me.

'*Got you now,*' they screeched.

The sky was twilight-dark when I straggled into the front yard, Gumtree Cottage's old-person's face scowling at me. The gales severed branches from the eucalyptus tree and blew them, like witches' brooms, across the corrugated iron roof. So there was some truth after all, in Nanna Purvis's "widow-maker" stories of dangerous gum tree boughs.

The waratah buds drooped pale pink instead of crimson, the jasmine creeper clinging to the fence like a kid trying to hide. But the gusts caught the fragile pink and white flowers, ripping them off. And from the Andersons' fence across the street, came the harsh, almost human, '*Ah-ah-ah,*' caw of a crow. That mournful cark had to be the ugliest noise of all the birds I knew and it chilled my soul with its ring of flies, stink and death.

* * *

I banged on the front door, wondering why it was locked. We never locked doors. I knocked again. No answer from Mum, and Dad would be down the pub. No noise from Shelley either, but the dogs started barking. Nanna Purvis didn't holler at Bitta and Billie-Jean to shut up, so she must be out at her hairdresser's.

I turned on the tap, let the hot water trapped in the hose coil run out. When it cooled, I drank and drank, moaning with the relief as it slaked my thirst, dulled the chiselling in my brain; washing that jumble of confusion from my mind.

I held the nozzle over my head, the wind spraying water over me, all around me. Soaked and refreshed, I turned off the tap but the heat trapped in the dense clouds sneaked up on me like a thief. It stole my dampness in a flash, so that I was hot and dirty again, and stripped of my skin. I swayed about on the grass, powerless against the wind pushing me where it wanted.

I was a mouse, the sky alive with crows.

I hurried onto the front verandah, crouched down out of the worst of it. The worn floorboards groaned and creaked beneath me, the gusts swirling around Gumtree Cottage as if they wanted to pick up the house and take it away. A Wizard of Oz house.

Still hunched over, I swivelled away from the road. I traced my forefinger around the animal-paw etching on one of the bricks — a banker's mark, my father had told me, identifying the convict mason who'd made the brick.

'It's a dingo's paw,' Dad had said, when he told me that his ancestors were amongst the first of Australia's sandstone brick-makers.

Ten minutes later Nanna Purvis hobbled out of a taxi, the wind twitching her tightly-permed blue curls. She limped up the verandah steps.

'Why're you soaking wet, Tanya?'

'It's hot, that's why. And since nobody will ever take me for a swim, there's only the hose. Why's Mum locked the door? Why won't she let me in?'

'Ya mum decided it needs locking if she's home alone. Maybe she's having a nap while Shelley's sleeping.'

'A *nap*? When did Mum last have a nap? And when does Shelley sleep?'

'Anyway, where've you been?' my grandmother went on, sliding her key into the lock. 'Skiving off without telling a soul where you've gone. My bet is you went to see the *Eyetie* girl?'

I hesitated. The truth sat on the edge of my tongue but the words died in my mouth. With my mother so strange and miserable and Dad down the pub more than ever since his car accident, Uncle Blackie was the only person I could count on, the only one I trusted.

I pushed past my grandmother, down the hallway and into my bedroom. No, I'd never tell her about my secret uncle. I'd never let her try and stop me seeing him like she kept trying to stop me seeing Angela Moretti.

I dumped my sodden dress onto the bedspread, leaving it to make a wet patch over the rose pattern. I slipped into a dry frock thinking, with a smug smirk, that this gross bedspread would never give me any more of those silly kid's nightmares.

… you're almost a grown woman now, not a silly kid anymore …

As I marched back down the hallway I felt strong. Proud and oozing power. I could do anything now I was grown up. Oh yes, I felt good. But at the same time a teensy bit bad.

Chapter 19

Casuarina she-oaks lined the wide driveway curving up to the Morettis' brick home which looked over all the other houses in Bottlebrush Crescent. Tall, white, palace-like columns enclosed the front verandah. Hydrangea shrubs, their flowers the same blue as our kookaburra's wing tips, circled the base of each column, and lizards darted between the sun and shade of the dark leaves.

'Hello,' I said to a man mowing the lawn, and to another trimming the hedges.

'G'day,' they both said, then Angela was skipping down the steps, her mother following.

Mrs Moretti kissed me on each cheek and I wished my mother still brushed her hair, wore rouge and lipstick and nice pantsuits like Angela's mother.

'Come inside,' Mrs Moretti said. 'You and Angelina are eating a biscuit before your swim.'

I followed them into the cool, tidy and silent palace and we sat at a vast wooden kitchen table, shiny with polish. Far more sophisticated than our ugly black Formica table and equally ugly black and white chairs.

'You are liking almond and chocolate biscotti, Tanya?' Mrs Moretti placed a plate of biscuits in front of me.

'I don't know but they sure look good.'

'They are *divine*,' Angela said.

The Moretti family had immigrated to Wollongong, along with so many other Italians and Europeans, because there were jobs going at the Port Kembla Steelworks.

'World War II devastation left the country in ruins,' our teacher had explained. 'And when the Italian soldiers returned from the war fronts there weren't enough jobs. Moving to Australia — a beckoning, hospitable land with endless prospects — was an enticing alternative to poverty, especially after the recruitment and assisted passage agreement between the Australian and Italian governments in 1952.'

Angela told me that after a few years working at the Port Kembla Steelworks, her father had started up a carpet-laying business, which — from the looks of his home — was obviously successful.

'Your mamma knows you here, Tanya … yes?' Mrs Moretti said, waving her arms about as I munched on the biscuits, so delicious I couldn't stop scoffing them. 'She is not worry for you?'

I washed down a mouthful of biscotti with the sweet and tangy ginger beer, which Angela had told me her mamma made herself, aching for the mother who used to worry where I was. Even if that had annoyed me.

'Oh no,' I said, 'she's not worried.'

Dad was already down the pub when I left the house so I'd only had to sneak past Nanna Purvis, swimmers and towel stuffed into my Indian bag. But that nosey, bossy grandmother must have seen me leave, as the phone rang a few moments later and Mrs Moretti hurried into the living-room to answer it.

'Your nonna is wanting you speak to her, Tanya.'

I dawdled into the living-room, decorated with religious-looking statues and fancy dolls perched on lace doilies on wooden shelves. I picked up the receiver.

'What do you want, Nanna Purvis?'

'What are you doing over there?' Her voice was a sharp needle through my eardrum.

'Angela's my friend. She asked me over for a swim. I told you, remember?'

'I can't have any granddaughter of mine mixing with foreign drug-dealing mobs. As if we haven't already got the strain and worry of Shelley's colic and your mum … your mum the way she is. And Dobson wearing the wobbly boot. You understand I'm just looking out for ya, Tanya, since nobody else seems to be able to right now?'

'Yes.'

'So you better get home before I can say, "Ain't no more gold in Kalgoorlie".'

'Okay bye, Nanna Purvis.'

'All is good?' Mrs Moretti asked as I sat back down.

'Yep. My grandmother says I can stay as long as I want.'

Upstairs, in Angela's bedroom, we changed into our swimmers. The whole room was white and frilly, every wall covered in posters of top models: Veruschka, Twiggy, Linda Morand, and other posters, of David Cassidy.

I wished I had a nice bedroom. I wished my pale and pudgy skin was smooth and olive like Angela's. Velvety as Golden Syrup.

'Why does your mum call you Angelina?' I hitched my Indian bag up over my shoulder as we hurried outside into the warm afternoon, across the shiny verandah tiles — so much neater than Gumtree Cottage's wobbly boards — and beneath the shade of thick grapevines, rather than our hot-as-hell corrugated iron eaves.

'Because that's my name, silly. But I prefer Angela, sounds more Aussie.'

'Angelina's a groovy name,' I said, following my friend down the backyard, alongside squawking chickens fluttering their feathers, and a row of silvery-leaved olive trees, down to a vegetable patch bright with tomatoes, capsicum and zucchini, and herbs which Angela said were basil and parsley.

'Why would you want to be more Aussie?' I said. 'I'd rather

come from some far-off ancient place like Naples … so much more exciting than boring old English convict ancestors.'

Angela shrugged. 'Aussie kids don't get called "wog", "dago" or "*Eyetie*".'

Beside the pool at the end of the yard a boy with hair as dark as Angela's lay sunbathing on a towel. Roberta Flack's hit single, *The First Time I Saw Your Face* blared from a radio beside him.

'This is my brother, Marco,' Angela said.

Marco glanced up at us. 'Hi, you must be Tanya?' His bronzed body rippling with muscles and his smile, full of straight white teeth, melted any words right off my lips. I couldn't even nod; could only stare at him in amazement.

Angela giggled and nudged me. 'Aren't you going to say hello?'

'Oh … oh yes. Hi, Marco.' I was aware of the silly grin spreading across my face, right to my bat-wing ears.

'Have fun, you two.' Marco picked up his radio, slung his towel over one shoulder, and I couldn't keep my gaze off him as he swaggered back to the house.

'All the girls think Marco's a total spunk,' Angela said with a laugh. 'And I can see you're no different.'

'Don't be a goon,' I said as we slid into the clear water. 'He's just your brother. Anyway he wouldn't have got up and left if … if he wanted to talk to me or anything.'

We slid along the bottom, eel-like, the silky water parting then closing behind us without a sound, sweeping back arcs of hair from our faces as we surfaced.

'Is Naples nice?' I said.

'I wouldn't know. We came to Australia the year before I was born. I guess I'll go there when I'm older but you could ask Mamma and Papa. They just *love* going on and on about Italy.'

Gripping the pool edge, our faces turned up to the sun, our legs bicycled underwater. 'Maybe they miss it?' I said.

'They do, but their lives are in Australia now. They'll never move back to Italy, especially because Papa's brother, Zio Ricci, and my aunt, Zia Valentina, are here too. Papa and his brother would never live apart.'

We had breath-holding contests, we shrieked with laughter gossiping about Stacey Mornon and her moron friends. I lifted my arms above my head, floated on my back and gazed at the bleached-out blue sky, bright orange and pink stripes hanging low, signalling the start of sunset.

And in those moments it all vanished: my blubbery body, my mother's miserable cleaning, Shelley's colic, my father leaving for Mount Isa, Nanna Purvis's bossiness. And my jitterbugs about Uncle Blackie's photos.

'Wish I could stay here forever,' I said.

'Yeah, it'd be fun if you could come over every day,' Angela said.

'At least you've got a brother. I can't wait till Shelley grows up so I can play with her. Then Gumtree Cottage might be less boring.'

'But Marco never hangs around with me,' Angela said. 'He's always off driving around with his friends. He just got his licence and Dad got him a groovy purple car.'

'Okay, I'll come over every chance I can get away from Gumtree Cottage. But I might have to go back to my uncle's soon, for another photo shoot.'

'He already took the photos? You didn't show them to me.'

'I've only seen one of them … the one he gave me.' From my Indian bag, I pulled out Uncle Blackie's shot of me on the red bike.

'Groovy,' Angela said. 'Whose bike is that?'

'Mine. Uncle Blackie's always giving me stuff, but this is the best present by far. It's even got handlebar streamers and a flowered seat.'

'Wow,' Angela said. 'Why didn't you ride the bike over here to show me?'

'I told you, I have to keep Uncle Blackie a secret otherwise my bossy grandmother will stop me seeing him. So the bike has to stay at his place.'

'That sounds weird,' Angela said.

'Nanna Purvis *is* weird.'

'No, I meant the secret business is weird,' Angela said with a frown.

'Not really. You don't know my grandmother.'

'Anyway, don't worry,' Angela said. 'You'll probably look just as groovy in all the other photos.'

'Oh, I bet I'll look fat in them,' I said. 'Especially in the ... in the naked ones.'

* * *

'*Naked* ones?' Angela's eyes widened, like large brown chestnuts. 'He took photos of you without your clothes on?'

'Oh, only some. I had my clothes on — my underwear at least — for most of them ... about half-half.'

'But he shouldn't do that, Tanya! It's ... it's wrong. Men who do that are filthy pervs.'

'Don't freak out,' I said as we scrambled from the water and lay on our towels. 'Uncle Blackie reckons it's fine, that photographers are used to it. That they don't even *see* the naked bodies.'

Even as I spoke, the doubt, guilt and fear knotted inside me again. But I couldn't tell Angela about that. What if she thought I was stupid and didn't want to be friends with me anymore?

'It sounds suss to me,' she said. 'Real dodgy.'

'He's my uncle. He's kind and nice. No way can he be a filthy perv.'

'Why won't you believe me, Tanya?' she went on. 'Men like him are *bad* news. Anyway, did you tell your parents about the photos?'

'As if ...' I breathed deeply. 'My father spends his life at The Dead Dingo's Donger and Mum's become this misery-guts, housework-crazed person. If only my sister would get better, then my mother would stop being miserable, and my father

128

would stop guzzling beer. Then we could be happy again, I just know we could.'

'So did your uncle tell you where he was, when he was away all those years?' Angela said.

'Not exactly, but Nanna Purvis reckons he was locked up somewhere for doing something to some girl. But you can't take any notice of what she says, since my grandmother talks pure rubbish.'

'Doing something to some girl?' Angela said, her voice gone all screechy. 'This uncle sounds like a *very* bad person!'

'Uncle Blackie's not a bad person,' I shouted back. 'He really cares about me ... look at this flashy bike.' I shoved the photo under her nose again. 'If he didn't, why would he buy me something like *this*?'

Angela fell quiet, looked away into the dense bushland behind the pool. 'Sorry I shouted at you,' she said.

'Sorry I shouted too.'

'This Uncle Blackie stuff just sounds all wrong,' she said.

Angela was older and smarter than me, and seemed to know more about everything. But as I let the sun lick the water from my body, I realised she couldn't know Uncle Blackie like I did, and I flicked her doubts from my thoughts.

'You can't tell anybody this,' Angela said after a few moments, 'but Marco reckons my father and my Zio Ricci can make bad people go away.'

'What bad people? And away where ... from Wollongong?'

'I don't know where exactly, but yeah, probably away from Wollongong. Marco told me about one of Papa's carpet workers whose daughter was attacked by some creep. He sent the creep away and nobody, including the girl, ever saw him again.'

'I don't want Uncle Blackie to go away. He's the only one in my family I can count on, especially since my father's going away.'

'Where's your papa going?'

'Up to Mount Isa ... for work. Says he's going to earn us lots of money. But I know it's just to get away from Nanna Purvis who he's always hated, and because he can't stand my misery-face mother anymore, or Shelley's crying. He even shook my sister the other day, to try and get her to shut up. Dad's never rough like that.'

'People do things they wouldn't normally do when they're fed up or exhausted,' Angela said. 'Maybe your papa won't be away for long. And your sister will surely stop the crying soon and then your mamma will feel better.'

'Yeah, probably,' I said. 'Anyway, you won't tell your brother or your parents — anybody — about Uncle Blackie, will you? We swore to keep each other's secrets, remember, so promise?'

'I promise,' Angela said, as sunlight flashed from the chrome fittings on Mr Moretti's black Valiant pulling into the driveway.

Angela's parents came out onto the verandah and Mr Moretti raised an arm in a wave. We waved back, then, arms linked, they disappeared back into the big house.

I wondered if he had drugs hidden in his rolled-up carpets. Mr Moretti didn't seem to have any carpets with him at all. And he didn't resemble a criminal in the least. Angela's father looked groovy (for a dad that is) in his smart, knife-edge creased black pants and black shirt. Nothing like my father's brickie gear.

When the sun slid behind Mount Kembla I told Angela I should get home. 'Nanna Purvis'll be hollering up and down Figtree Avenue if I'm not back for tea time.'

'You are come again soon, Tanya.' Mrs Moretti kissed my cheeks and Mr Moretti glanced up from his newspaper and gave me a friendly smile.

'Oh yes, I'd love to,' I said, and set off down the driveway, waving goodbye to Angela. I already missed her lovely pool, the luscious vegetable garden, the smell of baked bread hot from the oven, olive oil in metal tins, nutty biscuits and happy, smiling people. All that was different from Gumtree Cottage.

Half an hour later though, as I neared Figtree Avenue, images of the photo shoot fuzzed out every trace in my mind of the Bottlebrush Crescent palace. But even if it was wrong and Uncle

Blackie *did* end up being a perv, I hoped Angela wouldn't let on to her father about him. I did not want my secret friend to be sent away from Wollongong.

* * *

'Didn't I forbid you to hang around those *Eyeties?*' Nanna Purvis called as I came inside, the dogs barking and racing around my feet.

'You're such a racist. Angela's my friend and her parents are nice, real friendly. Unlike you.'

My mother stood at the kitchen bench, staring at what looked and smelled like a burnt apple pie. I wrinkled my nose. 'Oh, what happened?'

'Ya mum wasn't paying attention and scorched the pie to blazes, that's what happened,' Nanna Purvis said, opening up *Only for Sheilas.* Then, to the yelping dogs: 'Oy, quit that racket … youse're giving me a headache.'

'Headache … headache. I've got a headache too,' my mother said to no one. She opened the flyscreen door and hurled the burnt pie — dish and all — down into the backyard.

'What the …?' Nanna Purvis shook the blue curls. 'Strewth, Eleanor, what's got into you? And not even a care your own daughter's hanging about with a drug-dealing mob —'

'Stop talking rubbish,' I shouted, which made the dogs bark louder. Steely meowed and rubbed his head against my knees. 'Don't you know that after World War II those Europeans were so poor they had to leave everything behind — *everything* — and make a new life in a strange country?'

'This ain't got nothing to do with making a new life,' Nanna Purvis said, flipping her magazine pages faster. 'But everything to do with *destroying* life … with drugs. Look, I'm just worried about ya, Tanya.'

'I already said, you have no proof of any drugs.' I grabbed a packet of stale-looking cream buns from the pantry. 'Mr Moretti made it rich in Australia by working hard, nothing else.' I stuffed a bun into my mouth, barely chewed it before swallowing.

'What's so good about us Australians, anyway?' I went on, cream oozing from the corners of my lips. 'We all started as convicts. The Randalls did, at least.'

'Them New Australians're bludgers what paid bugger all to get over here,' Nanna Purvis said, gathering the whimpering Billie-Jean onto her lap.

'After the war, our country — *your* country — needed those migrants,' I said, echoing my old fifth-grade teacher's words. 'We had to find workers for all our new industries, and those migrants — Angela's dad — were really hard workers.' I sneaked Bitta a Pooch Snax.

'Seems I can't give you advice on anything these days, Tanya. And what've I said about wasting good Pooch Snax on that mongrel?'

'Why should Billie-Jean get them and not Bitta? That's prejudice.' Another often-used teacher's word. I stuffed two more cream buns into my mouth. I'd never be a skinny Twiggy model but I couldn't stop shovelling them in. My belly gurgled and I wished I could heave back all that bun and cream, but down it stayed, sitting heavy and sickly in my stomach.

Fat pig girl.

Later, when my father came home from the pub, drunk and red-eyed, he didn't say a word to anyone. He lurched down into the backyard, scraped out the pie into the rubbish bin and scrubbed the blackened dish until his hands were red and flaky.

'Am I adopted?' I asked, as he grabbed a tea towel to dry the dish. I knew it wasn't the right time to ask that question — it never was — but I just wanted him to talk to me. About any old thing. Anything was better than talking at all.

Dad's eyes widened, sort of crossed and his voice came out hoarse, hushed, as he put the pie dish back in the cupboard. 'Whatever keeps giving you that idea, Tanya?'

'Because Stacey Mornon reckons I am.'

'Don't listen to the rubbish people tell you,' he said, walking away from me.

I wanted to yell at him to come back, to tell me the truth. But if I was adopted I didn't want it to be true. And since, yet again, Dad did not directly say "you are not adopted", I still didn't know.

Chapter 20

'Why the bleedin' banjo's Shelley's pillow in her pram? Over her *face*?' From the kitchen, Nanna Purvis hobbled out to the verandah and limped down the steps as fast as she could with arthritic knees, and varicose veins the same colour blue as her slippers.

It was the morning of Australia Day. Friday, January twenty-sixth, 1973, the sun a lemon sliver over the Pacific horizon glimmering like steel. Mr Kooka was perched on his usual branch. But he was silent this morning, as if the heat had dried up his tongue. He was simply staring, with one sharp, white eye, down at Shelley's pram.

Dad had just driven off somewhere. Steely and the dogs were dozing in the morning sunshine on the verandah beside me, as I dangled my yoyo for "around the world".

'Shelley!' Nanna Purvis ripped off the netting and shook my baby sister. 'Wake up, Shelley. She's not breathing. God, oh god, oh god!' Each "oh god" was louder than the previous one.

Mum, dragging her Venetians outside for hosing, dropped the blinds in a heap. We both rushed to Nanna Purvis, beside the pram.

'Why? Why isn't she breathing?' Mum's voice was shrill. No trace of sluggishness. A hand clapped over her mouth, her scream came out stifled, damp. The dogs got nervy, barking and running around the pram, nipping at Shelley's pillow Nanna Purvis had chucked aside.

'Give her the kiss of life … bang on her chest.' Nanna Purvis was yelling and Mum was lifting Shelley from the pram and laying her on the dead brown grass and running her hands over her body, stroking, rubbing. She lifted Shelley's singlet and slapped my sister's chest.

'Call the ambulance, Tanya,' Nanna Purvis said. She turned to my mother. 'Go on, kiss of life, Eleanor!'

'Oh gosh, is the number triple 0? What if they don't answer?'

'Yes! Go now, course they'll answer.' My grandmother flapped her arms at me.

Legs marshmallow-squishy, heart bursting from my chest, I rushed inside as Mum's quivering lips covered Shelley's baby ones.

'My sister's stopped breathing,' I barked into the phone, and told them our address. 'Hurry, she's only a baby. Please hurry.'

Hopping from foot to foot, a hand pushing on my cowlick, I waited out the front for the ambulance. It took forever to arrive, though later the neighbours would say it was only ten minutes.

'She's out in the backyard,' I said, hustling the two ambulance men down the hallway, through the kitchen. Almost pushing them across the verandah.

'Is she breathing again yet, Mum?'

My mother was still kneeling beside Shelley. 'Not breathing, no … please … please help my baby.' She looked up at the men, wrung her hands through her cleaning shift. The dogs kept up their barking.

'Enough, youse two,' Nanna Purvis screeched, and overhead, a cockatoo screeched back, its crest a yellow fan opening against the hard blue sky.

'What happened?' one of the men asked, the other checking for a pulse in Shelley's neck, and pressing his palm against her chest.

'Nothing *happened*,' Nanna Purvis said. 'She'd been sleeping — whimpering — in her pram for the last half hour, then I saw her pillow was over her face.'

'Mum never leaves the pillow in the pram when Shelley's sleeping,' I said. 'Says it's dangerous. She always stores it on that shelf.' I pointed to the lower part of the pram.

'... only use the pillow to prop her up in the pram,' Mum said, 'when she's awake.'

'Never when she's sleeping,' Nanna Purvis said.

'Perhaps you forgot just this once?' the ambulance man said.

'No, never forgot.' Mum hugged her arms around her trembling body. I wanted her to hug me too.

Lenny Longbottom's crinkled face appeared over the fence. 'What's going on, Pearl?'

'None of ya business, Old Lenny,' Nanna Purvis snapped.

'Crikey, Pearl, only trying to help.'

Mad Myrtle and Mavis Sloan poked their heads over the other side fence. 'Anything we can help with?' Mavis asked.

'Youse mind your own bananas too,' Nanna Purvis said. 'And where's ya father when he's needed, eh?' she said to me, as if it was my fault Dad was always at the pub. 'Typical man, never home when there's a crisis. That's what me hairdresser, Rita, reckons.'

Nanna Purvis and I helped my mother clamber into the back of the ambulance with Shelley, the whole of Figtree Avenue came and stood out in the street, whispering behind cupped hands.

As the ambulance drove off, the blue tips of Mr Kooka's wings flashed as he came swooping from the backyard, over the roof, dipping and soaring. Dipping and soaring, and starting up his ghostly '*Garooagarooagarooga*.'

* * *

Eventually Dad's Holden pulled into the driveway and I rushed out to meet him.

'Shelley stopped breathing,' I said, 'but the ambulance took her to hospital to bring her back to life.'

'Stopped breathing? What ambulance?' Dad removed his Akubra, ran his forearm across his sweaty brow and swiped away a fly. 'Where's your mother?'

'I don't know why Shelley stopped breathing, but don't worry, they'll revive her … they can do that. I know all about the kiss of life.'

They must … they have to!

I followed Dad's work boots *thud, thud, thud* up the verandah steps, and inside.

'Pearl? What the bloody hell's happened to Shelley?'

Nanna Purvis told him about finding Shelley with her pillow over her face. 'Eleanor's gone with the ambulance, drivers said for us to wait here. They'll ring … let us know.'

Dad paced the kitchen. 'Bugger waiting here, I'm going up the hospital.' He slapped his Akubra back on.

'They said to wait here, they'll ring,' Nanna Purvis repeated. 'No use the whole lot of us going up there. We'll only get in their way.'

Dad hurled his hat back onto the table and lit a fag. 'Jesus bloody Christ, Shelley was fine this morning … well, fine apart from the usual colic fiasco.'

He kept walking right through Gumtree Cottage, from one airless room to the next, smoking and flicking ash, the thump of his work boots breaking the silence between his sighs.

'I always knew it was a bad move, me coming to live in this unlucky house,' Nanna Purvis said. 'What with all that's happened here. And now *this*. Our own little gumnut girl.'

'Just stupid legend and rumour,' Dad said. 'We don't know if any of those stories are true.'

'All the neighbours reckon they are,' Nanna Purvis said. 'Them Sloan sisters and Lenny Longbum … and others in Figtree Avenue.'

'And you're dim enough to listen to them?' Dad said. 'One you call "Mad Myrtle" and the other "that gaol bird"? Besides, where else would you have gone after Pop Purvis died? A nursing home? Jesus bloody Christ, Pearl, I can just see you loving that life.'

My head was aching, dizzy from my father and Nanna Purvis's arguing. My legs wobbled, and I slumped down into a chair.

And why are they taking so long to bring our baby back to life?

Chapter 21

Several hours later — and still no phone call from the hospital — a police car pulled up in front of number thirteen. Two policemen got out of the front seat, one tall and thin, the other short and stout.

They opened the back door, helped out my mother, and walked towards the house. The policemen each gripped one of my mother's arms because her legs kept crumpling beneath her.

'Constable Lloyd,' the tall one said as my father came hurrying out onto the verandah. He nodded to his partner. 'And this is Constable Adams.'

'Is my baby sister okay now?' I said.

Dad took my mother's arm; she fell against him. 'What's happened to Shelley?' he said, herding Mum, Nanna Purvis and the constables into the living-room. 'Go into the kitchen and get yourself some Anzac biscuits and a glass of milk, Tanya,' he said in a stuttery voice, closing the sliding doors behind him.

How dare my father shut me out of this important conversation about my sister? Munching on an Anzac biscuit, I slid the doors open a crack.

My mother, Nanna Purvis and Dad were slumped on the white sofa sheets. The policemen stood together on the other side of the living-room, arms stretched down their fronts, wrists crossed, hats in hand.

I listened, in mounting horror, to the thin line of talk that trickled out, each word a drop of poison seeping through the door crack.

'Very sorry,' Constable Lloyd was saying. 'The child is gone. The Casualty doctor pronounced life extinct on arrival at the hospital.'

'Sorry ... nothing they could do,' Constable Adams said.

Nothing they could do, gone where? Course they could've done something! They revived that boy in Real Life Crime.

A cold fist of fear tightened around my guts, squeezed until I was on the brink of vomiting up the Anzac biscuits. Bitter liquid spurted into my throat. I swallowed hard, hurtled into the living-room and hammered my fists against Constable Adams's arm.

'Liar, they could've got Shelley back to life ... they *could've*.' He did nothing to try and stop me, just stood there and let me carry on hitting him. 'You go and get them to bring her back to life ... try harder!' The sob grew inside me, swelling and exploding in a boom like Guy Fawkes Night fireworks.

'Tanya, quit that,' Nanna Purvis said, and Dad was kneeling beside me, gripping my fists.

'She's not gone, is she, Dad? They *can* bring Shelley back to life ... can't they?'

Dad squeezed my clenched hands and Constable Adams patted my head as if I was some little kid. 'I'm so sorry for your baby sister.'

My father slumped back onto the sofa and lit another fag. 'Jesus bloody Christ, what happened? I don't understand.'

Nanna Purvis shook her head, hair rollers bobbing like moths around a light. 'Whoever could suffocate a baby with her own pillow?'

'We're not a hundred percent certain the baby was suffocated,' Constable Lloyd said.

'Shelley ... her name is Shelley,' Mum said barely above a whisper, her first words since she'd returned home in the police car.

'Though we're obliged to suspect as much,' Constable Adams went on, 'because from a forensic point of view it's almost impossible for a baby to suffocate itself.'

'Her,' my mother said. 'Herself.'

'And,' Constable Lloyd said, 'because the doctor noted bruising around the child's mouth.'

'Shelley ... her name is Shell — '

'If the doctor hadn't detected the bruising,' Constable Lloyd said, 'we'd have thought it might be a case of this new cot death thing. There'll need to be a post mortem, investig —'

'Cot death?' Nanna Purvis said. 'What the bleedin' banjo is that?'

The constables looked at each other. 'A recent ... theory,' Constable Adams said, 'why babies die for no apparent reason in their cot, or pram.'

'You going to take everyone's fingerprints?' I asked.

Nanna Purvis rolled her eyes at Mum. 'I told you she's too young to be reading that damn crime magazine, didn't I?'

'Yes, fingerprinting,' Constable Lloyd said. 'And the pillow will be taken away for forensic examination.'

'But all our fingerprints will be on that pillow,' Dad said. 'We've all handled it at one time or another.'

'Yeah, don't see the point of that,' Nanna Purvis said.

'That might be true,' Constable Lloyd went on, 'but we'll still take the pillow. If fibres from it are found on the baby's lips ... in her mouth or lungs that would support the suffocation theory.'

'Had the baby been ill?' Constable Adams asked.

'Shelley ... her name is Shelley,' my mother mumbled.

'Nope. Fit as a mallee bull,' Nanna Purvis said. 'Except for a touch of the colic.'

'A *touch* of colic?' I curled my lip at Nanna Purvis. 'She's been screaming with colic pain for over three months.'

The constables glanced at each other again and asked us if we'd seen anybody lurking around the backyard.

'We saw nobody,' Nanna Purvis said.

'Shelley was asleep in her pram under the gum tree ... I was about to-to ...'

My mother was crying now; couldn't stop the hiccupping sobs. I sat beside her, circled my arms around her. Dad stayed upright, smoking and staring down at Mum.

'... clean the Venetian blinds,' she went on. 'Once a w-week, hang them over the Hill's Hoist to h-hose them down ... Shelley's pillow over her face ... not breathing.'

'We'll be asking the neighbours if they saw anything,' Constable Lloyd said.

Nanna Purvis huffed. 'Won't get anything sensible out of them.'

'Why's that, Mrs ...?'

'Pearl Purvis is me name. Them Longbottoms next door,' she said, flinging a gnarly hand in the direction of number eleven, 'are boozers who watch the footy and cricket on telly all afternoon. Right racket it makes. And another thing,' she began, as if the thought had just jumped into her head.

'What other thing?' the constable prodded.

'Lenny Longbottom, the old codger, is a convicted murderer, did youse know that? In gaol for years ... bashed some bloke to death.' A quick breath and on she prattled. 'Claimed he never meant to kill the bloke, but murder is murder, ain't it? Once done you can never take it back. Once a gaol bird always a gaol bird, I say. Once a killer always a killer. And he *was* always whinge-ing about Shelley's crying, said he couldn't stand the noise ... couldn't hear his telly.'

'We are aware of Leonard Longbottom's past,' Constable Adams said, 'and we'll be questioning the family.'

'And the Andersons over the road at number ten are *Catholics*,' Nanna Purvis said. 'So youse won't get much sense out of them either.'

'That's enough, Pearl,' Dad said, with a glance at the frown-ing policemen. 'They don't want to hear about every resident of Figtree Avenue.'

'Could've even been them mad Sloan women what suffocated her,' Nanna Purvis said, jerking a thumb at number fifteen. From her screechy voice it was obvious my grandmother's thoughts had run away from her and she was jibbering any old rubbish.

Dad glared at her. 'Sock in it, Pearl.'

'Mrs Purvis,' Constable Lloyd said, 'we are still not a hundred percent certain someone suffocated the baby.'

'Shelley ... her name is Shelley,' Mum said, her voice thick as mud.

'They know what her name is, Eleanor!' Dad said.

The living-room fell silent, save for my mother's muted sobs.

'Well, if that's all,' Nanna Purvis said, 'youse'll have to excuse me, the dog'll be wanting to go outside to do his business.'

'We'll be in touch,' Constable Adams said as the policemen let themselves out.

'Who would do such a thing?' I said, looking at my parents, my grandmother. 'Whoever would suffocate my sister?'

But none of them could give me an answer.

* * *

Nanna Purvis and I dawdled into the kitchen, as if changing rooms might make us feel better. We brewed tea, one cup after the other, but it didn't soften the blow. The shock was still an axe chopping into my skull, over and over.

I hunted through the pantry, ripped open a packet of TimTams — my favourite chocolate biscuits — and crammed five or six into my mouth. Nanna Purvis didn't make a single comment.

But the biscuits did not make me feel better. My guts were sick, puffier than a full-blown balloon.

Mum was still sitting on the sofa, droopy as a wet cloth someone'd forgotten to dry out. Her hands clasped in her lap, she never moved; just stared at the windows, bare without their

Venetian blinds, which still lay on the verandah where she'd heaped them.

Dad wandered from room to room, a beer in one hand, a fag in the other. Nobody said anything.

'Shelley won't ever come back to life, will she, Dad?' My father coughed, shook his head like an open-mouthed fair clown waiting for the ball.

'No … no she won't.'

'Do you reckon that dead people can look down from Heaven and see what's happening on earth?' I said. 'Could Shelley tell us who did that to her? We *have* to find out who did this.'

Dad didn't answer; just kept smoking and staring down at the lino.

'If only I'd helped Mum more,' I said. 'If only I'd been watching over Shelley ….'

'You did all ya could,' Nanna Purvis said. 'For a kid your age.'

'This was not your fault, Tanya,' Dad said. 'Don't you ever think that.'

'Whose fault is it then?'

Dad dragged on his fag, shook his head. He shuffled into the living-room, put his hand on Mum's shoulder, shook her gently. Her gaze dropped from the windows down to her thin white hands.

'What happened to Shelley?' he said.

Dad grabbed her shoulders, held her chin, forced her look up at him. 'Answer me, Eleanor … how did our baby die?'

'Why are you asking Mum how Shelley died?' I said. 'She doesn't know. Or she'd have told the police.'

'Go and lie down, Eleanor,' Dad said with a huge sigh. His hand slid away when she still didn't move, not even a blink. Zapped into a trance.

* * *

146

As if it was any ordinary afternoon, the *Illawarra Mercury* lay open on the kitchen table.

HAPPY AUSTRALIA DAY. January 26th, 1973.

165-year anniversary of convict ships arriving in Sydney.

The same ships that had brought the Randall family convicts to Australia; convicts who'd built Gumtree Cottage.

The home in which, generations later it was said, a man's young wife had died. The tale went that he'd wandered from room to room looking for her, night after night, and never found her. He wasted away through longing for her.

Like that man, I kept looking for Shelley; listening for her gurgles and cries, sometimes believing I *could* hear her but then realising I couldn't. Maybe I was hearing the ghost of that lonely man still trapped in his misery, and I feared that one day I too would waste away through longing for my baby sister.

'Is Shelley a Gumtree Cottage ghost now?' I said to Nanna Purvis. 'How long does it take a dead person to become a ghost?'

'Crikey, Tanya, what kind of a question is that?' Nanna Purvis rolled her eyes skyward. 'Just drink ya cuppa.'

'I hate tea,' I said, pushing aside my cup, slopping milky tea across the table.

My tear-blurred gaze skimmed the rest of the front page of the *Illawarra Mercury*, not reading the words, just staring at them.

Prime Minister, Gough Whitlam launches national anthem competition to replace "God Save the Queen".

'Who cares about the stupid national anthem?' I stroked Steely, hard. Nanna Purvis took Billie-Jean outside and, except for the humming fridge, the kitchen was silent. A sudden, unbearable silence.

I looked out through the flyscreen at the tangle of Venetian blinds, and beyond the verandah onto the heat-weary yard where the sun burned the leaves and flowers, purling their perfumes across the yard. And at Shelley's pram, still parked beside the gum tree trunk.

I craned my neck, peered inside. No Shelley. Only a single red blossom trapped in the pram netting.

I opened a bottle of milk, scraped the cream off the top and let Steely lick it off my finger. I poured a glassful, took another pile of Anzac biscuits from the tin, sat at the kitchen table and tried to think who could have done such a thing to Shelley. But, as in loads of *Real Life Crime* stories, I couldn't come up with a single suspect.

A pair of pliers twisted into my temples, the pain searing through my head. I had to stop thinking about Shelley, stop the agony.

I tried to concentrate on something else — a nice thing like swimming with Angela in her pool. Then when I came around to thinking of Shelley again, she'd have come back to life, somehow. She had to. My baby sister could not be gone for good.

I drank the milk and ate the biscuits, the voice of my fifth-grade teacher ringing through my mind, telling us about the Australian and New Zealand Army Corps troops landing at what would be named Anzac cove, at Gallipoli on 25th April 1915. I imagined them lying on the beach eating the Anzac biscuits their mothers had sent from Australia, whilst gloriously defending the Empire. Then the Turks shot them down, leaving a trail of half-chewed biscuits strewn across the sand.

'Such an achievement for the Anzac troops to land on a dark coast and hold the country while reinforcements followed,' the teacher had said.

I supposed the mothers forgave their soldier sons for the Anzac biscuits that went to waste. Same as Mum would forgive Shelley for the stroller she'd got on special which would go to waste since Shelley hadn't used it. Not once.

Steely sprang onto the table. I pushed biscuit crumbs under his nose. 'Poor Shelley ... poor little gumnut girl. Poor us!' And when the biscuit tin was empty, I swiped it onto the floor, loathing myself even more.

'Aw strewth, Tanya,' Nanna Purvis said, looking at the tin as she came back inside.

'Why do you hate Catholics?' I said. 'Same as you hate foreigners.'

'What a question to ask, the very day we've lost Shelley.' She gave Billie-Jean a Pooch Snax, and spooned out his kangaroo meat. 'They're people we just don't talk to … they just don't see things the same way as us.'

'Dad told me it's because Pop Purvis's family were Catholics,' I said, as Billie-Jean snuffled into his meat. 'And because my grandfather used to hit you. That's why you hate Catholics.'

'Best not to listen to everything your father says, Tanya, especially when he's been down The Dead Dingo. Besides, let's not bring all that up today, of all days.'

'*Hem, hem.*' We both looked up to see Old Lenny standing at the back door, dressed in the blue singlet stretched tight over his paunch, and the shorts from which his thin legs poked like a bird's. He cleared his throat again. '*Hem, hem.*'

'Can't ya see we're in mourning, Old Lenny?' Nanna Purvis said. 'Not to be disturbed.'

'I saw the cop car and guessed the worst had happened,' he said. 'Thought I'd bring youse a little something.' He held up a yellow fold-up sun lounge. 'Spanking new banana lounge, Pearl. Got it cheap off a mate. Noticed your old chair was getting saggy about the middle … bit like you and me eh, Pearl?' He let out a raspy cackle and patted his round belly — the only part of Lenny Longbottom with the slightest wad of fat.

'Speak for yourself, Old Lenny.' Nanna Purvis opened the door and took the banana lounge from him. 'Nothing saggy about my middle.'

'Aw, I just thought a small gift might make youse all feel a bit better in light of … of the tragedy.'

'Yeah, righto, thanks and all,' Nanna Purvis said, and when she sat back down, her gaze creeping back to the *Illawarra Mercury*, Old Lenny hobbled off.

'You told the police you believed Old Lenny might've killed Shelley,' I said. 'How can you take presents from him? '

Nanna Purvis didn't look up from the newspaper. 'I need a new banana lounge, that's why.'

Chapter 22

'Doc Piggot'll come and see your mum shortly,' Dad said as he put down the phone. He took two bottles of KB Lager from the fridge and sat on the front verandah, smoking and drinking until the doctor pulled into the driveway behind the Holden.

Doc Piggott looked at Mum, still perched on the sofa, rigid as the unbroken heat. Not speaking, not crying, simply staring at her blindless windows.

'She's been like that for hours,' I said as the doctor sat beside her, took her limp wrist and counted her pulse rate.

'Your mum's in shock … understandable given the circumstances,' Doc Piggott said. 'These pills should help.' He scribbled something on his prescription pad. Nanna Purvis took the paper.

Dad snatched the prescription from my grandmother. '*I'll* get her pills, first thing Monday morning.'

'Need to hose the Venetian blinds,' Mum said.

We all stared at her as if she was a mute person uttering words for the first time.

'Jesus bloody Christ, Eleanor,' Dad said, 'our baby's gone, forget the damn blinds.'

'Can't leave them outside — '

'Shelley is *dead*.' Dad couldn't stop shaking his head.

'Didn't even get the beds changed …'

'Eleanor!'

'Don't shout, Dobson. Can't bear you shouting.' Mum gripped

the hair at her temples, tugged so hard I thought she'd rip out clumps of it. 'Leave me alone … I'll be better if you just leave me alone.'

Doc Piggott frowned as he got up from the sofa. 'Call me if there's anything more I can do, anything at all.'

Once the doctor left, Dad grabbed his hat and car keys.

'Where you off to, Dobson?' Nanna Purvis said.

Dad strode towards the door. 'None of your business.'

The phone rang again. It rang a lot in those hours after Shelley died — a shrill and persistent intruder into our private grief. Later, when the sun was ripe over Mount Kembla and the sky turned amber, the phone stopped ringing. Probably because nobody ever answered it. My mother was still slumped on the sofa staring at her windows.

The pub was closed on public holidays so I wondered wherever Dad could be. Nanna Purvis said he was "God only knows where".

Finally, a fag jammed between his lips, his eyes scrunched against the curling smoke, Dad came in. His eyes were bloodshot and glittery, from crying or drinking too much beer. Or both.

'Looks like we'll have to make sandwiches for our tea, Tanya,' Nanna Purvis said, 'since ya poor mum can't move from that sofa and ya dad's in his usual state.'

But in the end no one was hungry so Steely licked the Vegemite off the toast and left buttery crumbs scattered over the table.

After nobody ate tea, Nanna Purvis turned on the telly and poured herself a nip of sherry. My mother was still sitting on the sofa but no one had the energy to try and convince her to move.

'Jesus bloody Christ, Pearl, our baby died today,' Dad said. 'And you go on with your normal television routine as if nothing's happened?'

'Don't you dare try and make me feel guilty, Dobson. We're all coping as best we can. If this is my way of dealing with the tragedy, far be it from you to criticise.'

Dad ignored her and turned the channel dial to the ABC News.

Pictures were flashing onto the screen of marching people wielding banners: *GET OUR DIGGERS OUT OF VIETNAM*

'... people demonstrating in Sydney ... police ...' the newsreader said.

'Turn that channel back, Dobson, *Matlock Police* will be coming on soon,' Nanna Purvis said.

'You don't think our soldiers in Vietnam are more important than some fictional crime show?'

'No I do not. I reckon most of us true blue Aussies don't give a wombat's willy about a war in some far-off Asian country. Mark my words we'll all be saying: "not my bowl of rice" instead of "not my cup of tea".'

And for once Dad let Nanna Purvis win the television argument, because all the fight had been sucked out of him.

I couldn't bear to be inside the house a second longer with him and my grandmother cutting at each other like a pair of blunt scissors, *snip, snip, snip.* The endless bickering a drill on my nerves.

I slipped out onto the back verandah and stared into the floral-scented dusk hanging heavy over the yard, the fateful gum tree, the pram. As if the pram was waiting for its owner to return; that Shelley was simply busy playing or having her nappy changed or being bathed. She'd be back soon.

Nobody moved the pram; I don't think anyone dared. While it stayed beneath her gum tree, a part of Shelley was still with us. But if the pram went, Shelley would truly be gone.

Cicadas whirred, continuous and irritating, mosquitoes buzzed and fruit bats squealed — soft and urgent — mini aeroplanes swooping low across the yard. I looked down at the hard baked ground. My life was as ragged as the mounds of brittle leaves littering it.

In the darkness, I couldn't see the red blossom inside Shelley's pram but I imagined it there — thirsty now, whimpering for water, and, when there was none, wilting in the heat. The creamy white fading to dirty brown. All shrivelled up and dead.

* * *

For our first night without Shelley, and since we couldn't get the new tablets till Monday, Nanna Purvis gave Mum two of Doc Piggott's old pills, and popped another into her own mouth.

'Come on, you need to sleep,' she said, pulling my mother upright from the sofa.

Mum's eyes were almost swollen shut and there were scratches around her mouth as if she'd been clawing at herself.

Gaze low, shoulders hunched, her hands jammed into the cleaning-shift pockets, she shuffled from living-room to hallway to bedroom. Each step was forced and unsteady — wading out to sea against a too-strong current.

'And half a pill for you, Tanya,' Nanna Purvis said, breaking one of Mum's tablets in half. 'I swear by these for any crisis.'

'So it must be true,' Dad said, 'seeing as you're the expert on *everything*.'

'Enough of your cheek, Dobson,' Nanna Purvis said. 'Now we all should try and get some sleep.'

Before I went into my bedroom, I looked in on my mother. She was facing away from the doorway, curled on the bed like the baby in a womb that our teacher had shown us in her anatomy book.

She didn't move or make a sound as I crept in and leaned over Shelley's cot. I pressed my face against the sheet, trying to smell her lovely baby scent: her own smell mingled with Pears' soap and Mum's washing powder that was always trapped there. I mashed my nose into the sheet, my nostrils twitching mad as a beagle's, but I couldn't find her. There was only the sour odour of things gone wrong.

The scream welled inside me but it couldn't get out — the wild and useless fluttering of a netted butterfly.

There was no way around it. Shelley was gone, her short life wrapped up in a sheet in a metal box in the hospital mortuary. Same as a *Real Life Crime* story.

My mother still didn't stir, and as I shuffled into my own room, the ache of her lost kisses cut even deeper with Shelley gone.

Sleep would never come. I knew it, but wanted it so badly, imagining Dad would shake me awake in a few hours.

'It's all right, it was just a dream,' he'd say. 'Shelley's not dead. It's over, Tanya … it's over.'

And then I cried, really bawled for the first time. Tears for Shelley, and how frightened she must have been, fighting the pillow held over her face; for how she must have suffered. For how she'd never crawl or walk, or blurt out her first word. How I'd never push her on a swing or a seesaw, or dive under the waves with her at North Beach. I sobbed because she'd left me as an only child. Even after all my mother's lost babies I never imagined I'd grow up without a brother or sister. But mostly I cried for myself; for how I was going to keep on living without her.

How dare some evil person steal away our happiness!

I fumbled around under the bed, reaching for the Barbie dolls I'd kicked there. I dragged them out, lined the Barbies in a row, my gaze resting on Twiggy. Dark and sultry eyeliner-eyes, long lashes, pouty mouth. Thin body. I looked down at my fat ripples and spat on Twiggy Barbie's face.

Dad came in and checked my flyscreen was closed. 'Mozzies're bad tonight,' he said as if mosquitoes were our only worry. He sat on my bed, took my hand from my cowlick. 'Will you be all right, Princess? I know we've had the most god-awful shock.'

'Will the police find out who killed Shelley?'

'We're still not certain someone killed your sister,' Dad said. 'Might be this … this cot death thing.'

'But what about the bruises around her mouth?'

'I dunno … I just don't know what to think.' He kissed my

brow and his fag smell mixed with sweat, bricks and beer hung in my nostrils.

After he'd gone I flung the nightmare bedspread behind my door and lay on the sheet thinking, once again, who could have killed my little sister. I knew my father also suspected murder, rather than this cot death thing. Those constables too, from the way they'd looked so suspiciously at us.

I must have fallen asleep because I dreamed I was standing on the edge of a cliff, the sound of the sea below like funeral music.

Teetering on the cliff edge, the sea below me rose in waves, heaving and folding in rhythm to the sickness at the bottom of my guts. Then a wave — bigger than all of them — rolled right up the cliff face, smashed over me.

The pain crushed my chest and when I could no longer breathe, I collapsed and tumbled off the edge. Faster and faster I fell, the world whizzing past me. I tried to grab hold of something to stop myself but there was nothing and I crash-landed, a baby again, in a pram the same as Shelley's.

I was in a row of babies in prams and Mum and Dad were walking up and down deciding which baby to adopt. The person selling the babies said to my parents: 'This one's on special because she's tubby and has bat-wing ears. "Batgirl" you could call her. Or "Ten-ton Tanya". And if you don't take this one it'll be junked … thrown out.'

'We'll take this one then,' Mum said, counting out coins from her housekeeping purse.

She wrapped me in a Venetian blind to take me home to Figtree Avenue because Dad's brickie work didn't earn enough to buy baby clothes as well as the baby.

The slats were sharp and cut into me and I ended up all wet because my mother had hosed the Venetian blinds beforehand. I started crying and Mum said: 'Be quiet, Tanya, let me get this house clean.'

My eyes snapped open, my heart juddering like a lizard trapped beneath a rock, my pillow soaked with tears.

Chapter 23

'The baby died from suffocation,' Constable Lloyd said on the Monday afternoon. Constable Adams stood beside him, serious and solemn.

'Shelley … her name is Shelley,' Mum said.

The policeman nodded. 'The child, Shelley, was suffocated with her pillow. Autopsy showed pillow fibres in the airways and lungs. So, combined with the mouth bruising ...'

'We're so sorry,' Constable Adams said. 'CIB'll take over the enquiry now, examine and photograph the crime scene.'

'CIB?' Mum said.

'Criminal Investigation Branch,' he said. 'The coroner is bound by law to conduct an enquiry when there are criminal or suspicious circumstances.'

My sister died on a Friday public holiday, so we'd had to wait the entire weekend and most of Monday for the autopsy results. Days that passed in one long, thick fog. But not real days, rather images from one of my faded picture-books; as if someone had pressed a button and time-frozen us.

I'd spent most of that time slumped on the back verandah with Steely and Bitta, staring at the empty pram, and eating. My father spent most of Saturday at the pub. He was out all day Sunday too, though he didn't say where he'd been. Billie-Jean curled up in her lap, Nanna Purvis had stared at the television screen — even after *God Save the Queen* played, signalling the end of ABC transmission for the night. And, as if a blustery wind had raked her over, my mother teetered through the house in silence, her arms wrapped about herself. She seemed always to be searching for something but never remembering what. And she looked dead, herself.

I'd wanted to go back to Albany and see Uncle Blackie. I wanted to see Angela too. Anything to get away from Gumtree Cottage and its old-person's face mortared in sorrow, but I didn't dare leave my mother alone, terrified she might topple from this almost-dead state into a real-dead state.

'Whoever'd suffocate an innocent baby?' Nanna Purvis said to Constable Lloyd.

'Yes, Jesus bloody Christ, who?' Dad lit a new fag from the butt of the last one, dragged deeply and exhaled. The smoke encircled my mother like a dirty halo.

'Anybody we could call?' the policeman asked. 'Friends, relatives, a priest?'

'*Priest*? Won't be no Catholics in this house,' Nanna Purvis said.

Dad shook his head and Mum stared, motionless, at nothing, avoiding everyone's gaze on her.

And later, when it got dark, we all sat at the table and tried to eat the baked beans she'd plonked onto slices of toast.

'Yuck, the beans are cold,' I said, my fork clattering onto the plate.

My mother jumped, her palm held over her heart as if the noise of a fork on a plate was the most frightening thing ever.

'Can't we have meat pies or sausage rolls?' I said. 'Why don't we ever have nice food anymore?'

'Just eat the beans, Tanya,' Mum whispered as if it was too much effort to talk properly, or she couldn't remember how.

No, my mother couldn't talk to me, or even look at me these days. My father was forever running off to the pub to get away from me. I was no longer his "princess". It was obvious my parents no longer loved me. Maybe they never had, only I was too young and stupid to realise it. Which all meant I probably *was* adopted in the first place.

'I don't want you to be my mother anymore,' I blurted out.

Mum got up from the table, grabbed hold of the bench side and started to cry. I didn't care. Let her cry, this thin, sad stranger who could only clean and scrub and wring her hands through her cleaning shift.

Clinging to the flowered fabric, she slid down the front of the cupboard onto the floor. Sprawled across the black and white lino, she reminded me of a *Real Life Crime* hit and run victim, mown down on the false safety of a pedestrian crossing.

That made me cry too even as I fought the tears; didn't want her to see me upset. Then we were both sobbing. Two separate, sobbing heaps on pedestrian-crossing lino.

'Crying is good for you,' Dad always said. Now he didn't utter a word, just stared at both of us. 'It lets out the hurt. If you don't let it out it'll just get worse and make you sick.'

I was already sick; sick in my guts. Rats gnawing at my heart, my liver, my kidneys, and soon there would be no more insides of me.

Eventually Mum stopped crying and dragged herself up, and back to the table. 'Sorry,' she said.

I didn't know why she was sorry; it wasn't her fault Shelley was gone. And I didn't know what to say to her so I picked up my fork and shovelled down the cold and pasty beans.

My stomach heaved and folded, the ache of it all coming freely, threatening to spill over into a vomit. I couldn't go on gathering the pain like this.

After tea, Mum slunk off to bed. Nanna Purvis switched on the telly and Dad went out — he didn't say where — and I lay on my bed because there was nothing else I could do.

In that heavy, stifling air, Steely and Bitta curled up beside me, I could hardly breathe. I opened the Venetians, slid up the window as the lights of a car shone over the Figtree Avenue hill. It came closer and I saw it was Uncle Blackie's rusty old

Kingswood. But he drove right past number thirteen, which was strange. Surely he wanted to see me; to say something comforting about Shelley?

But he must have turned around at the cul-de-sac because there he was again, coming back down the road, slowing in front of Gumtree Cottage.

I thrust an arm out the window, waved at him. As Uncle Blackie looked about, up and down the deserted street, I crept from my bedroom, eased open the front door and skittered over to the Kingswood.

Uncle Blackie leaned over the passenger side and spoke to me out the window. 'I heard about your baby sister, Tanya. I'm so sorry.'

'Yeah.' The word snagged in my throat, threatened to turn into a sob.

I wondered how he'd found out about Shelley so quickly. Old Lenny, too, had known straightaway. At least one thing Nanna Purvis said was true then: bad news travels fast.

'You know you can always come back to Albany if thing get too tough here,' he said. 'Just for a break, and to ride your new bike.'

'Okay, I might come ... soon.'

'In the meantime, I brought you this.' Uncle Blackie handed me a paper bag. 'Salt dough. You could try making your own sculptures, something nice for Shelley's funeral maybe? Keeping busy with a hobby can help take your mind off ... off things, you know. And if you need help, just come over. How does that sound?'

'Yep, sounds all right.'

'Good, well I'd better be off now, Tanya. See you real soon, eh?'

I waved at the Kingswood disappearing down the hill and hurried inside clutching the paper bag. An uncle who drives all the way over to say sorry about my sister, and to bring me salt dough, can't be *that* bad. Can't be a filthy perv. Maybe Angela — and I — were being unfair to him.

* * *

'Our baby has *died*, Eleanor,' Dad said as he came in from The Dead Dingo. 'Only four days ago. And all you can do is scrub the floor?'

He took in her greasy hair, plastic gloves and cleaning shift, the rag she clenched as she scrubbed the lino Cinderella-like. 'Look at that cloth, Eleanor … go on, look at the bloody thing. It's clean. Spotless. There is no dirt left to scrub.'

She stared up him as if he were a Martian wandered into her kitchen.

For the last three days I'd been hiding out in my bedroom, trying to mould Uncle Blackie's salt dough into shapes: a dog, a fish, a bird, a horse. But they were hopeless attempts, all resembling nothing, and now the dough had become brittle, impossible to shape into anything.

I wanted to go to Albany and ask Uncle Blackie to help me, but still it seemed wrong, somehow, to leave Gumtree Cottage. As if I should stay locked up inside, mourning Shelley like my mother and my grandmother. That rule, however, obviously didn't apply to my father.

My mother had not snapped from her trance, and only three days after Shelley died, she'd gone back to her household chores. As if against some deadline known only to her, she worked more frantically, and there was no reaching beyond an absent nod from that hunched back, those never-still feet, as she work, work, worked. As if she'd forgotten how to rest.

'What's happened to you, Eleanor?' Dad said, his voice low and husky as he took a KB Lager from the fridge. 'Where've you gone … and what the hell happened to Shelley?'

'Why do you keep nagging Eleanor about what happened to Shelley?' Nanna Purvis said, voicing my thoughts. 'How would she know?'

Ignoring Nanna Purvis, Dad sat at the table with us, in front of his plate of spaghetti — a tangle of cold worms on cold toast.

'We're all suffering too,' he said. 'Don't run away, love. Stay with us.' He sighed, picked up his knife and fork. 'Maybe I should get Doc Piggott to come again … get him to change your pills or something. Anyway, come and eat tea with us at least.'

Mum kept scrubbing as if he hadn't spoken.

'I'd kill for a cuppa,' Nanna Purvis said when we'd finished eating the cold worms. 'Dry as a nun's nasty I am.'

'As if cups of tea can fix the world,' Dad said rolling his eyes at me.

From the day Nanna Purvis had come to live at Gumtree Cottage, I'd been my father's ally in his ongoing war with her, so often caught in the no-man's land of their battlefield. But right now their arguing was worse than ever — a hatchet chopping my nerves into tiny pieces.

Mum shuffled across the lino, put the kettle on and made Nanna Purvis's cuppa.

'And god only knows why you let *her* order us around.' Dad jabbed his finger at my grandmother.

'Can't you see I'm only trying to get her to come back to us, Dobson?' Nanna Purvis said. 'From wherever she's wafted off to.'

'You do realise your mother's insisting on putting Shelley in the Purvis family plot, Eleanor?' Dad said. 'In that ugly cemetery down by the Sewage Treatment Plant?'

'Bury Shelley?' Mum shot Dad a bewildered look as if he'd suggested burying a live person.

'I don't want our baby there,' Dad said. 'Much nicer up at the cemetery at the northern beaches where the Randalls are buried. Say something, Eleanor, back me up … agree with me.'

Mum frowned, said nothing. Fingers kneading the scrubbing cloth, she stood there as if dazed to find herself in combat with the man she loved — or had once loved — baffled at being forced into an argument about where to bury her baby girl.

'Shelley should go in with the Purvis side of the family, Dobson,' Nanna Purvis said, sipping her tea. 'Best she's not associated with youse Randalls. After all, youse are the ones with the weird family … the perv brother. Not that we ever want *his* name mentioned in this house.'

'That business was just stupid bush-telegraph gossip,' Dad said with a sharp glance at me.

'And it wasn't only the Carter girl,' Nanna Purvis said. 'There were all those others — other young girls — who came forward after … who claimed they'd suffered the same thing.'

'Again, just vicious rumour,' Dad said. 'Anyway, what the bloody hell's all that got to do with burying Shelley?'

'They don't lock people up in Macquarie Pastures Asylum for the Criminally Insane on rumour alone, Dobson,' Nanna Purvis carried on. 'That's if Blackie's still there. When you were away with the pixies after the accident you were mumbling on about seeing him. So maybe he *is* out? God help us.'

'What's an asylum for the criminally insane?' I said, though I had read about one, in *Real Life Crime*.

Despite Angela's words swarming through my head: … *he's a filthy perv … a filthy perv … a bad person*, it was almost impossible to believe my nice and caring uncle had been locked up in an asylum for mental criminals.

'And who's that Carter girl?' I said to my grandmother. 'You wouldn't tell me before, but now I want to know.'

'Better you know nothing about all that vile business,' Nanna Purvis said, dragging the whining Billie-Jean onto her lap.

'Why not?'

'When you're older,' Nanna Purvis said, 'when you can understand those sorts of things.'

'So why do you always talk about things in front of me,' I said, 'but never tell me the whole story?'

Neither Dad nor Nanna Purvis replied. My father dragged on his fag, coughing, his face grim. *Click-click*, *click-click* went the ashtray. Nanna Purvis fed biscuit crumbs to Billie-Jean. My mother went back to working at a stain on the lino — a stain so small I could barely see it, but she fussed over it, grinding away, stubborn as the stain itself.

She became breathless, panting, crimson blotches flaring on her thin cheeks. Circles of sweat curled the armpits of her shift, and a trickle oozed down the side of her face, leaving a moist and glittery slug trail.

Nanna Purvis hobbled over to the phone and called her hairdresser. 'Funeral's in three days, Rita,' she said. 'Can't turn up with these grey roots, you'll have to fit me in for the blue rinse somehow … you can? Aw, knew I could count on you. Thanks, yeah, bye … cheers.'

'What'd I tell youse all?' she said on a note of triumph as she hung up the phone. 'Once ya find a good hairdresser, stick with her. Don't go chopping and changing, you'll only end up with some freak hairdo you wouldn't be seen dead with. Been going to Rita over forty years so I guess that merits some privileges.'

'Don't you think we've got more to worry about than your hair?' Smoke spurted from Dad's mouth with each word. 'Jesus bloody Christ, Pearl.'

'Do you know how to make salt dough, Nanna Purvis?' I asked.

'Why do you want to know about salt dough?' she said.

I want to shut up you and Dad bickering.

'To make a sculpture to put in Shelley's coffin with her. An animal or something … a cat, yes, that's what I'll make.'

'Come on then,' Nanna Purvis said and started measuring out salt, flour and water. 'We'll make the best bonzer salt-dough cat this side of Kalgoorlie.'

Dad shook his head and stomped out with his beer.

Chapter 24

'Why're them foreigners turning up to Shelley's funeral?' Nanna Purvis pointed at the Morettis' black Valiant pulling up outside the mud-brown brick church which, in the shade of a jacaranda, looked even more drab. '*And* in that drug car. Youse surely didn't invite them?' She glared at Mum and Dad.

'That drug story is spiteful neighbourhood gossip,' Dad said, his voice lost on the hot wind stalking in from the western plains. 'Your bush telegraph working overtime again, Pearl.'

'I know for a fact that Lorenzo Moretti conceals the drugs in his rolled-up carpets,' Nanna Purvis said. 'That's what a woman at the hairdresser's told me when I was sat beside her at the dryers.'

'Can't you just give over for once?' Dad said with a weary shake of his head. 'If the Moretti family are good enough to come today — people we hardly know — we'll accept their condolences gracefully.'

'Yeah, give over,' I said. 'You talk such rubbish.'

'What *has* got into ya, Tanya?' Nanna Purvis shook her newly-blued curls. 'Never this cheeky before.'

Mr and Mrs Moretti and Angela slid from the Valiant. Everyone else's clothes were already sweat-clingy, but Angela's parents looked elegant in their black clothes, except for Mr Moretti's crisp white shirt. No sign of Marco. I guess he thought he didn't know us well enough to come. Angela hugged me, pressing against my chest the bouquet of red blossoms I'd plucked from Shelley's gum tree.

'I'm ... we're all sorry, Tanya,' she said, the chestnut eyes shiny with tears. 'So sorry.'

On account of Shelley's death, I hadn't started sixth grade at the beginning of the week with the other kids, and Angela had been allowed today off to come to the funeral.

'I'm really glad you're here,' I said to her, as she took my hand and squeezed it.

Without speaking — I guess there just weren't any right words to say — Mrs Moretti kissed my mother on each cheek. Then, heads bent, my Italian friends walked into the church.

The Andersons from number ten arrived. Old Lenny Longbottom too, mopping his brow, hair pulled back in the thin grey plait. He'd swapped the singlet and baggy shorts for a pair of beaten-up Levi's slung low over the protruding belly, and a T-shirt with the words "Deep Purple" sprayed across the front.

Mavis and Mad Myrtle Sloan came, the sisters' red and puffy eyes bulging like a frog's behind their thick glasses. Despite the heat, they both wore lilac-coloured cardigans, and kept fidgeting with the pearly buttons.

The recently-divorced Mr and Mrs Mornon from up at number twenty-five arrived separately. Stacey came with her mother, silent and refusing to look at me, which was better than her taunts.

Mrs Mornon stood beside my father, splayed her pink fingernails on his arm, and patted it, whispering something in his ear. She kept her hand on his arm until Nanna Purvis gave her a withering look. My mother didn't glance up at Mrs Mornon or at any of the other people. She just teetered — a feeble sparrow in the rising wind.

I caught Mrs Anderson's whisper to Mavis Sloan, as she nodded at Stacey's father. 'Did you hear Gordy Mornon's moved in with his secretary? Right tart she is, apparently.'

Mavis Sloan raised her eyebrows and turned to whisper something into Mad Myrtle's ear.

'I'll eat me slippers, if it isn't the rellos,' Nanna Purvis said, nodding at Dad's twin sister, Uncle Bernie and my hateful cousins, Sharon and Vicky, arriving from Ballina, on the northern New South Wales coast.

Nanna Purvis nudged my mother in the ribs but Mum was scratching at an imaginary stain on her frock. 'Look at That Bitch Beryl, would you, Eleanor? Like some King's Cross brothel madam, prancing about in her red lipstick and her mini skirt, as if *she*'s the star of the show. And Bernie in his long socks and sandals. Whatever was Beryl thinking, marrying a Pommie bast — '

'Beryl's my sister in case you'd forgotten,' Dad said. 'Of course she'd come to her niece's funeral.'

That Bitch Beryl kissed Dad, leaving a red lip mark on his cheek, and fake-smiled at Mum and Nanna Purvis. I slunk behind Dad.

Don't kiss me. Just don't.

'Still a fatso then,' Vicky hissed at me, exchanging an ugly glance with her sister.

I curled my lip, felt my insides boiling up. I wanted to punch my cousin and shut her stupid mouth for good.

'Manners, Vicky,' her mother said, the lips a red drawstring purse.

Dad's brickie mates arrived and some others from The Dead Dingo. The pub mates smelled as if they'd already downed a few schooners and the brickie mates looked awkward dressed in funeral clothes instead of shorts, singlet and dusty boots. They all removed their Akubras and gazed towards the sea as if it might tell them why a little girl could die before she could even walk.

Sharon pointed to the two constables who'd come to Gumtree Cottage twice. 'Why're the cops here?'

'Don't you know anything?' Vicky sneered at her sister.

'Everybody knows the murderer always goes to the funeral, so the cops come too, so they can check out all the suspects … work out who might be hiding something.'

Nanna Purvis wobbled over to the constables in her "funeral shoes" — the ones she'd bought for Pop Purvis's funeral. Her only outside shoes. 'Suppose youse still got no leads or suspects? Anyway, didn't youse say it was a CIB job now?'

'Nothing yet, Mrs Purvis,' Constable Lloyd said. 'And yes, it's a CIB job. We've just come to give our condolences.'

'Righto, well I guess we can't hope for too much,' Nanna Purvis said, 'given Australia's first police force was made up of twelve bleedin' convicts.'

'Maybe *our* convict ancestors?' I said.

'Ya father's ancestors,' Nanna Purvis said, with a sharp glance at Dad and That Bitch Beryl. 'Not ours.'

'I'm sure the police are doing everything they can, Pearl,' Dad said. 'They've questioned all of us and every resident of Figtree Avenue but nothing's come of it. Remember they told us nobody had seen anything and, at present, there are no suspects.'

'*Humpf*,' Nanna Purvis said.

Shelley had been murdered a whole week ago and I'd learned from *Real Life Crime* that the longer a murder is unsolved the less likely the police are to find the culprit. I would not be able to bear it if they never found out who suffocated Shelley, if no one was punished for this terrible crime.

A black hearse pulled up and two sombre-looking men wearing equally sombre suits carried Shelley's white coffin into the church, and the organist began playing slow and sad music. I knew there were normally four pallbearers, but this coffin was so small that the funeral home hadn't likely seen the need to put four men on the job.

'Come on, girls, it's about to start.' That Bitch Beryl beckoned Sharon and Vicky into the church. Her fingernails were the same fierce shade of red as her lips. Tiny blood clots flicking through the air.

My mother clung to Dad's arm. The hand of grief had swiped every trace of loveliness from her and she looked tiny, her sea-swell eyes sunken holes, face deadly pale as if dusted in powder, framed in wilted-flower hair. Her legs quivering — sandpipers' legs on a swamp edge — could barely hold her up.

Dad shuffled along, a worn-out old hunchback, his suit coat ridden up behind him, the misery almost bending his body in two. I looked into his dark sad eyes, mirrors of the pain inside me.

He hung onto Mum too, as if they had to hold each other up. I couldn't recall seeing them like that — touching, holding each other — since before Shelley's colic. And in that moment I felt a brief, guilty gladness at the tragedy that had united them, fusing them into the same grieving body. As if someone had shot them both with a single bullet, injuring them as one.

Just as quickly that thought curled me inwards with hatred and shame, and I despised myself. But maybe my father wouldn't go to work in Mount Isa after all. He'd never leave us now, not after this. He couldn't!

I turned from my parents, unable to witness their agony. I rubbed at my tears and tried to think angry thoughts to stop them spilling.

'... pray together for Shelley,' Reverend James was saying. Everyone closed their eyes and I shivered in the hollowed-out quietness.

Then, as if I'd missed the whole service — because I couldn't remember a single minute of it — that silent arc of mourners was perched on the thin brown lip of Shelley's grave, beneath the flimsy shade of a few old gums.

Bossy Nanna Purvis had won the cemetery argument, which I put down to my parents being too shocked, too shattered with grief, to put up much of a fight. So we were about to bury the loveliest baby sister in what must be Australia's ugliest graveyard: a wide space of flat sun-burned earth littered with weeds, dried bush and the bleached skeletons of dead trees.

And, amidst the patchy wisps of grass tussocks, old and abandoned headstones leaned towards the ground as if they too longed to lie down like the dead.

* * *

'Council put the bunnies here to eat the grass,' Nanna Purvis said, nodding at the clusters of rabbits hopping around the graveyard, white powder puffs flashing. 'So nobody has to mow it and make noise and disturb the dead.'

Vicky and Sharon's sniggers were the only sounds apart from the dry wind blasts that whipped up dust veils, and the distant noise of breakers crashing onto the shoreline.

The pallbearers looped straps under the coffin, lifted it a little. The undertaker slid out the four-by-twos. Beneath the windy sunlight the mourners wavered. Insects hummed around me, blowflies darting like arrows into my eyes, gathering in the corners, up my nose, in my ears.

I stared into the deep hole; too deep surely, for one undersized white box. Sweat broke out on my forehead. Dark spots jiggled before my eyes. The wind kept up its eerie whistle as if the far-off Australian deserts were all dumping their fine dust on me at once, moaning as if they hurt as much as I did.

A voice all around me cried out. It came from one side, the other, the front, the back, overhead. *'Help me, help me!'* becoming louder until it was a hammer pounding at my brain. I reached out to it but the voice had no body, no face, no mouth.

I looked down. My arms were stretched at the coffin being lowered into the ground, one hand still clutching the posy of gum tree blossoms. And when I couldn't reach my baby sister I wanted to fall into the hole with her so the earth would swallow me and I'd never have to think about Shelley being gone forever.

Dad gripped my arm, his voice shaky. 'You okay?'

I managed to nod, and lifted my gaze to my mother. Her

face was so stretched I hardly recognised her. Her head dangled from the little white triangle of her neck, her eyes bulged and her body drooped.

Like a flower someone had forgotten to water, her face crumpled, each petal collapsing into the centre. Her mouth opened and out came a low moan that built to a wail. On and on it went, like the wind that couldn't blow itself out. I was sure if Dad let go she'd belly flop into that hole. And everyone just stood there as she cried and tore at her hair and fought my father's consoling arms.

Dad started coughing the fag cough. His rasp, mixed with Mum's wailing, burrowed into my mind and soon became the only noise. The sound of my parents' grief churned my guts, squeezed its way up through my body, spilled into my throat and filled it up until I couldn't breathe. And Dad was holding up me as well as my mother.

A few people cast in single roses. I threw in my bunch of red blossoms, and the salt-dough cat that Nanna Purvis had helped me make.

The cat sculpture hit the wood with a thud. Everyone jumped, stared at me.

'Heavens, Tanya, you could've cracked the coffin,' That Bitch Beryl said.

'I made it especially for my sister … she would've loved to play with a cat. A cat the same as Steely…' My voice trailed off as I caught Vicky and Sharon's lips hitched in sneers. The salt-dough cat suddenly seemed childish and uncool.

'It's a beaut cat, Tanya,' Nanna Purvis said, glaring at That Bitch Beryl. 'Shelley would've loved it.'

The first shovelfuls of earth on the coffin clattered dry, echoing across the beachside graveyard. Nobody looked at anybody, except the two constables who were looking at everyone and whispering to each other. No one tossed soil onto the coffin like on television or in *Real Life Crime*. We all just turned and walked away.

Chapter 25

Billie-Jean and Bitta danced around the mourners traipsing into Gumtree Cottage. Nanna Purvis took off her funeral shoes and slid her feet into the blue slippers. After standing graveside all that time, her varicose veins bulged so much it looked like someone had squeezed up bruises into bumpy ridges along her legs.

'Do you have to wear your slippers?' Dad said. 'We've got guests.'

'If you had to contend with very cow's veins, Dobson, you'd wear slippers too, guests or not.'

'*Varicose* veins,' I said. 'And can you two stop arguing for once!'

Dad shook his head. 'Do what you want, Pearl, you always do anyway.'

'Why're these people in my house?' Mum looked around at the crowd as if they were intruders. 'All staring at me … all talking so much I can't work out what any one person is saying.'

'They've come to help, love,' Dad said. 'Offer sympathy and support.'

'Don't want help … better on my own … tell them to go away.'

But they didn't go away. They buzzed around her. Flies to a roadside corpse.

'Can I help put out the food, Eleanor?' Mrs Mornon asked.

'Where do you keep your knives and forks?' someone else said.

'Sit down, Eleanor ... make you a nice cuppa.'

'Don't want to sit down ... no tea,' Mum said. 'Can't breathe ...'

Elbows jutted out, she fought her way through the congested house. I followed her into the bedroom, shut the door.

'Where's my baby?' she said, gripping the cot bars as if her legs were too weak to hold her up. 'Why aren't you sleeping in your cot, Shelley? Oh that's right ... asleep in the pram in the shade of the gum tree ... you'll be cool and safe there. Yes, safe.'

The agony of it — of not knowing who had made the gum tree unsafe — pressed hard. A boulder crushing my lungs. The pain wouldn't shift, the blood wouldn't stop tunnelling through my head. I leaned against the door, staring at my mother sobbing and shaking Shelley's cot bars. Her legs collapsed and she folded, floppy doll-like, onto the carpet.

'Get up, Mum.' I tried to pull her upright. She looked right through me, up at the ceiling, a shaky finger pointing.

'Cobweb ... in the corner.' Her eyes flickered across the ceiling. 'Another in that corner ... the Venetians rail, dusty ... grime spots on the window. How could I've missed ...?'

'No, no, Mum, not this again!'

She shook off my arm and snagged her cleaning shift from the door hook. From under her pillow, she grabbed her nightdress, climbed on a chair and reached for the ceiling. Up she stretched, towards the dust and cobwebs, breath held in. Straining, flicking the nightdress at the cobwebs, but not quite reaching them.

'Nearly there ... wipe away cobwebs. No dust, can't have dust.' She shook her head. 'Filth everywhere. Terrible housewife ... useless mother.'

Dad came into the bedroom.

'She's acting like a lunatic, Dad,' I said. 'Cleaning cobwebs with her nightdress. Do something!' I clutched the dressing table side to stop myself trembling.

'Get down, Eleanor,' Dad said in a stern hiss. 'Take off that bloody shift and come into the living-room. We've got people.'

'No, no. Got to stay here … clean everything.'

'Jesus bloody Christ, Eleanor, these people care about you … we all want to help you.'

My father dragged her along the hallway, my mother scratching at his hands, his face. But he managed to get her into the living-room, where she crumpled onto the sofa like a used tissue. He took off her shoes, lifted her legs up on the sofa. A few people gathered around though most stayed well clear.

'Thanks, yes, cuppa might help,' Dad said. 'Strong, lots of sugar. And a few of Doc Piggott's pills … do the trick.'

My mother lay there, helpless, as everyone mingled about trying to touch her, pet her. I didn't know how to help her so I went into the kitchen to make her cuppa. Someone closed the sliding doors behind me but I caught smatters of their whispers.

'… lost it …'

'… can't cope.'

'… what Eleanor's done.'

What Eleanor's done? My mother hadn't done anything except lose the one, perfect baby after years of flushing away failed ones.

I took the tea in but Mum had disappeared again. I hurried to the bedroom, tried to urge her to drink her cuppa and take the pills. Dad leaned against the bedroom doorway, shaking his head. Stacey's mother stood beside him, her palm patting Dad's forearm.

'Leave the tea there, Tanya.' Mrs Mornon pointed to the dressing table. 'Your father and I'll try and coax her to drink it.'

I wandered back to the kitchen where Nanna Purvis and the women mourners were laying out the food.

'Go and play with your cousins, Tanya,' Nanna Purvis said, 'and quit mucking with that cowlick. Gives me the heebie jeebies the way ya do that.'

I picked up Steely, stroked him. 'I hate the cousins, they're nasty little bitches.'

'True,' Nanna Purvis said, 'but as I know only too well, you can't choose ya rellies. Besides, you have to be extra tolerant in situations such as funerals.'

'You, tolerant?' I'd have howled with laughter if I hadn't been so wretchedly sad.

'Stay here and help me then,' she said. 'Put them mini meat pies and sausage rolls on plates. No, paper plates, we'd best save on washing up what with all these geezers, eh? That's it, Tanya, bonzer job ... and the coleslaw in a bowl.'

Dad was handing out beers to the men and they all lit fags, lumbered out onto the back verandah and lowered their Akubras against the fiery sun.

'No sign of a break in this heatwave,' someone remarked.

'... rent a TV for two bucks a week down at Lavis's,' one of them said, 'no deposit even.' Another man said Norman Ross was having a sale on Victa lawnmowers. 'Only seventy-nine bucks.'

They spoke of everything and anything. Except Shelley.

* * *

'Youse lookin' for a good lawnmower?' Old Lenny's voice crackled from outside. 'I got a garage full of lawnmowers. Got 'em cheap off a mate. Willing to let them go for a better price than any shop.'

The men muttered between themselves, several shuffling off with Old Lenny. I often wondered where he got all those items that filled his garage-flat. A different thing each month: lawnmowers, Wringer washing machines, fridges, chairs and tables. Anything you wanted, it seemed.

I put out the chicken sandwiches along with the food people had brought: a tomato and cheese salad (warm and soggy) from Mavis and Mad Myrtle Sloan, a three-bean salad from Coralie Anderson. Mrs Mornon had made cucumber (yes, really cucumber!) sandwiches.

Old Lenny loped back in with an Esky full of beer.

'And where did all that beer come from, Old Lenny?' Nanna Purvis said.

'Think of it as a little something to help youse with the funeral costs,' Old Lenny said, winking at Nanna Purvis as he stashed the beer in the fridge.

'There'll be no winking at me, Old Lenny.' Nanna Purvis started at him, a hand raised. He hurried back outside, arms full of beer bottles, plait slapping the back of his neck like a rat's tail.

Mrs Moretti appeared at the front door holding a basket filled with Tupperware containers. 'I no stay, Mrs Purvis, is not my place for this family sadness. I just bring you meals for the family.' As usual, she waved her arms about as she spoke. 'Lasagne, cannelloni, gnocchi, ravioli.'

'That's very nice of you,' I said. Angela's mother gave my arm a squeeze and before Nanna Purvis could argue about foreign grub again, Mrs Moretti was loading the Tupperware containers into the freezer.

Dad came inside for more beers. 'Thanks, Sofia ... much appreciated.'

'A big pleasure for me,' Mrs Moretti said and, as she turned to leave, 'Angelina is liking Tanya come at our home again, very soon. It help not to think about ...?'

'Oh yes, please Dad?'

'Beaut idea, Sofia,' Dad said, dragging my fingers from the cowlick.

Nanna Purvis opened her mouth to put up some kind of argument, but one look at my father's glare must've made her think better of it, and her furry slippers shuffled across the lino as she followed Dad into the living-room.

'Bog in,' Nanna Purvis said, pointing at the buffet table, 'plenty of tucker for everyone.'

The mourners sat on the white sheets covering the sofa and armchairs, balancing paper plates on their laps. They all seemed thankful for the excuse of food, to avoid speaking. There was still no sign of my mother and Dad made no more effort to force her out of the bedroom.

That Bitch Beryl pulled out *Only for Sheilas* from under a cushion. She waved the magazine about, and it fell open to a full two-page picture of a naked man. I tried not to gasp, suddenly understanding why Nanna Purvis always tried to hide the magazine from me when she was reading it.

My aunt let out a snuffly-pig guffaw. 'Yours, Pearl? How pathetic, at your age.'

'And if that isn't cocky calling the kettle black,' Nanna Purvis said, snatching *Only for Sheilas* from That Bitch Beryl.

'What's that supposed to mean?' My aunt puckered her lips.

'You waltzing around like some tart, that mini-skirt what shows off ya map 'a Tassie to all and Sunday,' Nanna Purvis said. 'I've said it before, I'll never understand why my daughter married into the Randall family. Eleanor could've done a darn sight better than an alky brickie. But then I suppose I should be thankful she *did* end up with Dobson rather than that bad egg brother of yours, Beryl. That was a near miss, if ever there was one.'

Mum, end up with Uncle Blackie ... the summer of '57-'58?

As if Uncle Blackie had known we were speaking about him, he appeared in the living-room at that very moment. No knock on the door, not a word. He was just standing there, tall and lean in the Driza-Bone coat. Oh gosh, what was *he* doing here?

Uncle Blackie didn't look at me and nobody said anything, probably because most of the people didn't know him. How strange it was, seeing him here with this crowd. Not just the two of us.

A horrifying thought struck me then, as I imagined Uncle Blackie pulling the nude photos of me from his pocket. He'd show them around to all the mourners, like That Bitch Beryl showing Nanna Purvis's magazine photos to everyone. And they'd all laugh at fat, naked Tanya. A hot iron scalded my legs, my belly, my chest, and I felt myself shrivelling up, shrinking away from the shame, the pin-stabbing guilt.

'Who let *you* out?' Nanna Purvis said, staring at Uncle Blackie.

'Blackie?' Dad moved towards his brother and, seeing them side by side, I saw how alike they were. 'I thought I saw … hospital … no hallucination …?'

'Is it really you, Blackie?' That Bitch Beryl tottered over to him, gave him a bear hug. 'Why didn't you call, let us know you were …?'

'Who's that?' Mad Myrtle whispered to Mrs Anderson, who shrugged. Other people were whispering amongst themselves, darting glances at Uncle Blackie, trying to work out who he might be.

Uncle Bernie held up his whisky glass and stuck out his chest like a proud cockatoo. 'This is Blackburn Randall,' he announced as if he was some important bearer of top-secret information. 'Beryl and Dobson's brother.'

My mother must've heard Blackie's name because she came wandering out from her bedroom, barefoot, a frown creasing her elfish face. And when she saw it *was* him, she pressed a palm to her heart and her breaths came out quick and nervy.

'Blackie?' Through the crowd gaping at the newcomer like a hooked fish, Uncle Blackie's gaze found my mother's. He smiled, the same soft and dreamy smile he always gave me. Something thumped against my chest, like my yoyo bouncing up too fast and whacking me in the ribs.

I was surprised to see my mother smile back — a furtive one she didn't want anybody to notice — dull eyes flickering with a pinpoint of light, dim at first, then brightening.

'I heard the tragic news, Eleanor,' Uncle Blackie said, patting my mother's arm. 'Just wanted to drop by and say how dreadfully sorry I am … give my condolences.'

Nanna Purvis kept glaring at Uncle Blackie but I don't think even my grandmother dared argue with sibling rights, so bottoms shifted on the sofa, and Uncle Blackie squeezed in between

Dad and Mrs Mornon, who looked especially miffed at having to make room for him.

Uncle Blackie rested a *therapeutic* gardening hand on my father's shoulder, gave it a squeeze. That Bitch Beryl spoke to him in a low and whispery voice; I couldn't catch the words.

When Uncle Blackie had drunk a beer and eaten a few sandwiches, Nanna Purvis said in a loud voice: 'Righto, you've been, given your condolences, now you can be on ya way, Blackie. We've got ... got young girls in this house.'

I wanted to ask my grandmother why she didn't want him in a house with young girls. Was it because he really was a filthy perv, and did something awful to that Carter girl? But I sensed now, in front of all these people, was not the moment to ask. I would make my grandmother tell me later. Somehow I'd force it out of her.

'What are you insinuating, Pearl?' That Bitch Beryl said. 'That was all just some trumped-up charge against my brother. Not a grain of truth in it.'

'Truth or not,' Nanna Purvis said. 'I'm not comfortable having him in my house.'

'Let me remind you this isn't your house,' Dad said. 'And my brother'll stay as long as he chooses.'

That Bitch Beryl threw Nanna Purvis a triumphant glare.

Blackie held up his hands as if in surrender. 'I don't want to cause any squabbles. I'll be on my way now.'

'So soon?' That Bitch Beryl said. 'You only just got ... '

But before she, or anyone else, had a chance to stop him, Uncle Blackie was striding down the hallway towards the front door.

Even if he was a perv, I felt a bit sorry for Uncle Blackie, my grandmother bossing him around like that, making him leave. I scurried after him.

'Thanks for coming,' I whispered, as he opened the front door.

He swivelled about, threw me a magical grin — a bright light shining up his whole face.

'That's okay, I wanted to come. Mainly to see if you were holding up okay.' He touched a finger to my cheek, trailed it down to my mouth. I froze, didn't know whether to try and run or stay put.

'You've suffered a terrible tragedy, Tanya, but you're a strong girl, you'll come through this. And when you *are* feeling better, you can come back to Albany and see the photos we took. I developed them in the bathroom … they're fabulous. You look like the most beautiful model.'

They're not in his pocket then. No, of course he wouldn't show them to anybody. He'd promised they were only for me. I'm just being a ridiculous idiot.

'Beautiful, really?' Warmth rushed to my cheeks.

But I felt dizzy too, like standing up too quickly, and the giddiness became blotched up with everything else: confusion, guilt and fear. And doubt, as Angela's words echoed back at me.

… he can't do that, Tanya … it's wrong. Men who do that are filthy pervs …

The hot iron turned glacial, so cold I shivered. And in that instant I hated myself for worrying if I truly was beautiful — for wondering about stupid photos with a man who might be a perv. All I should be thinking about was my baby sister. Poor dead and buried Shelley.

'Yes, really beautiful, cross my heart,' Uncle Blackie said, making the sign over his heart. 'And I can take more photos, any time you want.'

I looked at my uncle and I just knew it — he was hanging out for me to say yes I'd come for more photos. He *so* wanted me to come.

'*Hmn*, maybe. Maybe I'll come,' I said after a moment, trying to appear all thoughtful and undecided. 'But I'm not certain.'

And as he wriggled his fingers in a small wave and sauntered off to the Kingswood, one of those huge beach dumpsters arced over me. But I was strong, powerful, and it didn't knock me down. It simply curved, harmlessly, over the top of me.

Chapter 26

'Has Auntie Eleanor gone crackers, Mum?' Sharon nodded at the bedroom into which my mother had fled as soon as Uncle Blackie left.

'Nothing wrong with your aunt,' Nanna Purvis snapped. 'She's just got the miseries because her little one died, only natural.'

'Seems like she's gone crackers to me,' Vicky said.

'Same as that lady up Darwin way who went crackers and killed her own kid,' Sharon said.

Mavis and Mad Myrtle Sloan gasped, their eyes extra froggy.

People stopped eating mid-chew and the living-room fell silent; a silence as white as the sheets covering the furniture.

Their faces curved into arcs of suspicion. Enormous question marks. Like they all wanted to say it was my mother who'd suffocated Shelley but were waiting for someone else to suggest it first. Then they'd all nod their heads. 'It was Eleanor,' they'd say. 'Shelley's crying sent her crackers.'

'We all know Eleanor *is* miserable and unsociable,' Mrs Mornon said. 'But to suffocate her own child?'

Mrs Anderson was whispering to Mavis and Mad Myrtle. '... odd for months ... that house-cleaning frenzy ... muttering to herself, never leaving Gumtree Cottage.'

'At least there *are* special places nowadays,' That Bitch Beryl said with another red-nail jab, 'for women who commit such atrocities.'

'How could you think such a thing!' I shouted at her. 'Mum

would never've hurt Shelley. She never even got angry at her for all the crying … never slapped or shook her or anything. Ever!'

'Yeah, that's my daughter you're slagging off, Beryl,' Nanna Purvis said. 'Shows what kind of people youse lot are. It's no wonder we only see youse when we're forced to. Stands out like dog's balls.'

'I'm not accusing Eleanor, but the way you're reacting, Pearl, makes me wonder if you're not hiding something.' That Bitch Beryl sniffed, lips twisting like sausage ends. 'You might go on about Eleanor marrying into the Randall family but my brother was a good man before he married into the Purvis family. We'll never understand why Dobson did that.'

Nanna Purvis picked up Billie-Jean, trembling with all the raised voices, and held him against her bosom.

Dad strode in from the kitchen. 'Stop your ridiculous bickering, this is my daughter's funeral.'

'Well, I do find it hard to believe the police still haven't found out who killed little Shelley, Dobson.' That Bitch Beryl shook her head, and nodded towards my parents' bedroom. 'Surely it's obvious to the police … when it sure is to the rest of us. I mean, who else could've done it?'

'Eleanor had nothing to do with Shelley's death,' Nanna Purvis went on. 'As Tanya says, she never lost her temper once with the baby … and that constant crying could've pushed anyone over the edge. So I don't appreciate your nasty insinuations … leave my daughter be, she's not a well woman.'

Nanna Purvis'd stuck up for Mum. Cool. Sometimes my grandmother wasn't so bad after all.

But it did not escape me that my father hadn't said a word to defend his wife.

'You simply can't accept the blinding truth, Pearl.' My aunt crossed her arms, tapped fingernails against elbows. 'When everybody else can see it, even your friends and neighbours.'

Nanna Purvis wobbled on her bird legs towards That Bitch Beryl.

Lenny Longbottom clamped a hairy paw on my grand-mother's arm. 'Don't let her get to you, Pearl.'

'I'm not letting her *get* to me, Old Lenny, and I need your advice like I need a hockey stick in me head.' She turned back to my aunt. 'Anyway I've had enough of youse Blythes … just hoof it off home right now, why don't youse?'

'I knew this was a mistake, thinking we could get along just once, for the sake of little Shelley,' That Bitch Beryl said, gathering the family's belongings — bags, cardigans, my cousins' sandals. 'Come on, Bernie, Sharon, Vicky, we've stayed long enough in Figtree Avenue.'

She gave Dad a peck on the cheek, threw Nanna Purvis a dark look and strutted to the front door, the bitchy cousins and Pommie Uncle Bernie in tow. 'Goodbye, everyone.'

Once the Blythes' car zoomed off down the road, Nanna Purvis looked around at the rest of the mourners — the ones who hadn't sidled off when the initial argument with That Bitch Beryl had broken out. 'Those rellos've exhausted me,' she said, 'so if you all don't mind leaving us in peace now.'

Everyone got up, clutched bags, murmured last words of sympathy.

'Strewth, glad that's over with,' Nanna Purvis said, closing the door behind the last straggler. 'Now let's get this place cleaned up, Tanya, I'm gasping for a cuppa and a sit down.'

Mum floated back into the living-room, looking around as if she wondered where everybody had gone, or she'd forgotten there'd been a crowd gathered for her baby's funeral — the crowd that had virtually accused her of *murder*. She started picking up paper plates, shovelling scraps into a plastic bag. She fumbled, dropped a clutch of dirty plates. Bits of meat pie and globs of tomato sauce splattered across the carpet.

'Oh … the carpet, oh no!' My mother's hands flew to her mouth and she stood, wide-eyed, staring at the stains.

'Leave it, Eleanor, we'll clear up,' Dad said with a sigh, as if he knew it was pointless telling her that food stains on the carpet didn't matter, especially when you'd just buried your baby girl.

He cupped a hand under Mum's chin, tilted her face to his. 'Jesus bloody Christ, what's happened to you? What've you done?' His hand dropped back to his side and he backed away from her as if she were some alien monster.

Once I heard the bedroom door close I said, 'Mum didn't suffocate Shelley, did she?'

'Course she didn't,' Nanna Purvis said. 'What a thing to say.'

'I don't know who did this to your sister,' Dad said as we cleared away the food.

He didn't directly say he did *not* think it was her, so I was certain my father was starting to believe — like those mourners — that it was my mother who'd suffocated Shelley.

But he didn't come right out and say he thought it *was* her. Maybe because, like me, he so badly did not want that to be true.

* * *

'I'm off down the pub,' Dad said a few hours later.

'*Again*?' I said. 'Why don't you stay here with us anymore?'

My father didn't look at me, didn't try to explain himself; didn't call me "Princess". He just shook his head and slid out the front door.

I knew he was in deep grief over Shelley, and worrying about my mother's sadness — not to mention her possible crime! — and that a natter down the pub with his mates and Kev the barman about the cricket or footy cheered him up. But I was starting to bear a grudge against him for always escaping the misery of Gumtree Cottage when I could not.

I fed the animals, wandered about the house. Twilight fell, then darkness. I flopped onto my bed, exhausted but knowing there was no chance of sleep.

I could not believe my mother had suffocated Shelley; could not acknowledge something so horrifying.

Why would she do such a thing?

Because Shelley wasn't a boy. Need a boy to make up for …

I still did not know why she needed a boy. But even so, it didn't make sense. She hadn't suffocated me, a girl baby. So maybe she *had* gone crackers; just couldn't bear Shelley's crying any longer and had to put a stop to it.

The blood thudded through my heart, gushing from it, up through my neck, down my arms, tingling my fingertips.

I slid *Real Life Crime* from inside *Dolly* magazine and read about the Moors murderers: Myra Hindley and Ian Brady who murdered five children between 1963 and 1965. How terrible, to murder a child. Even more terrible than killing an adult who could defend themselves, unlike a child.

At the sound of low voices out in the street, I slid off the hateful bedspread and cracked open the Venetian blinds. Dad and Uncle Blackie were standing on the footpath facing each other like some kind of cowboy showdown.

'You know that Carter bitch asked for it,' Uncle Blackie was saying. 'Thought I could count on you to defend me. Same as you tried to stand up for me against sleazy old Uncle Ralph … may the bastard be rotting in Hell.'

In the pauses between their words and the whirring of the insects, I sensed a shiver beneath that hot air. *Flick, flick* went Dad's cigarette lighter and a wisp of smoke spiralled into the night sky.

I wondered who Uncle Ralph was, and why Uncle Blackie was calling that girl a bitch. She must be someone as horrible as Stacey Mornon-the-moron. It sounded as if Uncle Blackie had a number one enemy too, and that made me a bit sorry for him.

'You haven't forgotten, surely, Dobson?' Uncle Blackie went on. 'All those outings with Uncle Ralph to console little Blackie for his mother dying … her death birthing *me*?'

My father dragged on his fag, exhaled a long stream of smoke. 'No, I haven't forgotten. But … but the Carter girl was only twelve years old. *Twelve*, Blackie!'

'No buts, I paid dearly for killing our mother; then paid again for that prick-teasing bitch. You have no idea what it was like locked away in Macquarie Pastures all those years.'

Macquarie Pastures Asylum for the Criminally Insane — the place Nanna Purvis had mentioned.

Dad shook his head. 'No, I have no idea.'

'Be nice to turn the clock back, wouldn't it, Dobson? Back to when we were kids — me four years old, you and Beryl five — tumbling on the hot sand on Bulli beach, thrashing about in the waves?' He sighed, swiped messy hair from his face. 'And we'd walk up to the kiosk, you holding one of Dad's hands and Beryl the other ... because he held *your* hands. And we'd eat fish and chips straight from the newspaper, and anything else we could afford, because there was no mother to cook. Because the cook was dead!' Uncle Blackie breathed out, long and slow.

He looked so sad standing there facing Dad, but I couldn't stop thinking whatever he could have done to that Carter girl to get locked up in some criminal asylum called Macquarie Pastures.

'I should've guessed what was going on,' Uncle Blackie went on, 'when you brought Eleanor up to Macquarie Pastures, in the early days, that is. Before you both stopped coming altogether. Should've guessed you were stealing my girl away, leaving me to rot in that hellhole on my own.'

'There wasn't anything we could do, Blackie. We tried, remember? But nothing ever came of it.' Dad rubbed his brow. 'I've always been sorry for that ... always. But don't tell me this is *still* about Eleanor, after all these years?'

'No!' Uncle Blackie shook his wild hair. 'But look at her now, the state she's in. And it doesn't strike me you're doing much to help her. A drunk who can't take care of his miserable, sick wife. Bloody shame, it is.'

My hands balled into fists. Ants crawled across my neck, down my backbone. I wanted to rush out and yell at Uncle Blackie that Dad was doing all he could to help my mother. But he wasn't. My father's constant absences at the pub were not helping my mother at all.

'What the hell do you want me to do about Eleanor?' Dad spread his arms wide. 'What?'

'Get her some proper treatment,' Blackie said. 'Go back to the doc, insist he does something. Anyway, I've decided I'm leaving Wollongong. I only came back because I thought we could work things out … could be a family again. But it's obvious that's never going to happen.'

Despite the heat, he dragged the Driza-Bone around himself and started walking away towards the beat-up Kingswood. I thought it odd that my uncle always wore a work coat when he never seemed to go to work at that TAB.

'I'm moving over to Perth,' he said. 'Far away from all the Randalls and Purvises … make a new life somewhere nobody knows about the old one.'

'Wait!' Dad called. 'Blackie …'

But Uncle Blackie had jumped into the Kingswood, revved it up. He pulled away from the kerb. Going off to Perth, leaving me here on my own.

Good. I was glad I wouldn't have to worry about any more naked photos.

But who would call me beautiful? Who would buy me such far-out presents?

Chapter 27

'That was *so* boring. Whoever wants to learn about cooking and housekeeping budgets?' Angela said, as we hurried out of our new sixth-grade classroom. Well, the girls at least. The boys were already outside, playing cricket on the back oval, while the girls learned how to be homemakers.

'No way I'm going to be a boring housewife,' I said. 'I'll have a career.'

'Me too. What career do you want?'

'Dunno.' I shook my head. 'Someone who helps people who get sick in the head … maybe.'

It was a week after Shelley's funeral, a week I had no idea how we got through. Inch by inch, I supposed. Climbing a steep cliff, but never reaching the top.

February had begun as hot as January, the temperature rising to thirty-eight degrees. The sky was a hard blue as if it had to be to compete with the powerful sun, and the last of Shelley's gum tree blossoms floated to the ground and died. The word "heat-wave" lingered on everybody's lips as we sweated and swiped at the endless clouds of flies.

My little sister had been gone from us for ten days when I started sixth grade, which I quickly concluded would be no better than fifth grade. Stacey Mornon-the-moron and her friends still sniggered about me, and Angela was still my only friend.

But far worse than Stacey's taunts were her whispers; the vicious blather about baby-killer mothers which she'd sparked up right after Shelley's funeral.

I heard the rumour everywhere: behind the cupped hands of huddled groups of schoolkids, on the lips of housewives at Eastbridge Shopping Centre, on our neighbours' faces when I passed them in the street. It rustled through the sun-burned leaves of the trees, wound around the parched flower stems and became trapped in the thirsty, closing petals. The smoke-stained wind of the Steelworks scattered it like dust across the streets, into yards and homes. There was no escaping the air swarming with those terrible, invisible words.

'So have you seen your uncle again?' Angela said as we sat back down at the desk we shared, after recess. 'After he turned up at Shelley's wake?'

'No, but I heard him talking to my father outside, the night after the wake. It turns out people reckon he did do something to a girl called Carter. I'm not sure what, but they locked him up in Macquarie Pastures Asylum for the Criminally Insane.' I picked at a bit of peeling varnish, on the desk, scraping at it with my fingernail. 'But it could've been a huge mistake. I'm really not sure if Uncle Blackie's a bad person. Anyway I probably won't ever see him again because he's moving to Perth.'

'But he *must* be a bad person,' Angela said. 'He surely got locked up for raping this Carter girl. They don't imprison you for that many years for anything besides rape. Except murder. You know what rape is, don't you?'

'Course I do,' I said, recalling *Real Life Crime* stories, though still not a hundred percent sure what it was. 'But I know Uncle Blackie, he's so kind and generous, he'd never do something as awful as rape. Never.'

'But, apart from the asylum business, he *has* to be a bad person,' Angela went on. 'Taking photos of someone who's only eleven. That's wrong.' She took a quick breath. 'I'm glad he's going away to Perth, even if you're not.'

'I don't know if I *am* glad,' I said. 'Or not.'

'You should be. Good riddance to that filthy perv. Anyway, are you still going to enter Miss Beach Girl 1973?'

'Oh that, I'd forgotten all about that stupid beauty quest, what with Shelley … you know.'

'Quiet please!' the teacher said, walking in with a loud clap of her hands.

The classroom fell quiet, but my mind whirled with thoughts of my baby sister who I'd mothered and loved, and the grief snagged me once again. The space in my mind she'd occupied was still full of her. I still felt her warm weight over my shoulder, against my chest. It was terrible to know she'd never rest there again.

* * *

That night, sleep refused to come. A mosquito buzzed in my ear, the jumble of confusion and guilt over Uncle Blackie's photos clotted my thoughts, and the moonlit rose-patterned bedspread looked like a small and bleeding animal hunched up in the bedroom corner.

But I must've fallen asleep because I drifted into a terrible dream. Drop by drop the image burned before me, bright and so alive, etching the nightmare onto my mind.

Shelley was fighting the pillow Mum held over her face. Her chubby legs thrashed about as she struggled for air, her fisted hands pummelling as if she were trying to punch her killer. So strong for a baby. But soon the breath was squeezed from her body, her short limbs stilled and limp, feet turned outwards. Then Shelley was lying in her pink frilly dress in a white box deep beneath the sun-roasted earth of Australia's ugliest graveyard.

The judge banged his hammer so loud it deafened me. *Bang, bang, bang.*

'Eleanor Randall is guilty … guilty … guilty. Life

imprisonment … life imprisonment for Eleanor Randall.'

The courtroom crowd screamed, 'Not life, off with her head, off with her head!'

'Okay,' the judge said. 'Off with her head.'

The masses jeered and clapped as they placed my mother's head beneath the guillotine. The blade rushing towards her thin and snowy neck, I searched her hollowed-out eyes, pleading with her to tell me if she was guilty. Or not. She tried to open her mouth to speak to me, but her lips stayed tight as if cement had set them.

I was still panting when I woke, and clammy with sweat. And hurting so much, as if some invisible force had ripped my heart from my chest. Outside Gumtree Cottage, cicadas whirred. They smashed about in my brain, my temples throbbed so much I pressed my fingertips into them.

I shivered, tried to shrug off the dread that squeezed my neck like strangling hands. And from that waking moment, the fear too, awoke in me; the terror that someone — one of those mourners, That Bitch Beryl, Dad, a neighbour — would tell the police what they all thought. And the police would march into Gumtree Cottage, handcuff my mother and lock her up. I'd never see her again.

But if she is a murderer, she should be punished for what she did to Shelley.

No, no! She's not a killer. She's my mother.

Chapter 28

When Doc Piggott returned to Gumtree Cottage a few weeks later Dad had, once again, abandoned us for The Dead Dingo's Donger. Nanna Purvis opened the door, Billie-Jean and Bitta barking and racing around the doctor's ankles so he had to edge his way inside, holding his black bag up high.

'Quit that racket, youse two,' Nanna Purvis said.

'Dropped by to see how Eleanor's coming along,' Doc Piggott said.

Nanna Purvis motioned the doctor into the kitchen. 'Outside with you, Tanya, we need to talk about your mother ... about adult things.'

'I hate it when you treat me as if I was a kid.' I slammed the flyscreen door behind me. 'As if I've got no more sense than a six-year-old.'

Dusk was falling over the yard like bruised sunlight as I sat on the back verandah listening to their conversation. After all, it was my mother they were talking about. Of course I wanted to know why she was so ill and if she really had committed such a horrific crime.

'Are the new pills helping?' Doc Piggott asked.

'Well, the funeral was over three weeks ago,' Nanna Purvis said. 'And Eleanor still either cries or stares into space. She washes Shelley's clothes and bed sheets as if the little one is still with us ... bless her soul. She scrubs this house over and over, and in between all that she lies in bed with no idea what's going on around her. I don't know about you, Doc, but I wouldn't call that *helping*.'

'*Mmn*,' Doc Piggott murmured.

'Me hairdresser reckons it's that neurotic sickness what can come over a woman after having kids. Baby blues or ... postnatal depression, ain't that what youse call it? Happened to her sister after she dropped number three. She reckons Eleanor needs treatment, you know, special pills. '

'As I said before,' Doc Piggott said, 'I believe Eleanor is merely suffering from a severe dose of grief. Only natural, given the tragedy. I'll increase her sedative to make her sleep better. After a few good sleeps and time to get over the shock she'll come around, I assure you. And you must try to encourage her to keep her chin up.'

'Far be it from me to argue with the expert,' Nanna Purvis said, 'but I reckon Eleanor should see one of them psycho docs. Can't even look after her daughter. And running around cleaning like a headless chook, is that part of the grief too? What with Dobson an alky and me a near cripple, who does that leave to look out for me granddaughter? Tanya'll be turning twelve this coming August, on the verge of the difficult years.'

'I keep telling you I can look after myself,' I called through the flyscreen. 'And Dad's no alky.'

'Sometimes you gotta face reality, Tanya,' Nanna Purvis called back.

'*Mmn*,' Doc Piggott said again, and disappeared into the bedroom to see my mother.

A few minutes later he lumbered back to the kitchen table, wrote something on his prescription pad and gave the paper to Nanna Purvis. 'See Eleanor gets these please, Mrs Purvis. And call me if you need anything else.'

The front door closed and Doc Piggott's car reversed out of the driveway.

Nanna Purvis hadn't said a word to him about people suspecting Mum had suffocated Shelley. My grandmother might be bossy, and talk rubbish, but at least she didn't believe my mother had killed her own baby.

I dawdled into my parents' bedroom. Mum was curled up on the bed, facing the window. She remained motionless as I crept over to Shelley's cot which, like her pram under the gum tree, nobody dared move.

Still empty. Still no Shelley. Only her pink pyjama suit Mum laid out for her every night, straight and smoothed on the sheet. Perfect, except the baby inside the pyjamas was missing.

She'd been gone a month — four weeks that stretched as long as forever. Looking into her cot, an image of my sister's little face flickered before my eyes: the corners of her strawberry-coloured lips creasing up when she cooed and kicked her legs in the air, and rolled onto her tummy. Her eyes, big and dark, as she tried to ram Billie-Jean's plastic bone into her mouth. Her laughs and gurgles when I spun that transparent ball for her.

I had watched them lower her small white coffin into the ground but still I hadn't taken in the terrible reality that Shelley, once here, was now gone. Her sweet face, her pained cries, everything about her just gone.

But gone where, I had no idea. A witch or magician could have magicked her away for all I knew. It was as confusing as that.

I glanced across at my mother.

Did you suffocate Shelley?

Too fearful of the cruel truth, I still couldn't ask her, so I trudged back to the kitchen to help Nanna Purvis make tea.

* * *

Dad staggered in from the pub, took a KB Lager from the fridge and flipped the lid. Without a word, he sat at the kitchen table and glanced at the front page of the *Illawarra Mercury*.

Monday, 26th February, 1973.

OUR DIGGERS COMING HOME

Prime Minister, Gough Whitlam has announced the establishment of diplomatic relations with the Democratic Republic of Vietnam (North) while retaining diplomatic recognition for the Republic of Vietnam (South).

I wasn't exactly sure what that meant but it sounded as if the fighting sides were making up and had agreed to stop killing and maiming each other.

The last elements of the Australian Army will have left Vietnam by June this year. There have been more demonstrations … large number of Australians believe their deaths to be pointless, scandalous.

Yes, pointless and scandalous, like Shelley's death.

The pain of my baby sister's death was not easing. It wasn't true what Dad said: that time heals wounds and grief. Time was not healing mine. The grief pain wasn't fading; it was getting worse, and in a colder, uglier way.

How long is time, anyway? I wondered if different wounds and griefs took longer to heal — a simple knee scrape from banging into a Hill's Hoist clothesline, compared with a gunshot wound smack in the guts. And the grief of a baby sister dying, how long does that take to heal?

Perhaps time can never heal those most agonising wounds. They need something more, a thing that doesn't exist. And, in that case, my life would simply become one long continual wave in this sea of agony.

'S'pose your mum's in the bedroom again?' Dad said, snapping over another newspaper page.

I gave him a quick nod as I topped slices of bread with ham, tomatoes and cheese, and slid them under the griller.

Dad got up, opened the freezer and took out one of Mrs Moretti's Tupperware containers.

'Gnocchi,' he read from the label. 'Might be tastier than

cheese on toast. Want to try some, Tanya? And what about you, Pearl?' He laughed, but it wasn't real laughter, rather an odd high-pitched shriek, as if Nanna Purvis might actually want to eat the Italian food.

Ignoring my father's jibes, Nanna Purvis took two slices of cheese melt into the living-room.

'Tasty grub,' Dad said, loudly enough for my grandmother to hear over the television. 'Lucky Nanna Purvis doesn't want any, eh? More for us.' He nudged me and winked, but the flash and sparkle had gone from his eyes — the eyes of a dead old man.

'What's a drug dealer, Dad? Is Mr Moretti one?'

My father finished his mouthful of gnocchi before he spoke. 'It's someone who sells illegal drugs to people. But there's nothing to say your friends are involved in any of that business, Tanya. Take no notice of your grandmother's racist gossip. Narrow-minded people like her are just jealous of the Morettis' wealth. Think they don't deserve it because they're not true-blue Aussies. Which is a load of bullsh … rubbish.'

'Can I watch *Number 96* tonight?'

Dad shook his head. 'Nope. You're still too young for those kinds of telly shows. We could play Monopoly, eat some Lolly Gobble Bliss Bombs?'

'Don't want to play Monopoly … stupid kids' game.'

I didn't want to play any game. All I wanted was the truth: did my mother suffocate my baby sister? And if not, then who did? It was terrible not knowing. It was making me sick, stuck in my belly like gobbling too much bad food.

No doubt that Dad, too, yearned to know if my mother had killed Shelley. But he was shying away from it, avoiding the terrible truth that could make everything even worse than it already was. Because however could you explain or accept your wife killing your baby?

I took the Lolly Gobble Bliss Bombs and while Dad drank beers out on the back verandah, I munched through the whole packet, until it was time for bed.

I kicked off the nightmare bedspread and lay on the sheet. In that hot, quiet dark I heard their hushed voices. The sound of soft crying. Mum and Dad. Were they crying together, holding onto each other, bound in their grief?

I closed my eyes, saw them loving each other again; no longer guerrillas stalking each other in dark forests like the Vietnam War. Happy, like when the sun still filtered through the Venetian blind slits before Shelley's death snapped out all the light and left only darkness.

But things between my parents were not all right; things only got worse. They barely spoke to me or to each other or Nanna Purvis, and never about Shelley. Nor did they mention the police enquiry, of which we heard nothing more anyway. Still no suspects, no arrests.

In fact things got so bad that my father ended up fleeing a lot further than The Dead Dingo pub. Several days later, when I woke up, he was gone from Gumtree Cottage. His Akubra hat, most of his clothes, the Holden. Almost everything except the push-button ash trays.

It was Nanna Purvis who told me he'd left for Mount Isa. 'Don't look so surprised, Tanya, he did warn you he was hoofing it.'

She said Dad had driven away from Gumtree Cottage by dawn light. He mustn't have wanted to wake me, but I was certain he'd have left me a goodbye message. I searched the house for his note but there was nothing. Just an unbearably silent and smokeless house.

'I thought after Shelley d-d ... went,' I said to my grandmother, 'Dad wouldn't really leave.'

But even as I spoke I knew I should have seen it coming; should have read it in my father's bloodshot eyes, which had become sort of transparent too, unable to hide his sadness, or his useless yearning to help Mum; to bring her back from that crazy, mournful seabed. Unable to snap her out of it, he'd been clinging onto their happy past, but now he'd given up on her. He'd given up on his family, and dared to leave me on my own!

Chapter 29

'This is Zio Ricci and Zia Valentina,' Angela said, introducing me to the aunt and uncle she often spoke of — the relatives who'd come with them from Naples to start new lives in Australia.

Angela had told me that Zio Ricci started working at the Port Kembla Steelworks with her father, but now he and Zia Valentina owned a popular Italian restaurant in downtown Wollongong, *The Greasy Fork*.

Zio Ricci was an exact copy of Angela's father, Lorenzo Moretti, and I wondered if they were twins. There was also her groovy brother, Marco, shoulders and chest muscles bulging against his T-shirt. I met Angela's cousins too: Tony, the same age as Marco, and Bella, who was thirteen and so plump she made Angela and me look almost thin.

It was a few days after Dad left for Mount Isa, and when Angela invited me over to Bottlebrush Crescent for tea I'd leapt at the chance to escape the misery of ghost-ridden Gumtree Cottage. The angry gods who stalked the place and sent poison clouds raining down on it.

When it was clear my father wasn't just out on a job or down the pub, that he'd really gone, my mother cried all day. So much that it seemed she'd always cried. Occasionally there was a pause in her sobs and Gumtree Cottage fell quiet. Then she'd break the silence with a moaning sob or a soft whimper and slip on her orange-flowered cleaning shift.

She'd jiggle her feather duster back and forth over the sofa, simply moving the dust around. She hoovered the same spot on the carpet over and over. She shook the plastic strips outside, and stuffed the furniture sheets into her washing machine so often that the wringers seized up. From that gloomy face, the haze of sleep that clung to her, she no longer saw me — The Invisible Girl — as she moved silently through her day, from bedroom to cleaning every room, plodding down to the laundry shed for the washing, and back to her bedroom.

Oh yes, I'd have moved into Angela's home on Bottlebrush Crescent in a heartbeat if I'd had the chance.

Tea at the Morettis' began with antipasto: bread, olives, artichokes, cheese and salami. Three lemonade bottles stood on the table — one filled with red wine, one with white and the other with Mrs Moretti's zingy ginger beer.

After the ravioli starter, with its delicious mushroom sauce, she brought out crispy roasted chicken and the salad she said Zia Valentina had made. I should have been full, but after the pasty stuff that now passed for meals at Gumtree Cottage, no way was I going to pass up such tasty tucker.

'This is so yummy,' I said. 'How do you say that in Italian?'

'*Molto buono*,' Mrs Moretti said.

'Italian food is *molto buono* then,' I said, which made them all laugh.

'*Grazie*,' Mrs Moretti said.

'What's in the salad dressing?' I asked Zia Valentina.

'Olive oil, lemon juice, garlic and oregano,' she said with a smile that showed off very white teeth. She patted her hair that was teased into a puffy twirl on top of her head, fastened with a gold clasp in the shape of a glittery feather.

'You just mix all together and shake up,' she said, waving her hands about, her gold rings with huge diamonds like flashes of sunset.

After the chicken and salad, Angela asked her mother if we could go for a night swim before dessert. 'I know it's already March, Mamma, but it's still so hot.'

'Of course,' Mrs Moretti said with a smile. 'You are enjoying this lovely night. we are eating dessert later.'

Tony and Marco said goodbye to everyone and left to go driving around in Marco's purple car that I'd seen several times in the driveway — the one with a strip of matching purple carpet in the back window and a dog that bobbed from the rear-vision mirror. I wished they'd asked Angela and me to go driving around with them.

Bella lumbered upstairs behind Angela and me.

'I can't go swimming,' Bella said with a pout. 'Got my rags.'

'Oh bummer,' Angela said. 'So glad I haven't got mine right now.'

We changed into our swimmers, and I wished I was wearing a bra under my singlet, like Angela was.

'Yeah, real bummer,' Bella said. 'But at least that means Angela and I are grown-up women now. Are you a woman yet, Tanya?'

I felt the flush heat my cheeks. 'It's only happened once.'

'Ha, it'll soon come *every* month,' Bella said with a laugh. 'But Mamma told me I can use tampons soon so I'll be able to go swimming the whole month.'

'Mamma says I can try them soon too,' Angela said.

We left the adults drinking wine and chatting, and Bella and her rags in the bedroom, listening to the cassette of David Cassidy and the Partridge Family's, *I Think I Love You.*

The flower-perfumed night air wrapping around me, there wasn't a hint of wind but the darkness seemed to move with the sounds of birds, bandicoots and possums as we hurried by the hen-house and the vegetable garden.

We dived into the pool and as I felt the water, soft and silky cool against my skin, I forgot Shelley's murder, my mother's misery, my father abandoning us. My fat vanished and I was a beautiful mermaid gliding along the seabed surrounded by bright fish, exotically-coloured coral and clear blue water. A flash of gleaming bosom, a twisting glitter of tail, lazily twirling fronds of hair. And a seductive smile for the sailor that looked like Marco Moretti.

'Oh, we forgot to bring towels,' Angela said, as Mermaid-Tanya surfaced. 'I'll go back up and get some.' She scrambled from the pool and padded off into the balmy darkness.

I floated on my back, gazing up at the starry sky. Bats dived and swooped through a cloud of gnats and I drifted my fingertips through the water, swirling it around in tiny whirlpools.

A rustle in the bushes startled me. Too loud for a night creature. My feet grappled for the pool bottom and I stilled my hands, my body.

'Hello, Tanya.'

The voice that had always sounded so warm, wavy and exciting, froze me.

* * *

'Uncle Blackie?' I called his name, my head whipping from left to right, searching the shadows; wondering why I couldn't see him, and what he was doing at Angela's.

From the bushland onto which the Morettis' house backed, his tall silhouette emerged. In the ankle-length, oil-skin Driza-Bone, Uncle Blackie reminded me of the bushranger, Ned Kelly in his armour at the final showdown at Glenrowan Inn.

'What're you doing here, Uncle Blackie?'

'I was just worried about you, Tanya. Wondered why you hadn't been back to Albany to see me. To ride your bike ... or for more photos?'

I didn't know what to say. Angela's words, the Macquarie Pastures asylum thing, had made me suspicious of Uncle Blackie.

I glided away from the pool edge, started treading water in the deeper, middle part, floundering in my self-doubt.

'Is something wrong, Tanya? You know you can tell me everything.'

'It's just that Angela reckons you shouldn't have taken photos of me without my clothes on. She says that's what filthy pervs do.'

Beyond Uncle Blackie's reach I was powerful, untouchable, confident. 'And I know you *did* do something to that Carter girl. That's why you got locked up in a mental asylum for the criminally insane.'

'Ah, Tanya, I thought you were too smart to believe such lies.' His voice grew softer, sad, as if my accusations had hurt him. 'Besides, you know we're great friends. And a girl needs a friend even more when she's lost her baby sister … if her father's taken off to Queensland.'

'How did you know about my fath …?'

Oh what was the point in asking? Uncle Blackie seemed to discover everything about us.

'I don't want you to take any more photos of me,' I said.

'I promise then, no more photos. Come back to Albany, Tanya. It's a bit lonely there on my own. And I know you're lonely too. If we're together, neither of us would be lonely. Don't you see that?'

'I guess so, maybe. But you said you were moving to Perth. That's what I heard you tell Dad.'

'I was going to, but then I wondered what kind of uncle would leave you and your mum on your own. Now your father's run off to Mount Isa with that woman — '

My hands moved faster, batting at the water as if I were caught in a dangerous ocean rip.

'That woman? What woman?'

'Don't worry, it's nothing,' Uncle Blackie said, walking around the pool edge, steps long, slow and steady. 'I shouldn't have mentioned anything. Anyway, it's not right a man leaving his sick wife and his child to fend for themselves after such a tragedy. That's the real reason I'm not going to Perth … to stay here and take care of you and your mother.'

'Mum and Nanna Purvis and I are fine on our own. Anyway, Dad'll be back soon.'

Uncle Blackie shook his head, his tongue making *tsk, tsk* sounds. 'It's hard to accept, but I'm sorry to say your dad isn't coming back. I'm here for you now. For you *and* your mum.'

Against the mosquitoes' incessant buzzing, Uncle Blackie kept strolling up and down the pool edge, with that kind of smile you could believe in. I trod water, glanced up at the house.

Should I believe him? Am I just being silly, and Angela is wrong about him? I wish I knew.

'You're jumpy as a kangaroo,' Uncle Blackie said. 'Don't be nervous. You know I'd never hurt you, I only want to take care of you.'

'I ... I know. I'm not nervous, just a bit cold.'

The water *had* turned icy. My teeth clack-clacked. My arms ached, my legs weakened, but something made me stay in the pool. Then Angela was skipping back down the yard with the towels and, as quickly as he'd appeared, Uncle Blackie vanished into the thick bush.

I swam to the side, grabbed the edge. Breathless and panting, I rested my head on my forearms, thinking about what Uncle Blackie had said.

... your father's run off to Mount Isa with that woman.

'Why're you puffed out?' Angela wrapped a towel around her middle and offered the other to me. 'What's up, Tanya?'

'He was here ... Uncle Blackie.' A shaky finger pointed at the bushes.

'Your uncle was *here*?' Angela squinted into the darkness, twisted back around. 'I'm going straight to tell Papa. He and Zio Ricci will get rid of him.'

'No, don't tell your father, please. Anyway, he's gone now.' The last thing I wanted was Angela's father and uncle to rush out and look for Uncle Blackie. And not find him. I'd look a right idiot then.

'I really *should* tell Papa.'

'Please don't ... you did promise we'd keep each other's secrets, didn't you?'

'Okay, but if he ever comes back I'm going straight to Papa.'

'Uncle Blackie said my father's run off to Mount Isa with some woman,' I said. 'That can't be true, can it?'

'I don't know.' Angela's gaze was still searching the bushland darkness. 'But for now don't worry about your papa. Or your uncle. Come and taste my mother's frittole. You'll just flip, and Zia Valentina's chocolate-covered pannetone too!'

I nodded, already feeling better as we hurried up the backyard.

Once inside the Morettis' fancy house, with her friendly and happy family, I was safe from anything. And anyone.

Chapter 30

'Shelley's gone … gone, Eleanor. Bless her soul.' From the backyard, Nanna Purvis's voice boomed over the rising wind and the growl of approaching storm clouds. 'You don't need to wash her stuff anymore. You gotta stop washing her clothes, carrying on as if she's still alive, or Doc Piggott'll lock you up with the crazies.'

I dumped my schoolbag, patted Steely and Bitta and stuffed three lamingtons into my mouth one after the other, almost groaning with pleasure at the mixture of chocolate, coconut and sponge cake.

Dad had been gone about three weeks, and still no letter. No phone call. Nothing. I'd not seen Uncle Blackie again, still not sure if that was a good thing or a bad thing. And when I'd asked Nanna Purvis about Dad running off to Mount Isa with some woman, she'd said, 'Wherever did ya hear that gossip, Tanya?'

'Just around … at school. Is it true?'

'Not that I know of,' Nanna Purvis had said.

I went out onto the back verandah and ate two more lamingtons. My guts heaved and I threw aside the packet. From the Hill's Hoist, Nanna Purvis was unpegging Shelley's cot sheets that were swaying like dancers to a wind orchestra, and her clothes: singlets barely bigger than a Barbie doll's, tiny, curled socks and rows of white nappies that Mum washed twice to make sure.

'Nappies less than perfectly white are the sign of a bad house-wife,' she'd say.

Each time my grandmother reached for a peg, her thin legs quivered, the varicose veins bulged and her furry slippers made her feet look like a duck's webbed ones, only blue.

The wind juddered Shelley's pram too, littered with the fallen eucalyptus blossoms, and I remembered, as a kid, walking back and forth beneath those petals, hoping one would land on my head and my luck would change. Back when I believed the falling petal legend meant good luck, before I came to realise it meant very rotten luck.

My mother stood beside the clothes line, arms folded, glancing up at the iron-grey clouds scudding in from beyond the mountain range. She did not appear concerned that my grandmother was removing what were now unnecessary clothes; she was only worried the coming storm would wet her washing.

Nanna Purvis shoved the bundle of Shelley's damp clothes at my mother, who clutched the garments to her chest, gaping at them.

I couldn't stand it, could no longer bear to see her like this, and I wanted to scream the hurt away.

The first thunder grumbled, deep and threatening. A gust raked the yard, the temperature dropped and goosebumps spiked along my arms. My mother still didn't move, didn't say a word.

'Give them here then.' Nanna Purvis snatched the clothes from her, hobbled over to the bin and shoved everything inside. 'That's it now,' she said, slamming down the lid. 'The end, bless Shelley's soul.'

Mum's arms stayed wide open as if she was still holding Shelley's clothes. They dropped, limp and useless, to her sides.

'Storm's coming … get washing in,' she said. 'Change the beds, dust furniture …'

She grappled with the hem of her cleaning shift, began picking at the flowered fabric.

I covered my ears.

Can't hear you. Not listening. Shut up. Shut up. Shut up.

I so wished she'd snap out of it, so wanted things to go back to like before. If only she'd stop all this housework and take me to North Beach. But I feared my mother would never take me to the beach again. Ever. Well, she wouldn't be able to, would she, from gaol?

The faces of Mavis and Mad Myrtle Sloan appeared at the fence.

'Storm's coming,' Myrtle said.

'You feeling better, Eleanor?' Mavis asked.

Huh, the answer to that was so obvious it almost seemed they were mocking us by simply asking. Besides, I knew they only wanted to know if my mother really was a murderess.

Mum didn't answer and I could tell she wanted Mavis and Mad Myrtle to go away. She didn't want to talk to them, or anybody else.

'I reckon youse two could mind your own bananas,' Nanna Purvis said, waggling a crooked finger at the sisters. 'If this country wasn't so full of nosey parkers we'd be a lot better off. Besides, we can take care of our own.'

'Just trying to be neighbourly, Pearl. We know it must be hard for you, losing Shelley and all. Have the police found out who did it yet?'

'Those hillbilly fuzz couldn't find a dick in a men's dunny,' Nanna Purvis said.

The coroner's findings, once they'd "completed their investigation", echoed in my head.

Death caused by suffocation from the pillow that Shelley had in her pram by the action of persons unknown. Enquiry left open.

'Now, if you'll excuse us,' Nanna Purvis went on, nodding at the western sky, 'we gotta get inside before this storm hits.'

'If you need anything … that's what neighbours are for,' Mavis said.

'As if we'd be asking anything of them two,' Nanna Purvis said as the Sloan sisters disappeared. 'Cunning as Queensland cane toads they are, trying to find out our private business. If you want my opinion, Eleanor, it could've been *them*.'

'Them?' Mum said with a faint frown.

'Them who killed little Shelley,' Nanna Purvis said. 'No, don't look at me that way. Think about it logically. Everybody knows Mad Myrtle couldn't have any kids ... that they had to take her ovaries. Rotten they were, the both of them. That's why the husband hoofed it with them Hare Krishnas. So wouldn't it be logical Mad Myrtle'd be jealous of anyone with kids?' Nanna Purvis's eyes brightened. A *Real Life Crime* sleuth stumbling upon the truth. 'She could've legged it over that fence, Mavis keeping watch while Mad Myrtle walked right up to Shelley's pram and suffocated her.'

Mum stared at Nanna Purvis. Pale-faced, lips trembling, tears clouded her eyes.

'Besides,' Nanna Purvis carried on, barely taking a breath, 'with those frog eyes, them two don't even look the full picnic.'

'Oh stop it, stop saying stupid things,' Mum cried. 'Stop, stop, stop.'

Stupid things, yes. Though I understood why. Like me, my grandmother could not accept that it might've been her own daughter who'd killed Shelley, so she carried on inventing suspects: impossible, improbable and downright ridiculous ones.

Nanna Purvis and I were both drowning in that sea of suspicion. Swimmers caught in a dangerous rip, flailing about for a life raft, some alternative — *anything* — we could cling to, and thus spare my mother.

The clouds assembled in a dark clump and the first splatters hailed the break in the heatwave. I jumped at a thunder crack, the hairs on the nape of my neck prickling as the rain pounded the parched earth. Yards and yards of fishing line connecting sky and earth.

Dried grass and wilting plants sucked up the precious water, petals opening like welcoming arms.

'Anyway, Eleanor,' Nanna Purvis hollered over the rain as she wobbled up the verandah steps, 'those coppers haven't come up with a single thing so it seems we'll have to figure it out for ourselves. And as for people saying *you* done it … well I never heard such gobblerot. As if you'd hurt Shelley after all you went through to finally get another kid. Now come inside, you're getting sodden. You too, Tanya.'

Mum couldn't stop shaking her head, lumps of hair whipping her face. I tried to drag her inside but her knuckles were hard white knobbles as she clung to the Hill's Hoist, her feet stuck to the grass. '… must get those things off the line …'

'There are no clothes left on the line, Mum. Come inside, out of the rain.'

She tried to shake off my hand. 'No, no, no.'

I was already soaked so I left her there and dashed for cover. Dripping puddles onto the verandah, the water collecting in the worn wood ruts, I watched the rain wash over my mother's tortured body: slapping at her ankles, lashing her legs and pooling in her sandals.

I kept pleading with her to come inside, but my words were lost in the noise of the rain hammering on the corrugated iron roof. The hooves of a hundred galloping horses, coming faster, closer; about to trample me.

But really, I thought, it doesn't matter if she stays outside. If the rain was cleansing her — some softer thing, an ache more bearable than the utter misery of before — just let her stay out in it.

I hurried into the kitchen, grabbed a towel. As I dried myself off, the whole of Gumtree Cottage creaked and groaned. The wind pulled at the Venetian blinds — a banshee wind that fled, screaming, up Figtree Avenue, thready rain chasing it.

* * *

My mother eventually came inside and stared, open-mouthed, at Nanna Purvis hobbling about, gathering Shelley's entire layette.

'What are you doing with my baby's things?' she said.

'You'll never get back to normal, Eleanor, while Shelley's things are still in this cursed house.'

Despite the storm, it was still warm, but my mother was shivering, her arms bent up in front of her face, fingers working her cowlick. Rainwater ran off her, collecting in small pools on the kitchen lino as Nanna Purvis plonked everything beside the front door: nappies, plastic pants with non-chafe leg bands, cuddle rug, cotton wrap, singlets, booties, matinee jacket, terry towelling bibs. Everything except the pram, which my grandmother couldn't shift on her own, and I was not about to help her remove that last link to my sister.

'Get away, youse two,' Nanna Purvis said, flapping her arms at the dogs that were yapping and racing in circles around the growing pile of Shelley's belongings.

I pushed a towel into her hands but Mum just held it, so I took it from her and wiped her face, her hair, dried her arms, her legs, her feet. She stood as still as an obedient child. I was glad she let me do it; felt better seeing her half-dry, like it did her good whether she felt it or not.

Instead of walking next door in the rain, Nanna Purvis picked up the phone. 'Got a load of things to take to the dump when you got a minute, Old Lenny,' she said. 'Thanks, you're a mate.'

Old Lenny lumbered over to number thirteen straight away. Thug that I believed Lenny Longbottom was he didn't ask a single tactless question as he packed Shelley's things into the back of his old van.

But when he finished he came back to Gumtree Cottage and said to Nanna Purvis, 'Instead of just dumping all this stuff at the tip, I reckon I could sell it off. Get youse a bit of money back, compensate youse a bit like? I'd only take a small commission. Whadya say, Pearl?' He sniffed, hitched up the shorts over his belly.

'Well, if ya think we could get a bit back, Old Lenny, be a shame not to try.' She jiggled a finger at him. 'But don't you go ripping us off. I'll know if ya do, I'll see it in them conniving little koala eyes of yours.'

'Koala?'

'You always make me think of some sneaky koala, Old Lenny, with that round bald top and hair fluff poking out your ears.'

Lenny's face crumpled into a look of mock-hurt. He flicked the plait and limped back next door.

'Now let's all of us sit down with a nice cuppa and a couple of Iced VoVos, and work out what to do with you, Eleanor,' Nanna Purvis said.

She pushed my mother down into a chair and set the tea and biscuits in front of her. Oh boy, my grandmother *must* have been feeling generous, to share her Iced VoVos.

'Nothing like a nice cuppa to make a person feel better, eh?' she said. 'But you'll have to snap out of this mood. It's a terrible thing what happened to Shelley. But life goes on, ya gotta stare the goanna in the guts. And quit fiddling with that cowlick, you're as bad as Tanya. Give me the heebie jeebies, the both of youse.'

My mother's fingers dropped to her lap and she nodded as if she understood, and she'd give it a try. But within minutes, still staring at the steam from her tea curl up, twirl in a waltz, then die away, I knew she'd slipped away from us again. She moved from quietly leaking tears — *plink, plink, plink* into the milky tea — to heaves and judders, and back again. Practising crying for once instead of doing it.

I wanted to make her better, but I had no idea how. All I knew was that this never-ending weeping was not helping her recover; it was just making her sicker.

I stroked Steely, curled in my lap. I glanced up, out through the flyscreen door, as if the answer would be there, somewhere in the thunder and rain, in the soggy quagmire of our backyard.

Nanna Purvis and I were so busy thinking how we might

help my mother that we paid no attention to her. We didn't notice her shuffle into the bathroom and take her bottle of pills from the cupboard.

Chapter 31

'Go and fetch your mother, Tanya,' Nanna Purvis said, slapping Spam slices onto bread. 'Time for tea.'

The rain still a thousand possums scuttling across the roof, I padded into Mum's bedroom. She was lying on the bed in her usual position, facing the window.

'Tea-time.' I touched her arm, jerked my hand away from the cool, moist skin. 'Wake up, Mum.'

I shook her harder. No answer.

'She won't wake up!' I yelled to Nanna Purvis. 'And her arms are all floppy, and she's breathing funny and drooling like … Shelley did sometimes.'

Nanna Purvis came rushing into the bedroom. 'Strewth!' She shook my mother, yelled at her, waved her hanky over her face, slapped her cheeks. 'Eleanor?'

She snatched my mother's jar of pills from the bedside table. Empty. As was the sherry bottle lying on the floor beside the bed. 'Hurry, Tanya, ring the ambulance. Say there's been an overdose.'

Nanna Purvis scuttled into the bathroom, opened the cupboard. 'At least she didn't get to the second bottle.'

I knew what an overdose was. A woman in *Real Life Crime* had taken one when she wanted to kill herself. Mum was not dead, though. When the ambulance men arrived and rubbed her chest and pinched her ear lobe, she twitched, and her chest still rose and fell. So she was definitely not dead. Just not awake.

Nanna Purvis ordered me out of the bedroom but I hovered in the hallway while they worked on my mother, still wearing her orange-flowered cleaning shift that clung to her like a second skin. But watching them only sparked the still-blaring memories of those ambulance men trying to revive Shelley.

'… pump out her stomach … not sure we can save her … all that sherry …' I heard them say to my grandmother.

'You have to save her,' I said. 'She *can't* die.' I scurried out the front door behind them as they took my mother away on a stretcher. 'My sister already died, just a few months ago, and my father … my father …'

'We'll do our best, sweetie,' one of them said, dodging rainwater purling from roof to eave, and jogging down to the ambulance waiting in Figtree Avenue.

Despite the rain, the neighbours were all standing in the middle of the street: Mavis and Mad Myrtle Sloan, Mrs Anderson, and her boys with their cricket bat and ball. Old Lenny and his son and daughter-in-law, and the rest of them, including Stacey with her father, Gordy Mornon who — so Nanna Purvis heard at the hairdressing salon — had moved back to the family home in Figtree Avenue with his secretary when his wife scarpered with some bloke.

They whispered amongst themselves, heads nodding, women's hands clamped on aproned hips. I was sure they were saying that after suffocating her baby, my mother had finally cracked up.

Which she had.

My hand fidgeted with my cowlick. That was it. Mum was gone. I felt like a baby animal trapped in a bushfire that had burnt its mother to death, alone, withering in the flames of a large and frightening world.

* * *

Dusk fell, with no news from the hospital.

'Why can't we phone them to see how she is?' I said to Nanna Purvis.

'Ah, ya sound like cocky fallen off his perch, Tanya, hounding me with the same thing over and over. I told ya, they'll call us. That's what the ambulance drivers said.'

I was certain Nanna Purvis was itching to phone the hospital too but, like me, was afraid of what she might hear.

'No news is good news,' she kept repeating, annoyingly.

The storm wrung out its fury, sidled away over the Pacific Ocean. Every sound became clear and sharp: the crack of a eucalyptus branch, a dog's bark, tyres hissing on drenched asphalt. The slam of a car door. The *whack, whack* of the Anderson boys' cricket ball against the bat.

Washed and dusted, the trees glittered. Rosellas flashed their rainbow bodies, back from wherever they'd gone while the rain fell. The pink-breasted galahs, too, fluttered into the yard.

Birds, trees, flowers and earth all revived. Unlike my mother.

Then the phone did ring, loud and shrill as an alarm. Nanna Purvis and I jumped, stared at the ringing phone. Neither of us made a move to answer it; just kept looking at it, listening to its echo down the hallway.

'Go on then, Tanya, answer it.'

I managed to get my legs working, raced to answer it. But the hospital wouldn't tell me a thing.

'They want to speak to an *adult*.' I handed the receiver to my grandmother, hovering, trying to hear what the caller was saying.

'Ya mum's critical but stable,' Nanna Purvis said as she hung up. 'They'll phone back when there's more news.'

"Critical" they'd said. They'd hadn't said "dead" which was the worst word to hear because I'd learned that was something you could never reverse.

'If Dad knows about the overdose, he'll come home from Mount Isa.'

'Don't count on that,' Nanna Purvis said, feeding Pooch Snax to Billie-Jean. 'I wouldn't be surprised if ya father stays up there for good.'

'He *will* come home …'

But even as I said the words I wasn't so sure. He could easily stay in Mount Isa with "that woman", whoever she was.

And what if Mum dies? Don't die, please don't die.

Then it hit me. Even if my mother did survive the overdose, once the police learned of everyone's suspicions, they'd cart her off to gaol. Or to some mental asylum for the criminally insane.

I sat cross-legged on my bed, scratching Steely's head as I wrote a letter to my father, telling him about Mum's overdose, and that he had to come home.

I didn't know where he was living so I addressed the envelope to Mr Dobson Randall, c/o Mount Isa Pub, Mount Isa, Queensland.

I sealed the envelope and lay back on my bed, listening to the *tick-tock* of the hallway clock. I thought of my mother. Perhaps already dead, like Shelley. The world was too horrible. It would be better if I, too, were dead.

* * *

Over the next dread-filled, limbo kind of day, when we still didn't know if my mother would recover, I spent a lot of time peering through the Venetian blind slats, my heartbeat quickening with every car that came up Figtree Avenue. I kept lurching out onto the front verandah, but none of the cars was Dad's Holden.

I didn't understand why he wouldn't want to come home to us after such a terrible thing. Perhaps he hated my mother because of what he, and other people, believed she'd done to Shelley. Or he really had found another woman, and no longer cared a thing about my mother; no longer cared about me. He was never coming back to her or to me.

So perhaps I *was* adopted, unlike Shelley who, being their own flesh and blood, my parents had truly loved.

After school on the second day, and still no sign of my father, I couldn't bear staying in that awful death house. Without letting Nanna Purvis know I was home, I grabbed a packet of Iced VoVos, hooked Steely's leash onto his collar and went back outside.

'Hey, wanna be wicket-keeper?' Terry said, bowling the ball to batter-Wayne.

'Not today, thanks,' I said, spying Stacey Mornon-the-moron riding her bike down Figtree Avenue.

Oh no. The one person I do not want to see.

'So they finally carted your murdering mother off to the loony asylum,' Stacey said, braking alongside me. She gripped the streamer-handlebars, her fingernails the same bright pink as the bicycle basket.

Once again I wished my red bike — newer, shinier and flashier than Stacey's — didn't have to stay at Uncle Blackie's. I was itching to show it off to her.

'My mother's no murderer. She's just sick, in hospital. She'll be better soon.'

'Is that what they told you?' Stacey gave a nasty little laugh. 'You're so dumb. Because your mum's gone loony, they can't put her on trial for her crime yet … they have to wait till she can answer the questions, face the jury. So,' Stacey went on, 'they'll keep her away from the public so she doesn't kill again. And when she's cured of the lunacy, they'll put her on trial and find her guilty. Then they'll gaol her for life.'

'You're the dumb one,' I said. 'You know nothing about our business anyway.'

'I happen to know a *lot* about your business.' She flicked a blonde curl from her face. 'I happen to know that your father's gone up to Mount Isa with …'

Stacey's voice shook as it trailed off, as if she regretted starting the sentence. Tears glittered in her blue eyes, which she swiped at with a fist. I'd never seen tough-girl Stacey weep in all the eleven years we'd known each other.

'He's … your father's run off to Mount Isa with my mother,' she said. 'It was probably his idea, and he just forced my mother to go with him.'

'Run off with …?'

I stared at Stacey, unable to say another thing as Uncle Blackie's words pealed through my mind.

… your father's run off to Mount Isa with "that woman".

My father would never do that. No, he wouldn't. Besides, Nanna Purvis still hadn't heard anything about it, and since my grandmother knew every scrap of gossip, maybe they were both lying — Uncle Blackie *and* Stacey. But even as I tried to convince myself, it sounded unlikely.

A horrible image flared in my mind: Stacey's mother patting Dad's arm at Shelley's funeral. And again, at the wake, in my parents' bedroom.

'I'll be going to live up in Mount Isa too.' Stacey's shrill voice startled me from my thoughts. 'With my mother. As soon as … soon as they get a house organised.'

Why's bloody Stacey going to live with them? Why hasn't Dad asked me *to go and live with them?*

'So, see you round someday,' Stacey said, trilling the bell as she cycled off down the hill.

'How do I know you're telling the truth?' I shouted after her. 'You're such a moron, I bet you're lying.'

'You'll see, Batgirl,' Stacey called over her shoulder. 'You'll see it's true.'

Once my insides stopped foaming, I looked around me. Heat-heavy Figtree Avenue was deserted, except for Terry and Wayne Anderson playing cricket. Steely still on his leash, I continued on up the hill and stopped outside number twenty-five, Stacey Mornon's house. The one with all the garden gnomes.

The house looked empty. Well it would be, wouldn't it, if her father and his secretary were at out at work — together — and her mother was in Mount Isa with *my* father.

I stole into the front yard, hooked Steely's leash over the letterbox, and picked up a stone. I hurled it at one of the gnomes. Its head broke in two. Another stone. Smash. I was strong, brimming with energy. One more gnome down. Bits of gnome strewn across the yard. More and more stones hurled at the gnomes. Bang, smash, crash. One after the other, gnomes flying and me feeling more powerful with each newly-smashed gnome.

When I'd smashed the last ones left standing — the dog and cat gnomes — something hot and heavy welled inside me. I couldn't believe what I'd done; wanted to glue them back together, those thousands, perhaps millions, of shards.

But some things you could never fix.

Chapter 32

'Children aren't allowed to visit,' the woman on the desk said. She had the same stuck-up and irritating voice as That Bitch Beryl.

'Why not?' I said, stamping my foot.

We'd got the good news this morning, a few days after her overdose: they were transferring my mother to the psych ward and she was finally allowed visitors. But only adults, apparently.

'She's my mother,' I said to the snobby woman. 'I want to see her.'

'I don't make the rules, dear.' With a hoity-toity look, she pointed to an alcove-type space with four chairs around a table piled with raggedy magazines. 'Why don't you wait there for … is it your grandmother? She'll be able to tell you how your mum's coming along.'

With a sigh, as if we were real nuisances, the woman got up from her desk. 'I'll have Mrs Randall brought to the lounge,' she said to my grandmother, nodding at the sign, with an arrow: Patient-Visitor Lounge.

'Why can't we see her on the ward?' Nanna Purvis said. 'Why do youse have to take her to a *lounge*?'

'No visiting allowed on the ward,' the woman said, strutting off down the corridor. 'The behaviour of some of our patients can be … can be distressing to visitors.'

Still boiling with anger, I hissed to Nanna Purvis, 'She can't stop me visiting Mum, can she?'

'Shut ya clapper,' Nanna Purvis whispered, hustling me into the alcove. 'Trust me, I'll work something out.' Off she tottered, following the woman and the Patient-Visitor Lounge arrow.

I sat on a chair, folded my arms and glanced over the magazines.

Boring, boring, all of them. It was so unfair. For the past days I'd been badgering Nanna Purvis nonstop to bring me in to visit my mother and now this woman wouldn't let me see her.

'I keep telling ya, Tanya, have a bit of patience,' Nanna Purvis had said. 'This'll take ya mum ages to get over, Shelley going like that, then Dobson hoofing it to Mount Isa all in the same year.'

'Dad *will* come back,' I'd said. 'You see, he will.'

True, he'd not yet returned from Mount Isa and he still had not written to me. I wondered if my letter hadn't reached him, or there'd been a glitch with the post. Or maybe he was too busy mining to reply. Or too busy with bloody Stacey's bloody mother.

I still didn't want to believe my father had gone off with her. With the sulkiest pout, I swiped at the pile of magazines, splaying them across the floor.

Nanna Purvis had been gone about ten minutes when she appeared in the corridor and beckoned to me, a fingertip against her lips.

'Snotty woman must've gone for a smoko,' she hissed, glancing up and down the corridor. 'Hurry now, if you want to see ya mum.'

With a stifled giggle, I scuttled into the lounge, where my mother was alone, slumped in a chair. She was not handcuffed or tied to a bed awaiting trial, but free to get up, walk around and do what she wanted.

My baby sister had been murdered almost two months ago, and still the police had not arrested her. I'd read enough *Real Life Crime* stories to know that — insane or not — they would have handcuffed and taken her away by now.

Then, like a worm breaking through dark earth into the light, my bewildered brain began to suspect that maybe my mother had not killed Shelley after all.

So who did?

* * *

Someone had hung paintings on the lounge walls and stuffed dried flowers in plastic vases to try and cheer up the drab-green room. But the pictures were faded and flaking, the flowers frayed and dusty.

My mother's ropy hair was slick with grease, stick-arms poking from the hospital gown, her skin dead-fish scales. She glanced up, as if unsure what to expect from me, but as I shuffled towards her she smiled, took my hand and squeezed it like I was five years old again. Oh gosh, did that mean she was better, that she was recovered?

I leaned over, took her in the small circle of my arms and felt her heartbeat, feeble and fast.

'How're you two getting along?' she asked. She let go my hand and started winding imaginary thread through her fingers.

'Tanya and I are fine,' Nanna Purvis said. 'Don't you worry about us.'

'But we want you to come home,' I said. 'When can you come home?'

Nanna Purvis's face creased into a wrinkly frown and she jabbed a finger to her lips, motioning me to shut up.

My mother's brow furrowed as if it hurt her to think. 'Soon … home soon.' She looked away, out through the window at a drooping willow tree. Her eyes came over all glittery and she was gone again, to her seabed world. Oh no, she definitely was not better.

I was so busy staring at her that I didn't realise another person had come into the lounge. But I caught Uncle Blackie's smell behind me — vaguely damp and dour like Albany. I swivelled around, stiffened.

'What're *you* doing here?' Nanna Purvis said.

'Merely showing concern for my sister-in-law,' Uncle Blackie said. 'My absent brother's wife.'

'Dad's not absent,' I shouted. 'He'll come back after he's made a packet of money up in the mines.'

'Shut ya gob, Tanya,' Nanna Purvis said, 'or we'll both get thrown out.'

'Well, for now,' Uncle Blackie said, his voice pleasant as ever, 'your mum needs someone to help her through this difficult time.'

He took a gift-wrapped box from his pocket and pushed it into my mother's clasped hands. 'Thought this might cheer you up, Eleanor.'

As if he was quite at home in the Patient-Visitor Lounge, Uncle Blackie sat in the chair beside my mother as she fiddled with the paper, fingers picking uselessly at the sticky tape.

After what seemed an age, all the while Nanna Purvis and I exchanging wary looks behind Uncle Blackie's back, she managed to get the paper off. From the box she pulled out a bottle of Cologne 4711.

'That's lovely, Blackie.' Mum's eyes closed as she sniffed the perfume, a violent pink flush spreading upward from her neck. 'You remembered it's my favourite.'

'Let's just say it's a little memento of our summer of '57-'58.' He gave her a knowing wink and my feet started sweating, sticking to my Roman sandals.

'Isn't it nice of Blackie to visit?' Mum drawled. 'And with Dobson … gone, he's offered to take care of the jobs at Gumtree Cottage: gardening, lawn-mowing … fix a few things.'

'Dad's not gone! He's coming back.'

'Stop shouting, Tanya,' Nanna Purvis said, glaring at Uncle Blackie. 'That snotty woman'll be back any tick of the clock.'

Before I could say anything more, a man wearing a white

coat and a solemn expression strode into the room. 'You must be Mrs Randall's mother and daughter?' he said. 'I'm her doctor, and we've started her on a new drug which seems to be helping a great deal.' He didn't mention anything about no children visitors.

'Tranquillisers don't help my mother,' I said. 'She's already taken heaps of them.'

'This is a different medication, young lady. Tryptanol is a true antidepressant — '

'So, Eleanor *has* got this postnatal depression thing then?' Nanna Purvis said. 'I said as much to Doc Piggott but he reckoned it was just the grief.'

'I feel it's manic depression rather than postnatal,' the doctor said. 'A disorder she's likely been suffering from for many years. Of course, the tragedy — and grief — only made it worse. So Mrs Randall will have to take the Tryptanol for at least six months, in increasing doses, to fully recover.' He glanced over at Uncle Blackie. 'And having her brother-in-law here every day is also helping her. It's marvellous to see such caring family members.'

But my mother had not been allowed visitors! I opened my mouth to ask this doctor why Uncle Blackie had been allowed to visit and not us, but Nanna Purvis shot me another warning glance.

Once the doctor left, we all sat in silence. I stared at my mother, refusing to meet Uncle Blackie's gaze wrapped across my face like a thick, grubby scarf. From the corner of my eye, I could see Nanna Purvis scowling at him as she jiggled her crocheted bag up and down on her lap.

We gazed out the window at the droopy trees and shrubs. The jasmine, without its pretty pink and white summer flowers, climbed the wall; trying to escape over it.

When there was nothing else left to look at, and nothing more to say, Nanna Purvis stood up. 'We'd best be going, can't leave me little Billie-Jean on his own for too long.'

In her cool and distant manner, Nanna Purvis didn't kiss my

mother goodbye, not even a pat on the arm. She just said: 'Keep up the good work, Eleanor. We'll be back in a few days.'

Out in the corridor, she said, 'Wait in the alcove, Tanya, I need the dunny before we leave. Me old bladder'll never last the trip home.'

I sat back on the same chair, kicking my left heel against my right toes, Roman sandals making squeaking noises on the shiny lino floor still littered with the magazines. An annoying, grating noise. A shadow passed across my feet. I looked up to Uncle Blackie's frame filling the doorway.

'Why are you avoiding me, Tanya?' He sat beside me. 'I thought we were friends. And didn't you say you'd come back to Albany?'

'Why are you hanging around my mother all the time, and buying her presents?' I jerked away from his hand dragging my fingers from the cowlick. 'I told you, we can look after ourselves. And I could tell Mum about your photos, if I wanted.'

Though even as I spoke I knew my mother could never find out about the nude photographs. She was far too ill to bear such news. Besides, Angela might have convinced me it was wrong of Uncle Blackie to take them, but I also believed the photos had, somehow, been my fault; that it was me who'd really wanted him to take them. And that guilt, too, stopped me letting on to anyone besides Angela.

Nanna Purvis came out of the Ladies. She muttered something to Uncle Blackie that I didn't catch and hustled me down the corridor faster than I'd ever seen her move.

'Will you tell me now,' I said as we waited at the taxi rank, 'what Uncle Blackie did to that Carter girl?'

'Things adults ain't supposed to do to kids,' Nanna Purvis said. 'Keep away from that one, Tanya, you hear? There's one rotten egg in every nest and they should've kept that bloke locked up in Macquarie Pastures Asylum, and flushed the key down the dunny.'

'But if he committed a crime why wasn't he sent to gaol, instead of a mental asylum?'

'Because it was an asylum for criminals,' she said. 'And the judge ruled Blackburn was crazy at the time. Not only "at the time" if you ask me. That one's always been a nutter. Even back in that summer of '57-'58 when ya mum had the bad luck to meet him at the beach. And a black day that was.'

'Why did Mum and Dad stop going to visit him at the asylum?'

'Because I made them see sense,' Nanna Purvis said as we got into the taxi. 'Made them realise they should forget such a monster, not pay him visits like some ailing rello in hospital. Besides, by that time ya mum and dad had decided to get hitched. It would've seemed odd, them going to see him as a couple when it was Blackie stepping out with Eleanor in the first place.'

So my suspicions had been right. Uncle Blackie and Mum *were* boyfriend and girlfriend in the summer of '57-'58. And as the taxi struggled up the Gallipoli Street hill an ugly suspicion about my uncle and my mother sneaked into my mind.

But I could not yet be certain.

Chapter 33

'I saw her ... saw Shelley.' I couldn't help myself, and grabbed hold of Nanna Purvis's arm.

'What you on about, Tanya?' My grandmother didn't even shake off my hold.

I nodded at a dark-haired woman waiting in the supermarket check-out queue behind us. 'In her pram,' I hissed. 'I'm sure it's Shelley.'

My grandmother sidled back behind the dark-haired woman and squinted into the pram, ignoring the mother's bewildered frown.

She stared for a moment, and hobbled back to me. 'It might look like Shelley but it ain't her.'

'But I was *sure* it was,' I said, unpacking our groceries from the trolley.

'I know what ya mean, Tanya, I've seen a dozen babies I thought were Shelley. In prams everywhere: the supermarket, the hairdresser's, along the street. It's all part of the grief.'

My mother had been in hospital for a few weeks, and that Friday after school, the month of March blowing itself out on a refreshing cool wind, Nanna Purvis and I had caught the bus down to Eastbridge to stock up the pantry.

I knew my grandmother was right, that I had just been imagining Shelley might still be alive somewhere and well. She was simply away from us; not ours any longer but living happily with another family, unaware I was searching for her the whole time.

Nanna Purvis slipped *Only for Sheilas* into the trolley, then, to my surprise, threw in the latest issue of *Real Life Crime*.

'Oh?'

She winked and I started packing our purchases into the bags — all the specials Nanna Purvis-the-bargain-hunter had found: a barbecued chicken for one dollar, fifty-five cents, mustard pickles for twenty-three cents a jar, the cool posters she'd let me get for my bedroom wall, and a double-pack of Iced VoVos for "cheap as mice".

'How much do mice cost?' I'd asked, with a smirk.

'Watch ya cheek, girl,' she'd said, poking me in the ribs.

Despite missing Mum and Dad, it was easier now the strain was gone from Gumtree Cottage, which settled into a peaceful kind of place as if its ghosts too were absent. Gone away on holiday.

It was strange at first without my mother shuffling about — a fairy lost in the woods — her feather duster quivering like a useless wand. It was lighter too, without my father's heavy despair, though his smoke-tinged scent of sweat, beer and baked bricks clung to the walls, his gravelly voice scratching about in my head.

Bath time, Princess. Teatime, Princess. Leave that cowlick alone, Princess.

I'd expected Nanna Purvis to become even more of a tyrant but she didn't. Her hard shell softened, as if the sun that came blinking over the horizon every day was thawing her cold heart.

We never house-cleaned or hosed the Venetian blinds. We dumped the white sheets covering the sofa and armchairs in a pile in the corner of the living-room. To avoid washing up, we used paper plates, and I drank straight from the milk bottle.

I spent most afternoons after school at Bottlebrush Crescent with Angela, eating Mrs Moretti's *molto buono* food and darting secretive glances at Marco's rippling muscles.

Nanna Purvis didn't even make too much fuss about me hanging around "that foreign mob".

'Italians are just the same as Aussies,' I'd told her. 'People are just people … whatever country they come from.'

'*Humpf*,' she mumbled, and left it at that. No arguments, no more racist comments.

We'd bought far too many groceries to lug back on the bus so Nanna Purvis and I caught a taxi home.

'Reckon we deserve a treat after that effort, eh, Tanya?' she said, as we dumped the shopping bags on the kitchen floor.

I stored the food in the pantry and the fridge while Nanna Purvis wriggled into her slippers and made a pot of tea, the dogs hovering about her ankles.

The last thing I took from the shopping bags was the training bra — on special, of course — that my grandmother had picked out for me. 'Go on then, try it on,' she said with a wink.

My cheeks burning, I sloped off down the hallway to my bedroom. My grandmother buying me a bra was the most embarrassing thing ever, but I was secretly glad my boobies would no longer bounce more than the Andersons' cricket ball.

'Come and show me how it looks,' Nanna Purvis hollered.

'No way! As if …' I pulled on my T-shirt over the bra and stood in front of the mirror patting my new womanly chest, and giggling.

'What if I make hamburgers for tea?' I said once we'd drunk our cuppas.

'Bonzer idea,' Nanna Purvis said, feeding biscuit crumbs to Billie-Jean.

I dragged Mum's mincing machine from the cupboard and Nanna Purvis said, 'None of them gadgets around when I was a young wife: mincing machines, sandwich makers, food processors and them new frog things … what're they called? Fondue pot, that's it.'

She carried on chatting as I poked raw meat hunks into the top, and turned the handle. 'And the only recipe book we had was *The Kookaburra Cookery Book* from the Committee of the Lady Victoria Buxton Girls' Club of Adelaide. Which is a hell of a mouthful but did us just fine.'

Nanna Purvis shrieked at the pink worms of meat oozing from the end of the mincer. 'Looks like poo coming out a bum, eh, Tanya?'

'Let's call them poo burgers, then.' And we were both laughing far too crazily for something as moderately funny as that. So much that tears flooded our cheeks, my sides ached and my arm got sore from turning the mincer handle.

* * *

After tea, I stood on a chair in my bedroom to put up the new David Cassidy posters, Nanna Purvis handing me bits of sticky tape.

I stuck the last tape in place, jumped from the chair and stood back to admire them. 'Groovy, huh?'

'Groovy all right,' Nanna Purvis said with a smirk. 'Now come on, it's telly time.'

She switched on the television and patted a place beside her and Billie-Jean. 'Reckon you're old enough to watch *Number 96* now, Tanya.'

'Can I, really?' Nanna Purvis's favourite show, *Number 96*, was Australia's biggest soap opera, with — so I'd heard at school — lots of sex, nudity, racism, gay people and drugs.

Bitta, Steely and I sat with Nanna Purvis and Billie-Jean, and I managed to finish off the whole three-pound packet of jelly beans we'd got at Kmart for one dollar. Nanna Purvis didn't say a word about me gobbling, and even poured me a nip of sherry, along with her own.

I sipped the sherry — heavy and tart but not unpleasant; a taste I could probably get used to.

I threw the empty jelly bean packet onto the coffee table, disgusted with myself. 'I'll never be a skinny model like Twiggy.'

'Why you wanna look like that sickly-looking creature?' Nanna Purvis said, and swallowed a mouthful of sherry.

Sickly-looking creature who probably has to have photos taken in the nude. No, I do not *want to be like Twiggy.*

'Don't worry, you'll slim down,' she said with a slap on my thigh. 'If ya quit scoffing all that food, that is.' She turned her attention back to the telly, her knobbly hand still resting on my leg. I'd never known the feel of her skin on mine, and it was strange.

'So *did* Pop Purvis belt you?' I said. 'Dad said … some things …'

She pulled away her hand, fingers closing around Billie-Jean's collar. 'He could be a bit free with the fists now and again. When he got too much grog under his belt.'

'Did he hit my mother too?'

'Not a chance, I'd have killed the bastard if he ever laid a hand on Eleanor. Though I didn't give him much of a chance — packed your mum off to that posh boarding school up Mittagong way soon as she was old enough. Ya mother might have learned to speak all proper, but fat lot of good that fancy school did her in the end.'

She took another sip of sherry. 'Never really wanted kids meself. Didn't want them to have that kind of a father.'

'But you had Mum?'

'Bit of an accident that was,' she said. 'Don't get me wrong, I wasn't sorry I had Eleanor, but I was thirty-two years old, an old woman to be having a baby, in those days.' She sighed and swallowed the last of her sherry.

'You wouldn't *really* have killed your own husband, would you?'

'You bet ya cotton socks I would've, Tanya. Even had it all planned,' she said as *Number 96* finished and I switched off the television. 'But that's only for your ears, mind.' Nanna Purvis's face lit up in a mad kind of grin. 'But then the old codger keeled over on the dunny and whoosh, all me troubles over. Dead and buried.' She poured herself another shot of sherry, topped up my glass. 'Let that be a lesson, Tanya. Ya gotta pick the right one to get hitched to. Don't get caught up with the wrong bloke, like your mum almost did.'

'You mean Uncle Blackie?'

She nodded, took a sip of sherry.

'What did you mean "fat lot of good that fancy school did her in the end"?'

'Because your mother still got herself in a spot of trouble. But if I tell you, don't go blabbing your mum's secret, okay?' She wagged a finger at me. 'She don't want no one to know about the kid.'

'I know how to keep my mouth shut,' I said. 'What kid?'

'The one she had with that monster, Blackburn. I was all set to help Eleanor out, bring the kid up as me own, but soon as her father — Pop Purvis — found out she was preggers he made me pack Eleanor off to this *Catholic* convent in Sydney.'

'What happened to the baby?'

'Those nuns tricked your mum into signing the adoption papers before she knew what she was doing.' She swallowed more sherry. 'Never even let her get a look at the kid — a boy it was, apparently — snatched him away quick smart, and she never set eyes on him again.'

The bathroom scene came hurtling back to me: Mum's terrible cries, her blood everywhere, another baby flushed down the toilet. And that seabed sorrow made more sense to me — the sadness that had swamped her after each lost baby. Each one that might have been a boy.

Then the overdose. I understood that too. When Shelley died, she'd had enough; just couldn't take any more sadness.

'I have a brother ... how old is he?'

'Half-brother,' Nanna Purvis said. 'Born around the end of '58, so he'd be turning fifteen this year.'

'Just three years older than me.' I became excited at the idea of this unknown brother; that I might not, in the end, have to grow up an only child. 'Where could he be? Maybe we could find him ... get him back?'

'Gawd, not a chance,' Nanna Purvis said. 'Once a kid's adopted out that's it. And no point searching, you'd never find him.'

'Did Uncle Blackie know about the baby boy?'

Nanna Purvis nodded. 'Wanted to marry Eleanor, he did … get himself a proper family: him, Eleanor and the kid. But she was only sixteen. Too young to get hitched.' Another gulp of sherry. 'Then, when ya mum was at the convent, the Carter girl thing happened with Blackie,' she said, 'and they locked him away. Anyway, ya mum had it tough on the baby front, that's why all them miscarriages got to her so bad.'

Still stunned at my mother's secret, I helped Nanna Purvis up off her banana lounge. She limped off to her bedroom, Billie-Jean under one arm, and said: 'So remember, don't go spouting a word of this to anyone.'

I nodded. I could keep a secret, though I was tempted to blurt out the Uncle Blackie secret, his photos, to Nanna Purvis.

No, no, I can't! She might blab to my mother.

I took Steely into my bedroom, shoved the red-rose bedspread onto the floor and lay on my sheet. 'Poor Mum,' I said, cradling my cat against my chest, stroking his soft grey fur.

Certain the first letter to Dad had gone astray, I began another one. I had to convince him to come home to us. Not just for my sake, but for my mother's too. I was certain that was the only way to bring back the happiness to our family.

I explained to Dad that thanks to the new Tryptanol medication, Mum was recovering after the nervous breakdown. I told him not to worry, that Nanna Purvis and I were fine and I was having a fun time with Angela. I didn't ask if he'd run off to Mount Isa with Stacey Mornon's mother as I didn't want to accept the terrible truth of that. I said nothing about Uncle Blackie flirting with my mother, or annoying me about going back to see him at Albany. Besides, I didn't like talking about Uncle Blackie. Or thinking about him.

But that soon became impossible, when Uncle Blackie started coming around to Gumtree Cottage.

Chapter 34

'You go on into bed, Tanya,' Nanna Purvis said, as Lenny drove his van into the driveway of number eleven after our tea down at the RSL club. 'Just gonna share a nip or two with Old Lenny here. Can't let the poor bloke drink sherry on his own, can I?'

Lenny let out a crackly laugh, revealing the gap where one tooth was missing.

'Oh no,' I said, smirking at my grandmother. 'That would be so mean to leave poor Old Lenny on his own.'

'The cheek of ya,' she said with a slap on my arm. 'Now off ya go, I won't be long. And don't even think of giving Billie-Jean's Pooch Snax to that Bitta mongrel.'

With a laugh, I jumped out of Lenny's van and hurried across to number thirteen.

Nanna Purvis always called Lenny Longbottom "Old Lenny", though he was a whole year younger than her. But what did one year matter; they both looked about a hundred years old to me.

'Why would you want to have tea with Old Lenny?' I'd said to Nanna Purvis, when she told me he'd invited us both to the club. 'You don't even like him.'

'Ah, ya gotta be a bit tolerant sometimes, Tanya. If Old Lenny's pining for me sparkling company, what choice have I got?'

I skipped up the front porch steps into Gumtree Cottage, started to walk down the hallway. Ahead of me, the kitchen light spilled into the end of the hallway though I clearly remembered switching it off before Nanna Purvis and I left for the club.

I stiffened, pressed a palm against my thudding heart. 'Hello … anyone there?'

'Don't be scared, it's only me, Tanya.'

Uncle Blackie was sitting in a kitchen chair, a large package before him, on the table.

'Uncle Blackie, what …?' I stammered, trying to mask my fear. 'What are you doing here? And since when do you walk into somebody's house without knocking?'

'Since they leave the door unlocked,' Uncle Blackie said with a wink. He stood up, looking down at me with that friendly smile. 'When I realised you and your grandmother were out, I thought I'd just wait here, to give you this.' He pointed to the box on the table.

'What is it?' I said warily.

'Why don't you open it and find out?'

'I'll wait till Nanna Purvis comes back,' I said. 'Then I'll open it.'

'You know your grandmother doesn't want us to be friends, Tanya. Why not open it now, before she gets back?'

'I'm not sure,' I said, picking at the brown paper.

'Don't be silly, you know we're mates. And I know you'll just love what's inside this box.'

'Isn't it my mother you're mates with? The one you buy presents for?'

He raked a hand through the curly black nest, threw back his head and laughed — taunting, mocking. 'How innocent you are. How young and sweetly naïve.'

A blood-hot rage simmered inside me. I pushed the parcel away. 'How dare you make fun of me!'

'I'm not … I'm not,' he said, still laughing. 'I'd never make fun of you, Tanya. And you'll see just how much I care about you once you open your present.' He nodded at the package again. 'Go on, you'll see.'

I ripped off the brown paper, took the lid off the box.

'Oh wow, thanks,' I said, pulling out a pair of white boot-roller skates, lacing them up over my sandals. 'They fit perfectly. How did you know my shoe size?'

'Just a hunch. And I bet you'll be the star skater of Wollongong.' Uncle Blackie ruffled my hair, patted it down it over my ears, his eyes warm, his smile happy.

I stood there, staring at the groovy skates, barely hearing Nanna Purvis's voice chiming up the back verandah steps.

'Yeah, you too, sleep tight, Old Lenny,' she called. 'Don't let them bed bugs bite.'

Without another glance at me, Uncle Blackie sidled down the hallway and out the front door as quickly and soundlessly as a Gumtree Cottage ghost.

But from then on he started coming regularly to fix things around the house and yard. I could tell his presence annoyed my grandmother, though, thankful to have the jobs done, she just let him go about his work, never speaking to him.

In all that time, Uncle Blackie didn't mention the photos, or ask if I wanted him to take some more. He never asked me to go back to Albany. All he did was bring me presents: a shiny glow mesh handbag the same as Mum's, my own bottle of Cologne 4711, a pair of cork-heeled platforms.

He put my red bike in the back of the Kingswood and brought it over to Gumtree Cottage. I rode it around the neighbourhood — especially outside Stacey's house — the streamers flashing behind me.

I wondered however I could have doubted my caring uncle or imagined he could be a filthy perv. Angela's warning words faded from my mind, and when I went to her place in Bottlebrush Crescent I never brought up the subject of Uncle Blackie.

* * *

'Look, Steely, a letter from Dad!' I'd written the second letter almost a month ago, and had just about given up hope of a reply. But I hadn't checked the letterbox for a few days; it could've been sitting there for ages.

I pushed the envelope under the cat's nose. 'I bet Dad will say he's coming home.'

The Anzac Day breeze in my face smacked of autumn. No school today because April twenty-fifth was a public holiday commemorating the loss of over eight thousand Australian and two thousand, seven hundred New Zealand soldiers at Gallipoli in 1915.

I sat in the sun on the front verandah step, shooed away a fly, and, forgetting for the moment I was still cranky with my father, ripped open the envelope.

Dad's writing was shaky, which was odd as he'd always had neat handwriting.

C/o Wingfield House,
Mount Isa
Queensland
My dearest Tanya,

How are you, Princess? I'm fine up here in Mount Isa. There's heaps of money to be made in the mines so I'm busy working hard all the time.

Mount Isa's a really hot place, so hot sometimes I think the sun'll shrivel those mines right up. There's a nice lake though with shady, grassed areas and barbecues, where everybody goes swimming and boating and has picnics. I'd love to take you there sometime, to see the cormorants, the galahs, the pelicans.

You're probably wondering why I haven't phoned. Well, Mount Isa is so far away that the phones don't work very often.

I was sorry to hear about your mum's nervous breakdown but it sounds like she's finally on the right pills and will be home before you know it. Don't worry I'm sure they'll take good care of her in the hospital ... look how they fixed me up after that car accident.

I'm thinking of you all the time and hope you and Mum and

Nanna Purvis are okay and that you're working hard at school.

Be a good girl, give a pat to Steely, Billie-Jean and Bitta and I hope to see you soon.

Love forever,

Dad xxx ooo

He hadn't mentioned Mrs Mornon, or Stacey going to live with them.

I ran inside, taking the milk bottles from the doorstep on my way and waved the envelope at Nanna Purvis.

'See, I told you Dad hasn't abandoned us. "Soon", he says … "hope to see you soon".'

'Don't hold ya breath, Tanya. Hard that it is to get your head around, Dobson's done a bunk. Wearing that wobbly boot made his brain go funny.'

'Dad hasn't done a bunk.'

Nanna Purvis kept her gaze on the television screen, one hand stroking Billie-Jean. 'Look at these dickheads, would ya? Trying to beat that bloke, Bob Hawke's record of sculling two and a half pints of beer in eleven seconds and getting themselves in the Guinness Book of Records. Rita reckons that bloke'll be prime minister one day. I said to her, I don't know what this country's coming to, letting in all them foreigners, and packs of women marching about burning their bras, and boozers wanting to become prime minister.'

'Is Mum ever coming home?' I said. 'She's been in that mental ward for ages.'

'She'll be home soon enough, but I told you, ya gotta understand it takes a long time to recover from this kind of illness. And when the doc does let her out, you'll mind to be good and not bother her with silly questions like "am I adopted?" Give your mum time to recover.'

I wondered how long it took to recover from trying to kill yourself. Or from murdering your baby.

Could you ever *recover from that?*

Chapter 35

Two months later, around the end of June, I was sitting on the verandah with my yoyo, Steely swiping a paw at the string. Nanna Purvis was over at number eleven watching telly with Old Lenny.

'Hey, Tanya,' Uncle Blackie said, loping outside from where he'd been repairing the leaky kitchen tap. 'The hospital just rang. Good news, your Mum'll be coming home tomorrow.'

'Really? Did you hear that, Steely? Mum's better!'

In the months of my mother's absence, while Uncle Blackie was at Gumtree Cottage clearing the yard, repairing broken taps and toilets, he'd never touched me. Not once. He always spoke in that soft and friendly way, so I was surprised when he sat cross-legged beside me on the wooden boards and his hand slid onto my knee.

'Thought I'd varnish these old verandah boards,' he said. 'And paint the railings and posts. This old paint's all peeling away. Pretty new paint would brighten up the whole of Gumtree Cottage. What do you think, Tanya: green, blue … red? I know you love red.'

'Whatever you reckon,' I said, clutching the yoyo in both hands as his index finger rubbed at the Hills Hoist scar on my knee. I didn't move, my neck and face burning up.

His gaze skated over my body, easy, familiar. 'You're a woman now, not a little girl anymore. Those hips could almost bear a child.' He moved closer, the whispery voice burrowing through my ear. His finger still rubbing at the knee scar, my whole leg trembled. 'Don't be scared, Tanya, you know I'd never hurt you.'

He inhaled so deeply as if he were breathing me right inside him. 'You like the perfume I got you then?'

I nodded, couldn't get any words out, just sat there. A cement statue.

The *therapeutic* gardening hands were bristles on my face. A finger tracing the outline of my lips, the curve of my nose, my brow, finding the crevices in my ears. Scraping down one arm, across to a small breast, making circles around the nipple.

I sensed it wasn't right. That despite his floaty sea-ripple voice what Uncle Blackie was doing was all wrong. I should get up and run but I couldn't. My body tingled, a heavy throb pulsing low in my groin. A feeling I did not want to stop.

'She left me ... chucked me aside like dirty rubbish.' Uncle Blackie's voice was a cracked whisper, his breaths coming hot and fast on my face. 'Not you though, Tanya. You're mine now, aren't you?'

I shuddered. A bolt of white-hot lightning shot through me. A shard of ice froze me. I leapt up and ran inside, slamming the flyscreen door behind me.

* * *

It was Uncle Blackie who drove my mother home from the mental ward. After yesterday on the verandah I never wanted to see him again, didn't want him to notice my embarrassment as I remembered his hand on my breast. He could never know I'd kind of enjoyed the feeling.

I was walking home from school up Figtree Avenue when the rusty Kingswood swept into the driveway as if it were a limousine. The Driza-Bone reeling about him like Heathcliff from *Wuthering Heights*, a book we'd had to read at school, Uncle

Blackie hurried from the driver's side and opened the passenger door. He half-bowed as my mother stepped onto the driveway as if she was a queen and he her servant.

He carried her bag, one hand cupped beneath her elbow, gripping my mother tighter as he ducked to avoid the Anderson boys' wayward cricket ball. We all ignored Coralie Anderson's gawping stare from her front yard.

'Are you better, Mum … truly better?'

She nodded, blinked away tears, smiled, frowned — a jumble of emotions tumbling from her all at once, like she was anxious how I'd be: pleased she was home or despising the mother who couldn't look after her daughter when she'd needed her most.

'I'm getting there. Look at you, how grown up you are,' she said, as if she'd been gone three and a half years rather than three and a half months. And especially since I'd seen her several times during her absence when Nanna Purvis managed to sneak me past the hoity-toity desk woman.

I linked my arm through hers, and with a gentle tug away from Uncle Blackie's grip — and avoiding his weirdo stare — we walked up the verandah steps and into Gumtree Cottage.

'Gosh, isn't that snazzy,' Mum said, nodding at my bicycle, leaning against the wall. 'Uncle Blackie told me he'd got you a bike … what a lucky girl you are, Tanya, having such a generous uncle.'

Mum stood just inside the doorway, looking about her as if seeing her home for the first time. She bent down and patted the yapping dogs.

'Stop that racket,' Nanna Purvis said. 'At least let her get inside before youse start bothering her.'

'They're okay,' Mum said. 'I've missed them … missed everything.'

'I'll leave you to get settled in then, Eleanor,' Uncle Blackie said. 'I'll get busy mowing the grass. It could do with a good going over.'

With a pat on her forearm, Uncle Blackie strolled through

the kitchen as if it was his own and down the backyard to the garage, where Dad kept the mower.

He'd mowed about half the backyard, taking care to mow around Shelley's pram rather than move it to one side, when Angela and her mother arrived.

'Tanya is telling Angelina you coming home this day, Eleanor,' Mrs Moretti said. 'You looking well, I am very happy to see this.' She thrust a heavenly-smelling basket of food at my mother. 'I am thinking you would enjoy things to eat, just until you get back on your legs.'

She set the basket filled with still-warm bread, strong-smelling cheese, and olives, on the kitchen table. 'And cannelloni for your tea, and other meals.' She began stacking Tupperware containers into the freezer, like at Shelley's funeral.

'Now, Sadie —' Nanna Purvis started.

'Sofia,' Mrs Moretti said.

'Ah sorry, I get confused with ya funny names. As I was saying, I don't generally condone foreign grub in this house, though I will admit the last lot was quite tasty.'

'You said Italian food made you sick, that it messed with your insides?' I said, exchanging a wink with Angela and her mother.

Nanna Purvis cleared her throat, bellowed her fake laugh. 'Just a manner of speaking, Tanya.'

Mrs Moretti smiled and shut the freezer door. 'My big pleasure, Mrs Purvis.'

'Let's all sit down and have a nice cuppa,' Mum said.

I went to fill the kettle but Mum placed her hand over mine. 'It's okay, I can do it, Tanya.'

Moving across the lino like a normal person, no longer stuck to the chair, sofa or bed as if they were part of her, Mum made the pot of tea against the background whir of the lawnmower. Nanna Purvis was frowning at Uncle Blackie, and stroking Billie-Jean faster, harder.

Sitting at the table she'd scrubbed at, slumped and cried on, my mother sipped tea and chatted with Mrs Moretti. I was pleased to see her doing something as simple as drinking tea with a friend in her kitchen; happy to hear her talking properly — almost, for I knew the Tryptanol dried her mouth and made her drowsy — in real sentences that made a kind of music instead of dull words in a straight line.

As always when she spoke, Mrs Moretti waved her arms around. She told Mum about all the nice times I'd had with Angela, as if reassuring my mother I'd not suffered while she'd been away.

'Your Tanya is loving our Italian food,' she said. 'I am learning her make the capsicum and eggplant with stuffing. I am sorry to say, you Australians know nothing of food.'

'And her favourite,' Angela said. 'Meat balls in Mamma's homemade tomato sauce.'

'I'll make some for you, Mum,' I said. '*Sooo* yummy.'

'Maybe you should give me cooking lessons too, Sofia?' Mum said with a laugh. 'As you say, we Aussies could do with a change from the same old food we've eaten for years.'

'Why's your uncle mowing your lawn?' Angela said, as I took her out to the front verandah. I certainly wasn't going near the backyard with Uncle Blackie in it.

We dangled our legs over the edge, sipped the green cordial. Steely stretched himself out between us in the warm sun and a spider carved its web between the dusty old verandah rafters.

'He's taking advantage of my father being away ... for his work, to try and get my mother to be his girlfriend again. Like she was before she married Dad,' I said. 'I sussed *that* out the first time we visited Mum in the mental ward, when he came and gave her perfume. But Mum's not that stupid. Anyway, how dare he use Dad's lawnmower? I could mow it, or it could just wait till my father comes home.'

'So since your mamma's come home,' Angela said, 'that must mean nobody, including the police, believe she suffocated your sister?'

'Nanna Purvis said the police went to the mental ward several times to question her but that they decided "not to take matters any further." No evidence I guess. Anyway I don't think Mum suffocated my sister ... I reckon it was someone else.'

'Who then?' Angela said.

* * *

'That creep.' I nodded at Uncle Blackie, who'd come around from the backyard. Casting me brief, sharp glances, he started mowing the grass in front of us.

'Oh gosh!' Angela's chestnut eyes widened. 'Why do you think it's your uncle?'

'A few reasons. Firstly because my mother was in no state to have a boyfriend while she had a crying baby, so he had to get rid of Shelley.'

'No, that's *terrible.*'

'And secondly,' I went on, stroking Steely so hard he nipped my hand, 'he started hanging about Gumtree Cottage around the time Shelley died. And we both know he did commit some crime on a girl named Carter — the reason they locked him up in Macquarie Pastures Asylum for the Criminally Insane. And one crime leads to another, you know.'

I took a swig of cordial, a deep breath. 'And thirdly, he knew Shelley had died without me or anyone else telling him. Three days after it happened he drove over here to give me some salt dough to make that cat sculpture for Shelley's coffin.' I drained my glass. 'He just seems to know everything that happens with us: my father's car accident, my mother's cleaning frenzies. Shelley's colic and crying. How can he know all that unless he's here, hiding in the yard, listening to everything that's going on?'

'It sure sounds suss,' Angela said.

'And yesterday he touched me, here.' I pointed at my breast; didn't mention that I'd enjoyed it, sort of.

'He touched you *there*?' Angela gasped, her eyes wide and chocolaty, like Maltesers.

'You were right,' I said. 'Uncle Blackie *is* a bad person. And how dare he come back here after touching me like that!'

'That is a totally and completely bad thing for a man to do,' Angela said. 'He should be locked up for that, and if he did suffocate Shelley, well ...'

'But how can the police arrest him?' My gaze narrowed on Uncle Blackie. 'There's obviously no evidence against him. I just wish he'd go home and leave us alone. Come on, let's go back inside so we don't have to look at him.'

Angela and I chatted in my bedroom for a while, and when we returned to the kitchen for more drinks, Uncle Blackie came inside, mopping the sweat from his brow.

'Oh, Sofia?' He looked surprised to see Angela's mother sitting at the kitchen table as he took a KB Lager from the fridge — uninvited! — and guzzled it down. 'Lawnmower broke down,' he said. 'I half-expected it, Dobson should've replaced that clunky old model years ago.'

Beside me, Angela tensed; her nostrils quivered. 'We should go, Mamma. I've got loads of homework. Come over again soon, Tanya,' she added, with a glance at Uncle Blackie.

And as Mum closed the door after them, I wondered if she had sensed that hesitation: Angela's unspoken words hanging in the air. A smell gone sour in the heat of a still day.

'I'll be off too, Eleanor,' Uncle Blackie said. From the corner of my eye, I knew he was staring at me but I refused to look at him. 'I'll come back tomorrow and trim those bushes; it's a bit hot now.'

It was almost winter, not at all hot. Just a clever excuse to come back tomorrow.

Uncle Blackie had barely shut the front door when Nanna Purvis started on about him.

'It's a bad idea him coming around here, Eleanor. I didn't like it when you were in the hospital, but there was always some job needed doing so I could hardly send him packing what with Dobson gone.'

'Oh no, don't start on about Blackie again,' Mum said. 'We went through all this years ago. Things have changed now.'

'Have you forgotten there's a young girl in this house?' Nanna Purvis nodded at me. 'They should never've let him out of Macquarie Pastures. Monster should be kept away from civilisation … from young girls.'

'Stop saying those things about him,' Mum snapped, fingernails tapping against her empty teacup. 'He's nice, a gentle person. All that business was an awful mistake.'

'Never trust a bloke with a murky past, I say,' Nanna Purvis said. 'And what Blackburn was accused of was more than murky.'

Uncle Blackie's photos, his caresses. It was on the tip of my tongue but once again I stopped short. Apart from my guilt — the embarrassment-tinged doubt that the photos, the touching, had been all my doing — I did not want to worry my mother. Something like that could tip her back into the nervous-breakdown abyss.

But I couldn't believe she was defending Uncle Blackie, and I knew he'd tricked her too, same as he'd tricked me.

As a kid I'd thought my mother was perfect. Well, not perfect, because sometimes she'd refuse me things and we'd argue. But I'd believed her smart. I never imagined she could be wrong or silly. But seeing Uncle Blackie deceive her so easily made me think she wasn't so clever after all.

Chapter 36

'Guess what, Tanya? I've got a job interview at Jim's Jeans 'n Johns,' Mum said, almost bouncing on the spot with excitement.

Jim's Jeans 'n Johns was a shop down at Eastbridge that sold jeans and underwear. 'Only till I finish my typing and short-hand course,' she went on, 'then I'll get a better, secretarial job. Anyway, Sofia and Angela are coming over to drive us down to Eastbridge ... Sofia said she'll take you girls shopping while I'm at the interview, so let's hurry and get ready.'

Preparing herself for the job interview — slipping into her bell-bottom flares, shaking them down over her slim, hairless legs — was the first time I'd watched Mum get dressed up since before Shelley's colic. I guessed this show of fancy clothes and make-up wasn't only for her new job. It was also for Uncle Blackie.

It was late July of 1973, and he was still waltzing into Gumtree Cottage all the time, a persistent blowfly around my mother. Apart from fixing everything that broke, he took my mother shopping in the Kingswood, and paid for our groceries, and whatever other bills came in, with his TAB-job money. And while he helped her unpack the shopping, he was always touch-ing her. A pat here, a stroke there. As if he owned her. How I hated that.

But when Nanna Purvis and my mother weren't paying

attention, that black gaze swept from her to me. He'd drink me in from my head to my toes like a person gasping for water. I began to sense that each caress he lavished on my mother was meant for me; that it was me he wanted, rather than her. I took to avoiding him, and never let him corner me on my own.

Shower-fresh, smelling of Pears' soap and wearing her satin dressing-gown, Mum patted her powder puff against her cheeks, her nose, her brow, the powder clinging to the fine hair above her lip and along her jaw, like flour on pastry.

She turned to me, sitting on the edge of her bed, smiling as she reached over and patted powder over my face. The sun streaking through the Venetians lit her hair golden beige. She drew black liner around her eyes — no longer hollow sea swells but the hazel colour of grass at a dewy daybreak. Leaning towards me, she traced eyeliner around my eyes.

'I want a good job when I leave school,' I said, as she brushed mascara over my lashes, and hers. 'So I won't have to depend on a husband to bring home the bacon.'

'I thought you wanted to be a model,' Mum said. 'Like Twiggy … the "Face of '66". Maybe you'll be the "Face of '76"?'

I felt uncomfortable, like running from the surf with my swimmers full of sand. 'Oh no, I'd *hate* to be a model.'

Mum patted my arm. 'Well I hope you get what you want. Now purse those lips.' She made kissing lips and we were both smacking our pink, glossy mouths.

She smiled at my reflection in the mirror. 'Don't you look the real young lady?'

I tilted my chin, stuck my chest out. 'Hello,' I said to the real young lady.

Just as quickly, my shoulders slumped. 'But look how my ears stick out.' I pressed my fingers against the tips of each ear, pushing them against my head. I scraped my hair over them. 'Why can't my ears be flat, like this?'

'Those pageboy hairstyles are coming back in fashion,' Mum said. 'Perfect for hiding sticky-out ears.'

'Okay, I'll get a pageboy ... maybe I could go to Nanna Purvis's hairdresser?'

'Ha, your grandmother thinks Rita's exclusively for her,' Mum said with a laugh. 'Probably best we try Percy's Pin and Perm.'

'And I *am* fat, you can't deny it, Mum. I'm not called Ten-ton Tanya for nothing.'

'Two women in my typing and shorthand course are on Weight Watchers,' she said. 'The pounds have just dropped right off them.'

'Maybe I could go on Weight Watchers?'

'Why not?' Mum put her head next to mine in front of the mirror. 'You look so much like me when I was your age.'

'So I'm not adopted?'

'Why do you keep asking that?' Mum frowned as she slipped on a pretty flowered blouse, and Nanna Purvis hobbled into the room.

'Because I didn't inherit Dad's dark genes ... the dominant ones, like Shelley did. And because Stacey Mornon's mother said you weren't in Wollongong Hospital having me when she was having Stacey.' My chest felt caught in a vice as I imagined Stacey Mornon's mother and my father *together*. 'Her birthday's the same day as mine so she reckons I must've been adopted. I always asked, don't you remember?'

'But I never thought you really believed it,' Mum said. 'Oh dear, I should've spelled it out. I'm so sorry. You were born three weeks early. We were up at the Blythes'. Vicky's birthday, I think. We still saw them back then. You were born in the hospital up there.'

'You or Dad or Nanna Purvis have never actually said, "You are not adopted". If you'd only said that.'

'Anyway, how would that Mornon woman know anything?' my grandmother said. 'She was too busy having her seizure.'

'Seizure?' Mum said.

'Didn't they have to do a seizure to get that bird-brained Stacey out? Wasn't her head too big for her mother's fanny?'

'Oh, I see.' Mum giggled. '*Caesar* … short for *Caesarean* section.'

'Whatever,' Nanna Purvis said, and Mum and I smirked behind our hands cupped over our mouths.

'Anyway, it doesn't matter,' I said. 'I know now that mothers can love their adopted kids just the same as natural ones.'

'I wish I could've been a better mother.' Mum sighed, laid a hand on my arm. The dewy eyes filled with tears, which she tried to blink away.

She was going to cry again. Oh no, I'd seen her cry enough.

'Sorry I got sick, Tanya. Sorry I couldn't look after you properly like a mother should.'

'You couldn't help it. Too many sad things happened to you.'

She looked away, out through the Venetian blind slats, one hand rubbing at her cowlick. 'You make it sound so simple. If only…' She sighed again. 'I felt so useless; knew you needed me when Shelley … and your dad drinking more and more. But the sadness, those pills, took all my energy. I needed them to get through the day but they made me so sleepy. I was too weak to fight.'

'It's okay, Mum.'

'And I don't blame your father for leaving us. I did try to give him what he needed, what every person needs, but I couldn't fill that gap between us and it just got wider every day.' She exhaled, her top lip quivering. 'He tried so hard at first, but I kept pushing him away. As if his tenderness might melt me to some cold, liquidy … *nothing*. Oh, I don't know how to explain it.'

'He knows you couldn't help it,' I said. 'Anyway he'll be back soon. You can make it up to him. Cook him one of Mrs Moretti's yummy Italian recipes?'

'You and Nanna Purvis, and I, have to try and forget what happened to Shelley,' she said, wiping away the tear sliding down her cheek. She shook her head, as if she, too, wished things had not happened as they had. 'And — for the moment — don't think too much about your father.'

'Dad'll be back,' I said, which made Nanna Purvis roll her eyes. 'Then Uncle Blackie can stop coming around.'

'I don't know what you've got against your uncle,' Mum said, popping her lipstick into her glow mesh handbag. 'You're so unfriendly to him, always scowling or pouting. So ungrateful after all the nice things he's bought you.' She slung the handbag over one shoulder. 'I told you before, that Carter girl affair was all lies.'

'I just don't like him,' I said. The air between us grew hot and heavy, the guilt and frustration flaying me, the truth about Uncle Blackie's intentions for me — if I told her — threatening to rip apart those shreds we'd so lovingly woven back together.

No, she could never know about the photos, the touching. I could never tell her I believed it was Uncle Blackie who'd killed Shelley. I could not risk losing her again.

'Well, could you just try, please,' Mum said, glancing at her watch. 'Goodness, look at the time. Sofia and Angela will be here any minute.'

* * *

We left Nanna Purvis arguing with Old Lenny who'd heard about our broken-down lawnmower. Apparently he had one left in his garage.

'Only the one, mind,' he'd said.

Nanna Purvis was Old Lenny's haggling match and negotiations, underway for some time, were still in deadlock.

'Hey, Tanya, wanna play cricket with me 'n Wayne?' Terry Anderson called out.

'No thanks, I hate cricket, it's just for kids.'

At the shopping centre, Mrs Moretti, Angela and I waved Mum off, wishing her good luck, and began trundling from one clothes shop to the next.

Mrs Moretti bought Angela and me velour hot pants, flared

denims and a T-shirt with our names printed on the front. She seemed to have a lot of money in her housekeeping purse, so it was obvious that laying carpets earned far more money than laying bricks. Or mining in Mount Isa.

'I got the job ... start next Monday!' Mum's face was bright and cheery as she joined us at our table at The Cozie Café. 'And the boss is letting me work special hours so I can fit in my typing and shorthand classes.'

'Good on you, Mum.' I was happy for her, sensed this job was one of the final bends she had to negotiate in her long and winding recovery road.

'You be the best saleswoman,' Mrs Moretti said, kissing my mother on both cheeks.

Mum drank tea, Mrs Moretti had a coffee and Angela and I ordered a milkshake and a chocolate éclair.

I pulled the latest issue of *Dolly* magazine from my Indian bag and Angela and I flipped through the pages, poring over the clothes, makeup and jewellery. The good-looking boys.

When we arrived back at Bottlebrush Crescent, Mrs Moretti and my mother went outside to relax on the deck chairs by the pool, with ginger beer and cannoli, whilst Angela and I thumped upstairs to her bedroom.

We pulled the new clothes from the bags, held them up against our bodies, admired ourselves in the mirror.

'Any more letters from your dad?' Angela asked as we tried everything on, flinging clothes about her bedroom. 'Is he coming home soon?'

I shook my head. 'I haven't heard from him in ages. And I can tell my mother's given up on him coming back ... and flirting with that perv, Uncle Blackie, who still always tries to touch me when Mum and Nanna Purvis aren't looking.'

'Yeah, what an old perv. But remember what I told you Marco said — that my papa can make bad people go away from Wollongong.'

'Uncle Blackie would just come back from wherever they

sent him. But I can't stand him being at Gumtree Cottage all the time … can't bear to see him with my mother when I know he doesn't really like her; that he just wants to get to me.' I took a deep breath. 'And if he *did* suffocate Shelley, what if he does the same to me?'

'That's just too awful! Are you *sure* you don't want me to tell my papa?'

'Definitely not,' I said as we left that sea of tangled garments and made our way down to our mothers sitting beside the pool. 'If all that got back to Mum it would destroy her. I'll have to find my own way to stop him coming around to Gumtree Cottage.'

Chapter 37

A few weeks after Mum started her job at Jim's Jeans 'n Johns, I went to change out of my school uniform and found a framed certificate hanging on my bedroom wall beside the David Cassidy posters.

Certificate of Birth.

Where Born and When: Ballina, New South Wales, August Twenty-Second, 1961.

Sex: female. Name (if any): Tanya Pearl.

Mother: Eleanor Daisy Randall.

Father: Robson Randall. Profession: Bricklayer.

Still grinning like a happy fool, I sat at the kitchen table and got out my homework.

'Give you a hand with that?' As usual, Uncle Blackie had crept up on me, and he settled his bulk into the chair beside me, his raspy breaths hot on my cheek.

'No thanks.' I kept my gaze fixed on my pen, moving it across the page and trying to concentrate on the words.

His hand was on my thigh, a pat, stroking. I jumped from the chair and moved to the other end of the table.

'Stop being silly, Tanya, please. I know you enjoyed it before.' His voice was soft as always, but wheedling now. 'You know you want us to be together as much as I do, so stop acting like this.'

I was trying to think what to say to him when Nanna Purvis and Mum burst through the door. Mum was jabbering on to my grandmother about how many pairs of jeans she'd sold that day at work, Nanna Purvis butting in with what her hairdresser had said about someone going travelling around Australia in a Kombi van.

Mum smiled at Uncle Blackie, took off her jacket, kissed my forehead and put the kettle on to boil. Nanna Purvis scowled at him.

'Just weeded all the flower beds, Eleanor,' Uncle Blackie said. 'New lawnmower from Old Lenny's working like a dream too. And I've been thinking, it's about time we got rid of Gumtree Cottage's old corrugated iron roof. What do you say to a spanking new tiled roof?'

'No,' I snapped. 'I like the roof the way it is … the sound of the rain on it. Why do you want to change everything at Gumtree Cottage?'

It might have been a bit rundown and shabby-looking, and even though I envied Angela Moretti her Bottlebrush Crescent palace, I wanted Gumtree Cottage to stay the way it was; the way I'd always known it. How it was when Shelley was alive and before Dad left, when we were all happy together.

'Don't let him change the roof, please Mum.'

'If you're so against it, Tanya,' Uncle Blackie said, 'of course I won't.'

'Blackie's only trying to make Gumtree Cottage a nicer home for us,' Mum said.

'Anyway, you have a think about it, Tanya,' Uncle Blackie said. He laid a hand on my mother's shoulder. 'I thought I'd hang around, Eleanor, give you and Tanya a lift to the cemetery?'

Mum looked at me, eyebrows raised. 'Sure you still want to go, Tanya?'

'I do, but do *you* still want to go?'

Mum had said it would be good for us to visit Shelley's grave. Her psychiatrist believed it would help us "move on", but I was afraid it would simply recall to her all those terrible seabed memories. I still imagined her as a frail flower petal which the slightest gust could swoop up and blow any which way. But she gave me a firm nod.

'Okay, almost finished my homework. We'll catch the bus. We prefer to go on our own to see Shelley, don't we, Mum?'

'Righto, if that's what you both want,' Uncle Blackie said. 'And just so you know, Eleanor, I got rid of Shelley's pram for you … thought it best.'

'Got rid of her pram?' Mum's face creased into a frown. The boiling water she was pouring into the teapot splattered over the benchtop and I could see she was shocked too, that he'd removed it without asking her. But she never argued with anything Uncle Blackie did or said. As if he'd stolen away not only Shelley's pram, but my mother's mind too.

'But … but why would you do that?' she said.

I flew to the flyscreen, looked out into the backyard, at the sad and empty space beneath the gum tree.

'Why did you take her pram away?' I snarled at Uncle Blackie. It had been comforting seeing it there every time I went outside. A silent reminder of Shelley. A memorial to our little gumnut girl.

But now the pram was gone, along with her clothes, toys, cot and the rocking chair, another piece of her was erased. Soon there would not be a single snippet of her left. It would be like she'd never existed.

* * *

'I'd best get off to work then,' Uncle Blackie said, giving my mother's shoulder a squeeze. 'All those punters'll be waiting at the TAB to throw their money away.'

Mum stared, wordlessly, into space, her eyes slightly crossed and misty.

'Thanks for the birth certificate,' I said, mainly to try and stop her thinking about Shelley's pram. 'But *Pearl*? I didn't even know I had a middle name.'

'Be thankful we gave you "Pearl" and not "Beulah Fannie",' Mum said, pouring herself a cup of tea, and one for Nanna Purvis.

'Beulah Fannie?'

'Nanna Randall's name … poor woman.' Mum held her cup with both hands and blew on the hot tea. 'Poor, because she bled to death.'

'It must be so awful to bleed to death,' I said, wondering if that was worse than suffocating.

'It happened when she was giving birth to Blackie. "Poor Beulah Fannie, that last baby was far too big", everyone said. Blackie told me his father — Pop Randall — was never the same after she died. Something snapped inside him that couldn't be fixed. He blamed her death on poor little Blackie.' She sipped her tea, blew on it again. 'Pop Randall ignored Blackie his whole life. Never wanted anything to do with him … his own child.' Another sip of tea. 'Then, and Blackie didn't tell me this, it was your father who told me about Uncle Ralph years later, after Blackie was sent to Macquarie Pastures.'

'Who's Uncle Ralph?'

Even as I asked the question, I recalled the name from Uncle Blackie's conversation with Dad, the night of Shelley's funeral.

… like you tried to stand up for me against sleazy old Uncle Ralph … may the bastard be rotting in Hell.

'He wasn't a real uncle,' Mum said. 'Just some friend of Pop Randall's who took Blackie under his wing after his own father had rejected him. Sadly, this Ralph did terrible things to Blackie … awful things adults aren't meant to do to children. Pop Randall must've known what was going on … your dad as good as told me he did, but he turned a blind eye.' She paused for breath, placed the teacup on the saucer. 'Anyway, what I'm trying to say, Tanya, is that's maybe why Blackie's the way he is … a bit *unusual*. He's never got over that terrible childhood; never got the chance to grow up properly. But he's good at heart. Give him a chance, you'll see.'

I pressed my lips together, my hand tightening around the pen poised above my homework composition.

Uncle Blackie had brainwashed my mother. That was clear. I'd never be able to count on her to help me stop him coming to Gumtree Cottage.

'So,' Mum said, with a small smile, 'how's that homework going? We should catch the next bus if we don't want to get home too late.'

'Almost finished, it's a composition about yellow peril.'

'Yellow peril?'

'Our teacher told us that in January of this year, England, Denmark and Ireland joined the European Economic Community. She said Australia had counted on Britain as a market for our meat products, but that now we were forced to find other export markets, such as Japan. So we must all be on the alert for yellow peril.'

'Yellow peril all right,' Nanna Purvis said, shuffling in from the living-room. 'Before we know it, there'll be no more good old Aussie Iced VoVos, meat pies or sausage rolls. We'll all be munchin' on rice and noodles. Now, outside for a widdly-woo for you,' she said to Billie-Jean and carried her dog out the back as if he had no legs of his own.

'What do you reckon's worse,' Mum said with a smile. 'Yellow peril or Nanna Purvis peril?'

'What about Pearl peril?' I said. 'Or the peril of Pearl Purvis?'

We both exploded into giggles.

'What's so funny, youse two?' Nanna Purvis said, coming back inside.

'Oh nothing,' Mum and I said together, neither of us able to stifle our laughs.

'What if I make poo burgers for tea?' I said. 'When we get back from the cemetery.'

'*Poo* burgers?' Mum said.

Nanna Purvis clapped her hands. 'You'll see, Eleanor. Best burgers this side of Kalgoorlie. I could even get Old Lenny over to taste them.'

'Don't you hate Old Lenny?' I said, with what my grand-mother would call a "cheeky grin". I'd guessed by now that Nanna Purvis had a warm spot for him in her cool heart, but that she just wanted us to believe she despised him, fearing we'd tease her for associating with a ratty-haired gaol bird. '*And* you suspected him of suffocating Shelley. That's what you told the police, at the time. "Murder is murder" you said. "Once done you can never take it back. Once a gaol bird always a gaol bird, once a killer, always a killer."'

'Ah well, sometimes people say things in the heat of the moment, things they don't mean. Anyway, maybe it was an acci-dent; that other bloke just pushed Old Lenny too far. You gotta learn forgiveness in this world. Besides, you know the police questioned him, same as the rest of us, but the son and wife gave him a solid alibi — he never left number eleven that whole morning Shelley was killed.'

'Who did suffocate Shelley then … who?'

'Dunno, Tanya, and the sad fact is we might never know.'

'But we have to find out. I couldn't bear it if …'

Since Mum had started her job and the typing and shorthand course, I'd been cooking lots of teas: omelettes, lamb chops, green beans, mashed potatoes. I helped her with the housework too. Not that she cleaned anything like before. Now we did what she called "a lick and a promise", and I never again saw that ugly orange-flowered cleaning shift.

Of course I only helped with the inside jobs. I hardly ever went outside, with Uncle Blackie always loitering around the yard, ready to corner me. A squeeze of my shoulder. A pat on the head. A stroke of my hair.

And the rising panicky fear that I was at the mercy of a ruth-less child-killer.

I itched to blurt out my suspicions about Uncle Blackie suf-focating Shelley, but I had not the scantest proof. Nothing. There just wasn't a thing to pin it on anyone.

Chapter 38

As the bus rumbled along to the cemetery, our shoulders bumping, Mum pulled a book from her bag — *The Female Eunuch* by Germaine Greer. 'A woman at the jeans shop gave this to me,' she said when she saw me peering at the cover. 'Told me I needed to learn about feminism.'

'I've heard of that book ... some girls at school were talking about it.'

'Apparently it's caused loads of domestic fights,' Mum said. 'Some wives are even throwing the book at their husbands. And one woman had to keep it wrapped in brown paper because her husband wouldn't let her read it.'

'I don't want to be like that,' I said, nodding at the cover of *The Female Eunuch* — a woman's body without face or limbs. A woman incomplete. 'I want more than a husband and kids. I want to be a *somebody*.'

Mum smiled, patted my knee. 'But a husband and children are still important. You don't want to grow old alone, Tanya. Nothing worse than ending up a twisted old maid.'

Better a twisted old maid than growing old with Uncle Blackie.

'What was it like, Mum, at Macquarie Pastures Asylum for the Criminally Insane?'

'A hell on earth. A terrible place full of sad, lost people wandering up and down spooky corridors. Most of them wore these flimsy gowns, all open at the back, so everyone could see their stained underwear, or bare bums, and the staff yelled at them till they covered their ears and cringed. They all resembled skeletons. Rumour had it that the staff pilfered their food, chickens especially, which turned up in the local pub chook raffle.' She let out a sigh. 'Your dad and I went up there a few times, before Blackie got so ... so ... Anyway, we thought it best to stop going.'

'Sure sounds awful.'

'A good thing they closed the place down in the end,' she said.

My mother felt sorry for Uncle Blackie. She couldn't stop making excuses for him; couldn't see that the summer of '57-'58 was a thing of the past and I was his target.

But still I remained mute for fear of spoiling our new, happy time. Nothing could ruin it. Especially not Uncle Blackie.

The late afternoon sunlight slicing through the window onto our shoulders, she went back to reading her book, then stuffed it back in her bag as the bus reached that wasteland cemetery down by the Sewage Treatment Plant.

As I glimpsed the sombre rows of tombstones, my courage faltered. I thought of sweet little Shelley, dead in her white coffin, and the blood thudded through my skull so fast I was afraid it might burst open.

'No, I don't want to go ... I can't.' I sat there, glued to my seat, and my mother had to almost drag me off the bus.

As I crouched down and laid the bouquet of white roses on my sister's small stone rectangle, the agony drowned me again.

I wondered what Shelley would look like now. Still a perfect little girl with raspberry lips, the dark hair and eyes that made her skin look even whiter? Would the frilly pink dress and matching matinee jacket still be whole, or would insects and rodents have gnawed it to shreds? Or was she all rotted away to a thin scatter of separated bones?

Six months ago, and it was still so unbelievable. So not real.

'She's gone, Tanya.' Mum bent down beside me, squeezed my hand. 'Nothing we can do to bring her back. We have to try and live our lives without her. Can we try, together, to be happy?'

A slimy fish slid down my back, and I shook all over. We can only be happy if Uncle Blackie is away from Gumtree Cottage, I wanted to say to her.

In the falling winter twilight, my mother blew a kiss at Shelley's grave. 'Goodbye, my sweet little gumnut girl ... I'll never forget you.' She sniffed, didn't swipe at the tears running down her cheeks.

I folded my hand over my mother's, squeezed it, and blew my own kiss to Shelley. I pulled Mum upright. We walked away, her arm curving around my shoulder as I glanced back to where Shelley would always be asleep. Never crying, only sleeping.

We took the next bus home. I slumped into the seat, looked out into the dusk light, not seeing anything. Staring at nothing.

'There's something I've been meaning to talk to you about,' Mum said as the bus groaned its way up the Gallipoli Street hill. 'About Blackie and me.'

I stiffened. From her wary tone, I guessed what she was going to say about her and Uncle Blackie and I did not want to hear it. I snapped my eyes shut.

'Tanya?' Mum shook my shoulder. 'Are you asleep?'

I didn't move, not the slightest blink. I heard her sigh; kept my eyes shut.

* * *

I dreamed of my father that night. He'd taken me to the beach but raced into the water without me. I was chugging along the long, empty shoreline, breathless and calling out to Dad, craning my neck over the gigantic waves to catch a glimpse of him.

'Why didn't you wait for me, Dad? Why did you leave me on my own with Uncle Blackie?'

My voice echoed against the harsh blue sky, went hoarse with the screaming and the frustration when I got no answer from him.

Then, from the inky water beyond the breakers, his dark

head rose. He caught a ride in on the lip of a breaker, waded towards me, smiling, water beads sparkling like diamonds on his sun-bronzed chest. And that moment seemed to last forever. Fairy-tale time. Until I woke, sweating, tangled up in the sheet. And hating my father again.

'Everything all right, Tanya?' I stiffened as Uncle Blackie sat on the side of my bed, one hand dragging my fingers from the cowlick. 'I heard you call out ... bad dream?'

In the moonlight slicing between the Venetian blind slats, I caught Uncle Blackie's sympathetic smile. His finger trailed from my cowlick to my cheek, my mouth. Tracing around my lips.

'I'll bite your finger off,' I hissed, pushing away his hand.

'You'd never do that, Tanya, you like me too much. Anyway, listen, I've had this great idea.'

'What idea?'

'What about if I do go to Perth ... and you come with me? We could go together, just you and me.' He spoke in a low, urgent whisper. 'We'd have such a beaut time: the beach every day, visiting the city, going to fun fairs. We'll eat meat pies and fish and chips whenever we want. We'll go everywhere, do everything together. We'd be best friends.' He took a breath. 'You know deep inside how much I care for you, Tanya ... how much we truly care for each other.'

His hand was sliding up my thigh, making small circles as he reached higher and higher until the hand was at the top of my thigh, fiddling with the elastic of my undies. I shoved it away, opened my mouth to yell, no longer caring whether my mother discovered the truth, and fell ill again.

Uncle Blackie pressed a palm against my lips. He didn't raise his voice a single notch; spoke in the same low and gentle tone. A voice I'd once loved and trusted.

'You wouldn't, Tanya. I know you aren't stupid ... I know you're a clever girl, really.'

As he got up and crept away, I fought back my tears of cold rage. Gumtree Cottage was my house. This was my bedroom. Somewhere I'd always felt safe. How *dare* he?

But as Uncle Blackie slid out the front door and into the beat-up Kingswood, I knew it was no longer safe. Gumtree Cottage had become a treacherous place.

Chapter 39

'Blackie's going to cook us a barbecue for tea tonight,' Mum said a few days later. 'We'll eat it out in the yard, then I'll tell you the news ... the surprise.'

'What surprise?' From her shy glance at Uncle Blackie, I suspected it was what she'd wanted to say on our way home from the cemetery — something she was hesitant to talk about — and my gut twisted and knotted.

'You'll find out soon enough.' She sounded all girly, mysterious.

After school, when Mum came home from her typing and shorthand course, she laid a blanket on the grass that Uncle Blackie kept almost shaved with Old Lenny's bargain lawnmower.

It was warm for August; the sun's final burst of heat had bleached the sky pale. Orange and pink cloud ruffles hovered over the last sliver of sun, the leaf shadows drunken ballerinas swaying across the back fence. From that fateful backyard, Nature's beauty seemed to mock me.

'Old Lenny's son and wife've gone down the coast for a few days,' Nanna Purvis said. 'He wants me and Billie-Jean to go next door to share his tea. So I won't be joining youse all for the barbecue.'

'Don't you hate Lenny Longbottom?' I said.

'Just showing a spot of neighbourly goodwill,' she said, ignoring my teasing tone once again. 'If Old Lenny's lonely ... wants a bit of intelligent company, who am I to refuse him?'

Off she shuffled next door in her slippers, with Billie-Jean. I bet it was nothing to do with keeping Old Lenny company but rather to avoid eating tea with Uncle Blackie and hearing my mother's "surprise". His presence at Gumtree Cottage seemed to disturb my grandmother almost as much as it did me, and she too must have suspected the shocking news that was coming to us.

Dusk had turned the light a deep mulberry as my mother plonked the tomato sauce, slices of bread, and paper plates onto the blanket, next to a cask of wine.

'Want to try some wine, Tanya?' Mum asked, filling her glass.

'Okay.' I'd got used to the taste of Nanna Purvis's sherry, so why not wine too? Mum poured an inch of wine into a glass and handed it to me. She took another glass over to Uncle Blackie, where he was cooking sausages on the new brick barbecue he'd built — the barbecue that Dad should have built since *he* was the bricklayer.

Uncle Blackie slapped the (overcooked) sausages onto a plate and sat beside Mum on the blanket.

A twinge of fear gripped me. I edged away from Uncle Blackie, as far as possible, so that I was no longer sitting on the blanket, but on the grass. Blades of it pricked my legs like needles.

Uncle Blackie made my mother a sausage sandwich and Mum gazed up at him, eyes shining. 'Ooh, thanks.' She giggled as if he'd cooked some gourmet meal instead of a stingy pack of snags.

I wanted to refuse all food Uncle Blackie had cooked, but as usual I was famished, so I slapped a sausage between slices of bread, squeezed on tomato sauce and gobbled down my sarni. Steely lapped up the tomato sauce that kept oozing out the end.

We ate in silence. I started on my second sausage sarni.

'Look at that bold thief,' Mum said, pointing to a butcherbird stealing a stray morsel of bread.

'But listen to his lyrical song,' Uncle Blackie said, a finger behind one ear, head cocked.

'Why's it called a butcherbird?' Mum said. 'Seems so barbaric for such a sweet-sounding bird.'

'Because he impales insects and lizards on thorns and tree forks,' Uncle Blackie explained. 'To support his prey while he eats it, or to store it for later.'

Mum smiled. 'You know about *everything*.'

Uncle Blackie threw a bit of sausage to the bird and when it sang he told us it was the butcherbird's "thank you song".

What a load of rubbish!

From his branch, Mr Kooka started up his eerie cackle: '*Garooagarooagarooga*.'

'And there's another bold thief,' Uncle Blackie said, nodding up at the bird. 'Watch your sarnis, girls ... kookas have a keen scent for all kinds of meat. Quite creepy, in fact, aren't they?'

'Mr Kooka's our friend,' I said. 'He's not creepy.'

You're the creepy one.

Mum rested her sandwich on her plate, swallowed a mouthful of wine, and took a deep breath. 'Blackie's going to be living with us from now on, Tanya. Here at Gumtree Cottage.'

Clods of sausage spurted from my mouth as I choked on it, coughing and gasping great, heaving breaths. My hands were jelly, the last bit of the sarni dropping to the grass. 'But w-why? Wh-what about Dad?'

'Blackie's here most of the time anyway,' Mum said, making no effort to soften the blow of her words. 'Helping around the house ... why not save his Albany rent money and move in to Figtree Avenue with us?'

A witch stirred her cauldron inside me. Simmering, boiling, and witch brew spurting into my throat. About to puke, I swallowed hard.

'No, no, no! Dad'll come home soon, *he's* your husband.'

Mum and Uncle Blackie exchanged desperate glances, as if they'd expected this outburst, but just hoped it wouldn't happen.

They might have been desperate but I was in total despair, leaping to my feet and stamping my foot. 'I don't want him to move in.'

I flew through the twilight, purple as a bruise, up the verandah steps, and into the kitchen.

* * *

I listened through the flyscreen, looking down at them on the blanket in the middle of the yard.

'Don't worry, Ellie, she'll get used to the idea,' Uncle Blackie was saying. 'She feels I'm taking her father's place ... only natural.'

Ellie?!

'I know you'd never do that.'

'Are you happy?' he asked Mum, 'because that's all I want, you to be happy. You *and* Tanya.'

How false were his words. Paste drying in my mouth.

'I'm happy. Finally I'm happy,' Mum said with a firm nod. 'And I know Tanya will be too, as soon as she gets used to having you around.' She rested back on the blanket, her wine glass dangling from her hand like fake jewellery. 'Did I ever tell you about that outback trip when I was at boarding school? I must've been about twelve. Somehow I got separated from the group ... lost.'

Uncle Blackie stretched out, curved his body around hers. He caressed her arm, his dark gaze travelling all over her. I didn't know which was worse: watching him fawn over my mother or trying to stop him doing it to me.

'I walked and walked, trying to find the group,' Mum said, rolling over to face him. 'It seemed I walked forever ... struggling through endless ravines, up slippery granite escarpments. So thirsty, so hot, so exhausted.'

Uncle Blackie smiled down at her, flipped a dark clump of hair from his boxy face.

'Finally I reached the top of a ridge,' she said. 'I stood there, crazed with thirst, staring at a pool of water in the distance, shimmering like silver. Exhausted as I was, I started running. But no matter how many slopes I scrambled up or how many ridges I stood on, I never reached that silvery pool.' Mum took another sip of wine. 'What I mean is … what I'm trying to say, is that I felt just like that for so many years — lost.'

'My poor Ellie.' Uncle Blackie kissed the top of her head.

'Then Shelley arrived. Perfect, beautiful Shelley. I imagined my silvery pool would be there, stretched before me, glinting its welcome. But then she got sick and I'd stare at the baby in her cot, screaming in pain, and unable to stop it. That silvery pool receded further and further, then vanished altogether.'

'It's over, Ellie. You're better now. I'll help you reach your silvery pool.'

Like the actors in Nanna Purvis's TV show, *Number 96*, they kissed passionately and suddenly my head felt too big for my neck. A sunflower dangling on its thin stalk. The pain was buried so deep I hadn't known it was there, waiting quietly alongside my other pains. As if I had a line of them, one for every occasion — Shelley dying, my mother's misery, Dad leaving. Uncle Blackie taking photos of me naked, touching me. And now moving in with my mother. All those pains ached right down to my soul.

Uncle Blackie was still lying on the blanket beside my mother, almost on top of her. The fearsome Ned Kelly-lookalike — the bushranger who had died by hanging at Melbourne Gaol in 1880.

If only Uncle Blackie could die by hanging. If only Uncle Blackie could die by any old way.

I skittered to the phone in the hallway, dialled Angela's number and told her the revolting news.

'How could my mother do this to me? I can't bear to stay at Gumtree Cottage with that creep. What if he tries to do to me — rape me — same as that Carter girl? Or suffocates me, like Shelley … or kidnaps me off to Perth?' My words fell from my lips in a mangled garble. 'Did I tell you he wants me to run away to Perth with him?'

'To Perth? Oh boy … oh gosh!' Angela said. 'I told you I'm not supposed to know about Papa's business, but Marco *did* say he and Zio Ricci can make bad people go away from Wollongong.'

'But *how* would your father make him go away?'

'I don't know exactly, but why don't you let me tell my parents, and you can stop worrying? Hey, come over to my place now, for a sleepover … Papa will come and get you.'

'Oh yes, please.' I inhaled deeply. 'And okay, you can tell your father about Uncle Blackie. I hope he'll make him go away.'

I replaced the receiver, relieved to be able to share the burden of those bitter Uncle Blackie-secrets with adults who seemed to know what to do about everything in life. And to care about me.

* * *

'*Mio Dio!*' Angela's mother said, glancing at Mr Moretti as Angela and I finished telling them about Uncle Blackie's photo shoots.

'Is sicko!' Zio Ricci said, and Zia Valentina nodded, her gold earring hoops wobbling.

I was sitting beside Angela at the polished kitchen table, the warm and sugary frittole taking away some of the sickness at my mother's "surprise". Melting on my tongue, sultana and apple taste lingered after I'd washed it down with Mrs Moretti's zingy ginger beer.

'You must be telling us everything about this uncle, Tanya,' Mr Moretti said, looking at Zio Ricci as Angela's mother refilled my glass.

'Tanya's uncle was here that night we had the swim,' Angela said. 'Down behind the pool, in the bushes … he made her nervous.' My friend turned to me. 'I could tell he'd scared you, when I came back with the towels, you were all puffed out and acting weird.'

'The man was here, at our home?' Mr Moretti frowned.

'*Merda!*' Zio Ricci said, propping an elbow on the table, his thumb and index finger stroking his chin. He looked serious, as if he was in deep thought about something.

'Why you not tell your papa then, Angelina?' Mrs Moretti said.

'Because Tanya didn't want to tell anybody about her uncle, and I promised to keep my friend's secret,' Angela said. 'Papa always says friends' secrets are important, and never to betray them.'

'Is true,' her father said with a nod. 'But this is different, Angelina, this … '

'So this Uncle Blackie, he still frighten you, Tanya?' Mrs Moretti said, her hand on my arm.

'I guess so.'

So much attention — Angela, her parents, aunt and uncle all concerned about me — was a bit embarrassing. I wondered if I was making a fuss about nothing. But their faces and voices remained serious, so I carried on.

'He's always nice and caring but sometimes he looks at me with these kind of faraway eyes, and his face goes all hard, and I can tell he's angry … but he never shows it; never shouts or screams or anything. And he keeps touching me, every time my mother's back is turned.' I drank more ginger beer. 'I can't tell Mum about any of it, though. I'm too worried she'll get sick again.'

'Poor Tanya,' Zia Valentina said, sipping her wine. 'You not worry, we look out for you now.'

'And he wants to take me away to Perth,' I went on. 'Just the two of us.'

'To *Perth*?' Zio Ricci slammed his glass onto the table, his dark eyes widening. 'Why this Perth?'

'So we can start new lives together,' I said. 'But I'm not going. I'd never go anywhere with Uncle Blackie. Not unless he forced me.'

'And,' Angela said, 'Tanya thinks it was Uncle Blackie who suffocated her baby sister.'

'*Mamma Mia!*' her mother gasped, patting a palm against her heart.

'But I have no proof of that,' I said. 'Just a suspicion … because of a few reasons.'

Mr Moretti and Zio Ricci frowned at each other again.

'You are not frightened no more,' Angela's mother said, dishing me out another serving of frittole. 'You are trusting us, everything be all right now.'

'Will you call the police?' I said.

'No police,' Angela's father said. 'We are having no proof of anything about your uncle.'

'No, we don't need the police,' Zio Ricci said. 'We — the Morettis — can take care of ourselves … *and* our friends.'

Chapter 40

It was almost my twelfth birthday, and Uncle Blackie had been living with us for about a week, when I saw the Mercedes for the first time. It glided past me, dark blue and shiny, as I walked up Figtree Avenue after school.

I only noticed the car because I wondered who owned it. I doubted anyone in or around our street could afford such an expensive-looking car. It wasn't that kind of neighbourhood.

I reached Gumtree Cottage and pulled an envelope from the letterbox, hoping it was another letter from Dad. But the heavy sadness welled inside me as I saw it was addressed to Blackburn Randall, Gumtree Cottage, 13 Figtree Avenue.

Why's Uncle Blackie getting his mail sent to our place? Oh yeah, because he lives here now!

And, besides taking up the garage and storage sheds with his Albany junk, how easily he'd slotted into our lives. His soft and caring words lifted up my mother and carried her somewhere else, so she was always swirling about Gumtree Cottage, silly and dizzy.

She would lower her eyes, lashes stiff with mascara, showing off the eyeshadow that made her eyes look like glass beads in a doll's head, and kiss him with a tiny pecking movement of her lips. And all the time he accepted those kisses from my unguarded mother, his dark roving eye would be seeking me out.

Nanna Purvis barely spoke to him, throwing him the glare

she reserved for foreigners and Catholics, but my mother trusted him. She'd come to depend on him, leaning on those strong shoulders the way she should have been leaning on my father, miles away in Mount Isa.

With or without Stacey Mornon's mother. I still didn't want to acknowledge the awful reality that my parents might truly be separated, that they didn't need or want each other anymore. No longer my parents, somehow.

Dad's smoky smell of sweat, beer and hot bricks lingered about the house as if he'd been gone only a day. I imagined him walking through the door any minute, Akubra in hand, fag dangling from his lips. But he didn't, and I resented him more and more for leaving us to the mercy of Uncle Blackie.

I wanted to write to him again, to tell him Uncle Blackie had moved in with us, convinced that news would make him run home. But I also feared it might make him hate my mother for allowing Uncle Blackie to take over his side of the bed. I just didn't know what to do for the best, and that uncertainty exhausted me.

On and on it whorled, a deep and swift river carrying me along, taking me somewhere I couldn't see, could only imagine. There was nothing I could do about it. Just live in fear of him. And in terror of my mother discovering the reason for that fear. Or Nanna Purvis finding out and telling her.

I walked inside, almost chucked Uncle Blackie's letter straight into the rubbish bin, but I was curious to know what it was. I flipped it over. No sender's address. I left it on the kitchen table beside the *Illawarra Mercury*.

'Whoever'd send Blackie a letter?' Nanna Purvis said, looking up from the Specials page of the newspaper. 'The man ain't got a single mate that I know of.'

'I'll give it to him when he's finished fixing the fence,' Mum said, from where she was stirring a delicious-smelling chicken stew on the stove. 'When he comes in for tea.'

'Uncle Blackie's staying for tea again?' I said.

'Of *course* he is,' Mum said, 'now he's living — '

'Yeah, bloke's here so often,' Nanna Purvis interrupted, 'anyone'd think he *lived* here.'

'He does!' Mum stirred the stew faster. 'I told you, Tanya … last Friday before you ran off to Angela's again.' Her face creased, almost crumpled, and I feared she might break down in tears. 'So could you two please stop being like this, ignoring the fact that he's moved in? Blackie's so much help, fixing, tidying things — *paying* for everything — I don't know how we'd cope without him. Besides, I thought you'd both be pleased for me to be happy.'

'*Humpf*,' Nanna Purvis muttered. 'You know what I think of that rotten egg, Eleanor, unless you want me to repeat myself till me hair turns pink?'

Oh yes, part of me *was* happy that my mother — the bright and normal one — was back. The mother who no longer flew into frenzies of house-cleaning. The one who kissed my brow after school, asked how my day was, made my sandwiches for school lunch and cooked teas that no longer featured baked beans, spaghetti or Spam. But another part of me couldn't look past the single dark cloud threatening that sunny reunion at Gumtree Cottage: Uncle Blackie.

As if he knew I was thinking about him, Uncle Blackie strolled into the kitchen, Akubra in hand, pearls of sweat fringing his brow.

'Right, that's the fence fixed and the garage all cleaned out, Ellie,' he said. 'I tossed out all that junk Dobson had collected over the years. I'll take it to the dump tomorrow.'

I despised the way Mum smiled at him, as if she owed him everything. 'Letter for you, Blackie.' She nodded at the envelope on the table, touched her fingertips to his elbow and slipped off into her bedroom. She'd started doing that every day before tea — brushing on green eyeshadow, dabbing rouge on her cheeks, painting her lips with Tropical Coral lipstick.

Uncle Blackie pulled a KB Lager from the fridge, picked up the envelope and turned it over. Nanna Purvis and I raised our eyebrows at each other.

He ripped open the envelope, pulled out a single sheet of paper and unfolded it.

'What the —?' A frown knotted his brow.

'What the bleedin' banjo does that mean?' Nanna Purvis asked.

I peered over Nanna Purvis's shoulder, at Uncle Blackie's letter. A hand print. Just a single black print with words in bold black capitals beneath it:

LEAVE WOLLONGONG
NOW

* * *

'You gone and upset someone again?' Nanna Purvis said to him. 'Besides us, that is? Done some other vile thing to a girl?'

Ignoring Nanna Purvis's taunts, Uncle Blackie crumpled the paper into a ball and flung it at the bin, which he missed. 'Probably just stupid kids playing jokes.'

Uncle Blackie didn't believe it was kids joking. And me neither, because my suspicions had leapt straight to the Moretti family.

Nanna Purvis picked up Billie-Jean and the second she disappeared out into the yard, Uncle Blackie gripped my shoulders.

'We should go now, Tanya. Leave for Perth right now, today.' His eyes were two hard black stones. His hands squeezing, I couldn't jerk away. 'We don't want to wait forever, to start our new lives, do we?'

There was that quiet rage again; the fury that came and went in flickers, lingered about him, but which Uncle Blackie never really showed. It unnerved me.

'I don't want to go to Perth with you, or anywhere,' I whispered, afraid Mum would overhear us. 'And if you don't go away from Wollongong — like that letter says — and leave me alone,

286

I'll tell my mother all about you … about the photos, about Perth.' I took a deep breath. 'And I'll tell her you don't like her; I'll say you're just tricking her, to get to me.'

He bent down, spoke close to my ear, his voice still soft, but with the edge of a hissing snake.

'We both know you wouldn't say anything that might upset your poor, fragile mum, don't we, Tanya? That would be so selfish of you, after all the effort she's made to get better, to come home to you, wouldn't it?'

The caterpillar eyebrow rose in an inverted "v" over his eyes as if he was truly concerned for my mother's well-being.

'I could tell Nanna Purvis then,' I said, heat scalding my cheeks. 'She'd never put up with you here, if she knew the truth.'

Uncle Blackie's face creased into a confident grin as he swaggered off to my mother in her bedroom. Of course he knew I wouldn't say anything to Nanna Purvis either, for fear of my grandmother tattling every last thing to my mother.

Chapter 41

I fed Steely and Bitta, snagged a packet of TimTams from the pantry, and sat at the kitchen table. I worked my way through the biscuits, listening through the flyscreen to Nanna Purvis next door, talking to Old Lenny as they watched his telly. I imagined them sitting on the ratty sofa together, a blanket wrapped about their hunched shoulders against the August chill.

That brought a wry smile to my lips, which dropped as soon as I glanced out into our own backyard. Uncle Blackie was standing beside the gum tree with a team of men who, by the looks of the big sawing machine, were about to cut it down. Mum stood beside him, her arms crossed over her chest.

That witch's cauldron brew surged from my belly into my throat. I pushed open the flyscreen door and shouted from the back verandah: 'No, stop! Don't you cut down the eucalyptus. That's Shelley's gum tree ... Mr Kooka's home. How dare you?'

'My dear Tanya,' Uncle Blackie said, as I rushed into the yard so fast I tripped over Bitta and sprawled onto the grass at his feet. 'Don't you understand, it's the best thing? We need to remove all reminders of your sister so we can move on ... start over.'

'Don't you "dear Tanya" me!' I jumped to my feet, still shrieking, and batting away my mother's hand as she tried to brush off grass bits from my front. 'Where would our kookaburra live if you cut down his gum tree?'

I stood against the tree, circled my arms around its trunk.

'If you cut down this tree, you'll have to cut down me with it.' I glared around at the arc of men, all of them staring, wordlessly, down at their boots.

'Come on,' Uncle Blackie started again. 'Don't be a silly girl.'

'Tanya —' my mother started.

'And how could you let him do it?' I snarled at my mother. 'How could you? I'm *not* moving, you hear? I'll stay here as long as I have to. Nobody's cutting down this tree.'

Still gripping the trunk like a beloved teddy bear, I called out to number eleven. 'Nanna Purvis, come quick, they're trying to cut down Shelley's tree!'

My grandmother appeared within a minute, Old Lenny hobbling along behind her.

'What the bleedin' banjo you up to now, Blackburn?' Nanna Purvis threw Uncle Blackie, and the tree-fellers, her fiercest glare. 'Now youse can all just piss off home,' she said to the men, making flapping motions with her hands. 'There'll be no tree-cutting at Gumtree Cottage. Not today, not any other day. Youse hear me? Now skedaddle … shoo.'

Nobody moved. The tree cutters all looked at Uncle Blackie, started muttering between themselves.

'Go on, get off with you, before I kick youse all in the unmentionables,' Nanna Purvis went on, shrugging off Old Lenny's hand on her arm.

Uncle Blackie shook his head and, still mumbling to each other, the men sloped off out of the yard, lugging the cutting-machine with them.

I couldn't look at my mother, or at Uncle Blackie. Trying to stamp down the burning anger, the hurt, and calm my trembling body, I stomped back inside and finished off the whole packet of TimTams.

Mum and Uncle Blackie stayed in the yard beside the tree, whispering to each other. But I was still shaking so much — so fired with rage — I didn't want to know what they were saying; didn't care.

I screwed up the biscuit packet, hurled it onto the floor in disgust at myself, and scribbled a note to Mum, saying I was going to Angela's for another sleepover.

I phoned my friend, stuffed a few clothes into my Indian bag and went out onto the front verandah to wait for her and Mr Moretti.

As I kept watch for the black Valiant, the sun lengthened along the side of number thirteen, the leaves playing their last mellow shadows across Gumtree Cottage's old-person's face. Birds flitted through the web of shadows and the house stood mustardy yellow in the afternoon sun.

Then I saw it again, the same dark blue Mercedes cruising up Figtree Avenue. Making an arc at the top of the cul-de-sac and cruising back down. Up and down again.

I screwed up my eyes against the slice of sun across the western horizon, but still I couldn't recognise the driver through the tinted windows. He sat low in the seat, a hat partially hiding his face. He glanced neither left nor right, and he didn't look the type who'd wind down his window and call out '*Cooee*' to friends or neighbours.

So intent on the Mercedes, I wasn't aware of Uncle Blackie sidling out onto the front verandah. But I recognised his voice, behind me. My heartbeat started up a chip-chip-chip, like a woodpecker at a tree trunk.

'Please don't be angry with me, Tanya. I'm so sorry about the gum tree. I didn't realise … Can't we still be friends?'

'How dare you even think of cutting down Shelley's tree? Dad said that tree was here when our ancestors built Gumtree Cottage a hundred years ago. How *could* you?'

My blood swarming, I tried to push past him, to dash back inside, but Uncle Blackie blocked my path; blacked out every trace of amber light from over Mount Kembla. He caught my arm.

'Let me go,' I snarled. He wasn't hurting but he wouldn't release me, and for a long and panicked moment I held my breath.

'You know what we have is real, Tanya ... our love.' He motioned to the bag slung over my shoulder. 'That will do, you don't need to pack anything else. Just hop in the Kingswood right now and we'll drive off to Perth. I'll buy everything we need, anything you want, on the way. We'll change our names and start a whole new life together. You see, it'll be so much fun.'

'I told you already, I don't want to go anywhere with you. I might not be able to tell my mother about your tricks, but I could tell the cops. Taking nude photos of eleven-year-olds is against the law. And sicko.' My fingers rubbed at my cowlick.

'Yes, you could tell the cops,' he said, 'but I doubt they'd believe you. Besides, what naked photos are you talking about?' He frowned as if he truly had no idea. 'I certainly haven't seen any.'

A road train was barrelling towards me but my feet were cemented to the middle of the road. No way to run, no escape. Just before that huge truck slammed into me, I realised something: I, too, had never seen Uncle Blackie's naked photos.

But they must be somewhere in Gumtree Cottage. Probably hidden away from Mum and Nanna Purvis in Uncle Blackie's junk, which was taking up so much space in the storage shed and the garage.

'It's not as if you're even that young,' Uncle Blackie was going on in the smooth voice. 'Look at those African girls — ten or eleven-year-old brides. There's even somewhere in America where girls can marry at about fourteen ... and time passes so quickly, you'll be fourteen before you know it. Come on, we'll have the best time together, away from here.'

I'd never been so relieved to see the Morettis' Valiant sweep up the hill. Uncle Blackie vanished back inside as the car pulled up alongside me.

As I slid into the back seat with Angela, I realised he was right. I wouldn't tell my mother or the cops about him, but I *would* tell Nanna Purvis, and I would convince her not to say anything to Mum. If anyone had enough sway to force Uncle

Blackie to go away from Gumtree Cottage, to leave me, and my mother, alone, it was Nanna Purvis.

Chapter 42

'Give me a hand to change my bed, Tanya?' Mum said when I got back from Angela's the next evening.

'Oh well, all right, if you really want me to.' I never went into her bedroom any longer; hated seeing the indent of Uncle Blackie's body on my father's side of the bed.

We removed the bedsheets, took fresh ones from the linen cupboard and remade the bed. Mum's face flushed pink as she smoothed a palm across the sheets that smelled of her washing powder. From her bedside table, she took one of her candles which were supposed to smell flowery but — to me — stank of old vomit. She placed it in the candle holder and stood back, head bent to one side, admiring it as if it were some artistic masterpiece.

'Can I go and live at Angela's?' I blurted out. 'I'm there most of the time anyway.'

'Oh Tanya, I know you're only trying to avoid Blackie, and he did apologise for trying to cut down the gum — '

'No, no, Angela's my friend. I just like being at her place.'

'Your dad's not coming back to us, and I don't know why you can't accept Blackie being around … be happy for me. For us.'

I shrugged, my fingers flying to the cowlick.

'I told you before, think about Blackie for a minute, Tanya, all those terrible things that happened to him.'

'But none of that's our fault.' I could almost taste the

desperation in my voice. 'Doesn't mean he has to live here.'

'Blackie's never had a chance in life. I want to give him that chance. Besides, I don't want to grow old alone.'

'You can grow old with Dad. What if he comes home and sees his brother here?' I looked down at the freshly-made bed.

Mum shook her head. 'He won't come back to us. I didn't want to tell you, but it seems I'll have to. Your father's gone to live in Mount Isa permanently, with Stacey Mornon's mother.'

I'd known all along it was true, but the cold harsh shock was still hard to bear. Ice shards spiked my arms, my neck, right down my back.

'I know,' I said. 'Stacey was boasting about going to live in Mount Isa with them. Her, not me ... why not me too?'

'For a start, you and Stacey don't get on,' she said. 'So why would you want to live with the girl?'

'That's not the point, Mum. They asked her to live with them, and not me. Why?'

'Because I wanted you to stay here with me, Tanya. I'd be ... I'd be lost without you.'

'Why didn't you tell me all this before?' I stamped a foot, glared at her.

Why I was venting my rage on her, I didn't know. Perhaps because she was, partly, the reason for my father leaving us.

'I didn't want to upset you.' She tried to take my hand but I brushed her off. 'Look, Tanya, I'm sure you'll get used to having Blackie around.'

All I could do was keep shaking my head; still I could not tell her the truth about that devil-man.

While Mum went off for her shower and Uncle Blackie nipped away for a whisky down The Monitor Arms, my brain raced yet again with schemes of how to get rid of him. But as I turned over each one they all sat, unlikely or impossible, in my mind.

So, clutching Steely to my chest, I went into the living-room, sat beside Nanna Purvis on her banana lounge and told her everything.

* * *

In unusual silence, with no interruptions, my grandmother listened to it all: Albany and the nude photos, the Perth runaway threats, my suspicions about him suffocating Shelley.

'And he's always trying to touch me,' I said. 'To catch me in the bath or while I'm taking my clothes off. Saying "nice dress", and stroking my hair. I keep wishing you'd see him but you never do … he's too clever for that.'

I also told my grandmother why she couldn't tell any of this to my mother.

Nanna Purvis's saggy bosom heaved against her chest. 'I just knew it was a bad idea having him here, around you — a young girl. Been saying as much to your mother, haven't I?'

She didn't holler or curse but spoke evenly, rationally. 'But you're right, we can't tell Eleanor, don't want to risk kicking off the miseries again.' She nodded at the television. 'Turn that thing down, will ya, Tanya? I need to think.'

Against the background television hum, Nanna Purvis fell silent, stroking Billie-Jean, the blue slipper of her top-crossed foot bobbing up and down.

'Angela's parents know everything too,' I said. 'She told me her father will make Uncle Blackie go away from Wollongong, but he's still here. You can't say anything about that to anyone, though. The Morettis' business is secret.'

Nanna Purvis's eyebrows shot up. 'Well, if that mob've offered to help, be rude not to accept, wouldn't it? And I guess they'd take care of Blackburn a darn sight better than our hillbilly fuzz. But we still have to tell the cops.'

'Tell the police? No!'

'Why not, Tanya? Blackburn Randall's a convicted child molester. They'll believe us about that, at least. But not much point telling them you suspect him of murdering little Shelley … bless her soul. They already interviewed, and cleared, him along with everyone else.'

'If the police know what he does to me then *everyone* will find out,' I said. 'They'd all be laughing at me — Stacey Mornon and the rest of them. I just know they would. Please, you can't tell the police.'

After a pause Nanna Purvis said: 'Righto, we won't tell the cops just yet. But in case your Italian friends can't help, I've an idea who *will* help us with that perv.'

'Who? And what'll they do?'

'Best you know nothing about it.'

While my mother was in her bedroom slipping on her nightie and plastering cream into her face, I crept down the hallway behind my grandmother, to the bathroom. Peering around the doorway, I spied on her as she opened the cupboard and slid Mum's old bottle of tranquillisers into her apron pocket. As she was about to turn around, I hurried back to the kitchen.

'Just taking Billie-Jean out for a widdly-woo,' she said, and I watched her trundle off outside and go next door to number eleven.

I looked up to the cloudless, star-blown sky and the Southern Cross winked at me as if it approved of whatever mad plan my grandmother was devising.

* * *

The next afternoon, while I was doing my homework at the kitchen table, Old Lenny was in the backyard yarning on to Uncle Blackie as if they were best mates.

Lenny Longbottom was at our place so often these days he no longer bothered knocking or even coming to the door. He let himself into the yard through the side gate and if nobody was outside he'd holler to Nanna Purvis from the back verandah.

'How'd you like to get first grabs on this latest homebrew?' Old Lenny said to Uncle Blackie, holding up two bottles filled with amber-coloured liquid. 'Best stuff in Wollongong, so me mates reckon … real cheap too.'

Uncle Blackie stood upright from where he was pruning the bushes, smeared earth across his brow as he ran a hand through his curls.

'Saw you running up a sweat out here,' Old Lenny said, flipping the rat-plait over his shoulder. 'Thought you might wanna try the stuff before you buy? I'll go snag a few glasses off Pearl.'

Before Uncle Blackie had time to answer, Old Lenny was climbing the verandah steps and barging into the kitchen, where my grandmother was sitting beside me, studying the Specials page of the *Illawarra Mercury*.

As if she'd been listening to the conversation in the yard, Nanna Purvis had three glasses ready on a tray.

I kept my gaze on my homework, shaky hands making my writing wriggly. Old Lenny opened both bottles and filled the three glasses: two from one bottle, and the glass on the left from the other bottle.

I pretended not to notice the glances he and Nanna Purvis exchanged. I took long, slow breaths, trying to soften the lump of wood wedged in my chest. Something was going on between those two and I was shocked, nervous and proud all at once.

Nanna Purvis followed him outside with the tray, placed it on the verandah and sat on her banana lounge — the other new banana chair Old Lenny had got her for a bargain. 'That way you won't have to lug the living-room one outside, Pearl,' he'd said.

I stood to one side of the flyscreen, watching.

'Ready when you are,' Old Lenny called. He sat on the verandah edge, hairy legs and bare feet dangling over the side.

Uncle Blackie swiped the sweat from his brow and loped across to them, smiling, as if pleased that Lenny had befriended him; as if any mate — even an old gaol bird mate of Nanna Purvis's — was better than no mates at all.

'Only got half a dozen bottles of the stuff,' Old Lenny said with his gap-toothed grin, as Nanna Purvis took her drink from the tray, and Lenny handed the glass on the left to Uncle Blackie. 'So, as I said, happy to give you a good price if the stuff's to your taste.' Old Lenny took the remaining glass and swallowed a mouthful.

Nanna Purvis sipped her homebrew. Uncle Blackie hadn't touched his yet.

'It'll go all warm, Blackie,' Old Lenny said, nodding at the glass.

I was certain Uncle Blackie was about to raise his glass to his lips when my mother bounced in from Jim's Jeans 'n Johns. Her steps were always bouncy now, and she bounded right past me, out onto the verandah and sat on Uncle Blackie's knee.

'Is that your tasty homebrew, Old Lenny?' she said, as Uncle Blackie kissed her on the cheek, one hand patting her back. 'I'm gasping after such a long day.'

'Have mine, Ellie.' Uncle Blackie pushed his glass over to Mum and got up. 'I'll get another one.'

Things happened quickly then, in a jumbled confusion of wrinkly old limbs. Nanna Purvis was leaning towards Uncle Blackie's glass. Old Lenny was on his feet, lurching at the tray, and suddenly Uncle Blackie's glass was knocked over, the home-brew leaking onto the wooden boards.

'Ah, ya clumsy old bugger,' Nanna Purvis said.

'Blimey, sorry about that,' Old Lenny said. 'You all stay put, I'll get more drinks.'

As Old Lenny came back to the kitchen, Uncle Blackie's gaze settled on Nanna Purvis, the caterpillar eyebrow a thick, steady line above dark and evil eyes.

And, as if he'd known all along that I was watching from the kitchen, Uncle Blackie looked up through the flyscreen. He winked at me, a grin spreading across his mocking face. As if he'd slapped me, I leapt backwards.

The fear bubbled inside me again, for now I understood how wicked Uncle Blackie really was. He would've let my mother drink that doped homebrew, knowing that it might kill her.

I knew for certain he *was* capable of murder.

The cold hand of terror gripped me, the horror that Uncle

Blackie might easily kill my mother, Nanna Purvis or me as easily as he'd killed our little gumnut girl.

Chapter 43

'How about I make you a special birthday cake like when you were little?' Mum said. It was my twelfth birthday, August twenty-second, 1973. But the winter chill outside was nothing compared with the ongoing iciness within me, the solid block of Uncle Blackie's menacing presence.

There was nothing I could do to get rid of him. Even Nanna Purvis and Old Lenny had failed, but still I could not allow him to keep sleeping on my father's side of the bed. That was all wrong.

'Or is twelve too old for funny cakes, and candles? Tanya … are you listening to me?'

Her voice snapped me from my thoughts. 'No, not too old,' I said to the working mother who I was sure no longer had time to cook birthday cakes. I didn't hold that against her though, rather admiring her for the long hours at Jim's Jeans 'n Johns, as well as the time spent on her typing and shorthand course. I would have been totally proud of this modern mother if only she hadn't let Uncle Blackie trick her with his romantic ways and his dreamy voice.

'But you don't have to worry about a cake, Mum. The Morettis invited us to Zio Ricci's restaurant tonight for my birthday, remember? Angela said they're organising the cake too.'

As she left for work, and me for school, I smiled to myself

thinking of the cakes, party pies and sausage rolls, buttered bread sprinkled with colourful "hundreds and thousands" — the parties I'd had as a kid long before Shelley came, before the misery of my mother's endless messy miscarriages, and her baby's death, tortured her body and her mind.

I recalled her laughing and kissing my brow as she laboured over the most complex dolphin or cat-shaped cake or whatever I'd chosen. And my father insisting she buy me a new party dress even if the housekeeping money was low.

'We'll scrimp on something else,' he'd say and make me put on the dress long before the party guests arrived, and parade up and down the verandah before him and twirl about on my toes.

'Prettiest girl in Wollongong,' Dad would say, which I soon learned was the biggest lie. But that had only been a small fib in the growing mound of my father's lies. His entire fatherhood had become one big lie since he'd given it up so easily for Mrs Mornon. And bloody Stacey.

* * *

Uncle Blackie would still be at his TAB job, my mother working down at Eastbridge, so I sprinted home from school, and down to the back-yard shed. For days, every chance I got, I'd been searching through Uncle Blackie's belongings for the photos. And now, finally, there were only three boxes left to sift through.

I climbed the ladder, and from high on the shelf at the back of the shed, I brought the boxes down, one by one. Breathing hard, I rubbed my cowlick, pushed at my brow. I opened the flaps of the first one. Inside it, beneath a moth-eaten pullover, sat a red box.

My quivering fingers lifted the lid from the red box, fussed with the tissue paper inside, folding it out. And there they were — a stack of photographs. Mostly of girls around my age, but as I flipped through them all, I saw that some of the girls looked only about seven or eight years old.

Who are they? Is one of them "that Carter girl"?

There were shots of the girls in their school uniform — different colours, different schools, but all in the same poses. The poses Uncle Blackie had taught me.

Then, beneath them, were more photos — all of the girls naked.

And, at the very bottom of the pile, I found Tanya: first in my uniform, then my underwear, and, lastly, fat and gawky-nude, trying to look like a model.

Swallowing back a hunk of vomit, I almost cried out with embarrassment, with the dirty guilt. I clamped a palm across my mouth, tried to slow my breaths, to stop my head spinning.

I took each photograph, one by one, and ripped it into a hundred tiny pieces. Then I shovelled all those tiny bits of paper into a plastic bag, and stomped down to the end of the yard.

Emptying the bag into the bin in which Dad used to burn leaves, bush and grass clippings, I took from my pocket one of the lighters my father had left behind, and stoked up a blaze.

I stayed and watched until the last paper morsel curled up and blackened. And when it was all a smoky mound of ashes, I went back inside and got ready to go out to The Greasy Fork.

Uncle Blackie's horrid photos would *not* spoil my birthday tea.

Chapter 44

That evening, sitting in the back seat of Uncle Blackie's Kingswood beside Nanna Purvis, in the long floral-print frock with its halter-neck top that Mum had got me for my birthday, I felt almost beautiful. The one ugly thing was Uncle Blackie, driving, and Mum sitting so close to him their shoulders touched. I hoped he'd be furious when he discovered I'd shredded his disgusting photos.

Nanna Purvis's arms were clamped across her chest. 'Old Lenny just got me a new telly and youse already drag me away from it. Besides you know that foreign grub messes with me intestines. Gives me the farts for the whole next day.'

'But it's my birthday tea,' I said with a giggle.

'And you might even enjoy the food,' Mum said.

'I doubt that,' Nanna Purvis grumbled as Uncle Blackie parked the Kingswood in The Greasy Fork carpark. He opened the door for my mother who slid out like a queen, glow mesh purse shimmering in the lamplight.

Angela and her parents, and Marco — whoopee, he'd come! — were waiting for us. Mr and Mrs Moretti kissed me on each cheek.

'*Buon compleanno* … happy birthday,' they said, and Nanna Purvis took two steps back like she was afraid they'd kiss her too, or say something else in Italian.

Angela's parents glanced at Uncle Blackie, at each other, but so quickly it was over before anyone noticed, besides Angela and me.

The Greasy Fork was crowded, with not a single spare seat. Ours was the largest table which Zio Ricci and Zia Valentina had set with an ivory-coloured tablecloth, silver crockery and white candles in swan candleholders, the candles rising from the swans' backs. The other tables had red and white checked tablecloths — simple picnic ones — and no swan candleholders. All the tables, though, had lemonade bottles filled with red and white wine.

'I got you a present,' Angela said as I sat beside her. She pushed the gift at me, wrapped in red smiley-faces paper, tied with a gold ribbon.

I opened it slowly, trying to make the good feeling last — that delicious sensation of a friend giving you a present.

I gasped as I pulled out *Ring-Ring*, the new single from the popular Swedish group: Björn & Benny, Agnetha & Anni-Frid, along with a giant poster of the four singers.

'Wow, groovy,' Marco said, the muscles in his arms and shoulders straining beneath his white satin shirt, the top buttons open to show off his suntanned chest and the sparkly gold cross he wore.

'Thanks, Angela,' I said, 'I'll put up the poster in my room as soon as I get home.'

The adults were drinking wine and chatting to each other, except Uncle Blackie, who remained wordless, beside my mother, obviously not wanting to be here.

'He got another one of those weird black-hand prints in the mail,' I whispered to Angela. 'Remember that first one I told you about?'

Angela nodded.

'Well, this was the same … same words telling him to leave Wollongong. I wish he'd take notice of them, but he doesn't, he just stays, and keeps trying to talk me into going to Perth with him.'

'I told you not to worry, didn't I?' Angela's cheeks turned pink. She glanced away sharply and I suspected that, like me, my friend had a good idea who'd sent those black-hand prints. But she wasn't going to tell me. Or couldn't, for some reason.

Zia Valentina brought out soft drinks and a plate of anti-pasto. 'Olives, mozzarella balls, salami and pepperoni,' she said. She was so tall in her corked high heels, slim and elegant in the tight black dress with gold sequins. She made me think of a film star, her hair teased up high like that, and I wished that one day I'd look so pretty. Angela's mother always looked nice too, with perfectly-curled hair, smart clothes and lipstick, but she was more homely than Zia Valentina, more *motherly*.

'You are trying salami, Mrs Purvis?' Mrs Moretti said. 'You are liking it, I am sure.'

'Okay, just a small piece, if you insist,' Nanna Purvis said. 'Only hope it don't mess with me intestines.'

Nanna Purvis swallowed a morsel of salami. 'Crikey, not bad at all. I might even have to give up Spam for this salami grub.'

Everyone smiled. Mr Moretti poured more wine, and Nanna Purvis leaned over to me and said: 'Don't slouch, Tanya. You're almost a grown woman, and you don't want to end up an old maid.'

You're almost a grown woman now.

I stole a glance at Uncle Blackie, who was staring straight at me. That dark gaze sent a chill through me — a cold wave flooding a warm rock pool. I sat up straight, looked away from him. 'Old maid?'

'I always said to me own mother,' Nanna Purvis went on, 'if I'm not married by the time I'm twenty-five, I'll cut off me own bosoms rather than be an old maid.' Angela and I tried not to giggle too much and Mum and Angela's parents hid their smirks.

'I should've made you read *The Female Eunuch*,' Mum said.

Nanna Purvis scowled. 'What would I want to read that for?'

'Get the Spaghetti Carbonara, Tanya,' Marco said, leaning towards me from the other side of his sister, as Zia Valentina took our order. 'It's Zio Ricci's speciality … *so* yummy.'

And when the meals arrived, I wound my spaghetti around the fork like Zia Valentina showed me, and held it on my tongue, savouring the creamy bacon taste before it slid down my throat. I swore I'd never again eat canned spaghetti.

I had a taste of Mum's Involtini — melty veal rolls with a cheese, parsley, garlic and breadcrumb topping.

After the meal, Zia Valentina brought out an enormous cake with chocolate swirls, frilly cream and twelve candles. Zio Ricci switched off the restaurant lights, and not only the people at our table, but everyone in The Greasy Fork sang "Happy Birthday", then *"Buon Compleanno"*.

The warm feeling rushed right up to the tips of my ears. I couldn't stop grinning. Mum took my other hand and squeezed.

'Happy birthday, Tanya.'

And in that instant, my eyes closed, the lilting Italian music making me feel like swaying, joyful voices ringing in my ears, a strange feeling settled over me. Happiness, it was. Something I'd almost forgotten existed, except for the brief moments I was at Angela's house.

Shelley was still alive. The colic gone, she'd grown up, and was tottering around Gumtree Cottage babbling in broken sentences and giggling and shrieking with a toddler's innocence.

How sad that I would never see her do that. And so unfair! I willed myself to stop dwelling on that sorrow, and imagined Uncle Blackie was still locked up in Macquarie Pastures Asylum for the Criminally Insane. He'd never been released. I'd never met him. I didn't even know he existed. My mother had never fallen ill and my father would walk in, on his own, through the door of The Greasy Fork the instant I opened my eyes.

I kept my eyes shut, wanting it to go on forever.

* * *

'Blow out the candles, Tanya.' Mum was nudging me. 'Everyone's waiting.'

'Make a wish … gotta make a wish,' they were all chanting.

I opened my eyes and tried not to spit on the cake as I blew out the candles.

'Don't tell us what the wish is,' Marco said. 'Or it won't come true.'

So I said nothing, though from the way he, Angela and their parents glanced at me, I think they guessed it was something to do with making Uncle Blackie go away.

'Bonzer cake,' Nanna Purvis said as I cut slices and served it out.

Everyone nodded and murmured, '*Mmn, mmn,*' dabbing chocolate and cream from their mouths.

'Well, knock me out with a cricket bat,' Nanna Purvis said. 'Look who's here, it's Rita.'

All gazes turned to the hairdresser with bright orange, spiky hair, as she came towards Nanna Purvis, smiling.

Neither Mum nor I had ever met Rita in all the years she'd been doing Nanna Purvis's hair.

'What're you doing here, Rita?' Nanna Purvis's bird eyes blinked at a woman in a long pink and yellow-flowered skirt, plaits hanging halfway down her back, who'd joined Rita.

'This is Vivian,' Rita said, laying her hand on the hippy woman's arm. 'My partner.'

'Partner?' Nanna Purvis said, shooting Vivian a dark glare. 'Hairdressing partner? Never seen you in the salon. Not once in the forty years Rita's been doing me hair.'

'Vivian and I've been together almost as long as I've been doing your hair,' Rita said. 'I'm sure I did mention it, Pearl. Maybe you weren't listening?'

Like a hooked fish, Nanna Purvis's mouth stayed open, one of the rare moments I'd caught my grandmother speechless.

I was pretty certain what Rita meant by "partner", but it took longer for Nanna Purvis to tweak. As the bitter realisation slowly came, my grandmother's curls trembled, the crease between her upper lip and her nostrils quivered. Nobody said anything, as if we were all waiting for something to happen, though nobody knew what.

'We're celebrating our retirement tonight,' Rita said. 'I've sold the salon and Vivian and I've bought ourselves a Kombi van. We're going travelling around Australia for a year. But I think I told you that too, Pearl?' Rita clapped her hands together. 'We can't wait, can we, Vivian?'

Vivian smiled.

Nanna Purvis sat there like a mute person.

'Sounds like great fun,' Mum said.

'You are having lovely trip,' Mrs Moretti said.

'Happy retirement,' Mr Moretti said, and we all raised our glasses to Rita and Vivian's retirement.

'Thanks, enjoy your tea … food's divine, isn't it?' Rita said, she and Vivian smiling as the two women turned away, bumping shoulders as they walked through The Greasy Fork's door.

Nanna Purvis stared after them, her mouth still wide open but no sound coming out.

'Never mind,' Mum said to her with a wry smile. 'There's always Percy's Pin and Perm.'

'I wouldn't go to that poofter if he was the last hairdresser this side of Goonoo Goonoo,' my grandmother said, far too loudly. Other diners turned, stared at her. 'I'd sooner shave it all off.'

'I can't imagine you as one of those skinheads, Nanna Purvis,' I said. Mum and Mr and Mrs Moretti chuckled and drank more wine and Angela, Marco and I exploded into giggles.

'Anyway, Percy's a *Catholic*,' Nanna Purvis said, with a bang of her spoon on the tablecloth.

'Maybe Rita's a Catholic too?' my mother said, with a laugh. 'Hardly practising though. The church does give those poor lezzos a nasty time.'

For the rest of the birthday tea, my grandmother remained silent. I kept leaning over and patting her arm. 'Don't worry,

Nanna Purvis, you just have to get with the times. Ya gotta stare the goanna in the guts.'

Chapter 45

I t was a week after my birthday dinner, Friday afternoon, and I was dreading another whole weekend with Uncle Blackie. Angela was busy with some family gathering so I'd have to stay at Gumtree Cottage on my own.

Mum wouldn't be home from her typing and shorthand course till later, and, walking up the front verandah steps, I heard Nanna Purvis's screechy voice coming from next door's driveway. Arguing about something with Old Lenny again, no doubt.

I was so busy sniggering to myself about Nanna Purvis and Old Lenny's constant bickering that I was shocked when Uncle Blackie grabbed me as soon as I walked inside.

Face beetroot-red, his eyes glittered with an icy anger I'd never seen before.

He must've known Mum wasn't here, planned his attack while Nanna Purvis was next door, since my grandmother never left me alone with Uncle Blackie for a second now.

'Let me go!' I kicked and squirmed beneath his hold, shivered with fright, couldn't free myself. 'If you don't let me go, I'll yell out to Nanna Purvis.'

'Oh you would, would you, Tanya? We'll see about that.'

One hand pinned me to the wall. With the other, he bound a smelly handkerchief around my mouth. He released his grip for a few seconds, knotting the gag at the back of my head, and

I tried to make a run for it. Two steps only, and both hands were clamped on my shoulders, pushing me back to the wall.

My scream caught in my throat, the gag muffling it. I breathed fast, through my nose. My belly tightened, bladder pressing.

His hand was on my breast, kneading, squeezing. I shrank from him, from the pain of his pressing fingers. I turned away, couldn't bear to look into those vicious-snake eyes.

I looked beyond Uncle Blackie into my bedroom, at the Venetian blinds. In the splices of sunlight darting between the blind slats, the dust was moving, floating where it wanted to go. Quickly though, each particle became trapped on the window sill, in corners, on furniture.

His breaths quickened, short and urgent. Gaze shafting mine like black drills. Body rigid, powerful.

'Ellie left me ... chucked me aside ... dirty rubbish.' He spoke in an ugly, cracked hiss. No trace of the floaty warmth. 'And gave away our son ... did you know that, Tanya? Just gave him away as if he was worth nothing. Turned her heart to Dobson. Can you imagine what that's like, the one you love switching her worship to another man?' His voice grew louder, his words rushes of steam. 'It's this roar that comes from deep inside you.' His hand fell from my breast to my belly, circling my navel. Dropping to my underpants, fiddling with the elastic. 'It burns your eyes and blasts your brain apart.' His voice was low again, soft, pleading. 'You won't leave me, will you, Tanya? You're mine ... almost a woman now.'

Rough fingers inside me, poking, pushing.

I wriggled, tried to kick out at his shins, swiped at his probing hand. With as much force as I could muster, I sank my teeth into one of his fingers staking me to the wall.

In the short, shocked silence that followed, my heart beat even faster. Every muscle trembled. He could smell my fear, the desperation engulfing me. Now he would lift the handkerchief over my nose. And he would suffocate me.

'You bit me, you little bitch,' he said, quite calmly. Still holding me to the wall, he squinted at his finger, reddened and puffing up, a blood blister appearing beside the nail. The dark eyes turned sad, like a puppy's, his shoulders slumping. 'How could you bite me? You know we love each other … this is it, Tanya. Real love.'

I tried to speak again, to scream, but could barely breathe through my nose, as if my nostrils had closed up and no air could get in or out.

The panic rose from my knotted gut, up to my chest, tight, pressing.

Can't breathe … can't breathe … going to die …

Terrified he'd kill me if I didn't let him do what he wanted, I closed my eyes, blocked out his face, his smell, the hot and musty fan of his breaths. Let his fingers wander where they wanted; let him press the hardness in his trousers against me. I closed my ears too, on his stupid talk of love, and my teacher was telling us about the ancient Greeks.

The human flesh-eating Minotaur had the body of a man and the head of a bull and grew into a ferocious monster. After getting advice from the Delphi Oracle, King Minos of Crete had a gigantic labyrinth constructed to hold the Minotaur at his palace in Knossos.

Every nine years, seven Athenian boys and seven Athenian girls were sent as sacrifices to the Minotaur, so King Minos would stop attacking Athens.

I was trapped beneath the Minotaur, bull horns threatening to poke out my eyes, ferocious face twisted, muscles twitching as it tried to rip apart its human sacrifice.

The handkerchief slipped from my mouth. I opened my eyes.

'Stop!' I tried to breathe normally, but each one was a sharp gasp. 'Please let me go, Uncle Blackie … I want to come to Perth with you. I promise … we'll go right now.'

The Minotaur relaxed its grip.

'Really?' Uncle Blackie's gaze was wary.

'Yes, really … truly. It's what I want.'

'Finally you've seen sense, Tanya,' he said, and pressed his lips to mine. A crinkled and mouldy lemon.

When he paused for a breath I said, 'Let me go, and I'll just get my bag.' I tried to keep my voice steady. 'Then we'll leave before Mum gets home, and before Nanna Purvis comes back from Old Lenny's.'

'No need to pack anything,' he said, pointing to a bag sitting beside the front door, which I hadn't noticed before. 'I've got everything we need, and if not, we'll just buy things along the way.'

He spoke like before: soft and sea-ripply, but I couldn't deny the harsh, panicky edge to it. I knew he didn't trust me not to make a run for it, and I didn't dare argue with him.

* * *

One hand holding my arm, he slapped on the Akubra hat, hooked the Driza-Bone coat over his free arm and picked up the bag.

He hustled me outside, across the front verandah. No sign of Nanna Purvis next door. She and Old Lenny must've gone around the back to watch telly.

Down the steps he hurried me, out into Figtree Avenue, where the Anderson boys were playing cricket outside number ten.

'You won't shout, or scream, will you?' he said.

I shook my head. 'Course I won't. I told you, I *really* want to come to Perth.'

The Kingswood was parked beneath one of the huge Moreton Bay figs. Uncle Blackie must have known there was less chance I'd notice it out on the street, as I came in from school. For I'd definitely have seen it parked in its usual place in our driveway — where Dad had once parked the Holden. In that moment, it was as if my father had never existed.

'Quick. In you get, Tanya.'

Pushing me into the front seat, pressing down the lock. Slamming the door and rushing around to the driver's side. I couldn't believe this was happening.

How could I have let him corner me … stupid, stupid.

Hands trembling on the steering wheel, Uncle Blackie fired up the Kingswood.

I smiled and waved to Terry and Wayne Anderson. Uncle Blackie zoomed off.

'You'll see, we'll have such a great time together,' he said, a hand patting my thigh. I forced myself not to swat it away. 'The best time ever. I love you more than you could know, Tanya. And now I'm going to prove that to you.'

I nodded, keeping my gaze on the road ahead.

We reached the end of Figtree Avenue. Uncle Blackie had to slow down to turn into busy Gallipoli Street, where husbands would be outside mowing lawns or enjoying a beer in the shade, mothers watching children play hopscotch, jumping rope, or twirling hula hoops.

He slowed the Kingswood at the intersection, stopped to let a car pass. Another car behind it. I flung open the door, tumbled out of the car.

My heart beating so fast I thought it would explode, I stumbled to my feet and ran and ran, as far from him as possible. Didn't look back; just kept running.

'Bitch,' Uncle Blackie shouted after me. 'Little prick-teasing bitch. Knew I couldn't trust you. You're just like that Carter bitch … you're all the same.'

I expected him to come after me, but people in Gallipoli Street were staring at me, at the Kingswood. I chanced a look over my shoulder. He'd turned the car the other way, heading down the street, in the direction of the beach road. I didn't care where he was going, as long as Uncle Blackie never returned to Gumtree Cottage.

But he did.

Chapter 46

'... and he gagged me ... I couldn't breathe,' I said. '*And* he said I was a little prick-teasing bitch.'

Half an hour after my desperate escape from the Kingswood, I was sitting at the kitchen table with Nanna Purvis, who'd set a cup of tea in front of me, and stirred in two sugars and half a Valium. I sipped the hot milky drink and, hands still shaking, I stroked Steely, curled in my lap.

My mother, who'd arrived home fifteen minutes ago, stood leaning against the kitchen bench, arms folded.

Nanna Purvis and I had told her everything — all about Uncle Blackie's naked photos; the way he'd snaked his way into Gumtree Cottage and slid beneath her skin just to get to me. And his attack that very afternoon.

But through the entire account, Mum hadn't said a word. Her breaths came quick and shallow, her knuckles whitening as her fingers clung more tightly to the bench top.

Nanna Purvis poured a cup of tea for herself and one for my mother. 'Say something, Eleanor, and come and sit down ... drink your tea.'

But Mum remained silent and I feared the worst: the truth about Uncle Blackie had pushed her back down to that miserable seabed.

'I didn't want to tell you,' I said. 'Didn't want you to get sick again. But I ... I couldn't keep it a secret any longer.'

'It can't be true.' Mum fidgeted with her cowlick. 'It just can't be … not Blackie. You're over-reacting, Tanya, still grieving Shelley, and your father leaving us. Jealous of our love for each other. All Blackie wants is to be a good stepfather to you. Besides, where are these supposed naked photos of you?'

'I … I burnt them. But they were here, in a box of his stuff in the storage shed. Not only me, lots of girls. It's true, you have to believe me, Mum.'

'All of it's true,' Nanna Purvis said. 'Bit of a shame Tanya burnt the evidence, but good riddance to the bad egg, I say. And if you've got any sense, Eleanor, you'll just be thankful he didn't truly harm your own daughter.'

'But he did,' I said, swallowing the last of my tea. 'He did harm one of her daughters.'

'What do you mean?' My mother turned her wide-eyed frown to me. 'You — *apparently* — escaped from this so-called fiend.'

'He suffocated Shelley. I … I'm sure of it.'

'No, no, no!' My mother clenched and unclenched her hands. 'It's all lies. You've both hated him from the moment he started coming here, and now these … these vicious accusations. How could you try and turn me against him, the man who loves me? The man who's been waiting for me all these years, unlike my own husband who left not only his grieving wife but his daughter too?'

My mother stared from my grandmother to me. She shook her head, as if waiting for Nanna Purvis and me to say we were sorry, that it all *was* just callous lies.

'Ask the Morettis if you don't believe me,' I said, gesturing at the phone. 'Go on, call them. I've told them all about Uncle Blackie.'

'No, no! Why would you tell them such things, Tanya?'

'And why isn't Blackie here then, Eleanor?' Nanna Purvis said. 'Why're his clothes, his Driza-Bone, his Akubra gone? The Kingswood? Tell me that.'

'Oh god, why?' My mother's face crumpled and she sank to the floor. Thinking this was some shocked acknowledgement of our accusations, Nanna Purvis and I dashed to her side, helped her into a chair and forced her to drink the sugary tea.

'Well, Tanya doesn't have any proof he suffocated Shelley,' Nanna Purvis said, 'so we can't expect the cops to do anything, especially as they already questioned him. But who else could've done such a thing? It's gotta be him.'

'We should tell the police,' I said, 'even if there's no proof. They might be able to find some evidence against Uncle Blackie if we tell them we're sure it was him.'

'Too right we should call the fuzz,' Nanna Purvis said, hobbling over to the phone. 'Alert them a crazed child-attacker's on the loose.' She picked up the receiver, started dialling.

'Nobody will call the police,' my mother said. 'Put that phone down.'

For once Nanna Purvis obeyed Mum, and placed the receiver back onto its cradle.

'And both of you will shut your mouths now,' my mother went on. 'How dare you utter such vile things about Blackie?' Tears filled her eyes, thin body trembling, her hands balled into fists. She leapt from the chair, knocking over her teacup. 'Just shut up, both of you! Shut up … shut up … shut up!'

She banged a fist onto the table which made Nanna Purvis and me jump. Steely sprang from my lap, skittered away. Billie-Jean started yelping and Bitta barked from the doorway as my mother stamped off to her bedroom and slammed the door behind her.

Nanna Purvis and I remained sitting at the table, staring at each other, not knowing what to say or do. Milky tea leaked across the table and dripped onto the lino. Drip, drip, drip.

Soon afterwards, my mother still locked away in her bedroom, Uncle Blackie lurched through the front door. He stank of stale sweat and whisky breath, the dark eyes watery, red-rimmed. He stood there swaying, and glowering at me.

* * *

The dogs barked and dashed about Uncle Blackie. He kicked out at Billie-Jean, who yelped.

'You kick my dog,' Nanna Purvis said, 'and I'll kick you.' Her hand hovered over the phone. 'Tanya and I've told Eleanor all about you and I'm calling the police. Calling them right now if you don't leave this house and never come back. Ever!'

I gathered Bitta into my arms, held him against my chest like a shield. My mother came scurrying down the hallway, snatched the phone from Nanna Purvis and jammed the receiver back down.

'Can't you see Tanya's lying, Ellie?' Uncle Blackie spread his arms at her like he was shocked and insulted. 'You know she's always tried to turn you away from me … not happy for her own mother to have found love, finally. You know she's hated me from the start. She'd do anything to turn you against me. Don't you think you deserve to be with someone who really loves you?'

He looked at me with a fishy kind of gaze, and I sucked in my breath, staring at him in disbelief. Like a cyclone unleashing, a dark rage bloomed and I sprang at him.

'You're the liar!'

I turned to my mother. 'I told you before, just ask the Morettis if you don't believe me.'

My mother looked from me to Uncle Blackie, back to me again.

'Tanya's telling the truth,' Nanna Purvis said. 'He's the liar, the perv. You just don't wanna believe it, him layin' on that charm thick as cream. You're his victim too, not only Tanya.'

'Why would I lie to you, Mum?' I said. 'Why would I risk you getting sick again? I was so glad you'd got better, so pleased to have the happy mother back.'

My mother clamped her hands on her hips. 'Tell me the truth, Blackie. Is Tanya lying, or are you?'

Uncle Blackie let out a huge sigh. 'What can I say, Ellie? Her word against mine, but think about it … think about how she's been since I moved into Gumtree Cottage. Doesn't that answer your question?'

'Look at his finger,' I blurted out, suddenly remembering. 'When he pinned me against the wall, gagged me … touched me everywhere, I bit his hand.'

My mother took Uncle Blackie's arm, her gaze settling on the purple-red swelling on his forefinger.

'See?' I said. 'Do you believe me now, Mum?'

A terrible silence followed, broken only by our hard and fast breaths. My mother dropped Uncle Blackie's arm, stared down the hallway, beyond us. It was as if I could see into her mind; watching it trying to take in the truth of those terrible accusations about the man she'd grown to love.

She rubbed at her cowlick. The horror of it must have hit her like a hammer blow to the head: how Uncle Blackie had tricked her, to get to me. How he'd touched and fondled me and — the worst of it — how he'd held a pillow over her beautiful baby's face and snuffed the life from her.

The skin on her throat broke out in pink splotches. 'Turn around and go straight back out of this house, Blackie,' Mum said, jabbing a finger at the door. 'How dare you show your face back here, after all you've done? After what you did to sweet little …' She spoke low, evenly; an odd kind of calm.

How strong and assertive she sounded, though I smelled the terror beneath her brave words. How proud I was of my mother who, just a few months ago, couldn't have defended me against a fly.

'How can you believe them, Ellie?' Uncle Blackie said. 'I thought we loved each other?'

'So did I.' Her voice remained calm. Determined. 'But how mistaken I was, how foolish. Leave now, I don't ever want to see you again. And we're calling the police … just to make sure you *never* come back.'

Nanna Purvis picked up the phone again.

'At least let me get the rest of my things, and my suitcase,' he said, and started walking towards the bedroom.

'Out now!' She was shrieking, lunging at him.

Nanna Purvis dialled triple 0. 'I need the police,' she said. 'And quick smart.'

'Okay, okay, I'm leaving,' Uncle Blackie said. 'Put the phone down, Pearl, I'm going, see?'

'I will not,' Nanna Purvis said. 'Can't let a monster just waltz off into the night.'

In one long stride, Uncle Blackie reached the phone. He snatched it from Nanna Purvis. With a grunt and a tug, he tore the whole thing out from the wall, threw it onto the floor. The phone smashed into pieces.

His gaze still on us, Uncle Blackie backed out of the door, empty-handed, and vanished into the gathering dusk light.

My mother closed the door, swivelled around and leaned against it. She shut her eyes, her breaths still coming fast and hard.

I didn't know why but, for some reason, I had to let Angela know what was happening, and I raced out the back door, across the yard and into Old Lenny's place. Without even asking permission from Old Lenny's son and daughter-in-law, I picked up the phone and dialled Angela's number.

'Guess what, he's going!' I said. 'Leaving Gumtree Cottage right now!'

Chapter 47

I was back at number thirteen in less than a minute. My mother and Nanna Purvis were sitting on the sofa in the living-room, Nanna Purvis pouring nips of sherry into two glasses.

I dashed into my bedroom, peered through the Venetian blind slats. I had to make sure Uncle Blackie was truly gone. For good. But he wasn't, not yet.

Twilight had turned the trees to long silhouettes, the street lights illuminating no more than their circles of trunk, light slapping across Uncle Blackie's face, bruising it yellow and a deathly white. Coralie Anderson called her cricket-playing boys inside.

Figtree Avenue was deserted, except for Uncle Blackie headed for the Kingswood parked, once again, beneath the fig tree. But, as if he sensed me watching him through the blinds, he swivelled around to Gumtree Cottage's old-person's face.

He walked back a few paces; stood on the front verandah steps not six feet away from me.

Was that fear in his eyes, reflected in the street light? Fear, yes, and anger. And sadness.

'I know you're there, Tanya. You'll pay for this, little bitch. Little dobber … won't get away with it. How could you do this to me?'

I didn't answer, the terror stealing away my breath. Moths

flapped against the window as if trying to bat their way in, and, from the backyard, Mr Kooka cackled.

'*Garooagarooagarooga, garooagarooagarooga.*'

'Tanya … you all right in there?' Nanna Purvis's voice hollered down the hallway. 'Come in here with us, you'll be needing a nip of sherry too, I reckon.'

'Yes, fine, coming soon, just getting changed,' I said, looking at Uncle Blackie standing there, staring at my window. His eyes turned glittery. Was he crying? He swiped at them.

'We should've left before, Tanya.' Cobwebby voice. 'When we had the chance.'

I couldn't speak, couldn't move. How could he still not have understood I didn't want to go anywhere with him, that I hated and feared him more than anything else?

'We've should've left before they started watching me, before the moving shadows, before the black-hand letters, the threats … too late now.'

He sounded like a crazy person; a mad man who *had* known what those black-hand letters meant.

Tears leaked down Uncle Blackie's face, his gaze odd, faraway. 'I know you're watching me, Tanya, but look, all the others are here too: Ellie, Dobson, Beryl … Dad and Uncle Ralph.' He took a sobbing breath. 'But no, Uncle Ralph is dead … dead, buried and *rotted.*'

Mr Kooka laughed again. Uncle Blackie looked up and down Figtree Avenue, and in the light of the moon rising like a lamp, I saw the madness in his eyes.

'And Mum, is that you, Mum? So that's what you look like.' He turned back to my window. 'You see, I never knew her, Tanya. It was me who killed her.'

His voice was friendly again, the look in his eyes, which had so chilled me before, vanished.

'Nanna Randall died in childbirth,' I hissed, before I could stop myself. 'It wasn't your fault.' I had no idea why I was defending Uncle Blackie; trying to make him feel better.

Uncle Blackie's face tightened, his voice rising, panicky. 'Bloody hell, my mother's bleeding. Look, blood's gushing from her nose, her mouth, her ears, her eyes, her insides. Quick, Tanya, we have to help her. You and I together … must save her!'

But there was no Beulah Fannie Randall, blood gushing from her insides. Nobody, apart from Uncle Blackie. I shook all over, afraid for him; terrified for me.

He must have been this crazy when he raped the Carter girl; why the judge locked him up in a mental asylum for the criminally insane. Maybe the madness had never left him but I — and my mother — just couldn't see it.

'Hurry, Tanya, she's fading away, drowning in her own blood.' Uncle Blackie gripped his temples, tearing at the greying tufts of curls. 'Too late, she's gone. That last baby was too big for her. That's what they all said, but Uncle Ralph said it was my fault. All my fault.'

He hunched his back, bent over, cringing. A defenceless animal against Uncle Ralph's evil words.

'I'm a bad person. I killed my mother … did a revolting thing to a young girl … to you, Tanya. I deserve to die for that.'

I knew I should keep my mouth shut, just stay quiet and hope he got into the Kingswood and drove away for good, but I sensed this was my last chance to find out the truth, and I burned to know it.

'Did you suffocate my baby sister? Was it you who killed Shelley?'

'Shelley?' He frowned, shook his head as if he had no idea who Shelley was, or what I was talking about.

* * *

Uncle Blackie smiled — a strange, sad, lop-sided grin — as he turned and walked away from me, back to the road. I wanted to run from my bedroom to the safety of Mum and Nanna Purvis drinking sherry in the living-room, but something kept me there, stayed my fingers plucking apart the Venetian blind slats.

So stunned at this different — mad — Uncle Blackie, I paid no attention to the car slowly climbing the Figtree Avenue hill. As it drew closer to number thirteen I saw it was the same Mercedes I'd seen twice before. I was sure of it, with those tinted windows and the driver slumped low in the seat, a hat masking most of his face. But this time there were two more men, in the back seat.

Uncle Blackie stood on the kerb, teetering at the edge of it, staring at the Mercedes as if waiting for it to reach him.

He was about to step onto the road! My heart missed beats, thudded against my chest, my thoughts fluttering like trapped birds. Mr Kooka laughed, long and low.

'No!' I shrieked, as he walked straight into the Mercedes' path.

Then, in that briefest instant, when he could still choose between living and dying, he changed his mind. The Mercedes' headlights inches away, Uncle Blackie leapt back onto the footpath.

'How dare they blame me for her bleeding to death?' he said. 'How dare they lock me away in that hellhole, steal my youth — my life! — on nothing more than the wild accusations of one blubbering prick-teaser?'

His head thrown back, he spoke not to me, but to the night sky, the moon and stars, and to the sudden breeze that rattled the window panes. 'How dare you refuse me, Tanya? This is all your fault.'

Uncle Blackie turned around once again and strode back to the front verandah.

He was coming for me; he'd kill all of us.

He reached the verandah steps. Climbing up. One step. Two, three.

My whole body shook.

The two men from the back of the Mercedes leapt out, dashed

up onto the verandah. They each grabbed one of Uncle Blackie's arms. He had no chance to shout or struggle, as they shoved him into the back seat and the Mercedes drove off down Figtree Avenue.

My fingers found my cowlick, rubbing harder, faster, and that sound — of the Mercedes' car door closing — seemed so sharp and clear. And final.

Chapter 48

A week after those men took Uncle Blackie away in the Mercedes, his Kingswood disappeared from Figtree Avenue. No one saw who drove it away, or when, it just wasn't there any longer. Like Uncle Blackie: just not there any longer.

And, a little more each day, as the warm days of spring arrived, the winter chill carried off with it my terror of Uncle Blackie. Well, the worst of it.

Shelley would've been celebrating her first birthday, taking wobbly steps, cooing and laughing. Instead, we all still sagged under the pain of her young life unlived. Though we did celebrate one thing — my father's return to Wollongong.

No letter, no phone call. The Holden simply pulled into the driveway of Gumtree Cottage one afternoon as if he was back from work or the pub rather than from an absence of almost eight months.

Mum allowed him back into the house but refused to let him into their bedroom; she threw a pillow onto the sofa for him each night after tea.

At first I wouldn't speak to my father, too angry with him for leaving us alone with Uncle Blackie's evil madness. And for running off with Mrs Mornon. There was no sign of her, or of Stacey, and nobody asked him about them. Later, Coralie Anderson told Nanna Purvis that Mrs Mornon had returned to

Figtree Avenue just long enough to sell the house and pack her and Stacey off somewhere. I didn't want to know where, didn't care. I just hoped I'd never see that vile girl again.

Dad made a big effort to get me to forgive him. After carefully removing the David Cassidy, and Björn & Benny, Agnetha & Anni-Frid posters, he ripped off the ugly wallpaper patterned with violet posies from my bedroom walls and repapered them with the brightly-coloured flowery print I'd chosen.

He changed the kitchen wallpaper too, for one with a modern blue geometrical design. He ripped down all the Venetian blinds and replaced them with those smaller and lighter aluminium "Mini-Blinds" that were all the rage. He knocked down Uncle Blackie's barbecue and built a larger, fancier one.

My father found another brick-laying job but restricted his trips to The Dead Dingo's Donger with his work mates to Friday evenings only.

After about a week, my mother stopped putting out the sofa sheet and pillow. I supposed she thought Dad wasn't the only one who had to be forgiven; that she had her own mistakes that needed pardoning.

I lay on my bed that first night Mum let him back into her bed, admiring my groovy new wallpaper, catching snippets of their whispers.

'... missed you and Tanya so much ... made a big mistake. Couldn't bear your misery ... Shelley dying like that.'

'... not entirely your fault, Dobson, I'm as much to blame. How could ... let that monster ... our home? So ashamed.'

'Don't be ... you ... victim as much as Tanya.'

'Yes but ... the guilt ... idiocy!'

'... all in the past now, Eleanor.'

'I hope Tanya ... forgive me too.'

'Of course I forgive you,' I wanted to call out to my mother. 'That monster tricked us all.' But I think she knew both Dad and I — and Nanna Purvis — were just thankful Uncle Blackie was gone for good.

'... adopted ... search for the boy if you're still keen, Eleanor?'

'... don't know.'

'If I did find him ... constant reminder ... Blackie. Do you want that?'

'No, Dobson ... really don't know ... for the best.'

'Best thing we can do is help Tanya get over ...'

* * *

Danish architect, Jørn Utzon had won the competition held to design the new Sydney Opera House. Nothing so daringly inclined and top-heavy had ever been built and it took a decade and a half to finish. And this morning, October twentieth, my father was driving Mum and me up to Sydney for the official Opera House opening.

Nanna Purvis said she preferred to stay home and watch it on telly with Billie-Jean, at Old Lenny's. 'How can I refuse the lonely old bugger,' she'd said.

The sun warming Sydney Harbour heralded another hot summer on its way. Boats crowded the water, the sun's rays bounced off Sydney Harbour Bridge, and the crowd cheered as Elizabeth, Queen of England and Australia, officially opened the Sydney Opera House.

After the ceremony, Dad bought us fish and chips. We unwrapped the butcher's paper sleek with greased salt, and fended off the grey and white gulls that stalked around us, glassy eyes watching our every mouthful.

We walked along the quay back to the Holden, my parents' hands entwined, my father's other arm slung across my shoulder. We stopped at a booth and Dad got me some fairy floss, which the harbour breeze stuck to my cheeks.

We drove home to Wollongong via the Royal National Park where we set up camp for the night in the same spot as before Shelley was born.

Our teacher had told us that the park was once the country of the Dharawal people, Australian Aborigines who survived as skilled hunter-fisher-gatherers in clans scattered along the coast. But it had been named the Royal National Park after Queen Elizabeth's visit to Australia in 1954.

Dad pitched the tent while Mum and I kindled up a blaze and unpacked the food from the Esky.

Sulphur-crested cockatoos shrieked from the eucalyptus trees. Brightly-coloured rosellas whistled their musical '*ching-ching-ching*' and pink and grey parrots pecked the grassland for seeds and roots.

'Why do gum trees look blue?' I asked Dad, as Mum set the billy to boil.

'Because the oil from their leaves makes the air look a bit hazy,' he said. 'And, from a distance, kind of blueish.'

'Hey, it's the same wallaby as last time.' I pointed to the shy creature staring out at us from behind the large rock, ears pointed towards the paling sky.

'Such a sweetie ... as if he's been waiting for us to come back,' my mother said as we sat cross-legged by the campfire munching on the Vegemite sandwiches she'd prepared.

'Did you know, Tanya that Australia was home to megafauna twenty or thirty thousand years ago?' my father said. A thread of gooey marshmallow dangled from his lips. Mum swiped it away and kissed the sticky spot.

'What's megafauna, Dad?'

'Giant marsupials. Wombats the size of rhinos, kangaroos ten-foot long and seven-foot-long lizards.'

'What happened to the megafauna ... where'd it go?'

Dad shook his head. 'Nobody really knows. Prehistoric man likely hunted them to extinction, or their fires destroyed their habitat.'

'I heard it was the progressive drying of Australia that destroyed their environment,' Mum said.

Dad smiled, kissed her cheek. 'Back together ... all of us,' he said, threading more marshmallows onto skewers, and toasting them over the flames.

Yes, a happy family again, all of us back together. Almost.

I glowed with the heat of the flames warming my skin, and breathed in the scent of the gums, the bewitching aroma of wild-flowers. I could have almost convinced myself that everything that had happened was simply a nightmare of some distant past.

Except that Shelley was never coming back.

* * *

'Come on, Old Lenny Longbum, get ya saggy middle and ya ratty plait over here,' Nanna Purvis called over the side fence. She and Lenny were hosting a barbecue tea in our backyard this evening, for no apparent reason.

Old Lenny came hobbling across with a load of homebrew and a giant Tupperware full of chops and sausages. 'Got the meat cheap off a butcher mate,' he said, and my mother smirked and nudged my father, sitting beside her on the blanket, one arm draped across her shoulder.

'Wonder if Lenny buys anything he doesn't get cheap off a mate,' Dad said, which made Mum and me laugh.

People began arriving, bearing dishes of food: neighbours, friends and some dubious-looking mates of Old Lenny's. Lenny Longbottom took up his spot at Dad's fancy new barbecue, wearing an apron over his shorts and singlet with the slogan: *Don't like our grub? Then piss off home.*

Mr and Mrs Moretti, and Angela and Marco — yes, he'd come! — arrived with armfuls of lemonade bottles full of red and white wine. I patted my new pageboy haircut that disguised my bat-wing ears, sure Marco would notice it.

With Nanna Purvis's help, I'd made a salad with onions, pineapple and orange slices I'd seen in Mum's *Mother's Helper* magazine.

For dessert, Mad Myrtle and Mavis Sloan bought pink and white fairy cakes, to go with Coralie Anderson's chocolate-soaked lamingtons, and my mother's Pavlova that dripped passionfruit and cream.

Not that Angela or I would be eating any of those desserts. After only two months on Weight Watchers we were both thinner, and I was sure her brother would notice that Ten-ton Tanya had shrunk to Three-ton Tanya.

Mrs Moretti wasn't as keen on our diet us Angela and me.

'Ah my Angelina,' she'd say, throwing her arms in the air. 'You no more eat my good pasta ... the pasta I make for you with these own hands.'

Nanna Purvis settled herself on her banana lounge with Billie-Jean, who quivered with the excitement of a crowd. Steely had disappeared somewhere and Bitta dashed about yapping.

Old Lenny brought Nanna Purvis over a glass of sherry. Bottle of beer in one hand, he parked his bum on the edge of her chair. 'Pretty groovy banana lounge you got yourself, Pearl,' he said, patting the shiny, plastic yellow slats.

'Ah, some cagey old bloke got it for me,' Nanna Purvis said with a wink. Old Lenny slapped his hand on Nanna Purvis's leg.

'Oy, watch where you're putting them grubby mitts,' she said, swiping away his hand.

People laughed, lolling about on the new spring grass or slumped in one of the plastic chairs Old Lenny had got from somewhere, hands shading eyes against the glare of the westbound November sun.

Through the haze of barbecue smoke tinged with the smell of scorched meat, a flash of blue moved on a gum tree branch. '*Garooagarooagarooga.*'

I looked up through the tangle of leaves at Mr Kooka.

'Means we're in for a change,' Nanna Purvis said. 'That's what me old nanna always said, and she never told a fib in all her hundred and two years on this earth.'

'Your nanna lived to a hundred and two?' Coralie Anderson said. Everyone glanced at each other, eyebrows raised.

'Almost a hundred and three when she keeled over onto the kitchen stove,' Nanna Purvis said. 'She reckoned if a kookaburra laughed we were in for a change ... a storm coming, or a heatwave brewing. Goannas'd turn pink or kangaroos'd sprout wings and fly across the Nullarbor.'

'Seems like there's some truth in that kookaburra legend then,' Old Lenny said with a flip of the plait. He looked around at everyone. 'We got an announcement to make, a big change for me and Pearl.' He took a swig of beer, a deep breath. 'We, Pearl and me, we're movin' in together.'

Silence fell across the backyard, as if nobody was certain they'd heard right.

'Here's to living in sin,' Nanna Purvis said, raising her glass. 'Same as all them new-age women's lippers.'

'Li*bb*ers!' Angela and I cried, in unison.

'That's what she said,' Old Lenny croaked, and laughter tinkled in the warm evening air, the melting sun painting everything gold.

'So you won't be needing those *Only for Sheilas* nude centrefolds anymore, since you've got a real man now, Pearl,' Mrs Anderson said.

'Yeah for women's rights,' Mavis Sloan cried.

'Burn the bra!' Old Lenny said, for no logical reason I could see.

'Language, Old Lenny.' Nanna Purvis smacked his leg.

'Any more beatings and you'll not get your living-in-sin-present, Pearl Purvis.' Old Lenny hobbled over to the garage, lugged out a cardboard box and plonked it beside the banana lounge.

More giggles and glass clinking as she opened the cardboard box to reveal a portable television set. 'Perfect size for when we get our new bedroom, Pearl,' he said.

'Crikey, you're one for the surprises, Old Lenny.' Nanna Purvis cupped her hands over her mouth like a kid excited over a birthday present.

'Bet you got it cheap,' I said. 'Off a mate?'

Everyone laughed and cheered and raised their glasses to the future living-in-sin couple.

The excitement over Nanna Purvis and Lenny's announcement died down, and I sat on the grass with Angela and Marco, my plate of chop and salad balanced on my lap.

Mr Kooka was still there, the sun's last rays whitening his chest, shining on the blue feather tips peeking from the tawny mass, reflected in his bright, white eye. Looking for Shelley, wondering where she'd gone.

But I knew she was up there; up in the tree with our kookaburra, watching down on us.

I wonder what you'd look like now, little gumnut girl.

'Beautiful bird, isn't it?' Marco said, as the kookaburra flapped his wings and flew away into the softly falling darkness and the winking stars. Old friends in a velvety sky.

I nodded, my gaze turning to the empty place where Shelley's pram had once stood beneath the gum tree. There she was, smiling, waving her arms, stubby little legs bicycling in the air, the breeze lifting her pink frilly dress.

There was nothing more beautiful and perfect in the world and in that dreamlike moment of sounds and sights and thoughts mingling, the memory of my little sister was so bewitching I was certain it would never be lost.

The enquiry into her death was still open. But Uncle Blackie had vanished, so we would never find out if it was that monster who'd suffocated her. Or if it was someone else. And that need to know burned — a smouldering bushfire in my chest.

Chapter 49

Forty years on, I still have no idea what happened to Uncle Blackie that night the Mercedes took him away. But I do know that in those naked photos he stole my childhood. He bit into the forbidden apple, then held the juicy core in his palm, toying with it, savouring it, knowing all the time he was going to finish it off.

Many times over the years I've wanted to ask my husband about Uncle Blackie's black-hand letters, and that dark-coloured Mercedes. But right from the beginning I learned not to ask questions about Marco and his uncle and father's "business". I just enjoyed the wealth it afforded us: the easy lifestyle for our children, our elegant home in Bottlebrush Crescent near his parents' place. Besides I learned that some things are better left unknown.

Angela Moretti is still my closest friend, though we catch up only on special occasions. She's so busy with her jet-setting life, originally as a Milan fashion model, and these days as a successful business woman with her own brand of clothes and lingerie.

As my father did when he returned from Mount Isa, I forgave my mother her gullibility — Uncle Blackie's enchantment of her as he played the part of dashing saviour, rescuing her from loneliness; her husbandless predicament. I mean, how could she not have been so vulnerable, Uncle Blackie pruning her with the perfection of sculpted art?

But that didn't mean she'd stopped loving my father. I remember her asking me, years later, if I believed you could love two different men at the same time. She hadn't thought so before, but at that moment she believed it *was* possible, and — according to the tide of women's libbers at the time — entirely acceptable.

And forty years on, Shelley is still with me. Certainly everyone stopped talking about her after a time, except in passing. But like the new spring flowers blooming at Gumtree Cottage: the jasmine, wattle, bottlebrush, oleander and the red gumnuts, I came to learn that the cycle of life continued, without Shelley. My very youth buried it beneath the leaps of maturing into a teenager, an adult, a wife and mother, diminishing its conscious importance.

The pain of her death has never left me though. Oh there were times over the years — long periods even — when my memory slipped, as memories do, even those brimming with love; those you think will never leave you.

I stopped thinking about Shelley every moment of the day, but she was always with me. Often I wouldn't know it until she prodded me with a painful reminder. Then, as my mind could no longer contain it, the grief flared. And worse, when each of those agony-filled days was over, the pain would shadow me to my bed, slink into my nightmares. The fear of it became as unbearable as the pain itself.

Then, afterwards, there would be a long period of nothing.

Only now can I understand the depth of my shock, so profound I'd blanked out the days leading up to Shelley's death, the actual day, and the weeks after it. As if my subconscious was trying to protect me from the indescribable horror of losing a sister, the memory magician made of it all a shadowy phantom.

In hindsight I'd thought that maybe my mother had been

neglectful leaving Shelley alone in our backyard, sleeping in her pram in the shade of the gum tree. But no one accused her of neglect at the time; it wasn't even mentioned.

It was Australia Day, 1973 — the exact day, seven years beforehand, that the Beaumont children disappeared. Jane, Arnna and Grant, aged nine, seven and four, failed to return to their parents' home after a trip to Glenelg Beach, near Adelaide.

The public had been sympathetic, never suggesting the parents were negligent in allowing their young children to catch the bus and stay at the beach unaccompanied. Simply because at that time in Australia this was safe and acceptable.

We now regard the Beaumont children's disappearance as a significant event in the evolution of Australian society: parents no longer presumed their children were safe, and changed the way they supervised them.

But, like everyone else in the neighbourhood, I still wonder if Gumtree Cottage wasn't at the root of our problems. If you heard the stories of the tragedies that generations of my family suffered there, you too might be convinced that everything was the fault of that star-crossed house.

Now, here I am, back in Gumtree Cottage — solid and welcoming when my father's convict ancestors built it, then strange and harrowing after Shelley died — sifting through my family's possessions. And juggling with the memory magician.

Chapter 50

In my childhood bedroom, sorting through each box, the hot morning stretches into a stifling afternoon. Evening comes and outside the sea breeze arrives, welcome as a cool drink on a scorching day. The trees, bushes and flowers move gently. Dancers warming up for a show.

My gaze strays again to Nanna Purvis's box, and the newspaper headlines of Australia Day, 1973. I sit for a moment in silence, like the aftermath of something shocking. Something devastating that has no words. A great wave dumpster surprises me, jolts me from my reverie, submerges me in its obscure depth, and it seems not to be an aftermath after all. But rather a beginning.

The powerful memory magician is clawing at the edge of my consciousness — the magician who plays tricks on you that you can't understand no matter how hard you try — grasping for that all-important missing fragment of truth.

It started so quickly I didn't see it coming, and now it swells so fast I can't stop it. That remnant of childhood my eleven-year-old brain had simply erased — the truth, hard and dark as a bitter seed — is revealing itself to me.

I'm hot and clammy but my body freezes. I close my eyes as the force of it uncoils from inside me, stretching up, gasping for air, shrieking. Its scream is evil — a wild, tachycardic pulse. And as those flickering jabs of memory fight their way to my brain, my head spins with the enormity of it.

Dissociative amnesia they would likely label it: occurring when a person blocks out information usually associated with a traumatic event; a degree of memory loss beyond normal forgetfulness with long periods of memory gap. The memories are still there, though, deeply buried and stewing, only recalled when something in that person's environment triggers it.

How ironic — me, a psychologist who couldn't even see into her own psyche.

* * *

It is the evening of Australia Day, 1973. I'm lying on my bed. Through the Venetian blind slats, in the darkness of Figtree Avenue, cicadas buzz and mozzies throw themselves against the flyscreen as if they are desperate to get in and suck my blood. The full moon throws its brightness across the tangle of the blood-spatter bedspread, and from between the Venetian blind slats, the man in the moon looks down on me.

High on his gum tree branch in the backyard, Mr Kooka cackles: '*Garooagarooagarooga, garooagarooagarooga*.' Laughing, mocking. Knowing something I don't.

I run my tongue over dry lips, taste salt. I'm too old to play with Barbie dolls but the shock of Shelley's death has regressed me to a child-like state and I slide from the sweat-damp sheet, tip the box of dolls onto the carpet and line them up: Twiggy, Ken, Skipper, black Christie, Miss America and Sunset Malibu Barbie.

'You,' I hiss at Twiggy Barbie. I separate Twiggy from the others, reach over and take my pillow. I hold it over her face. I press, harder and harder, imagining Twiggy Barbie struggling beneath the pillow, gasping for breath, legs kicking, hands fighting mine. Bruises flowering on raspberry lips.

My tears blind me, the raw grief hurtles towards me like the wind from the western plains lashing Wollongong, crouched between the mountains and the sea as if it were defenceless as an infant.

I keep the pillow over Twiggy Barbie's face until my pain and fear boil up and explode into sobs.

Accidents can happen — bad, terrible accidents — though you don't mean them to, Dad always says.

But it's going to be okay. My baby sister won't stay dead. Those ambulance men will bring her back to life. Of course they will, they revived that boy in Real Life Crime.

I stare at my Barbie doll. Shake her, squeeze her, slap her face. I give her the kiss of life, bang on her chest.

'Breathe, breathe,' I hiss. 'Why won't you just breathe again?'

I want to scream at Twiggy Barbie to come back to life; to tell her she was never, ever supposed to die for real. But Twiggy Barbie stays dead.

The kookaburra stops cackling. The night is still again.

And there is only silence.

Author's Note

This is a work of fiction, a work that combines the actual with the invented. All incidents and dialogue and all characters, with the exception of some well-known figures, are products of the author's imagination and are not to be construed as real. Any resemblance to persons living or dead is entirely coincidental.

Acknowledgements

With grateful thanks to the writers and readers and friends who helped shape this novel: my Triskele colleagues Catriona Troth, JD Smith, JJ Marsh and Gillian Hamer; Beta readers Carol Cooper, Chris Curran, Tricia Gilbey, Courtney J Hall, Jane Hicks, Gwenda Lansbury, Lorraine Mace, Claire Morgan, Pauline O'Hare, Camille Perrat, Mathilde Perrat, Wendy Quiggin, Barbara Scott-Emmett, Claire Whatley; Pamela Bennett for checking obstetric facts; Dr Norman James for help with psychiatry information and treatment from that era; Det. Sgt Septimus Hergstrom, Victoria Police (July 1963 -January 1999) for police procedures; DP Lyle MD for forensic information; Maria Loschi for Italian food and customs information; Wendy Quiggin for "facts and feelings" from the 70s in Wollongong, and my other Aussie mates who helped with "blasts from the past"; Liz Hergstrom for advice on prams and baby clothes; Claire Whatley for final version edits; JJ Marsh for the blurb; Lorraine Mace for grammar tips; Shannon Page for proofreading expertise; JD Smith for the cover design. And finally, to my family for their ongoing support and encouragement.

Thank you for reading
a Triskele Book

If you loved this book and you'd like to help other readers find Triskele Books, please write a short review on the website where you bought the book. Your help in spreading the word is much appreciated and reviews make a huge difference to helping new readers find good books.

Why not try books by other Triskele authors? Choose a complimentary ebook when you sign up to our free newsletter at www.triskelebooks.co.uk/signup

If you are a writer and would like more information on writing and publishing, visit http://www.triskelebooks. blogspot.com and http://www.wordswithjam.co.uk, which are packed with author and industry professional interviews, links to articles on writing, reading, libraries, the publishing industry and indie-publishing.

Connect with us:
Email admin@triskelebooks.co.uk
Twitter @triskelebooks
Facebook www.facebook.com/triskelebooks

Other novels by Liza Perrat

Spirit of Lost Angels
Book 1 in *The Bone Angel* series

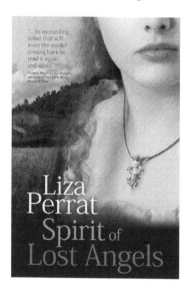

Available now as print and E-book.

Print book on Amazon: http://myBook.to/PBookSpirit
E-book on Amazon: http://myBook.to/EbookSpirit

Smashwords:
https://www.smashwords.com/books/view/161707

Nook/Barnes & Noble: http://www.barnesandnoble.
com/w/spirit-of-lost-angels-liza-perrat/1111399033?e
an=9782954168104

Kobo: https://www.kobo.com/fr/en/ebook/
spirit-of-lost-angels-1

Her mother executed for witchcraft, her father dead at the hand of a noble, Victoire Charpentier vows to rise above her impoverished peasant roots.

Forced to leave her village of Lucie-sur-Vionne for domestic work in the capital, Victoire suffers gruesome abuse under the *ancien régime* of 18th century Paris.

Imprisoned in France's most pitiless madhouse — *La Salpêtrière* asylum — Victoire becomes desperate and helpless, until she meets fellow prisoner Jeanne de Valois, infamous conwoman of the diamond necklace affair. With the help of the ruthless and charismatic countess who helped hasten Queen Marie Antoinette to the guillotine, Victoire carves out a new life for herself.

Enmeshed in the fever of pre-revolutionary Paris, Victoire must find the strength to join the revolutionary force storming the Bastille. Is she brave enough to help overthrow the diabolical aristocracy?

As *Spirit of Lost Angels* traces Victoire's journey, it follows too the journey of an angel talisman through generations of the Charpentier family. Victoire lives in the hope her angel pendant will one day renew the link with a special person in her life.

Amidst the tumult of the French revolution drama, the women of *Spirit of Lost Angels* face tragedy and betrayal in a world where their gift can be their curse.

***Spirit of Lost Angels* listed on "Best of 2012" sites**

http://darleneelizabethwilliamsauthor.com/blog/2012-top-10-historical-fiction-novels/

http://abookishaffair.blogspot.fr/2012/12/best-books-of-2012.html

http://thequeensquillreview.com/2012/12/10/holiday-picks-from-the-queens-quill/

Shortlisted Writing Magazine Self-Publishing Awards 2013
http://lizaperrat.blogspot.fr/2013/06/spirit-of-lost-angels-shortlisted.html

Winner EFestival of Words 2013, Best Historical Fiction category

Recommended at the 2013 Historical Novel Conference in "Off the Beaten Path" recommendations
http://thequeensquillreview.com/2013/06/26/the-mammoth-list-of-off-the-beaten-path-book-recommendations-brought-to-you-by-our-hns-conference-panel/

Indie Book of the Day Award, 13th July, 2013
http://indiebookoftheday.com/spirit-of-lost-angels-by-liza-perrat/

Spirit of Lost Angels **Editorial Reviews**

'... I LOVE, LOVE, LOVE when a book sucks me in and is so engrossing that I get ticked when I have to put it down. As a reader, it made me feel as though I was being written into the pages of the book. ... those who refuse to read indie-published books lose out on dynamic novels and this book is definitely an example of why I feel that way. I would not be surprised if this is a book I find in the collection of a large publishing house in the future ...'... Naomi B (A Book and A Review): http://abookandareview.blogspot.fr/2012/11/spirit-of-lost-angels-by-liza-perrat.html

'... how well written and detailed the book is as the author clearly outlines the path of a commoner's life and the hardship of Victoire's life from childhood to adulthood ... very intriguing ... an historical book about enduring, accepting, regret, love, loss, family, hope, coming home, and an angel pendant that held it all together for each of the women who wore it ...' ... Elizabeth of Silver's Reviews: http://silversolara.blogspot.fr/2012/07/spirit-of-lost-angels-by-liza-perrat.html

'... impressed with Perrat's knowledgeable treatment of the role of women during one of France's most tumultuous times, as well as the complexities of insular village life ...' ... Darlene Williams: http://darleneelizabethwilliamsauthor.com/hfreviews/spirit-of-lost-angels-by-liza-perrat-historical-fiction-novel-review/

'The writing is superb, the sights, sounds and smells of a city in turmoil is brought vividly to life ...' ... Josie Barton: http://jaffareadstoo.blogspot.fr/2012/08/author-interview-liza-perrat.html

'... a tale to lose oneself in ... persuasively combines fact and fiction in this engrossing novel. The peasants' fury, the passion building up to the Bastille storming, and the sense of political explosion are just a few of the vivid illustrations ...' ... Andrea Connell: http://thequeensquillreview.com/2012/10/10/review-spirit-of-lost-angels-by-liza-perrat/

'... a truly astounding book that will have you reaching out to the characters, feeling for them, and fiercely cheering them on ... engrossing, absorbing and you won't be able to put this down. ... a book not to be missed ... perfect for fans of historical fiction ...' ... Megan, Reading in the Sunshine: http://readinginthesunshine.wordpress.com/2013/04/05/spirit-of-lost-angels-by-liza-perrat/

'... escapist fun — Francophiles will want this one and those who enjoy historical fiction that doesn't focus on royals ... great fun for the summer read.' ... Audra (Unabridged Chick): http://unabridged-expression.blogspot.fr/2013/05/spirit-of-lost-angels-by-liza-perrat.html

'... brings to life the sights and sounds of 18th century France. Her extensive research shines through in her writing, from the superstitions of the villagers to the lives of the more sophisticated Parisians.' ... Anne Cater (Top 500 Amazon reviewer): http://randomthingsthroughmyletterbox.blogspot.co.uk/2012/09/spirit-of-lost-angels-by-liza-perrat.html

Wolfsangel
Book 2 in *The Bone Angel* series

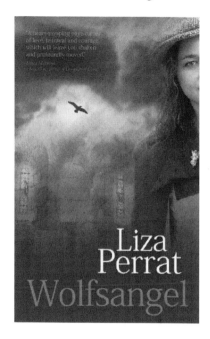

Available now as print and E-book.

Print book on Amazon: http://myBook.to/PBookWolfsangel

E-book on Amazon: http://getBook.at/WolfsangelEBook

Smashwords: https://www.smashwords.com/books/
view/363451

Nook/Barnes & Noble: http://www.barnesandnoble.com/w/
wolfsangel-liza-perrat/1117076332?ean=9782954168128

Kobo: https://www.kobo.com/fr/en/ebook/wolfsangel-2

Seven decades after German troops march into her village,

Céleste Roussel is still unable to assuage her guilt.

1943. German soldiers occupy provincial Lucie-sur-Vionne, and as the villagers pursue treacherous schemes to deceive and swindle the enemy, Céleste embarks on her own perilous mission as her passion for a Reich officer flourishes.

When her loved ones are deported to concentration camps, Céleste is drawn into the vortex of this monumental conflict, and the adventure and danger of French Resistance collaboration.

As she confronts the harrowing truths of the Second World War's darkest years, Céleste is forced to choose: pursue her love for the German officer, or answer General de Gaulle's call to fight for France.

Her fate suspended on the fraying thread of her will, Celeste gains strength from the angel talisman bequeathed to her through her lineage of healer kinswomen. But the decision she makes will shadow the remainder of her days.

A woman's unforgettable journey to help liberate Occupied France, *Wolfsangel* is a stirring portrayal of the courage and resilience of the human mind, body and spirit.

Indie Book of the Day: http://indiebookoftheday.com/wolfsangel-by-liza-perrat/

Josie Barton (TOP 500 AMAZON REVIEWER) Best books of 2013: http://jaffareadstoo.blogspot.co.uk/2013/12/books-in-my-year-2013.html

Wolfsangel Editorial Reviews

'A heart-stopping novel of love, betrayal and courage which will leave you shaken and profoundly moved.' ... Karen Maitland, bestselling author of *Company of Liars*.

'... one of the best books I have ever read.' ... Kimberly Walker, reader

'… captures the tragedy of betrayal and the constancy of hope. It brings home to the reader that choices made in youth, cast deep shadows. A superb story that stays in the mind long after the final page.' … Lorraine Mace, writer, columnist and author of *The Writer's ABC Checklist*.

'A beautifully laid-out spiral of unfolding tragedy in German-occupied France; a tale of courage, hardship, forbidden love and the possibility of redemption in times of terror.' … Perry Iles, proofreader.

'Once I picked this up I found it nigh impossible to put down … Loosely based on the tragic events of Oradour Sur Glane in 1944, this novel doesn't pull any punches and will remain with the reader for a long time.' … Lovely Treez (AMAZON TOP 500 REVIEWER): http://www.lovelytreez.com/?p=778

'Wolfsangel is a powerful story that has stayed with me since finishing the last page. Wow.' … Megan ReadingInTheSunshine (AMAZON TOP 100 REVIEWER): http://readinginthesunshine.wordpress.com/tag/wolfsangel/

'… an absorbing, well-researched and well-written novel ideal for anyone who enjoys reading historical fiction and like Liza Perrat's previous novel, Spirit of Lost Angels there are courageous female characters at the heart of the storyline.'… L. H. Healy "Books are life, beauty and truth." (AMAZON TOP 500 REVIEWER): http://thelittlereaderlibrary.blogspot.fr/2014/06/wolfsangel-liza-perrat.html?spref=fb

'… reviewed for Historical Novel Society … entertaining play on the familiar theme of love in the twilight of politics and honour and grippingly dramatic. The prose and the writing are beautiful, the central character conflict and the outcome are very satisfying and the book is a solid achievement.'… ChristophFischerBooks (AMAZON TOP 500 REVIEWER): http://historicalnovelsociety.org/reviews/wolfsangel/

Blood Rose Angel
Book 3 in *The Bone Angel* series

Available now as print and E-book.

Print book on Amazon: http://myBook.to/
BloodRoseAngelPBook

E-book on Amazon: http://myBook.to/BloodRoseAngelEbook

Smashwords: https://www.smashwords.com/books/
view/581151

Nook/Barnes & Noble: http://www.barnesandnoble.com/w/
blood-rose-angel-liza-perrat/1122873896?ean=2940151046091

Kobo: https://www.kobo.com/fr/en/ebook/blood-rose-angel-1

1348. A bone-sculpted angel and the woman who wears it—heretic, Devil's servant, saint.

Midwife Héloïse has always known that her bastard status threatens her standing in the French village of Lucie-sur-Vionne. Yet her midwifery and healing skills have gained the people's respect, and she has won the heart of the handsome Raoul Stonemason. The future looks hopeful. Until the Black Death sweeps into France.

Terrified that Héloïse will bring the pestilence into their cottage, Raoul forbids her to treat its victims. Amidst the grief and hysteria, the villagers searching for a scapegoat, Héloïse must choose: preserve her marriage, or honour the oath she swore on her dead mother's soul? And even as she places her faith in the protective powers of her angel talisman, she must prove she's no Devil's servant, her talisman no evil charm.

Longlisted, MsLexia Women's Novel Competition, 2015

Blood Rose Angel Editorial Reviews

Blood Rose Angel, from the spellbinding *The Bone Angel* series, tells a story of continuing family traditions, friendships overcoming adversity, and how *good* and *evil* are too often bestowed on fellow humans in the name of faith—*Zoe Saadia, author of 'The Rise of the Aztecs' and 'The Peacemaker' series.*

Medicine, religion, and love intertwine in this captivating, richly-detailed portrait of a young woman's search for identity as the Black Death makes its first inroads into Europe. Liza Perrat uses her training as a midwife and her experiences living in a French village to create a compelling and unforgettable heroine determined to heal the sick in a world still ruled by superstition—*C. P. Lesley, author of The Golden Lynx and The Winged Horse*

The balance between the darkness and the light makes this book so wonderful ... an emotional reading experience. I was deeply moved ... — *Magdalena (book blogger)*

I could not tear myself away … Liza Perrat has now joined the ranks of my favorite authors. The first few pages hook you and never let up. I tore through this book so quickly I was sad when it ended. Yes … that enjoyable — *Melinda (book blogger)*

For me Heloise represents those forgotten women, intelligent, brave and indomitable who have formed the heart and soul of every town and village throughout history. Wonderful — *Chris Curran, author of Mindsight.*

Liza Perrat paints an enthralling picture of the ignorance and superstition that allowed the plague to spread inexorably and unchecked. The author is particularly gifted at transporting you to the historical setting and everyday detail of people's lives — *Vanessa Couchman, author of The House at Zaronza.*

One of those books that once started was impossible to put down and yet at the same time one of those novels that you didn't want to pick up knowing that every page read was a page closer to having to say goodbye to some wonderful characters not to mention the end of an exceptional trilogy — *Tracy Terry (book blogger).*

Héloïse is a strong and inspiring main character; an amazing woman to guide you to a very dark chapter in history — *Maryline (book blogger).*

I loved Heloise's character … a strong woman … sure of her powers of healing. She oozes confidence through most of the book. I also liked how the author included a lot on the methods that Heloise would have used as a midwife during the time period — *Meg, A Bookish Affair.*

Liza Perrat has quickly become one of my favourite authors. In her new sweeping tale, *Blood Rose Angel*, emotions overwhelmed me right from the start and kept me on the edge of my seat with my heart in my throat right through to the last page, when I sat there stunned that it was all over. It was like leaving a best friend behind — *Cindy, (Book Blogger).*

… the author's medical background, her artistic brush strokes in language, and the so deftly integrated literary devices elevate this novel to a very fine work of historical (and literary quality) fiction … I was sad when the story ended — will particularly miss Midwife Heloise. Though well suited to the story path, the climax and ending of *Blood Rose Angel* did suggest a possible sequel. We can hope! — *Bernice L. Rocque, Author of Until the Robin Walks on Snow.*

With flawless and progressive characterization and each characters emoting to dot, the story was simply magnetic. I had to finish the book off! — *Shree, Book Blogger*

About the Author

Liza grew up in Wollongong, Australia, where she worked as a general nurse and midwife. She has now lived in rural France for over twenty years, working as a medical translator and a novelist.

For more information on Liza and her writing, please visit her website: www.lizaperrat.com
or her blog: http://lizaperrat.blogspot.com
Facebook: https://www.facebook.com/Liza-Perrat-232382930192297/
Twitter: @LizaPerrat
Pinterest: http://www.pinterest.com/triskelebooks/
Google +: https://plus.google.com/114732287937883580857/about

For occasional book news and a free copy
of *Ill-fated Rose*, short story that inspired
The Bone Angel series,
http://www.lizaperrat.moonfruit.com/signup

Printed in Great Britain
by Amazon